The DEVIL in the DOORYARD

The DEVIL in the DOORYARD

Gregory Blake Smith

WILLIAM MORROW AND COMPANY, INC.
NEW YORK

Library of Congress Cataloging-in-Publication Data

Smith, Gregory Blake.
The devil in the dooryard.

I. Title.
PS3569.M5356D4   1986   813'.54   86-12419
ISBN 0-688-06664-X

Printed in the United States of America

First Edition

1 2 3 4 5 6 7 8 9 10

BOOK DESIGN BY PATRICE FODERO

Acknowledgments

The author wishes to thank Phillips Exeter Academy, Stanford University, and James A. Michener and the Copernicus Society for their generous support in the writing of this book.

Contents

Voted, that the earth is the Lord's and the fulness thereof; voted, that the earth is given to the Elect; voted, that we are the Elect.

—An American

CHAPTER 1

My Wife in Seventeenth-Century Clothes

• 1 •

It was the fall before my captivity at the hands of King Philip that I discovered my wife was stealing from me. I started missing things at the dig: my vitamin pills, a mortise chisel, some wool socks. I tried to catch her in the act when she came to visit me, looked for bulges under her clothes when I ferried her from the island back to Boston, but my wife is secretive. At the dock she'd offer me her cheek, give my hand a squeeze and then hurry off into the dusky city with something hidden in her purse or bra; and I'd sail back to the island through the icy water, not knowing what it was I was minus until the next time I visited her, and after a little discreet snooping, found my chisel or my socks in a drawer or under a cushion. Why she didn't steal from me before we were married I don't know, except that her sort of stealing presumes a certain intimacy, and maybe she felt we hadn't yet got down the tricky ins and outs of each other's natures. Or maybe she felt it made up for our not living together. Still, I wanted to say to her: "Sweetheart, I've given you my

soul, more or less, why are you stealing my vitamins?" But
I didn't. Instead I started stealing some of *her* things and
bringing them out to the island with me. I meant it as a
vengeance, but she seemed pleased by it, as if this truly—at
last—was love.

Her name is Mehitible Constance Jenney; my name is
John Jenney Wheelwright. She goes by Hetty; I go by Wright.
We're cousins—first cousins—and though that might raise a
few brows, these are modern times, aren't they?

We were married last May—drove through a moody
drizzle up to my parents' summer place in Exeter, and after
a damp night in separate beds, stood side by side in the
Congregational Church. I remember Hetty all in white, her
face drained of color and her fingertips trembling. The
church interior was Puritan clean all around us—white-
paneled, white-pewed—and outside, through the paned
windows, enormous spring snowflakes drifted through the
drizzle like the falling lingerie of wanton angels. I was in a
daze when I said "I do." Hetty seemed nearly to faint at the
words. But back in Boston she went to her cellar apartment
on Commonwealth Avenue and I sailed through the night
harbor under a maple-colored moon out to the island. She
had Mrs. Steele's autistic twins to take care of, and I had
Samuel Mavericke, and we were both of us obsessive when
it came to self-enclosed worlds and seventeenth-century
ghosts.

· 2 ·

At first I tried to win her over to Samuel Mavericke,
showed her my model of his house, then when the full-sized
frame was raised, got her to run her fingertips over the
honest wood. I gave her appropriate presents—an oyster-
gray lappet cap and a moroccan-bound Hawthorne—sang
her an uncertain "Come Live with Me and Be My Love,"
and at the Massachusetts Historical Society showed her
Mavericke's letters to Governor Winthrop, pointed out his

civilized hand, the hope he expressed that God would enable him to walk inoffensively in the world ("To live a moral life," I explained; "To be isolated," Hetty murmured); and then showed her Winthrop's commendation of Mavericke, how he'd helped the Massachusetts Indians during the smallpox epidemic of 1633 when whole tribes were wiped out, helped them at great risk to his own life, burying their dead and taking their children home with him.

"He had a big heart, you see," I whispered to her in the quiet library.

"He lived on an island," she answered with a grimace.

"When the world needed him he came."

"But he went back," she said and pulled on her mittens, leaving me with the ancient paper and ink.

On our honeymoon night up in Exeter I got her drunk on my father's cognac and fit her into a seventeenth-century petticoat and cap bought at a Sotheby auction, dressed myself in breeches and buckled shoes. I got her to pretend to be some of our mutual ancestors, figuring I'd move us slowly into Mavericke and his wife. She looked maddeningly prim, her smallish breasts laced against her chest in Puritan denial (but still there!), and her gray gown concealing the heart shape of her hips. When she sat down the red petticoat showed just below the hem of her gown, the fancy embroidery and bright colors the perfect type (for a drunken typologist) of wilderness passion beneath a chaste and maidenly Hetty.

But when I tried it again a few months later in my boyhood bedroom on Beacon Hill, dressed her up and got her under the influence of liquor and Anne Bradstreet (even as I *thee*'d and *thou*'d her), I pushed it too far, asking her to give up her twins and come and live with me in my hand-built home in Boston harbor. She pulled away, and when I pressed her, told her the old story, that she lived amidst the whiz and howl of the American wilderness and that only on my (that is, Mavericke's) island could we lead a life of light and election, she got wobbly to her feet, and with a look of reproach and hurt, gathered up her clothes from around the room and started downstairs. I didn't try to stop her right off, kneeling at the top of the stairs while she flounced from floor to floor. But when I heard the street door shut, I went to the closet and pulled on a pair of galoshes over my buckled shoes.

I kept a block between us, ducking into a handy doorway from time to time, watching her as she ran lightly through the dirty city snow and past the disgorging doors of bars and taxis and noisy subways. She was like a sight out of one of my dreams, her maidenly clothes sprinkled with moonlight and the city lurid and hungry all around. When she reached her apartment I almost called out to her, but instead I waited until she was inside and then crept quietly up to the building. I wriggled my way behind a laurel bush and got down on my hands and knees in the snow so that I could see in through the grilled cellar window.

Over on the couch the girls lay in their autistic oblivion, their arms and legs entwined like the whisks of an egg-beater, their red hair snarled together. After a moment Hetty came out of the bedroom dressed in a nightgown and sat in a rocking chair near them. Then, like a ritual, she lifted her feet up in the air and held them there. I wondered at her, almost rapped on the window. But then slowly, almost imperceptibly, the twins let a small crevice open up between their knees so that Hetty could snug her toes in between them. They did it with barely an acknowledgment, without changing the dulled and inward-looking expressions on their faces. But Hetty had a look of gratitude, of victory, about her. She leaned her head back in the rocking chair, and when she felt my seventeenth-century cap still on her head, seemed to think of taking it off—but she didn't, and I went back to my parents' place blessing her.

• 3 •

"Hetty," I whispered the next night, allowed back into her bed. She was sleeping soundly beside me. "Sometimes I dream we live in an antique Boston, a Boston of pillory and stocks, of solemn divines parceling out God and His grace, and laws that tell me what to wear and worship and when to make love to you."

Beside me I could hear the soft lift and fall of her breathing like sweet assent. In the next room the twins slept wrapped in their love embrace, and above us Mrs. Steele entertained her lawyer.

"I dream of a settlement of light in a demon-dark wilderness," I told her, "of a moral hillside where I stand at dusk and see both the first faint fires lighting hearths in the village below, and the Indian fires like witchery on the tree trunks in the wilderness beyond. I stand on that hilltop and feel the lure of darkness, listen to the urgings of haunts and imps in the breeze. But in this dream, Hetty, just when I am about to give in to the wilderness, I drift downhill into the firelit settlement, searching out that one light that is yours."

CHAPTER
2

Samuel Mavericke in Twentieth-Century Clothes

• 1 •

I fell in love with Samuel Mavericke when I was thirteen. I used to stop off at the Boston Public Library on my way home from the Harrison Day School dressed in my gray blazer and gold tie, and in the huge vaulted reading room, dream over musty books about my namesake, John Wheelwright (1592–1679), and that old Indian-killer, cousin Isaac. I read their biographies, even made it through John's sermons, and in the Rare Book Room, fingered an original copy of Isaac's boastful account of King Philip's War. But from book to book, appearing out of nowhere, like a historical Flying Dutchman traveling without rhyme or reason from tome to tome, Samuel Mavericke nodded to me from the printed page. At first his was just another name in the broad patchwork of hotheads and dreamers, but after a while I began keeping an eye out for him, skimming the stories of Indians and antinomians and giving a little cry in the tomblike room now and then when I spotted his name. I started keeping a notebook on him, got my parents to take me on

17

the tour boat out to the harbor islands, out to *his* island, where I remember standing on a hilltop with the flash and steel of the Boston skyline within cannon range, thinking that *this* was where Mavericke must have built his house— the same hilltop where fifteen years later, during the preliminary dig, I found the faintly discolored earth where the postholes of his palisade had been.

He was born in 1602 in Devonshire, the son of a clergyman, and educated at Cambridge (where, if I can believe Mavericke's ghost, he once wore Oliver Cromwell's youthful socks after getting his own soaked in a downpour). No one is quite sure how or why he came to America, whether he was part of Robert Gorges's Episcopalian expedition in 1623 or one of the heady adventurers who tacked up and down the Atlantic Coast all during the first quarter of the century, but when John Winthrop and the Puritan elect arrived in 1630 ready to found a nation that would be a moral beacon to the rest of the world, they found Samuel Mavericke and his young bride, Amias, already there ahead of them. They had been living a quiet miracle at the edge of the wilderness, just the two of them a mile off the mainland, their house built with the aid of the Massachusetts Indians and a shipwright who had lain over one winter while selecting masts for the king's navy. Scouting for a likely site for God's new Israel, Winthrop had landed on the island to investigate a pearly screw of smoke twisting heavenward out of the firs and oaks, and expecting at any moment the whoop and cry of Satan's red imps, heard instead the tinkling, plangent sweetness of a Dowland pavane coming out of the greenery (pregnant Amias at her virginal), as if (as he wrote in his journal) "wee had come to Heaven's anteroom and not to the savage Wilderness' edge." With an air of admiration, awe and a bit of jealousy, he describes Mavericke and Amias, the clean and orderly house they kept, the candlelit windows, the clothed Indians living in a hut in the rear, the palisade and its quartet of bronze four-pounders, Amias's beautiful embroidery and Mavericke's trim pinnace (*The Royal We*) anchored in the lee of the island. He slept the night there, treated to hot strawberry pie and pignut tea, and in the morning—emboldened with the thought that if one man (and an Anglican at that) could so banish the wilderness from his hearth as well as his soul, what might not a thousand elect souls accomplish?—he crossed to the mainland with Mavericke guiding him to where a fresh spring gushed in the hollow of the three hills that later became Boston.

· 2 ·

In my gray blazer and galoshes, dripping puddles of October snow on the marble floor of the reading room, I played out the scenes of that first Boston winter in my thirteen-year-old head: the wigwams and the caves dug into the side of the Shawmut hills for homes, the teenage daughters of the elect scouring the tidal rocks in search of mussels, the Lady Arbella (with whom I had a momentary love affair) leaving the fine mists and green willows of Lincolnshire to die in a mud hut in the New England Canaan. That was the fall they were digging the cellar of the Hancock building across the way, the monolithic pile driver with its shuck-*chunk*, shuck-*chunk* making the old walls of the library tremble with each hit, driving the twentieth century into my head so that sometimes I awoke from my reading with the sense of having tumbled from the moral certitude of the past into the confusion of the present, from the light-and-shadow wilderness of Winthrop's New England (where at least you knew where you stood) to the cement-and-steel wilderness of our lost America. I traded rooms, carried my books from the first floor to the third floor, looking for some nook safe from that violent, inane, relentless hammering—shuck-*chunk*, shuck-*chunk*—but it invaded the entire library, rattling the glass cabinets in the Cabot Room and making the books creep forward on their shelves until they sprawled on the floor. The custodians finally had to wire the busts of Winthrop and Cotton Mather to their pedestals—John Endecott had fallen and shattered—winding the wire around their faces so that they looked as if someone had tried to truss up their souls inside of them, or as an eleven-year-old Hetty said on Hallowe'en afternoon: "Like someone had wrapped a hairnet around their ideas."

"Or cobwebs," I said.

"No, a hairnet. A hairnet is better!"

(She went as Joan of Arc that night; I was an all-gray Roger Williams.)

· 3 ·

As a member of the Church of England Mavericke was considered a papal mote in the Puritans' midst. Unable to offer proof of God's working in his soul, he was denied church membership, and along with it, any right to involvement in civic affairs. The aid he gave those first harsh winters, establishing trade alliances with the Indians and renting the settlers *The Royal We* so they could fish the bay for cod and mackerel, was forgotten when the better years came, when the grace-laden ships began arriving from England, flooding the lands surrounding the Mystic River with the elect. (Winthrop, to his credit, never forgot Mavericke's kindness, writing in his journal that he was "worthie of a perpetual remembrance," the *perpetual* being crossed out by some later, more dogmatic hand.) By the time my first ancestor arrived in 1636 (John, pastor of the Mount Wollaston church and brother-in-law of that redheaded heretic Anne Hutchinson), attempts were under way to have Mavericke's island confiscated and Mavericke banished. By 1645, after ancestor John was banished himself, Mavericke still had his island, but he lived there with Amias in a state of utter isolation, nearly forgotten by the community he had helped survive. By the time King Philip (not *my* King Philip; the *real* one) started his Indian uprising in 1675, Amias was dead. Six months later when Cousin Isaac ferried the first shipload of Indians out to Mavericke's island, informing the seventy-four-year-old Anglican that his island was to be used

as an internment camp and that the General Court had ordered quarters for him in town, Mavericke excused himself
and shuffled into a back room where he tied himself to
Amias's floor loom and sat waiting with his flintlock across
his lap.

When my corporal informed me of the matter [Cousin Isaac
wrote years later in *A Narrative of the Aweful Methods
and Mercies of God In the War with Satan's Red Armie,
1675–76*], *I went back to the old man's house. He had on
his person a waistcoat of great embroiderie, purples and reds
and golds that I think should have outdone the pope, and
which would have walked him before the Court had he been
seen in the streets of Boston towne with it on. I told him I
did not think a length of hemp enough to withstand the
efforts of my soldiers, to which he had nothing in replie. I
then told him I did not much care for church of Englanders
and did not much care if he put that hemp about his neck,
to which again he had nothing in replie. Then feeling the
unchristian smart of my words I meant to soothe him into
relenting, quoting him: "Oh that my people had hearkened
to me, and Israel had walked in my ways, I should have
subdued their enemies and turned my hand against their
adversaries." [*Psal. 81:13–14*] To which he replied: "The
Lord hath chastened me sore, yet he hath not given me over
to death." [*Psal. 118:18*] To which I replied he was welcome to Satan and left him on his island amidst the devilish
howls of the Indian Savages. He died, as I understand it,
in the general woe of starvation and disease the Lord effected that winter among the Savages, to his greater glorie
and to our better chastisement.*

· 4 ·

"To *his* greater glory?" Mavericke said last fall just before King Philip took Hetty and me hostage. "Who does he
mean by *his*? Me? Or the Lord?"

"The Lord, I think."

He took a sip of his Gatorade, and wrinkled his nose. "Your ancestor wasn't much of a writer," he said finally.

"Neither were you," I answered, waving a copy (Sotheby's, $340) of Mavericke's own *A Briefe Discription of New England and the Severall Townes Therein*. We were sitting in the parlor of his house (that is, in the parlor of his house as reproduced by me). Through the window I could see the tiers of the dig descending like steps down the hillside to the test trenches in the meadow below. From a distance my graduate students were like dabs of modernity against the sandy, colorless soil, dressed in the blues of their cutoffs and the bright T-shirts of MIT, sifting the dirt, spraying it with atomized water, looking for discoloration, for carbon, for the bone of crockery. The windscreen that buffered the site from the ocean wind (Mylar stapled to a snow fence) ran like a rickety backbone from the Quonset hut across the valley to a copse of poplars that exploded out of the bushy, gnarled meadow. Behind it the tourists who had come over on the one o'clock boat and were waiting for the four o'clock boat to take them back watched the lazy movement of the dig, picnicked on the mossy cowstones that littered the island, or tried to snap photographs of Fort Bentley (not visible from my window) or of the Boston skyline (all too visible).

"About Amias," Mavericke said after a minute. He was sitting in my Brewster chair and skimming through the first draft of my monograph on him. "I married her *in* New England. Not back in England like you've got it here. And she wasn't a young bride. She was a widow of one of the members of the Gorges expedition."

Through the window I could see Hetty come out of the Quonset hut where she'd wandered off half an hour ago (to sneak a cigarette). From a distance she looked like a teenager, short, with girlish knee socks on and only a puff of hips under her shorts.

"I like Amias as a young bride," I said eventually. We'd had this talk before.

"I know you have sources who make Amias a virgin," he said and he waved his hand at my stack of books, "but there are others who've got it right. And you're supposed to be interested in facts, aren't you? As a scientist?"

I watched Hetty making her way up the path.

"As a historian? An archaeologist?"

I turned in from the window and looked at him. "I like it my way, Mavericke. As for mere facts: I am my ancestors' descendant. Now, Hetty's coming, and you know the rules."

He made a face, drained his Gatorade and left by the back door.

• 5 •

"To what degree are ghosts and other parapsychological phenomena merely projections of our divided selves?" I asked Hetty once, hoping for a professional opinion, but she was busy puttering around in the back room, getting her things together to go back to the city—which is another way of saying she was waiting for me to get back to work so that she could steal something before she went.

• 6 •

In the reading room that first winter, while I wrote plays and biographies (even an *auto*biography) about Mavericke, I could see the welded skeleton of the Hancock tower rising floor by floor against the frigid New England sky. Like homeless ghosts, the winter clouds floated between the red beams, gliding in from the west and hovering a moment inside the bony building as if auditioning for its soul, and then drifting seaward out through the far side. Sometimes, stuck in Chapter Three (Mavericke picking wild strawberries for a pregnant Amias and tallying all the reasons for abandoning the island), or in the second act (Amias's monologue by moonlight), I left the library and crossed the street to the building site, then stood at a peephole while the early dusk of a deep winter folded around me. I watched the end-of-day work on the building, the spray of welding sparks falling like lost angels from the fourteenth floor into the gloom below, the dark cranes roaming the slushy landscape like Lowellian dinosaurs, and in the haze of dusk the workmen seeming mere hard-hatted shadows, or—fresh from my theater of saints and sinners—like underworld souls trudging across the land in the service of some welded, pile-driving Satan. I left with my bundle of Maverickalia under my arm, making my way homeward through the evening traffic, passing the dark-faced pedestrians, and trying to hold my soul tight to me for safekeeping.

Years later, when the Hancock building was finished, it made the national news for spitting its enormous panes of blued glass onto the pedestrians fifty stories below. For the next ten years James Avenue and Trinity Place were intermittently cordoned off while engineers talked about vacuum and wind sheer, and while thicker and thicker panes were tried and lawsuits bogged in the Boston courts. But John Wheelwright's dreamy namesake, an MIT undergraduate majoring in archaeology and ethics, knew that the falling glass was more than the shiny calculations of atmospheric pressure and vacuum, that a monument built by shades and unlit souls would have to spit out its devilry on the very shadows that had built it. Even today from Mavericke's Island, in spite of its skin of bright glass, I can see the iron-red skeleton underneath, standing like a colossus over the urban wilderness.

CHAPTER
3

The Virgin in the Sky

• 1 •

When summer came that first year of my infatuation with
Mavericke, instead of her usual weekend visits, Hetty moved
up with us to our summer house in Exeter. Her mother
drove up to visit from time to time (without her father), and
her father came at careful intervals (without her mother).
My mother and father—in earnest conversation under the
purple arch of magnolias in the backyard—would suddenly
fall silent when Hetty and I came near, though we might
catch a sad something about courts and a sadder "That's the
world today, isn't it?" My *wife* tells me now that she knew
that her parents were getting divorced, but my *cousin*, I remember, had a look of wonder and confusion in her green
eyes as we searched under the laurel for an orphaned croquet ball.

That was the summer when we used to go out into the
pasture that slopes away from the north side of the property and moo at the cows and do Indian dances to stir them
up (though the cows merely stared at us with their big, brown,
fly-confused eyes).

That was the summer too when we were learning the constellations, meeting in the upper hall at midnight and sneaking out of the house with our star chart and penlight.

And that was the summer when I made sure that when we went to church, I sat between Hetty and the aisle, so that when the deacon took up the collection I could take Hetty's quarter from her and for a moment feel how warm her hand had made it before dropping it into the silver plate.

When the hot weather came we all went swimming and sailing at Sagamore Lake, me in somber trunks and Hetty in a bikini (the top of which she was just beginning to need). I taught her how to handle a jib, drilling her in nautical terms as we sailed ("Port!" "Starboard!" "Come about!") and feeling a burst of joy when she cried "Aye-aye!" The summer sun sparkled along the boom, and as we tacked and heeled, skidding across the bright water, I told her about Samuel Mavericke, reciting bits and pieces of my unfinished novels and biographies. She listened and said he sounded like Daniel Boone and sucked on her Popsicle. I told her about Amias, said that she was short and had curly hair and green eyes, that she was pretty and that she was true to Mavericke right up to the end.

"Was she like Cleopatra?" she wanted to know. "Because I played Cleopatra in the class play. I was *very* good. *Everyone* said so."

"You've been in a play?" I asked.

"And I kissed Eddie McElroy. He was Julius Caesar."

I thought about that, and the next day brought two copies of my play up to the lake, and in a cardboard box some props from the house: a wool cap for Amias, a silk scarf with embroidery on it, a Chatty Cathy for their baby ("My name is Chatty Cathy and I love you!") and my BB gun for Mavericke's matchlock. Out in the *Protestant Ethic* (my father's name for our sailboat: He had a touch of his son about him—until he went deaf and forgot that the world was still there), out in our boat, I say, I talked Hetty through her part, filled her in on Amias, on the rightness of an island

life in a hostile world (or a fourteen-year-old's words to that
effect), and how Mavericke's pretty wife never lost her purity in the midst of the wilderness. She read her lines like a
natural, trying out different faces and voices (though she
got stuck in Cleopatra from time to time), and asking me
questions with a look of such sincerity and concern that at
the end of an hour I was abuzz with love and gratitude. I
watched her as she read, watched the dance of emotion on
her face, her voice rising into a scream from time to time
when the cold spray cut a dagger across her back and then
falling back into Amias. The wind kicked up her curly hair
and her lips were bright red from her Popsicle. I watched
her so much I began to lose my place in the script. At the
end of Act 2, I sailed the boat over to a float—the far float
we called it—and lashed it to one of the slabs of rubber tire
that rimmed its edge.

"This is our island, Amias!" I said, and then pointing to
the cluttered beach: "And *that's* Boston village."

"And this is your gun," Hetty said.

"My *matchlock*."

"And this is baby Samuel," she said, hauling Chatty Cathy
by the leg and stepping up out of the boat. She already had
Amias's cap on.

Dizzy with visions, I marched up and down the float saying my lines while Hetty tried to keep up. On the shore I
imagined Winthrop and John Endecott and that narrow-
minded bastard—Mavericke's nemesis—the Reverend John
Wilson throwing covetous looks our way. Behind them the
leafy Boston woods darkened and grew sinewy. I had a feeling of mastery, of potency: Hetty behind me, and the world
held off by the wide water. *This* was how you kept yourself
your self, I thought, how you kept the world away from
you. I pumped my BB gun up and when someone—a boy—
dove off the near float and started swimming toward us,
toward *our* float, I shot at him.

"Wright!"

I shot again. Whoever it was stopped in the water. Back

on the other float one of his buddies started yelling at him and pointing at me. I held the gun up high in the air so no one would make any mistakes. Behind me Hetty was searching wildly through her script.

"Act Two, Scene Three," I said. "The Puritans try to take Mavericke's island away from him."

"But did he shoot at them?"

"He didn't have to. He tricked them by deeding his island over to Samuel junior."

Hetty looked doubtfully at Chatty Cathy and then toward the beach. But everything was calm there; no one had heard anything. On the near float the town boys—four of them—were in a huddle, keeping an eye on me and talking. After a minute they dove into the water and started swimming shoreward, toward where the boats were moored.

"Wright . . ." Hetty said behind me.

"Never mind," I told her. I watched the boys swimming; they were headed toward one of the speedboats. "Sometimes you have to fight for what's yours."

"It's just a float, Wright!"

"It's an island! It's *our* island!"

"I'm getting back in the boat."

"You don't know how to sail yet," I said to her, but she left Chatty Cathy and climbed into the sailboat all the same. The boys had got their motor started.

"I'll untie it and just float away."

"Amias wouldn't have."

"*Cleopatra* would have! She was *smart*! She would have let them think they had the island and then come back and married them and poisoned them or something."

"Cleopatra," I said slowly, pumping up my gun, "did not lead a moral life."

When they came they came full speed, buzzing the float and nearly swamping the *Protestant Ethic* so that Hetty screamed. I got a few shots off and told her to get back on the float. When they came a second time, one of them leaned over the edge of the boat with an oar and tried to hit me, but I shot him in the chest and the sting made him cry out and drop the oar. The beach had woken up by now; the lifeguard was waving and yelling out to us, but I didn't even turn toward them. The speedboat made another pass, not at me but twenty yards out to pick the oar up. Then they idled a ways off. Behind me Hetty was standing stiff with fear. She had a dazed, unconscious look about her, and for the first time I felt a little rattled. When they came again they got Chatty Cathy, knocking her with the oar so that she skidded across the water and one of her arms flew off. The boat let out a cheer. From the shore there were shouts and waves; I thought I heard my mother ("Jay-jay!"). I was getting hot and confused, but I couldn't stop; I'd gone too far to stop. I pumped the gun up again and took aim. But just as the speedboat started again, in a quiet, vacant voice, Hetty spoke behind me.

"My parents," she said. "I think my parents are getting a divorce."

I turned to her. She wasn't looking at me. She wasn't looking at the speedboat. She was watching Chatty Cathy floating broken twenty feet off in the dark water. I lowered my gun and took a step toward her, but the roar of the speedboat was in my ears, and then the oar hit me in the head and all I saw was a shower of light before I hit the water.

· 2 ·

That night, after a scolding from my mother and an interview with my father ("Why a gun?" he wanted to know; "It's the American way!" I shouted into his hearing aid), I lay with my head at the foot of the bed and my feet on my pillow. I could see out the window that way, see the dark tops of the oaks and smell the sugary pines. From time to time I thought I heard something in the hall, something like footsteps, but when I looked, there was nothing except the shadows of the trees waving along the wall, and at the far end of the hall, the dark rectangle of Hetty's door. I took my pajama top off—it wasn't hot; I just felt better with it off—and stared up at the sky where I could see the bright *W* of Cassiopeia between the treetops. After a couple of minutes I thought I heard something in the hall again, and turning, caught a shadowy movement out of the corner of my eye. There was no noise, and no answer when I whispered "Hetty?" Still I kept my eye on the hall, and after another minute she moved out of the shadows and stood in my doorway.

"Are you all right?" I said, but she just stayed where she was. "Hetty?"

"You're sleeping upside down," she said.

"I'm just looking out the window."

She turned from me to the window and then crossed the room, hauling herself up onto the bed and sitting on my pillow so we faced each other. "How's your head?" she asked.

I felt the egg under my bandage. "Cassiopeia's out, you know."

She nodded in the dark. I could see her by the moonlight that spilled in at the window. She fidgeted with the pillow under her and then tugged at her hair, and then suddenly pulled her pajama top tightly against her chest.

"I've got breasts," she said, gazing straight across at me and keeping the flannel stretched so the tiny rise of her breasts was evident. "They're not rosebuds anymore."

"No," I murmured.

"I've got breasts," she said again as if daring me to say otherwise, and she peered fiercely at me in the dark. Then just as quickly, she let go of her pajama top and turned away, looking over at my model of the *Mayflower* on top of my bookcase. The moonlight made ghosts in the rigging, the shadows dancing from mast to mast.

"Maybe your parents *aren't* getting a divorce," I said after a time.

She acted as if she hadn't heard me, still looking at my ship model.

"Maybe they're just fighting."

She cocked her head from side to side and then threw me a look the length of the bed. "Someone whistled at me in town."

"Or maybe they're going on summer vacation alone."

"A man did. Actually he didn't *whistle* at me. He said something."

I looked at her and kept quiet.

"Something dirty."

"What?" I said finally. "What'd he say?"

"Something dirty, I said."

"What?"

"You want me to say it?" she asked, and in the moonlight I could see her brow arch.

"No."

"I will," she said. "If you want. I will."

"No."

"*I* didn't mind," she said. "I liked it. *I* didn't mind."

I put my pajama top back on and didn't look at her.

"Do you want to see one of my bras," she said next. "I've got three of them. Do you want to see one?"

I shook my head.

"Do you want to see one?"

"No," I said a little angrily.

"Here," she said, swinging off the bed. "I'll get one." And I heard the pat of her bare feet on the pine floor. She came back and put a bra on the bed between us.

"Mother calls them brassieres. That's French."

"We should go to sleep now."

"*Brassiere*," she said. It was white and starchy-looking in the moonlight.

"We should go to sleep now. It's late."

"Bras and panties," she said, and then suddenly: "*I* don't care if they get divorced. I really don't. *You* care. *I* don't. I really don't."

I watched as a branch waved up and across her chest, throwing her face in and out of shadow. Then I picked her bra up.

"It's soft," I said. She looked uncertainly at me. "It's pretty." And I patted it as if it were a pet and then left off, feeling stupid. But she seemed to smile in the dark, tucking her head down and then shaking her curls out.

"You can keep it," she said and she hopped off the bed. "You can keep it tonight."

I nodded and didn't say anything.

"I'll need it in the morning though. All right?"

"All right."

She waited a moment longer, and then turned around and went through the door and down the hall into her room.

But I couldn't sleep. Outside the window, I could see the leg and hoof of Pegasus making a bright arch between the dark trees. Hetty's bra was on the pillow beside me. I didn't touch it, but I could feel its presence. I tried to sleep, but the harder I tried the more awake I felt. After half an hour, I got up and walked quietly down the hall to Hetty's doorway and whispered in the direction of her bed.

"Is that you?" she answered.

"Are you sleeping?" I asked.

"No."

Her bedroom was away from the moon, dark.

"I thought we could take your star chart out and learn another constellation."

"Okay," she answered simply.

"Are you too sleepy?"

"No."

I waited until I heard her throw her bedcovers off, then turned around and went back into my room for my bathrobe. We met at the top of the stairs, and taking giant steps over the ones that creaked (second, fourth, ninth), made it safely downstairs to the back door.

Outside, the lawn was wet with dew and the grass clippings stuck to our bare feet. We ducked under the clothesline and made it through the lawn furniture over to the barbed-wire fence that faced off the cow pasture. Watching for cow flops in the moonlight, we started across the field.

Overhead the stars seemed to shower down upon us, zooming across the sky from horizon to horizon, spilling from the bright crown of Corona Borealis straight overhead to the reddish spray of Scorpius just rising in the south. We made it out to our favorite spot (a cluster of mossy stones), and wiping the grass off our feet, sat down and got out Hetty's star chart and my penlight.

"Okay, review," I said. "You do the north sky. I'll do the south."

"Polaris!" she said straight off, stabbing the sky in the north, and then describing the gentle arc of Ursa Minor, then Ursa Major, and then the serpentine tail of the dragon that coiled between them. In the wet quiet her voice made me shiver. She didn't say the stars' names the way I did— all pomp and textbook—there was always the scent of mystery, of awe and pleasure at the utter constancy with which the stars shone every night. At the beginning of the summer I'd tried to explain to her that Polaris would not be the polestar forever, that even though it seemed to be the only fixed star in the sky, it was moving an infinitesimal amount each year and after a couple of thousand years it would no longer be due north. She'd looked at me for a moment as if I were lying, and then with my penlight, scrambled through her book until she found the chapter on Polaris, telling me it was called the Steering Star, wasn't it? The Ship Star, wasn't it? The Stella Maris, wasn't it? I said okay, the Stella Maris, okay.

"Auriga," she said now, pointing to the kitelike constellation on the east horizon. (We'd made it through the Andromeda group with a little tussle over the Greek letters I tried to get her to use.) "Auriga is the charioteer. The brightest star, Alpha Aurigae," she said with a grimace at me, "is called the Goat Star, and the triangle nearby makes up her three kids."

"Also known as . . . ?"

"The charioteer's whip."

For a time we sat in silence, the meadow wet and dark

around us, and overhead, dragons and bears' tails and the wings of horses revolving in a bright circle. I remembered what the Preface said about the Greeks, how they thought the stars were attached to glass spheres, glass globes that moved in fine procession inside each other, ringing across the heavens and all around us if only we had ears pure enough to hear them. I looked at Hetty. Of the two of us I could read the star chart better, take coordinates off one constellation and find another, remember which stars were which—Delta Cephei, Alpha Herculis—but it was Hetty who could see the lovely tuck of Virgo's shoulder in the sky, see Cassiopeia's throne in the Milky Way and the chains that hang from Andromeda's wrists. When we talked about *why* there were such things as constellations, I told her what Father told me, that there was something in us that made us arrange things around ourselves. It was like Amias playing her virginal in the middle of the wilderness—but she cut me short and said no, no, and lying on her back, started linking up stars with her finger. It was because they were white all in blackness and if you could bring two of them together (Oh! I should have seen the twins coming even then!), if you *could,* then it helped you feel less alone. And if you could bring more than two, then that was better still. Because *there,* she said, pointing upward, there's Andromeda, and there's her mother, Cassiopeia, and her father, Cepheus, and her husband, Perseus, *all* in the same part of the sky. Right? *Right?* She wanted to know. *Wasn't that proof?*

"Do you think it all happened?" she asked suddenly beside me.

"What?"

"Do you think there really was an Andromeda who got chained to the rocks because of her mother? And a sea dragon *really* attacked her? And Perseus *really* saved her and married her?"

I wondered at her. It seemed so clear to me that there hadn't been.

"I don't know," I said finally.

"I'll bet there was."

"I don't know," I said again, and turned my penlight on and started studying the star chart. Beside me Hetty bristled a little.

"I'll bet there *was* because you can see the way Cassiopeia's got her hands thrown up in the air like she's upset that she did what she did to Andromeda, and Cepheus isn't hardly a father at all, he's just sort of dim and unimportant, isn't he?"

"Maybe we should learn Lyra next."

"And then Perseus has got Medusa's head in his hand and his legs thrown apart and his sword raised over his head like he'd save someone if they needed to be saved."

I shut the light off and looked at her. She didn't look at all like Amias, not at all spiritual. I felt angry with her. She wasn't following things properly, running off and thinking things on her own. There floated into my head a picture of Amias getting into Mavericke's sailboat and leaving his island without him.

"What *did* that man say to you?" I asked after a minute. I hadn't meant to say it, and when I saw how Hetty started, I knew I shouldn't have. But I asked again anyway.

"I can't tell you now," she said.

"Why not?"

She looked up at the sky. "I just can't."

"You were all set to back in my bedroom."

"I know, but I can't now. Not out here." And she turned from me so I couldn't see her face. I tossed the penlight down on the rocks and threw my head back and tried to find Cygnus, the swan, high overhead, but my skull started hurting under the bandage so I had to look back down. I picked the penlight up and turned it on and off to make sure I hadn't broken it.

"What *did* he say?" I asked after a minute, but this time Hetty just kept looking upward at the stars.

"They're *so* beautiful!"

"I'm asking you what he said."

She kept her back to me and said dreamily: "*I'd* like to be a constellation."

I could feel myself go cold. "*You'd* like to be a constellation?" I said; and then it was out of my mouth even before I thought to say it: "Do you think you could be? Do you think you could be when you like people to say dirty things to you?"

She spun around and flung a hurt look at me. "I didn't like it!"

"You said you did."

"But I didn't. I did a *little*. But I didn't."

I shone the penlight in her face. "Do you think you could be a constellation when you like men to say dirty things to you?"

"Wright!"

"Do you think you could be a constellation when you show your bras to people?"

She tried to cover the penlight with her hands.

"And talk about your breasts that way?"

"Wright!"

"Do you talk that way with everyone?"

She hit me with her fists, and then shouting, "They're *rosebuds!*" ran off through the high grass. I got up and started after her, caught her by the arm, but she shook me off and ran on. I stopped and watched her go, dazed and breathing hard, watched her trip and stumble across the pasture, skid under the barbed-wire fence and then disappear into the shadows in the backyard. When I heard the screen door slam I turned around and threw the penlight as far as I could across the pasture.

Then I went and sat back down on the rocks.

"You shouldn't have tried to leave this afternoon," I said after a minute. "Hetty," I said.

After another minute I saw the light in her bedroom turn on, and then turn off.

A couple of days later her mother came to take her to her new home on Martha's Vineyard.

CHAPTER
4

King Philip with Horns on His Head

• 1 •

And for ten years I saw her only on holidays and at family get-togethers, watched her hairstyle change from flip to ponytail to pixie, her summer shoes change from sneakers to sandals back to sneakers, her bathing suits from two-piece to one-piece. I remember a woolly cable-stitch sweater seen one birthday and gone the next, a Black Watch plaid worn on a teenage Thanksgiving, the herringbone suit she wore at my high school graduation, the Easter yellow gown she wore at hers. She talked to me still—summery talk across the hallway upstairs, or cozy talk around the dying fire at Christmastime—and I would hold on to whatever she'd said for three months, half a year, and when I saw her again, ask her about this or that summer thing, this or that winter thing. But she was always past it—Anita had replaced Margie, the job at Vineyard Hardware, the job at Casual Corner, Mt. Holyoke had taken the glow from Radcliffe, Radcliffe from Wheaton, Wheaton from Wellesley. My sophomore year at college I tried to get her to apply to MIT,

37

told her MIT's psychology department was one of the best in the country, but she said it would be all white rats and statistical analysis, and she was interested in something quite, quite different.

When it came time for me to do my graduate fieldwork, I chose a dig on Martha's Vineyard, eight miles from Hetty's mother's house, an excavation of Indian sites, one of which was a burial ground and the center of an Indian protest. And I think now I should have been able to spot King Philip, pick him out by virtue of some genetic radar from among the pickets before he put on antlers and a deerskin and married Hetty under the Maypole. I should have been able to feel his eyes on me, sense him hiding behind this tree, that rock, while I bicycled cross-island after a day of brushing dirt off Indian bones, feel him somewhere in the air when I pulled up to Hetty's mother's house and climbed up to Hetty's bedroom (she was still at college). I should have sensed him taking notes, memorizing, thinking, analyzing, planning. I should have known Philip before I knew Philip. I should have known him before I started getting the notes.

They started during my second winter down on the Vineyard when I was alone at the Squibnocket site cataloging bones and potsherds dug up the summer before. They were taped most of the time to the door of the trailer where I worked, but sometimes I found them tied to my bicycle handlebar or left in Hetty's mother's mailbox. They were handwritten quotes from seventeenth-century texts dealing with Indians—petitions, sermons, laws—all of them carefully selected to indict the writer by his own words. In the beginning I thought it was someone from one of the other sites trying to spook me, but when I saw them on Friday nights there was never any hint of duplicity or foolery. So then I figured it was Hetty, Hetty working with some weekday accomplice (maybe her friend Alice), and for some weeks running I made an idiot of myself when she came home to visit her mother on weekends, throwing sly comments her way and leaving certain volumes lying around the house with a page turned down. But come Saturday night she just trotted off in her tight jeans and Fair Isle sweaters while my volumes sat clumsy and untouched on the kitchen counter or on the hamper.

So then I *did* begin to get spooked. Bicycling down the icy path to the dig in the morning, the snow-covered field hushed all around me and the winter mist rising in drifts off the water, I had an eerie feeling of being watched, of eyes peering at me out of the laurel and juniper that ran along the meltwater channels down to the ocean. I looked for footprints in the snow, but found only the pentagonal grid of my own boots; started once or twice at the sight of myself—wool-helmeted and ski-goggled—in the trailer window. Inside, measuring the zygomatic bone of a fifteenth-century forebear of the Gay Head Indians, I'd suddenly stop working and listen to the wind scurrying along the corrugated ribs of the trailer or whispering against the windowpane. Sometimes I'd go out and walk around the building, check my bicycle handles, and after a long scan of the dig, ride into town to the hardware store or the diner; but never—even when I came back and found a note had bloomed in my absence—did I see even the hint of my antagonist.

So I started writing notes back. At first I just appended source and page cite to *his* notes, but as the warmer weather approached I got my own quotes together—Hannah Dustin and Cousin Isaac were favorites—countering each incident of white savagery quoted me with an incident of red savagery. For Miles Standish putting the head of Wituwamet on a pike atop the fort at Plymouth, I gave him Mary Rowlandson's baby's brains dashed against a tree trunk; and when he cited me the Reverend Solomon Stoddard's proposal that dogs should be raised "to hunt Indians as they do Bears," I finished the quote for him: "for they act like wolves and are to be dealt with as wolves."

Come April when the dig geared up and the Gay Head Indians came out in protest, I got myself a pair of binoculars and, squatting in the trenches like an infantryman, drew beads on each picketer, studying their faces, trying to Ouija who it was who was after me. I looked for the quiet fire of fanaticism, maybe an unblinking eye or a certain sharp way of walking, and I looked for intelligence, for education: Some of his quotes, after all, stumped me. There were certain souls I could damn and disregard: louts out for a lark, drinking beer and throwing clods of sod at us across the snowfence; teenagers on dirt bikes; older Indians rousted out of their Gay Head trailers and looking ill at ease; a Mashpee delegation that came only on the weekend ferry; and some idiot who'd bought a headdress on God-knows-what camping trip out West. That left ten or twelve others: a couple of women in snug sweaters and Revlon—both with the look of Puritan-baiters; a black Indian with atavistic welts on his back and cheeks, a sign bearer (I'M AN AMERICAN; ARE YOU?); a couple of racial tossed salads; and a six-foot-sixer with the right look of irony in the way he held himself. Home from college to plan her Maypole party, Hetty voted for the scarred Indian, said he looked sinister enough. I told her *she'd* look sinister with welts on her cheeks.

"Who, then?" she asked, letting the binoculars down and looking at me. They left two white rings around her eyes.

"I don't know," I answered and took the glasses from her. "But I'm working on it."

Later that week, coming out of the Rexall's in Vineyard Haven, I found Increase Mather pinched between my hand brakes and my tires slashed. It cost me $24.25 for new tires. I kept the receipt. At the dig they started calling me names, shouting across the sloping terraces that the descendant of the First American Fascist Butcher was butchering the bones of their fathers. (Not true: The First American Fascist Butcher was John Underhill, commander of the Puritan troops who massacred the Pequots on March 8, 1637; Cousin Isaac is third or fourth in line.) Calling from Wellesley, Hetty said I should ask to be transferred to one of the other sites, Hornblower or Cunningham, where there were no burial grounds being excavated, but I told her I'd tough it out, and then quoted her for the hundredth time Oliver Cromwell's statement that the only man he was afraid of was John Wheelwright on the Cambridge football field. But a couple of days later I woke in the middle of the night with a spooky feeling that someone had just been in my room. I lay absolutely still, listening, moving my eyes around the room, down the shadowed hall to the head of the stairway. I thought I heard the crush of a footstep on the carpeted stairs, held my breath and imagined someone holding theirs. I thought of pretending to turn in my sleep, of saying something, of clapping my hands to startle them. I waited instead. Minutes went by and there was only silence. Had it only been the creak and whisper of an old house? I pictured a dark figure standing stock-still on the stairs, in turn picturing me lying wide-awake above. But there was only the brush of branches outside my window and the shadows quivering across Hetty's clothes in the closet. I moved. The bed moved under me. I turned on my side and coughed. There was no answer. I closed my eyes, opened them, then closed them again, daring myself to keep them closed. A car rumbled comfortably past on the road out front.

But in the morning I found Cousin Isaac taped to the bedpost.

"I mean he just came into the house?" Hetty asked the next weekend, sitting at the kitchen table and looking the note over. "I mean holy shit!"

"Don't tell your mother."

"Did you call the police?"

"No."

"Christ, Wright. We can't just have people breaking into our house."

"He won't do it again."

"Why not? How do you know?"

"Because now he's proved he can."

She made a face and looked the note over again. "'. . . so is the night the planting-ground of his serpents,'" she quoted. "Suppose he comes in when you're down on the couch and *I'm* up in my room? Does he know about me? Does he know I come home on weekends?"

"I don't know. How should I know?"

"I'll bet he does."

"I doubt it."

"I'll bet he does," she said like a challenge.

I sat stupidly and watched her read the note over again.

"I went to high school with some of those guys," she said after a minute. I didn't answer. "Do you know any of their names?"

"No."

"I'm trying to remember." She fell to studying the note again. Then the intelligence of something lit on her face and she stood up. "You wait here," she said and hurried out of the room. After a minute she was back with a stack of cards.

"I was hiding these," she said, giving me one. "I was going to mail you one, formally." They were invitations to the Maypole party, printed and signed by her and her friend Alice. "I'll invite them," she said. "I'll invite them and then maybe they'll quit all this."

"I don't think they'll come."

"They'll come. They'll come if I invite them in person. I'll go down to the dig with you tomorrow."

"You think a Maypole party will make them forgive me for measuring their ancestors' fibias?"

She scrambled around and then knelt on her seat, leaning over me and pointing at the invitation. "Look," she said. I could see the ripple of her backbone where her sweater pulled away from her pants. "First we're putting up a Maypole at Mare's Point. Everyone's supposed to wear gay colors, maybe come in masquerade, in animal costume. That's historic, right? And then while the tree gets decorated with ribbons and flowers and stuff we elect a Lord and Lady of the May who preside over everything. In the afternoon we'll have a cookout at Tibbet's Field, softball and Frisbee. *Revels.*

And at night a dance on Alice's yacht. Alice's brother's going to rig his stereo up." And she turned her head abruptly so the hair about her ear brushed my cheek. "So why wouldn't they come?"

I shrugged. "*I* might not come."

"You? You *have* to come." And she stuffed one of the invitations into my shirt pocket. "We won't be inviting anyone else from the dig. And we need you for authenticity. We want an authentic *American* May day. You have to tell us what's right and what's wrong."

"Frisbee," I said. "Frisbee's wrong."

"Not *that*. I mean details. We need historic details."

I took up a pencil and, pulling out my invitation, crossed out the *May* in the Lord of the May and wrote in *Misrule*."

"Misrule?" she said, looking at it. "What's Misrule?"

"The lack of moral imperatives."

"I know what *misrule* is. What is it with a capital *M*?"

So I wrote out some sources for her—Johnson's *Pagan Rites and Rituals*, Morton's *New English Canaan*, even "The Maypole of Merrymount"—and told her she didn't want *me* there, I'd likely act out Endecott's part and chop down her Maypole. She said I ought to learn how to relax, and then like a poker dealer, squared up her stack of invitations.

• 2 •

But when May 1 came I was already awake downstairs on the couch before Hetty's alarm went off. I lay listening to her upstairs, the pad of her bare feet on the floorboards, her closet door rolling with a rumble back into the wall, a hanger spilling onto the floor. When the shower turned on in the bathroom, I got up, put on the somber clothes I'd laid out before going to bed and started some hot water in the kitchen. A robin snow had fallen in the night. It lay with a look of bemused treachery in the pockets and coves of the backyard, making long fingers in the lee of the tree roots, white pillows and rags on the matted winter leaves. On the lawn itself it had already begun to melt; dropped spat-spat-spat! off the tree branches; gargled in the eaves troughs. When Hetty came downstairs she threw one look at my clothes, made a face and crossed to the window.

"What's the temperature?"

I crooked my neck so I could see the thermometer out the window. "Thirty-nine."

"Shit!"

"But it's sunny. It'll get up to fifty."

"This is May!" she said with a vexed look.

"This is New England," I answered and took the kettle off the stove.

She was wearing a skirt with a violent print, madder rose with purple and ocher flowers, brownish stems and birds peeking out from behind aquamarine leaves. She had on a peasant blouse that very nearly gave her a bust, elastic-belted around her waist and with great puffy sleeves that snapped tightly about her forearms. There were ribbons tied brace-letlike around her wrists, ribbons in her hair, and bright knee socks and green-dyed sneakers with red shoelaces. When she walked she made a noticeable rustle and her ribbons floated behind her like streamers.

"Well?" she said.

"You look . . ."

"Yes?"

I waved my hands helplessly.

"*You* look like you're going to a funeral," she said.

I tugged at the gray homespun I'd put on. "I thought a reminder of the darker things in life was in order. I'm offering myself as an anchor."

"To what?"

"To everything. To your ribbons."

She studied me a moment and then went back to the window. "I'm supposed to wash my face with *dew*. That's what one of your books said."

"This is a *New England* May Day," I said, holding out a

cup of tea to her. "Wash your face with snow."

She grimaced, but took the tea. "Do you think anyone will come?"

"Sure."

"Do you?"

I nodded, and said again: "With snow. Wash your face with snow."

She peered at me as if trying to see whether I were kidding, and then putting her tea down, opened the door and skipped outside. I sat at the table and watched her pick her way across the soggy grass to an island of snow under a forsythia bush. She squatted beside the yellow buds, and cupping her hand together, scooped up a basinful of snow and threw it in her face. She rubbed her cheeks with it, then her forehead, then swirled a fingertip over each of her eyelids. She shook herself, her hair scrambling about her face, and hurried back to the house, patting her face dry with the hem of her skirt.

"Cold!" she said, rushing back in the door. "It's supposed to make me beautiful! Do I look beautiful?"

"Beautiful."

She stood shivering and stamping her feet on the rubber mat just inside the door. Her cheeks were bursting with red and there were ice crystals on her eyelashes. "Do I?" she said.

"You'll be Queen of the May," I answered, feeling turned about.

"Queen of the May," she repeated, and she smiled and stuck her cold hands under her arms. "You have to vote for me."

"I will."

"You *have* to."

"I will, I will,"

"Okay," she said, going for her tea. "Let's get sweaters. Okay."

We clipped some sprays of forsythia and got into the car, driving to where Hetty knew we could find some cro-

cuses and some cranberry sprigs. We wandered through a
bushy croft picking whatever looked springlike or decora-
tive, me in my Puritan getup and Hetty sparkling like a fairy.
The ground was soft underfoot, and the melting snow ran
in runnels and freshets through the matted grass. By the
time we reached Mare's Point the air was warming so that
drifts of mist rose out of the dunes and sea bracken, purling
heavenward and vanishing in the bright sun. We started down
one of the sloping, rutted paths toward the beach, Hetty
scurrying up a sandy hillock from time to time to see if she
could spot Alice and her brother or the Maypole. But we
seemed alone. There was just the sound of the invisible ocean
breaking and receding on the shingle, and the outraged gulls
floating overhead. We went down one path, then another,
then a third. I got sand in my shoes. Hetty said she'd *told*
me no one would come, and with each half a dozen steps,
started tossing things away, first a branch of forsythia, then
a crocus, then a fir cone. I walked behind her picking everything up and adding it to my armload of pine boughs. I was
thinking we'd have our own May Day, the two of us. But
just as the gray line of the ocean began to appear beyond
every second or third hummock, we heard the woody rasp
of a saw somewhere on our right. With a little cry, Hetty
veered off, tramping along the ridge of a dune. I stumbled
after her, my hopes sinking.

An hour later the Maypole, shorn of all but its topmost
limbs, had been hoisted and shored up in the sandy soil
with stakes and dutchmen. I put my pine boughs in a circle
at the base and stepped back, sitting on a sandy tussock and
chewing on some rush. I let Hetty run from person to person, welcoming them as they trudged through the bracken
or along the beach. By ten o'clock there were twenty people
in all, some dressed in street clothes but most in masquerade, gay colors and ribbons everywhere. The costume mistress of the Vineyard Haven Players showed up with a
trunkload of foolscaps and bells, Bottom's ass head, faun
and nymph costumes. Someone with an alto recorder played

"The Leaves Are Green" over and over while whoever could get hold of one of the long garlands that were tied around the top of the Maypole rehearsed dancing in a circle—first clockwise, then counterclockwise—plaiting and braiding their streamers with the other dancers. One of Hetty's Wellesley friends brought a cradle with a baby doll decked with hothouse flowers in it, setting it on my pine boughs and explaining that this was tradition, fertility and all, didn't we know? I watched with a growing sense of exclusion, the noise getting on my nerves, and the sight of Hetty dancing with so many people I didn't know—kissing men, kissing women, letting them feel her ribbons and her hair—making me feel in turn angry and then stupid for being angry. I tried to pull myself out of it, picked up a baseball someone had brought and for a few minutes practiced my pitching grips from my Little League days. But with each windup I just backed off farther from the Maypole, until finally I tossed the ball down, and ducking into the sea shrubbery, started back toward the road.

That's when I saw the horns.

They pricked above a dune not twenty yards from me, deer antlers, only they rose and fell with a human step. I stopped at the sight of them, and then without thinking (and yet, almost knowing *who* it was), jumped off the path and hid behind a tussle of laurel and weeds. I heard voices first, then sand-muffled steps. I could see their legs through a breach in the laurel, their feet cuffing sand as they went. I matched shoes to heads. The scarred black man was there, one of the women too, and one of the sod-throwers. In the rear was the antlered man, the six-foot-sixer, and on his feet—I realized with a shock of understanding—*were boots exactly like mine.*

I gave them a good couple of minutes to get past me and find the Maypole, and then got up and started after them. I picked up my baseball where I'd dropped it and let myself be drawn back into the party. Hetty was taking each of the Indians around and introducing him, everyone wild

over Philip's antlers and the deerskin he wore on his back.
I kept behind them so she wouldn't get to me. When I got
a chance I matched my boot print to Philip's, saw the same
heavy grid in the sand that I'd seen the past winter in the
snow and then backed off again. He didn't look at me once.
But I kept my eyes on him, watched how he looked at Hetty
with a chill, mocking smile while she took his hand and led
him around. He was taller than anyone else; the antlers made
him a good seven feet. His skin had no trace of red in it as
far as I could tell, and his features seemed European, but
he had that same ironic look that I'd first noticed with my
binoculars, as if everything around him were faintly amus-
ing, his own presence included. I sat on a hump of dune
grass and watched him, waiting for him to recognize me,
thinking: So you're him, you're the one who slashed my bike
tires, you're the one who broke into my bedroom. When
finally he caught sight of me, I threw my baseball at him.
But he caught it—caught it coolly with one hand—and then
tossed it aside and didn't look at me again.

When the voting for Lord and Lady of the May began,
I took the paper and bit of pencil handed to me, and while
Alice called out how we should *describe* the person if we didn't
know their name, wrote down THE INDIAN WITH THE
HORNS, and then without a second of hesitation: *Alice
Bromfield.* I tried to muster a smile when Hetty winked at
me while the ballots were being tallied, but I was praying
she wouldn't win. When she *did* win, and when I saw the
same clean flush of nerves and pleasure I'd seen on her that
morning, I felt a shiver of betrayal. I watched her feeling
vexed with myself—it was just a Maypole!—and yet feeling
as if the mimic and mock lawlessness of the May Day were
letting me see something in Hetty, something inchoate, un-
formed, but which had always been there. She had a wild,
hungry look about her, touching everyone, laughing, talking, dancing away from Philip and then running back and
tugging at his arm—and oh! the chill, damning smile he
gave her back! (Why *couldn't* you see it, sweetheart?) It was
as if she wanted to bring everyone into contact with her, to

void whatever was disparate and isolate, and to void it—to heal it—by *her* touch, by *her* presence. I watched with a black ache as they took her arms and led her over to the Maypole; watched while a crown of forsythia was put on her curly hair, a wreath of plastic ivy on Philip's horns; watched sitting desperate and alone on an island of sand and weeds while the garlands were taken up, and Hetty and this unknown, silent, ironical Indian—the Lord and Lady of the May—were set inside the pinwheeling ribbons and married by Alice. I listened to the clumsy recital of the Congregational ceremony (how different it sounded five years later, Hetty!), watched the laughing crew of foolscapped and flower-blighted souls, the blaze of ribbons wound out of order, the words wrenched and mocked about, and in the midst of it all: Hetty's shining, nervous face looking like the face of some virginal soul led into pagan heat and wilderness passion, frightened, confused, but determined to be led on no matter what.

· 3 ·

I skipped the cookout and the softball. Instead I went back to the house and, after an hour of yelling at myself, went upstairs into Hetty's bedroom and got her private letters out of their hiding place. I spread them around on the bed, then cracked the window an inch so if she came home I'd hear the car.

She had them in order by date: notes and letters from high school first and then her college letters, letters from her boyfriends, her roommates, and some of her own letters returned to her. I'd read a couple during the winter when I'd first found them, feeling sneaky the whole time, and finally put them back with a promise never to do it again. But back from the Maypole, I couldn't help myself. I got a piece of paper and drew a line down the middle so it made two columns. At the head of the left column I wrote: ELECT; and at the head of the right: DAMNED.

It took me hours. There was Randal J. and his *"night behind Coco's";* Christine's laughter over Benny and John; Randal again and his worry that she would eventually find him too ordinary. I had to unbox her *Larousse* to look up Jean-Louis's *"bite"* from her junior year abroad (couldn't find it), had to go sit for a while in the closet among her pretty summer things after deciphering someone's scrawl and finding *"You're the only woman I've ever fucked with my eyes open."* I found out that she loved to ride the subways at rush hour because of all the other bodies, the closeness, the humanity all packed in together, because you couldn't help but touch and be touched; that sometimes she'd give herself a pedicure, paint her toenails, put on her best stockings and go from shoe store to shoe store, just to have the salesmen and saleswomen touch her feet, feel her ankles, her insteps, hold her calves as they took off one pair and put on another. I found out too that she went through a period when she'd gone to confession (my Congregational cousin), not for absolution but for the anonymous intimacy of it, to confess her sins to someone—a man, a priest—and hear his deep and unknown voice on the other side of the screen, talking to her about her life, her sex, her love, her fear. Sometimes I could see her in her handwriting—*physically* see her—see her as she'd looked under the Maypole, and then in the next paragraph, how she'd looked that morning when she'd come in from washing her face with snow. I felt all stuffed up with jealousy and hurt and desire. But I kept on, dogging detail after detail, weighing and interpreting until I had six sheets filled.

The final score was Damned: 83, Elect: 79. I sat in the darkening room looking at the two numbers, recounted my tallies, then looked at the letters spread all around me. I started thinking about statistical error and then gave up. I felt stupid and lost suddenly. I crumpled up my tally sheet and threw it away, and then just as quickly, picked up one of her letters and peered at it in the reddening dusk as if to force some secret out of it. I felt in everything she wrote the same longing for connection, saw in between the neat loops and parabolas of her handwriting the same lost, searching look. Randal J. wasn't enough for her (she *had* found him too ordinary); Jean-Louis wasn't enough for her. Neither were Mark nor Chris nor *"your Candyman, Ernie."* But it wasn't mere physical promiscuity. It was as if she could only feel herself alive when she was having an effect on others, when she felt herself pursued and in pursuit. I could imagine her alone in her room and seeming suddenly without personality, vacant, voided. She'd said as much in one of her letters, that when she looked at herself in the mirror, she seemed to be without a third dimension, just as flat as the mirror itself. In the end I threw the letters down, got up and started pacing around the room. I was hurt, and yet I felt a sting of envy too. I could picture her aboard Alice's yacht, stringing party lights or making the punch, could imagine the others around her, livened by her, attracted by her. I started picking her letters up one by one, a little roughly, putting them back in order, but the thought of her dancing, getting a little drunk, touching everyone and being touched—Queen of the May!—got me so worked up that finally I just stuffed the last letters together and put them back in their hiding place. Then I ripped up my sheets of Elect and Damned, put on a coat and tie and headed for the harbor.

• 4 •

By the time I reached the water the western sky was a deep violet and Venus trembled on the horizon. I could see the yacht in the distance, moored at one of the large dockside slips. There were colored lights strung along its grab rails, and I could hear the thump of dance music over the harbor water. I kept along the waterfront, the streetlights dropping pools of light on me and illuminating from time to time a patch of snow left over from the morning's shoveling. When finally I got close enough, I stepped up into a store doorway where I could see without being seen.

She had her ribbons on still. I could see her on the fore-deck, her hand around the lofty radio antenna where the Maypole flowers had been tied, and Japanese lanterns swinging like pastel beehives over her head. Someone had put electric heaters out. They made an orange fire in the tangle of feet and shins. I looked for Philip, couldn't find him at first, then saw him disappearing into the forward lounge, and a minute later, coming out of the aft compan-ionway. Even with his antlers off he was a head taller than anyone else. I watched him clip coolly between dancing partners and make himself a drink. When I looked back to the foredeck Hetty was gone, but in between songs I heard her laugh—that cascade of bubbling syllables—and snug-ging up my tie, I left my spy spot and started toward the dock.

On board I poured myself a tumbler of gin and tonic and, hearing someone say, "There's the archaeologist," headed aft to where the lights were dimmer. I spotted Hetty dancing along the port passageway. She waved and mugged a surprised look at me, and then tugging at her partner's hand, started dancing toward me. I felt an uneasy urge at the kick of her hips and the scramble of hair around her head: I'd never seen her dance before.

"It's *you!*" she said, sidling up to me. "Where've you been?"

"I went home."

"Put on a tie, I see."

I nodded and looked at her partner behind her. He had on a wool scarf over a Hawaiian shirt.

"What're you drinking?" she asked, and she bit the rim of my glass and started motioning me to tip it up. I did, and she drank, but I tipped it too far and two rivulets sprung on either side of the glass, running over her lips and down her chin.

"Oof!" she cried and jumped away. She laughed and wiped her mouth. Behind her, the Hawaiian shirt was still dancing, gazing seaward past us.

"You missed the cookout," Hetty said, starting to dance again.

"Yes."

"And the softball game."

"Yes."

"I was captain. I struck out four times."

"Would you mind?" I said suddenly to the Hawaiian shirt, stepping in front of him and taking Hetty by the hand. I started waltzing her toward the port passageway. She threw a helpless look backward over my shoulder, and then she let me pull her along.

"But we can't waltz."

"You can *always* waltz. It's civilized."

"No," she said and tried to disengage herself. "The music's not even in triple time."

"Pretend it is," I said and started humming "The Waltz of the Flowers" to her. "How's that?"

"I don't know," she answered, trying to follow me and tripping. Her ribbons fluttered and caught about her. "It's like patting your head and rubbing your stomach at the same time."

"Just never mind the record."

"It's *loud*."

"But never mind it."

And I swung her around and along the starboard passageway. We bumped into people as we went. Hetty seemed flustered and embarrassed at first, and then started laughing and saying, "We're waltzing, we're civilized," to everyone we passed. Coming around the forecabin corner we brushed past Philip, standing tall and straight with one of his cronies. "Hello, King of the May," Hetty said to him over my shoulder. "We're waltzing, we're civilized." He tugged at one of her ribbons.

"He's the one, you know," I said as soon as we were a distance away.

"He's the one what?"

"The one who's been sending me notes."

She drew back and looked me in the face. "How do you know?"

"His boot print matches mine."

"That's evidence?"

"How else could he drop notes off at the dig and never leave a footprint in the snow?"

She looked over my shoulder at where he was standing and a curious light came into her eyes. "You mean he's the one who broke into the house?"

"I think so."

The look lingered. I turned her away so she couldn't see him.

"He's descended from Massasoit, you know," she said. "He said so this afternoon."

"From Massasoit?"

"That's the Indian who was chief when the Pilgrims landed."

"Sachem, not chief."

She shrugged her shoulders. "Anyway, he's descended from him."

"So *he* says."

"He *is*. He told us about it. Massasoit had two sons. The first one was poisoned by the English, and the other one was King Philip."

"No kidding."

"But there was a daughter," she said as if she had me. "Her name was Amie, and it's from her that he's descended. There's a big deal book about it. It traces Massasoit's lineage right down to the present. Philip recited the whole genealogy, details and all. It was when we were talking about the dig and the skeletons. You came in for some pretty rough treatment."

"From him?"

"No, from the others. He just let the others talk."

And she looked across my shoulder at Philip. I could smell the shampoo in her hair.

"This is the first time we've ever danced," I said, and I tried spinning her smartly around, but she just followed halfheartedly and kept her eyes on Philip.

"So he broke into my room," she said after a time.

"It was me he was after."

"Still," she mused. "I should have guessed it was him."

"How? How could you have guessed?"

"I don't know," she said as if she did know but couldn't say. I tried to turn her away, tried even to lead her back down the starboard passageway, but she balked.

"Let *me* lead," she said suddenly, reaching and taking my right hand from behind her back.

"No."

"Yes. Let me." And she took hold of my gin and tonic and then put my left hand on her shoulder so the drink spilled a little onto her dress.

"I can't follow."

"Just feel my movement."

"I can't."

"Come on!" And she started dancing me toward Philip. I bumped into someone and nearly knocked him off his feet.

"Hello, King of the May!" Hetty said when we'd drawn up to Philip. She laughed and danced me away again. Then she started back.

"Hello, Lord of Misrule!" she said, and she kicked her hip out at him and again danced away. He threw us a curious look.

She led me this way and that, yanking at the back of my suit coat for me to follow. With each revolution, I could see Philip watching us, watching Hetty's legs, the incurve of her back, her hair, her shoulders, her ribbons. I tried to hold her close to me, but she was so wild—jitterbugging one minute, polkaing the next—that I had all I could do just to stay with her. When the song ended, she pushed me away, laughing, and then pulled me back and took my gin and tonic from me.

"Gin," she said, drinking it and shivering. "I hate gin." She handed the tumbler back to me. "I need my own drink," she said, and she spun around and started across the deck. When she passed Philip, she tucked her shoulder in and said something that made him follow her. I watched them disappear around the cabin, and then feeling a dozen pairs of eyes on me, ducked down the companionway.

There was a crowd keeping warm in the lounge. The Red Sox were on the television and there was a foursome playing hearts. Over at the stove, Alice was stirring a huge pot of tomato soup. "To keep everyone warm," she said when I passed her, and she stretched up and tipped a spoonful into my mouth. I scouted for another drink but the gin bottle was empty, and when I tried to pour a couple of fingers of sherry, I couldn't find a clean glass. There was a half-full bottle of brandy, so I just took it and climbed back up the companionway.

On deck I stationed myself first along the port rail, looking townward at the squat shops and the Vineyard Bank sign flashing from 10:07 to 49°, then circled behind where Hetty and Philip stood at the center of a group of people and leaned against the starboard rail. On the horizon Vega was just rising out of the sea, looking blue and watery through the heavy atmosphere. The dance music had stopped, and behind me I caught snatches of talk, heard Hetty's scatter of words and imagined a certain low, precise voice was Philip's. I turned nonchalantly around and looked at them. He had a bored, patronizing air, as if the scramble of interest around him were nothing new. I took a swig from my brandy, and then slipping the bottle into my coat pocket, moved closer.

"He went to Harvard," Hetty was saying. "He went to Harvard *for free* because of an old rule that said that Indians could go for free. Right?" she said and turned to Philip.

"You owe me twenty-four dollars and twenty-five cents," I said, but no one heard me.

"Harvard—" Philip said slowly, deliberately, "Harvard built an Indian College in 1655. To convert the savages, you know," he said, and he paused to light a cigarette. He did it with a careless, easy air as if he were onstage and knew his audience wasn't going anywhere. "But there weren't many savages interested in a combined course of Latin and salvation, so in 1693 they took the college down and used the bricks for another building. But the commissioners stipulated that in case any Indian should present himself to the regular college equipped to study, he could do so for free."

"You talk like a lawyer," someone—Alice's brother—said with a laugh. Philip turned a humorless smile on him and then dragged on his cigarette.

"At the beginning of my sophomore year I found the stipulation mentioned in a book on Puritan-Indian relations, and after researching if it had ever been repealed, I got them to pay for the rest of my time there."

There was a murmur all around.

"You owe me twenty-four dollars and twenty-five cents," I said again, a little more forcefully this time. A couple of people in front of me turned and gave me a curious look—but Philip didn't notice.

"They had to pay for my room and board and my books. I took premed and prelaw courses on purpose because the books were so expensive."

They all laughed.

"And I got a refund for my first year."

"You owe me—" I said again, loudly so that people on either side of me turned around. "You owe me twenty-four dollars and twenty-five cents."

He looked at me. For an instant there was a flash of anticipation in his eyes, but the patronizing look quickly returned.

"It's the grave robber," he said.

"It's the housebreaker," I answered.

Hetty made a sign for me to never mind. Philip shifted his weight so his body was turned more toward me.

"Being the scholarly quack that you are," he said, "you no doubt know that in 1667 a Massachusetts man was fined, stocked and imprisoned for the barbarous—that's a quote—*barbarous* act of digging up the skull of an Indian and carrying it around on a pike."

I stood squarely before him and didn't answer. There was whispering around us; I heard the dig mentioned.

"What's the matter?" Philip asked after a moment. "You don't have a pike?"

"Being the moral renegade that *you* are," I answered, "you no doubt know that because of arson and theft, laws were passed forbidding Indians to hanker about—that's a quote—to *hanker about* English homes, especially on the Sabbath and *at night*."

He turned his body full to me. "If you read John Cotton—your ancestor's buddy—if you read his book *The Bloody Tenant, Washed, and Made White in the Blood of the Lamb*, you'll see the wholly immoral arguments for racist usurpation of native lands by reason of Christian dogma."

"Point for the Indian," someone said, and there was a smatter of laughter.

"But if you read Roger Williams's *answer* to John Cotton, *The Bloody Tenant Made Yet More Bloody, by Mr. Cotton's Efforts to Wash it in the Blood of the Land*, you'll see a moral white man, an outcast in his own society, arguing for the rights of the individual—Indian *and* American—against the hungry, manipulative, destructive corpus of society."

"Point for the archaeologist," someone else said, and there was a sprinkle of applause. Philip showed his teeth in a taut smile and took a step toward me. He started counting on his fingers.

"Metacomet's only son sold into slavery."

I held up my own fingers. "Mary Rowlandson's baby's brains dashed against a tree trunk."

"Wituwamet's head on a pike at Plymouth."

"Plymouth receiving a Pequot's hand from the Narraganset as a treaty."

"A Pequot tied to a post by the Puritans and torn limb from limb."

"Those same limbs roasted and eaten by the Puritans' Mohegan allies."

"The entire Pequot nation—women and children—massacred in 1637."

"*You owe me—*" I shouted, getting my wallet out of my

pocket. *"You owe me twenty-four dollars and twenty-five cents!"*
And I handed him the receipt for my bicycle tires. He took
the creased paper and held it up to one of the Japanese
lanterns. Beside him Hetty strained to see but she wasn't tall
enough.

"Mike's Bike Shop," Philip said with a snort and passed
the receipt around.

"I'll take check, cash or money order," I said.

He eyed me. "You are a direct descendant of John
Wheelwright, aren't you?" He asked after a minute. I kept
the receipt when it came back my way.

"That's right."

"John Wheelwright, antinomian?"

"That's right."

"Brother-in-law of Anne Hutchinson?"

"Right again."

"Swindler of Pennacook lands in Exeter, New Hampshire?"

"Twenty-four dollars and twenty-five cents," I repeated,
snapping the paper between my fingers.

He took a notebook out of his back pocket. At the sight
of it, one of his buddies from the protest started laughing.

"I think I've got you down," Philip said, licking his finger and, with a theatrical air, paging through the notebook.
"Wadsworth . . . Weston . . . Wheelock . . . Wheelwright.
John Wheelwright: nine million eight thousand and eighty-
four dollars."

And with a ferocious smile he handed me the notebook.
I took it and held it up to the blue lantern over my head.
My name was written in the same neat printing as the notes
I'd gotten, along with my father's name, my birth date,
birthplace, current address. There were various figures listed
under it. I skimmed through the rest of the book, keeping
a blank look on the outside but feeling turned about inside.
There were hundreds of names, all meticulously tracked
down and tallied up.

"So what?" I said after a minute.

"So that's the combined current appraised value of the lands in Exeter your ancestor ripped off my ancestors."

"*Your* ancestors? Those were Pennacook Indians. You're Wampanoag. And they weren't ripped off. They traded their land."

"What *I* am," Philip said, "is the only male descendant of Massasoit, father of King Philip, sachem of the New England tribes, the Pennacook included."

"The Pennacook told Philip to buzz off," I said and handed him the notebook back. "At best Philip united the Wampanoag, the Nipmucks, some plague-immune Massachusetts and the Narragansets."

"You owe me," he said, slapping the notebook across his palm, "nine million eight thousand and eighty-four dollars."

"*And you owe me,*" I answered, "twenty-four dollars and twenty-five cents."

We stood like that for a moment, faced off, and then Philip opened his notebook again.

"Adding up your land in Exeter," he said, "and your Beacon Hill house, you're worth two million seventy-thousand. Again, current appraised value."

I kept a stony look and didn't answer.

"Perhaps I should just start *hankering about* your property, torching it here and there and subtracting from your debt as I go along." And with the same ironic smile, he waited for me to answer. "Shall I start with your country house or your town house?"

"You can start with the twenty-four dollars and twenty-five cents," I said and handed him my receipt again.

"Small potatoes."

"It's all you'll ever get," I said.

"Small potatoes," he said again and made a dismissive gesture.

And then—almost simultaneously—we each realized my mistake.

"Does the subtraction of your bicycle tires legitimize the debt?" he asked quickly.

"Meaning?"

"Meaning you acknowledge it."

"No."

"I think it does," he said and took the receipt.

"It doesn't. It only acknowledges that you knifed my bike tires."

"That works both ways," he said and took a pen out. "Twenty-four dollars and twenty-five cents subtracted from nine million eight thousand and eighty-four dollars makes . . ." He paused to figure it.

"Nine million eight thousand fifty-nine dollars and seventy-five cents," Hetty said.

"Nine million eight thousand fifty-nine dollars and seventy-five cents," Philip repeated, writing it first on my yellow receipt and then in his notebook. He closed the book and put it back in his pocket, then handed me the receipt. "But I keep another book up here," he said and tapped his right temple. The loudspeakers crackled suddenly with music. He moved closer to me and shouted, "I keep another book of moral debts. And in that one you and your ancestor Isaac are on the first page."

"You'd better let God keep the moral debts," I shouted back. "You're going to have enough trouble collecting the financial ones."

"I'll collect," he said. "Don't worry about that." And he threw down his cigarette and turned to Hetty. "Do you want to dance?" he asked, and before she could answer, took her hand and led her away.

"That's my cousin!" I called after him. "A blood relative!" But he kept on and I only got thrown a furious look from Hetty.

· 5 ·

Twenty minutes later I'd assembled a cup of Alice's tomato soup, half a bag of Cheeze Twists and some celery, and climbed down the aft ladder into the tiny dinghy that was tied to the stern of the yacht. I set my brandy bottle and my tomato soup and my food on the aluminum seat in front of me and loosened my tie. I bailed out the bilgy water, put the oars in the oarlocks and just sat there.

" 'Abstract yourself with a holy violence from the dung heap of this earth!' " I quoted to the starry sky and took a sip of tomato soup.

On deck I heard Hetty's laugh from time to time, caught sight of the spin and furl of her bright skirt when I rowed the dinghy to the length of its painter. Mostly I just let myself rock behind the yacht's giant stern, studied the great gold and black letters before me: *VANITY FAIR, Vineyard Haven,* and drank my brandy and ate my celery. I gave up on the Cheeze Twists after half a dozen and instead tossed them one by one out into the water. I didn't even care when I saw Hetty and Philip run down the gangway, and playing a coquettish game of tag, head off together toward town.

When they started playing big band music, I got a life jacket from under the seat, and standing up in the bottom of the boat, started dancing. Somewhere between a fox-trot and a waltz I heard a low rumble of the engines start, and the gargle of the bilge pump. I sat out a few, and then when someone shouted, "All ashore that's going ashore!" got up and danced again. But I caught sight of something in the shadows over by one of the shops that fronted the harbor. I stopped a moment, and then as if to camouflage my having noticed, started in again. There was someone there, standing in the shadows and watching me. It took another verse before I was certain it was Hetty.

When the song ended she moved a little out of the shadow so the streetlight painted a bar across her chest, throwing her feet into light but keeping her head in darkness. I gestured for her to come over, but she stayed where she was. When I made a silly movement with the life jacket and beckoned again, she took a step into the light, and after hesitating a moment, started across the tar.

"What're you doing?" she asked when she drew near. She kept herself back, ten feet or so from the edge of the dock.

"I'm dancing."

She grimaced and tucked her head in, away from me. I put one of the oars in the water and maneuvered over to the dock, bumping the side of the boat against one of the tire slabs that were nailed along the facing beam.

"Come aboard," I said. "They're getting ready to put out."

But she held back. I thought I could see something, a smear or a smudge, just under her eye.

"Are you all right?"

She shook her head: first yes, then no.

"Come on," I said and nudged her feet with an oar. Someone from the boat was casting off lines. "Come on. We're going out."

She threw a look around that was by turns confused and angry, and then just as the boat began pulling away from the dock, ran and jumped into the dinghy. She stumbled, caught her balance and then fell onto the bow seat.

"He *hit* me!" she cried, throwing me a look of hurt and amazement, and then without warning, her face crumpled and she burst into tears. I shipped oars and crept along the boat bottom toward her. The yacht jerked suddenly and my tomato soup fell off its seat.

"He hit you?" I said and touched at her face. She pulled back, tucking her head down and letting her hair hide her. Her chest was shaking, and she was making queer hiccuping sounds. When I tried to touch her again, she let me, even pressed her face against my palm. There was an abrasion under her eye, the skin red and sore-looking, and her cheekbone was bruised.

"How did it happen? What did he do?"

But she was crying too much to answer. I swept her hair back from her face and tried to wipe her tears, but I hit the sore spot and she brushed me away.

"I'm in his fucking book too!" she cried.

"He hit you because of that?"

She shook her head.

"What, then?"

"We were playing," she said. "We were playing." She swept up her skirt and wiped her face. "You know how you play sometimes?"

I just looked at her.

"We were playing. We were kissing. And I was hitting at him. You know, like you do."

"All right."

"And then he hit me." She patted her face again. Her eyes were red and swollen.

"He just hauled off and hit you?"

"Well, no," she said and sniffled. "I mean he played a little bit too. He cuffed me a little bit. You know? You know how you do?"

"*I* don't do."

She looked sullenly at me. "Well, it was just playing. *I* was just playing. But he got rough. I told him he was hurting me, but he kept at it until he finally slapped me." And she looked across at me, bewildered and superbly innocent. "Hard! He hit me hard! And then he started telling me about Samuel Jenney and Plymouth and some land someone named Tispaquin or something sold him in 1667. Asnemscutt Pond he said." She stared at me with rage and impotence. "I don't even know where Asnemscutt Pond is!"

"It's near Middleboro."

"*You* would know," she said and dragged her fingers through her snarly hair. "You and your fucking antinomians and Indians."

"*I* didn't hit you."

"You and your fucking moral ancestors."

I just sat and looked at her.

"You and your fucking Cousin Isaac," she said. She'd started untying her ribbons. "You and your ancestor John."

"Hetty . . ."

"There." She threw a ribbon overboard. "That's for your Cousin Isaac."

The ribbon made a crazy striggle on the black water.

"That's for ancestor John," she said, throwing another.

"Hetty."

"That's for Asnemscutt Pond."

I got one of the oars out of its oarlock and started fishing for the ribbons. We were just passing the breakwater. The yacht's wake made a silvery crest on either side of us that swept the ribbons quickly out of reach. I managed to catch one and drop it back aboard.

"That's for your Puritan foundations of the American self," she said.

I fished out another.

"That's for the Maypole."

"Hetty . . ."

"That's for Philip and his antlers."

"Hetty, these are your *ribbons*."

"That's for my fucking ribbons."

"Hetty!" I said and tried to catch two or three, but they dipped and rolled away from me. "Well, Christ!" I said and threw the oar back in the boat. "If *you* don't care, *I* don't care."

"That's for waltzing."

"What did you expect, going off with someone you don't even know?"

"That's for nine million eight thousand and whatever the fuck it was."

"Going off with an *Indian*, for Christ's sake."

She started ripping ribbons out of the eyelets on her sleeve.

"Jesus, what do you expect if you change guys every two months? If every time you come home you run off an hour later in shorts and a halter? You and your candyman, Ernie."

She started to rip out the other sleeve and then stopped.

"What did you say?"

I sat suddenly dumb and witless. "I'm just telling you that you can't live like—"

"No, no," she said, confused. "How did you—?" And then

her face registered comprehension. "You've been reading my letters."

I just stared at her.

"You've read my letters. You read my private things." And she stood up dangerously in the boat. "You've been sleeping in my bed and reading my letters."

"Sit down."

"You've read all my goddamn letters!"

"Sit down, for Christ's sake."

"Don't tell me what to do! What makes you think you can tell me what to do all the time? What makes you think you've got the right to read my private things? *You're* not my lover."

I put the oars in the water and started rowing senselessly backward, pulling against the yacht.

"*You're* not my lover," she said again, almost spitting out the words. "You and your books and your Phi Beta Kappa and your Indian bones. You can't tell me what to do."

And she started unbuttoning her clothes. We were out of the harbor now, out past the headlands and coming into the ocean. I just kept rowing, straining my back against the propellers.

"I can go off with any fucking body I want," she said and threw her blouse at me. She took her green sneakers off and threw them into the bottom of the boat. "I can do any goddamn thing I want," she shouted. "Anything!" And she unwrapped her flowered skirt and threw it down. Then, in her bra and panties and bright red socks, she dove into the dark water.

I slammed the oars against the stern and whirled around. I saw her head pop above the water, the wake boiling all around her. I shouted to her, called her name, but even as I called, the yacht pulled me farther away. I leaped to the bow and tried to untie the line, but it was so taut I couldn't even begin to loosen the knot. I tried to pull on it, pull so the dinghy would edge closer to the yacht and the rope would slacken, but I couldn't keep it up. I looked back again for Hetty's head and then tried my pockets. I kept a pocket knife at the dig but I didn't have it with me. I turned around again and then shouted at the yacht, but they couldn't hear me. I stood frozen an instant, and then in a burst of inspiration, pulled the brandy bottle out of my suit coat pocket and broke it against the bow of the dinghy. In a minute I'd sawed through the rope.

"Get in," I said when I'd rowed back to her. She was swimming, taking smooth and regular strokes through the great swells. "Get in."

"No."

"What do you think you're going to do? You think you're going to swim all the way back?"

"What's it to you?"

I looked for the nearest land—the headland at East Chop—the lighthouse there winking and the sprinkle of shore lights shivering in the darkness. It was a good mile away.

"It's cold," I said. "Isn't it cold?"

She didn't answer.

"Do you think you're going to walk back through town in your bra? Is that it?"

Still, she didn't answer. Behind us, the yacht looked like an apparition, bright lights and brassy music floating on top of the black water. I rowed in silence for a while.

"I'm sorry," I said finally. "It was wrong of me to read them. I'm sorry."

She kept to her stroke.

"I just got mad at you. So I read them. It was stupid. I'm sorry."

But she still wouldn't answer. I watched her swim, watched her narrow body cutting through the water—rigid, methodical—and I felt suddenly angry with her again, with her knowing that ignoring me was the surest way to get to me, and that she wanted to get to me, not because of what I'd done but because of Philip.

"Do you think you're the only one who can do something stupid?" I said suddenly, and I said it in such a hardened voice that she stopped swimming and looked at me.

"Do you think you're the only one who's got feelings and gets angry and can do something stupid?"

She started in again, harder.

"Do you think you're the only one who can jump in the goddamn ocean?" And I stood up and started taking my clothes off: tie, shirt, shoes.

"Don't," I heard her say. She'd stopped again. Her voice sounded different, thin, a little scared. "It's cold."

"Of course it's cold!" I said. "It's May first, for Christ's sake!" And I threw my pants down, and in just my socks and boxer shorts, jumped in.

I wasn't prepared for the shock, for the peeling, scraping cold. I fought quickly for the surface, breaking through into the air. I looked around for Hetty, spotted her some feet distant—watching me—and began to tread water, dazed and breathing hard. When I'd gotten my bearings, I said: "Let's go," and started swimming for East Chop.

"You can't." She crossed to me and swam alongside me. Her voice was soft, almost solicitous. "You're not a good enough swimmer."

"I'll make it."

"You can't," she said again, and she reached out and touched me.

"If *you* can make it, *I* can make it."

"Wright." She touched me again—held on to my arm—so that I had to stop. I turned my face away. She reached across and touched me, touched me with her fingers and turned my face back.

"You read my letters," she said. I didn't answer. She'd said it without reproach, as if it were something that mystified her, but which in some vague way pleased her too. She came closer to me. I could feel her legs near mine, feel the currents she made. She reached out again and pushed the wet hair off my face. I tried to smile; and then before I knew what she was doing, she'd kissed me.

"Hetty . . ." I said.

"You read my letters," she said again, and this time her

eyes were looking at me with such secret wonder that I couldn't say anything. I reached out and put my hand on her, underwater, on her hip just where her waist curved in. She shivered and closed her eyes. In the distance I could hear the tinny bedlam of the yacht.

"We could never do this anywhere else," she said. Her voice was husky with the cold. She had her eyes closed still.

"No," I answered.

"Here," she said, "in the darkness, in the water, in the cold."

"Yes."

She opened her eyes. "Kiss me," she said. I stayed where I was. "Kiss me," she said and pulled herself closer to me. I felt her lips, soft and wet with seawater.

"Have you ever wondered what I kissed like?" she asked. "I mean, before."

"Yes."

"Have you?" she said. "Have you really?"

"Yes."

"And have you wondered what I looked like? I mean— you know . . ."

"Yes," I answered.

She smiled and closed her eyes again. "We could never say this anywhere else."

"Hetty . . ."

"Kiss me again. Come and hold me and kiss me. Kiss me like we're lovers."

"I can't. We'll sink."

"No," she said, and she put her arms around me. I had to peddle furiously to keep afloat. I could feel her body against mine, her chest, her bra. She kissed me, long and hard, and then let go.

"All right," she said, and she pushed herself off me.

"Hetty," I said and made a move toward her. But she shook her head, shook her head no, and then started swimming toward the dinghy.

CHAPTER
5

Whoring After Strange Gods

• 1 •

"Beauty is the visible fitness of a thing to its use," Jonathan Edwards said, "not entirely different from that beauty which there is in fitting a mortise to its tenon."

I fit my first mortise to my first tenon the fall after I'd left Martha's Vineyard. I'd finished my thesis and I was teaching part time and spending my spare time at the Restoration Lab at the Museum of Fine Arts. It was there, amidst the relics of an earlier America—cracked Bible boxes, uncrowned clocks, de-feeted wainscot chairs—that I learned a certain quality of moral salvage. For the next three years, while I wrote up my grant proposals for Mavericke's Island and watched Hetty move from man to man, loony ward to loony ward, I squirreled myself away in the museum's cellar, working on the abused, defiled and disfigured fingerprints of our national past. I repaired the split sides of lowboys never meant for the dry fire of central heating, relathed finials lopped off by the exigencies of seven-foot ceilings, scarfed, keyed, patched and otherwise hocus-pocussed

71

away hundreds of holes that had been bored to fit the pinched spans of modern hardware. Working in the peaceful, sawdusty room I felt myself in touch with the hands of workmen long dead, felt the nearby flutter of a soul whenever I discovered, say, on the back of a drawer the hard-learned arithmetic of some eighteenth-century journeyman, or saw where a finisher had tested the strength of his stains on the underside of a drawer blade. Every piece that passed through the shop gave testimony to its maker. I saw the whim and whiff of personality in the pert cusp of an acanthus leaf, in the fluid lip and leaf of a carved aster. I learned to recognize the New Hampshire hills in the interlaced cornice of a highboy, to sniff out the Connecticut River valley in carved tulips, Boston in the belly of a bombé. Bed, bowl, bench—they were the props of America, built of native wood by native hands: humanity left in the flutes of a quarter-column, in the rough plane marks on the underside of a drawer bottom.

Sometimes on my way over from MIT I stopped into the local Baal-built furniture store to inspect the offerings. Inside, with Muzak trying to peel off my skin, I pulled out bureau drawers that were joined together with staples and left them lying on the floor. I twisted butt-joined frames out of square, cracked the bottoms of drawers made of pressed cardboard, pried off plastic plant-ons and phony finials. I would lecture an occasional salesman into bewilderment, sermonize an assistant manager on the vulgarity of plastic beds, of headboards made out of press molds. I'd read them a jeremiad on how the moral interior of a people is reproduced in their environment, on how "the tribe which are not a people" prophesied in the Apocalypse might very well be the machines to which we have delegated our humanity, how the landscape of modern America is the landscape of impersonal horrors, to which they were adding by selling acres of ugly and illegitimate Home Furnishings. "The home is the home, after all," I'd say, and then I'd kick a final footstool and—with the Muzak like the devil's anthem in my ears—head down to my sweet maple and sharp tools.

So I spent a three-year novitiate in the embrace of beauty—at least, in the embrace of Jonathan Edwards's beauty, which is to say New England beauty, the fit of form to function, or to quality one last time: order. I cut my tenons straight and square, my mortises deep and true, and joining them together felt the full gratification of a snugly fitted joint: The friction and strain on the male member as it tries to slide into the mortise, the tight refusal of the female to let it in and the slow give of one to the other. When finally the lips of the mortise kiss the shoulders of the tenon there is a sense of completion in the act, of unity and order, as if the universe is right side up after all. The joint may expand and contract with humidity, swell in the rain and shrink under the sun, but it is married until it rots. It is what holds together the chair under you (that is, if you are one of the elect and not a Baal-built customer), keeps your bureau square, your window frames plumb, holds your bed together under the thrust of love. It is the footing of civilized life, what keeps your mind square, your morals rectilinear and your soul well swept. It is the preferred joint for all post-and-beam houses—and the one I planned to use in the framing of Mavericke's house.

· 2 ·

The first time I submitted my grant proposal to the National Science Foundation it was turned down. The second time I downplayed Mavericke and upplayed the Indian internment camp and it was approved.

It took me two years to get things under way, to get together a team of undergraduate and graduate students, enlist the Metropolitan District Commission and win approval for the permanent reproduction of Mavericke's house, the palisade around it, the well and the outbuildings. The first summer we concentrated on the burial grounds, digging up skeletons from King Philip's War, crockery and tools. But the second summer I broke off from the main dig, working alone on the postholes of Mavericke's house until I had a good idea of how it had been situated. Toward the fall, I started spending the odd night out on the island, the last tour boat gone, the twilight coming on and the city held off by the dark water. I was readying myself for what was coming. Just before Thanksgiving I had a load of timbers delivered, eight-by-eights for the posts and girts, a ten-by-twelve for the summer beam, four-by-sixes for the joists and studs. I took a leave of absence from MIT, bought myself the best Arctic gear I could find, stocked up on tins of food, jugs of fresh water, and then, just before Christmas, moved out to the island for good.

It took me a week in all. I had to ferry everything across the icy harbor in my sailboat and then harness myself to a sledge and pull it up the snowy path from the Parks and Recreation dock to the Quonset hut that sat at the foot of Mavericke's hilltop. They were subfreezing days, sunless and with the wind gusting out of the north. After each trip I thawed out in a tugman's café at the harbor's edge, the regulars looking me over and finally approving of me by virtue of the tangle of ice in my winter beard. At night I sat on the third floor of my family's Beacon Hill house watching the news, sat exhausted and aching while my mother worked in her greenhouse three floors above me and my father at his computer three floors below. By eight o'clock I was asleep.

On the third day I took a break from hauling the mundane matters of the body—clothes, food, blankets, table and chair—and instead delivered up a boatload of moral props: my model of the *Mayflower,* my practice mortise-and-tenon joint from my days at the Restoration Lab, and in six boxes, my library of Early American tracts, treatises and other sober treasures. On the fourth day I allowed certain concessions to the twentieth century: a space heater and a propane tank, the two of them so heavy that they sank the *Pilgrim's Progress* down to her gunwales. I rewaxed the sledge's runners

to move them cross-island, but even so, had to use block-
and-tackle to get them up the incline to the Quonset hut.
On the fifth day I ferried out my housewright tools—broadax,
adz, T-augers—and swept the snow off the pile of timbers.
Then, for the hundredth time since I'd discovered the discolored earth where the palisade postholes had been, I pictured the house frame raised, saw the sharp peaks of the
gables against the gray sky, the square and snugly joined
posts rising parallel to the Hancock building in the frozen
distance, the wide summer beam housed in its dovetail and
the ridgepole running straight and true from peak to peak.
I even took out my framing square and frame saw, and in
the purplish haze of the December dusk, squared off half a
dozen eight-by-eights and made a fire with the beam ends
to warm myself.

On the sixth day I said good-bye to my old life. I walked
through the corridors at the Harrison Day School just at
sessions change and got swamped by gray-blazered eight-
year-olds. At the Public Library I passed up the new wing
for the old reading room, visited the yellowish busts of
Winthrop and Cotton Mather (still sitting on their Doric columns—like America itself, an odd marriage of Puritan head
and democratic body). At the Planetarium I watched a delicate Andromeda rise on a beautiful autumn evening. Back
outside I swung around toward Mass General to the Baxter
School where Hetty was working with severely disturbed
children. Upstairs in her office, she said she didn't get the
point of this, this Thoreau act.

"Nothing to get," I told her. "It's part of the American
character."

"Just which American character is that?"

"The first one. The basic one. The one that says keep
your distance."

She had on her lab whites. There was a brownish stain
across her chest where one of her autistics had tried to throw
up God-knows-what out of his insides.

"So when are you leaving?" she asked.

"Tonight."

"And when arc you coming back?"

I shrugged. "I'll be in for groceries in the spring."

"In the spring?" she repeated. "You think you can last alone until the spring?"

"You don't think I can?"

"The spring?"

"Why not? Why not the spring?"

She searched in her desk for her lunch. "All right," she said, tossing me an orange. "I'll bet you can."

• 3 •

Back home I found my mother up in her rooftop greenhouse standing in front of a rich purplish-orange orchid with a broken stem.

"I don't know how it could have happened," she said, letting her delicate fingers flutter about the flower but never touching it.

"This is it," I said. "Today's the day."

"No one's been up here except me. Nothing's touched it. I don't understand." And she peered out the glass walls and up at the glass peak as if looking for something that had invaded the greenhouse. But there was just the familiar slope of snowy rooftops and in the distance the boxy skyline to the financial district.

"I'm taking my last batch of clothes with me, and I've left my room cleaned up and squared away."

"*Pogonia Jennia,*" she said, turning sadly back to the dying flower. Jenny was her maiden name. "It took me eighteen months to cross-pollinate *Pogonia Jennia.* Six earlier ones didn't take." And she touched the fragile orange petals. Her wrists were thin and her fingers quivered slightly with age and emotion. She looked helplessly at me, her blue eyes pale and misted, and then turned back to the orchid, pressing her forefinger and thumb around either side of the wounded stem so that it stood up straight and healthy. But when she let go, the flower fell over to one side.

"Today's the day," I said again, a little more gently, and I touched her on the arm. She smiled at the touch, and for a second her hands floated between us before she touched me back.

"You're leaving," she murmured.

"Yes."

"You're leaving," she repeated, and she gazed at me as she would at one of her prize crossbreeds. "But you'll come visit? Now and then?"

"I won't be far away. Just there in the harbor." And I pointed to the glistening water in the distance.

"Will you be able to come up to Exeter in the summers?"

"Weekends, maybe."

She nodded and tucked her head away. Behind her the dazzling rows of orchids seemed to incline their long stems toward her, toward her voice. "You'll be able to get a lot of research done on your island?" she asked after a moment.

"Yes."

"Good."

And again she was silent. She played with the pruning shears in her apron pocket.

"There'll be other people there? Your graduate students? Your friends?"

"No."

"Good."

Her hands had drifted back to the dying flower. She touched the bright, desperate petals and then palpated the liplike labellum, stroked the male anther, the female stigma. "Poor beauty," she murmured, and then as if caressing the wilting flower with her voice: *"Pogonia Jennia."*

"You can breed another," I said. She turned a look on me that was strangely pitying.

"Jay-jay," she murmured, using my childhood name. She took up her pruning shears, and turning back to the flower, clipped the orchid off at its wound. "Sweetheart," she said and tucked the green stem into one of my buttonholes. "Jay-jay," she said and she stretched up and kissed me on the cheek.

• 4 •

In the cellar I found my father at his computer terminal. He was working—as ever—on his unified number theory, a sort of grand numerology, a Pythagorean vision of the world as being at its deepest level mathematical in nature. He'd begun working on it as an undergraduate, and all during the forty years of his MIT tenure—in between teaching his classes on conventional number theory and fooling around with Fermat's last theorem—had refined and extended it, ascribing the world and everything in it—solid land and liquid abstractions; me, Mother and Elvis Presley; earthquakes, the Dow Jones, fats and carbohydrates—to numbers, or patterns of numbers, or elegant equations, or Gaussian integers. During my own undergraduate years he tried to haul me up the first few rungs of his theory but I kept slipping off, kept getting lost behind Minkowski's Lattice, or falling through the Sieve of Eratosthenes, or hiding out in a newly iterated class field tower. In the end he gave up, left me alone to play with my seventeenth-century toys and trudged on alone into Abelian fields, looking for revelation in numbers, for either the final principle of order in the universe or God's dice, for an explanation that was reducible to some avatar of one through ten.

"The number one," he said when I'd shouted into his hearing aid that today was the day, I was off on my own. "One: the universe, the sun, God, light, the primum mobile." He cleared his display and typed in 1 so it popped silently onto the green screen. "Powerful, mystical number of self, of solitude and purgation. The only number that can divide all other numbers, the ultimate prime."

I tried to sound matter-of-fact: "I'll be living in the

Quonset hut until I get Mavericke's frame up and closed in."

"Alone?" he asked, looking at the solitary number on his display.

"Yes, alone."

He nodded, as if approving. "The Babylonians believed that one was the most perfect number, for to go from zero to one was to go from nonexistence to existence."

"It's a *new* existence I'm after."

"Good enough," he said and started punching equations into his computer. "Watch," he said as lines and rows of numbers blipped onto the screen. "This equation ends with a congruent modulo *m*. Congruent but irreducible. But if you introduce . . ." And he typed in some bizarre equation. *"Presto!"* He turned to me with a smile at his own wizardry. On the screen—after all the hocus-pocus—was an equals sign and then the number *1*.

"What I'm after," I said, though not loud enough for his hearing aid, "is an existence where the moral variables are kept at a minimum."

"Newness, oneness," he said, turning back to the screen. "Union after all that. *Now* watch." And he slugged in a new battery of numbers. He had the look of a modern-day alchemist, his flyaway eyebrows lit with green fire, watching the numbers dance across the screen. "See?" he cried with delight. At the bottom of the display was another equals sign and again the number *1*. He looked at me for signs of persuasion.

"An existence," I said again, "a life lived along moral lines even when no one anywhere is keeping accounts anymore."

He turned up his hearing aid and smiled uncertainly. "Yes," he said and jabbed at the solitary *1* on the computer display.

"Neither God *nor* the devil."

"Yes," he repeated, looking lovingly at his numbers. "That's right. God."

CHAPTER
6

At the Edge of the Wilderness

• 1 •

Mavericke's Island lies .8 miles off the eastern landfall of
North America, latitude 42°20′, longitude 71°00′. To its north
is the roaring anvil of Logan International Airport; to its
south a string of sisterly vagrants: Spectacle, Thompson,
Peddocks and Bumpkin islands; to the east stretches the great
graveyard of the Atlantic; and to the west the glass and as-
phalt wilderness of America. The island itself is shaped like
a piece of popcorn, round-trunked with a collection of
stunted limbs exploding off it in every direction. The Harbor Islands guidebook tells me it contains 36.2 acres of
shrubby grassland, rocky outcrop and an occasional copse
of oak or beech or unexciting poplar. Indigenous shrubs
include juniper, bayberry and laurel; flowers to be met with
number daisies, jack-in-the-pulpit and rugosa rose; birds are
drawn from the usual North American species with accent
typically on the gull, the chickadee and, in the wintertime,
the grosbeak. The weekend hiker will find squads of home-
grown rabbits, squirrels and chipmunks underfoot—but no
people.

In 1965 the island was incorporated into the Harbor Islands State Park. A dock was built in the lee of one of its popcorn appendages, a cinder-block Parks and Recreation building was erected, and the small Civil War breastworks along the western crest of the island were restored and opened to the public. In the early 1970s a ferry began round-robin service to all the harbor islands from April until October and an advertising campaign was put on the radio (*"Our harbor has more than just water to offer!"*). The result was the devastation and desecration of Mavericke's grassy paths by platoons of trooping housewives and their cement-footed and onion-headed children.

But ah: From October to April the island is revirgined, the bruised paths purified by the ambers of autumn; the black-and-blued ground regenerated under a quilt of snow; the whisper of the ice-crusted junipers, the frozen roots, the sapless limbs: all a New England rite of winter. I have it straight from Mavericke that the island is as it was 350 years ago. Stand at dusk so the city is at your back, he says, and you can see Amias walking across the hill next over from where their house used to be, thinking herself unobserved and with each step kicking the powdery snow like a ten-year-old. He says the hills are the same, the ravines, the thread-like webbery of the thickets. He says the white-pelted rabbits are the descendants of his rabbits; the oaks are the sons of the oaks he framed his house with. He says life is life, Wheelwright, and for once I don't take the time to quibble and qualify.

So on the day before Christmas I began my new life of island solitude and winter antiseptic. I woke when the first shards of daylight appeared like stilettos in the crack around the Quonset hut door, buttoned and zipped and Velcroed myself into a suit of down, and taking up my trunk of housewright tools, stepped out into the white dawn. From that morning on I spent my days squaring up timbers, laying out and cutting the mortise-and-tenons for the posts and sills, chamfering the exposed edges of the beams and putting on a nifty lamb's-tongue stop that would show in the living room. I got in the habit of putting a couple of potatoes in a tin box atop the space heater at night, slipping them baked and hot into my pockets come morning and warming my hands with them until my ten o'clock snack— when a little butter made them go down all the sweeter for having served a thrifty double duty. In the afternoon I usually took a second break and went back inside the Quonset hut to warm up. Sometimes I melted snow in a big basin and did the laundry, roughing up yesterday's underwear and jeans on a scrubboard and hanging them on a washline I'd strung between cabinets of last summer's bones and potsherds. In late afternoon I was in the habit of taking a proprietary walk along the margins of the island, going from hill to hummock, reedy inlet to tidal islet. Sometimes I'd climb up the icy granite steps of Fort Bentley and walk along the earthen sentry walks, maybe stand at a cannon port and watch a tanker on the horizon grow smaller and smaller until it dropped silently off the edge of the earth. All around me the world was wet and white and possessed of a chaotic health. In the distance, sea met sky in a melt of gray water and cloudy violence. Landward the city sat like a great, glassy, crystalline growth on the edge of the continent, chuffing and crackling in the grayish dusk. The tall towers threw back crumpled reflections of the sky; cars moved like bugs along the elevated interstate; and Logan International sent the bellies of jets whining over my head. Amidst it all, silent and snow-swept, my island floated like a vision on the gray water, speechless but for the zagging track of my footprints going from hill to hollow, from hollow to hill.

I was alone.

Every day I made a little progress, ticked off a couple more of the 224 joists to be made, added to the neat stack of finished beams. I did everything as authentically as possible, using reproductions of seventeenth-century tools and relying on evidence from the dig and source material from other early Bay houses. I had to rig hoists and a two-wheeled trolley to move the three-hundred-pound beams around, made the most of my block-and-tackle and come-along. After a couple of weeks I could feel my arms muscling, my shoulders widening, my back hard and full. Lounging on a stack of joists, Mavericke wondered aloud if it wouldn't be easier with friends, with a community to help with the work.

"I had my Indians, after all," he said.

I told him Indians weren't what they used to be.

And I told him that the true New England (and so, American) soul, for all its disguise of democracy, of tolerance and humanism, was an island soul, cold, isolate and untouchable. I told him to be an American was to peg your thoughts to their own moral coordinates, to spurn any Greenwich Standard of ethics, to paint God in your own likeness and to banish any who painted him differently. For the true American is after purity—the purity of the wilderness soul—and he will walk on bones to get it. I told Mavericke I used to think he was the genius of the American soul, the original islander, but now I wasn't so sure. Because from everything I'd read and heard him say, he'd been able to keep himself away from the infections of the world without the accompanying violence and requisite bone-walk. And what kind of American was that? I told him I needed to know if his solitude was the communion of soul and self or merely a lonely sleepwalk: thirty-year-old Sam Mavericke banished, stripped, community-less, but still hungry for the touch of others.

"And what kind of American is it who walks on his own bones?" he said.

"Meaning?"

"Meaning never mind Indians, what kind of person does violence to *himself* to keep himself pure?"

"If it's not an American, I give up."

"What kind of person sterilizes himself by denying responsibility, brotherhood, human contact, and leaves his pretty cousin surrounded by monster children?"

"We're not talking about me," I said. "We're talking about

you. We're talking about whether you *chose* your life of solitude."

He picked up a handful of snow and started eating it. "Which solitude was that?" he asked.

"This!" I said, indicating the island around me.

"This," he repeated, mimicking my gesture, "was not *my* island."

"What?"

"*My* island," he said, "had Amias on it."

· 2 ·

My routine held all through January and into February. Sometime around Valentine's Day I passed the halfway point: more beams stacked on my finished left than on my yet-to-be-done right. I worked all the hours of daylight, quitting around five when the strobe atop the Hancock building began cutting its one-eyed swathe through the winter evening. I spent the nights until bedtime reading or writing my monograph on Mavericke. Sometimes Mavericke himself would help pass the time by telling me of the early days when America was a mere diccy idea, giving me thumbnails of Winthrop or John Cotton or Anne Hutchinson. He told me about the 1623 Gorges expedition that had brought him to America, how it had seemed doomed from the start, the trouble they had enforcing their patent to New England, collecting duty from the fishing fleets and trading shallops and trappers, the unbearable first winter, and the defections and deaths. I liked the sound of his voice in the close quarters, me on my cot, him in his hammock. We drank Old Mr. Boston brandy while he talked, the flickering space heater throwing devil's tails all around the room and the wind sending such drafts of wilderness into our cozy, gaslit home that we couldn't help but talk in terms of the polarities of things.

"We took half a dozen votes whether to stay or return to

England or sail south to Virginia," he said one night late in
February. "But no one paid any attention to them. Some of
the settlers slipped off into the woods with their traps, others drifted southward to Plymouth, most took passage on a
ship making a stopover on its way to Virginia. Gorges himself rounded up his retainers and set sail for England aboard
the *Swan* in early June. That left a few of us with the idea
of making a go of it. A handful stayed at Wessagusset. William Blackstone set up religious housekeeping on the west
side of the Shawmut peninsula. David Thompson and his
wife, Amias, moved to an island in the harbor, and I built a
hut on another island about a half-mile north of them."

And he threw me a quizzing look, as if to revive our old
argument of whether Amias had been married before, but
my head was pleasantly mulled in brandy, and I just held
out the bottle to him for a refill.

When he started in again I lay back and looked at the
ceiling while he talked so there was only the lulling sound
of his voice and the ragged spray of ice against the windows
when the wind blew. I could picture the island around us,
the dark drifts of snow, the ragtag army of junipers fighting
its way up the hill, the day's footprints beginning to vanish
under new snow, and all around the desolate sweep of winter: the cold, the hush, the darkness. I felt myself moored
to Mavericke, getting drunker and drunker, his voice like
an anchor, and the warm, lit Quonset hut our snuggery. I
put in a question from time to time, but mostly I just listened, listened to him tell of his first year on the island, of
his trading friendships with the post-plague Massachusetts
Indians, of his first few profits in fish and furs, and his
helping David Thompson with the building of a house for
him and Amias. I'd heard it all before, but I was always
ready to hear it again. I loved to picture the friendly sight
of Thompson's sailboat crossing the harbor, the late-night
games of snipsnapsnorum, a shared catch of cod drying on
the rickety fish flakes down by the water. By the time he got
to Thompson gashing his leg with an ax, and the gangrene

that followed, I had my eyes closed and I was fairly dreaming of an Amias become suddenly attainable in a virgin new world.

"She could've taken passage home on any number of fishing boats that happened our way, could've gone back to Wessagusset, or made her way south to warmer Virginia, but she stayed. I remember all during that winter seeing the pearly screw of smoke coming from her chimney and twisting against the deep-blue winter sky. As long as I saw it I knew she was all right. I sailed over from time to time, brought her fish and firewood and accepted in return some mussels she'd pried off the rocks at low tide. She was a small woman, not very strong but with snap in her movements. I always suspected that she straightened herself up just before I arrived, that she'd caught sight of my sail and stopped whatever work she was doing and put on a little lace or a finer cap. Because for all her ready smiles and the neat sweep of her hair on either side of her forehead, her fingers always seemed to be bleeding around the fingernails. She'd pour me some of her precious tea and ask me polite questions, whether I thought wheat could grow in the New England soil, and in general whether the American land could support an English world and—crossing her legs prettily—did I think the primary purpose of marriage was procreation as the Papists held or companionship as Calvin wrote. In spite of our earlier evenings at snipsnapsnorum I called her Mrs. Thompson and she called me Mr. Mavericke. But she always said it with just the faintest smile, maybe looking at me from under her brows, as if she knew what was what and wanted me to know that she knew."

I drank my brandy and listened to the showery spring of their courtship, watched the two of them pick wild strawberries on the daisied and dandelioned banks of Amias's island, wondered at the picture of Mavericke—the whole world a wilderness around him—dressing up in his best clothes and sailing every Sunday in his white sailboat across the water to a red-embroidered and waiting Amias. I envied them the theater of their love, the wild ocean, the wild land, the Indian eyes watching them from the wooded shore, and the two of them strolling along the neat boundaries of a world they'd chosen to inhabit— more than chosen—an island world they were constructing to the plumb lines and square aspect of their own selves. But even as I was getting excited about it—courtship in the wilderness!—I began to lose that snug, safe sense I'd had before—the brandy, the gaslight, the storm outside—and I began to feel alone in a new and frightening way. I tried to sit up in my cot to tell Mavericke, to ask him whether Amias was mere good fortune or a necessary prize, but I could almost hear his answer ("What's a tenon without a mortise?"), and a dim panic lodged inside me. I tried instead to lie still and concentrate on not being drunk, but my head kept turning over, then righting itself, then turning over again. I felt suddenly invaded by the cold, as if the Quonset hut had abruptly vanished and I was left lying in my cot on the *real* island, the frozen, ocean-eaten island. I put my drink down and again tried to steady myself. "Mavericke . . ." I managed to say, but I had to battle down my insides and couldn't say any more. I tried to listen to him, tried to concentrate on Amias at her virginal, on the white sails of Mavericke's boat, on the Reverend Blackstone in his Episcopalian robes marrying them under the trees with Indians in attendance—Indians in attendance!—but I couldn't. My head was spinning. In the end a rank taste like the taste of evil rose in my throat and I had to spill out of my cot and run for the door.

When my insides were done, I breathed deeply and ate a couple of handfuls of snow, and then knelt a moment to calm down. I could hear the crisp whistle of snow falling all around me, and in the distance the pound of the surf, and over everything the bladelike silence of winter. Across the harbor Boston was wrapped in the storm, its bright lights melded into a glowing dome that looked for all the world like a New England inferno: cold, isolate, unfeeling. I tried to pick out the hazy rise of Beacon Hill, wondered where

my parents were and what they were doing, and I wondered too where Hetty was. I could imagine her anywhere,
working late and sitting in the cell-like room of one of her
monster children, or out with one of her boyfriends, or in
the electronic cave of a video arcade, in a taxi, in a dark
movie theater, down along the littered streets of the Combat Zone, home alone. I felt a sudden urge to see her, to
get in my boat, reef sail and make it somehow through the
rough sea to the mainland. And I realized, imagining it,
that that was just what Mavericke would have done on some
unfit night when he was worried about Amias. But I realized too that Hetty was not on any island, pegged and easily
pointed to. She was somewhere in the snow-swept city,
monster children and modern lovers all around her. I felt
suddenly bereft, kneeling in the snow, as if my imagin-
ings—lonely Amias in a virgin new world—had been stolen
from me. Uphill, the timbers of Mavericke's house looked
like giant bones lying under a shroud of snow.

"I drank too much," I said back inside the Quonset hut.
Mavericke was leaning on his elbow in the hammock, watching me. I took off my wet socks and climbed into bed.

"Are you all right?" he asked.

"Yes."

"You're sure?"

"Yes."

He watched me a moment longer and then reached out
and turned the light down. "We'll talk of this some more,"
he said once the shadows had settled themselves.

The Mortise-and-Tenon in a Snowstorm

• 1 •

But I didn't give him a chance to talk of it some more. I threw myself back into my joinery, making such a clang and clash with chisel and mallet that after a couple of days of trying to sit on his stack of purlins and reason with me, Mavericke gave up and disappeared for a week. When he came back, he started leaving notes around the Quonset hut. They were notes on marriage: poems, biblical quotes, quaint letters from absent husbands to waiting wives, extracts from the marriage polemics of the seventeenth century, letters from old Dear Abby columns. I found them on my pillow at night, tucked under the molding of my mirror in the morning, found them taped to my adz head, folded and hidden in the well of a mortise, tucked into my shoes, into my shirt pockets. He kept himself hidden, coming and going behind my back. I'd catch sight of him from time to time— on a hillside, down by the rocks—but whenever I waved or gestured for him to come, he disappeared.

"What do you want from me, Mavericke?" I asked one

91

night in the dark, but he was nowhere around. In the
morning I found another note under my toothbrush.

> Where is the man this day living whose Virginity may
> be compared with Abraham's Marriage, in whom all
> the nations of the earth were blessed?
> —Alexander Niccholes, *Discourse of Marriage and*
> *Wiving* (1615)

And appended to the note:

> If you want to be celibate, become a Catholic. They
> go in for that sort of thing.
> —Samuel Mavericke, *Letter to a Young Fool*

"Mavericke," I said the next night, lying awake and eye-
ing the same dark. "I'm trying to live a moral life. With the
pop and whiz of America in my dooryard, it isn't easy."

> Marriage is itself a necessary civilizer of men. We must
> have no world, or but a beastly and confused world,
> if marriage were not; therefore it must needs be law-
> ful. And let it be taken away from any sort of man,
> and that man will grow, little by little, full of filthi-
> ness and uncleanness, by being forced to forbeare
> beyond strength. And in affecting an inattainable
> puritie, they fall into a most extreme impuritie.
> —Whatley, *A Care-Cloth* (1624)

(There are all sorts of impurity, Wheelwright.)

The next morning I gathered up every pen and pencil
in the Quonset hut and threw them into a snowbank. But
on my pillow that night I found my copy of Cotton Mather's
Eureka the Vertuous Woman Found with a leaf turned down.

> Ye Popish dogs, at Marriage bark no more;
> Unclean so Devils burn, and Single Roar,

Marriage, *that honorable Chastity,*
Let none but Filthy Antichrist decry.

I threw the book across the room.

After that the tone of the notes changed. There was a loving poem to her husband by Anne Bradstreet; Adam's bone of my bone; some gentle Latin erotica; a pun on marriage as *merry-age*; and there were testimonials to the sweetness of marriage, to the companionship of husband and wife in this vale of tears. But I didn't listen. I kept working, and when I was too body-tired to heft my timbers, found little jobs to keep busy—cataloging potsherds, measuring craniums, doing my laundry when I got desperate. I put on my all-weather gear and took the *Pilgrim's Progress* out, circumnavigating the island, and then breaking off and sailing down to Thompson's Island, docking and walking the island's paths, going this way and that. But there was nothing to see except the snowy hollows, the bushes shagged with ice, and over everything, the cold twentieth-century sunshine. Back on Mavericke's Island, I found three more notes strewn on my bed, but I threw them out without even looking at them. I went through three days of awful cabin fever, and on the fourth, the sight of a Metropolitan District Commission boat headed toward me was enough to set off an idea that Hetty was coming, Hetty bribing some MDC water cop through wile or wit or simple winsomeness and getting a free ride out to the island. When the boat veered off, I started shouting at Mavericke, wherever he was. But the next day, there was another MDC boat, again headed straight for the island. I tried to ignore it, but the sight of a smallish figure beside the pilot got me all turned about. When the boat skidded up to the dock, it was the blunt-headed administrator of the MDC Historical Preservation Department who hopped out onto the icy wood.

"You're a hard man to get hold of, Mr. Wheelwright," he said, handing me a folder full of papers. "Interrogatories. We're being sued."

"Sued?" I said. "By whom?"

"Indians, Mr. Wheelwright, Indians." And he tapped the interrogatories and suggested I read them through.

An hour later, back at the Quonset hut, I found a note in mariner's language about the wife as port in a storm, as sanctuary from the invasions of the world.

"Okay, Mavericke," I said that night, climbing into my cot, "this is it. Time to talk."

But there was only silence answering.

"They're trying to take your island away."

Still, silence.

"I'm being called as an authority. *As an authority*, Mavericke. You can't treat me this way."

But there was only the dark whisper of the space heater. I spent a minute tossing about, pulling at the covers and punching my pillow.

"But she doesn't *love* me," I said finally. "What about that? She doesn't love me." And I socked my pillow a couple of times more and then stopped when suddenly I heard the familiar sound of the hammock straining.

"How do you know?" came his voice out of the dark.

I sat up and looked his way but it was too dark to see. "I can tell," I said finally. "I've known her all my life."

"Then you have to *woo* her."

I fell back down in bed.

"She's wooable, I judge," he said.

"I'm no wooer."

"Sure you are."

"Let me build your house in peace, Mavericke. There is no sweet Amias on some near island changing her cap for me."

"There are all kinds of islands, Wheelwright, and I'd say your pretty cousin was stranded on one of them."

"We've grown apart. She's got her monster children and I've got you. Besides, we're cousins. First cousins. First cousins to the second power in fact. Offspring of married brothers and sisters."

"No big deal. It's legal in Massachusetts."

"I don't need you to tell me that."

"Aha."

"But legal doesn't mean possible."

"Ask her."

"I couldn't. I'd be a trembling idiot."

"Write her a letter then."

"Oh, God."

"Tell her you've loved her your whole life."

"Mavericke . . ."

"Tell her you've been to Babylon more than once and you know what's what. And what's what is she's the one for you."

"I've got to go to sleep now."

"Use some of that goddamn energy of yours, Wheelwright, and *win your love.*"

· 2 ·

The next day, in a gloom of defeat, I gathered up the sheaf of interrogatories, and hoisting my frozen sails, set out for the mainland for the first time in ten weeks. I felt like a barbarian in the city, walking up through the warehouses that surround the marina into the financial district, me in my grimy snowsuit, bearded, unbathed for ten weeks, and everyone around me dressed for the business world, men in herringbone overcoats and women with their rear ends high-heeled into the air. I felt queer and disoriented, as if I'd been away even longer than just the ten weeks, as if I'd stepped in from the legitimate seventeenth century and not my polished-up imitation. The feeling lasted the whole time it took me to walk to my parents' house, disappearing only when I stepped into the shower and saw the winter's dirt and sweat go down the drain like a 350-year-old patina.

At the Public Library I took up my old seat and got started assembling a deposition concerning the descent of ownership of the island. I tracked down document after document, answered each of the questions with reason and as many cites as I could muster, wording everything against anyone claiming ownership of the island. But all the time I wrote, I felt haunted by the ghost of myself: thirteen-year-old Jay-jay Wheelwright sitting in the same Windsor chair under the same green lampshade reading for the first time about Mavericke, about the island, about Amias's virginal. I had to keep looking at my hand as I wrote, to see there the care of thirty years and not the crispness of thirteen. From time to time in an old book or public record, I found notes written in the margins, notes so full of wonder and bloom that I felt as if I'd stumbled upon my young self, kept clean and eager and unaged in the yellowed pages. Outside, the Hancock building rose like an enormous glass tombstone, clean, rigid, sheer, exuding an indomitable right to be what and where it was. I got up and crossed to the window to look at it. What was so wrong in its construction and so right in my single labor on Mavericke's house? Mavericke himself might say the Hancock building was civilization solidified, a glass tower built by all levels of men, each not knowing what the others did but doing his job and so building a monument beyond himself, more than himself. But I couldn't help wondering about the cubicles of human souls inside the building now, not knowing how it was built or who built it, where the heat came from in the winter or where the air conditioning came from in the summer, who put the food in the Snak-o-Mat machines, and what an enormous and circuitous plunge their pee made when they flushed the toilets on the fifty-fourth floor.

"We are responsible for the comforts of our own bodies, are we not?" I managed to work into the interrogatory concerning the first permanent, habitable structures built on the island.

After lunch I got bogged down in a question concerning the colony's right to commandeer the island for an Indian internment camp in 1675. It seemed clear to me that the colony—the state—*didn't* have the right and that the island—far from falling to Boston after Mavericke's death as the State maintained, or falling to the Indians who continued to reside there after their internment as the Indians were claiming—the island was still Mavericke's. It had still been his when he died of starvation in the winter of 1676, and so, should be his heirs' now.

"Does he have any?" the MDC historian asked when I called from the first-floor phone.

"His son Samuel, but he disappears in history."

"So he doesn't?"

"Just a moral one."

"A moral heir?" he repeated, and there was a moment of silence. "I was warned about you, Wheelwright," he said finally. "Now just answer the interrogatories favorable to the government and don't try to horn in on the State Park system. We've got enough on our hands with these phony-ass Indians. Understand?"

I didn't answer.

"If the moral heir wants to keep playing around in the dirt out there, he'll understand," he said and hung up.

Down in the Periodicals Room, I started searching through recent copies of *The Boston Globe*. What I found made my heart stop.

KING PHILIP RETURNS
But This Time His War
Will Be In The Courts

BOSTON—Suit was filed today in Federal District Court by the New England Native Task Force (NENTF) on behalf of the Wampanoag Indian tribe. At issue is ownership of lands in Plymouth County, in Barnstable County—including the public golf course at South Carver—and of Mavericke's Island, part of the Harbor Island State Park.

And under a picture of Philip in a lawyerly three-piece, the article detailed the items of the suit, giving for background the recent government settlements with the Passamaquoddies and the Narragansets. Then, calling Philip the chief counsel for NENTF, it started in on the Wampanoag.

> According to chief counsel Safford, it is a historical irony that his tribe is not recognized by the United States government. It was the Wampanoag, and their leader, King Philip, who attempted to unite the Indians of New England against the encroachment of white settlers in the 17th century. They succeeded to the extent that King Philip's War is, to this day, the bloodiest war Americans have ever fought in, resulting in the largest proportion of the population killed.
>
> The new King Philip hopes to accomplish with law what his namesake was unable to accomplish with arms.
>
> To succeed he must first prove his own claim to be the descendant of Massasoit, the Wampanoag chief who aided the Plymouth settlers in 1620, and whose son was called King Philip by the whites.
>
> By proving his lineal descent from Massasoit, Safford hopes to circumvent the thorny question of whether he and the Indians he represents constitute a tribe. It was just such a question that torpedoed the recent Mashpee claim to land on Cape Cod. Because he is the male descendant of Wampanoag chiefs, Safford maintains he is the

rightful leader of the present day
Wampanoag—in effect, a tribe unto
himself.

The suit will be heard in Federal
District Court. No date has been set.

I read the article over five times, then put the paper down
and went back to the telephone on the first floor.

"Hello?" a woman's voice answered.

"Is King Philip there?"

"Is this a reporter?"

"No. Is Mr. Safford there?"

"He's in his study. Can I take a message?"

I thought a moment. "Tell him this is a death threat. If
he wants to hear more, I'll be at five-five-five-six-eight-four-
seven for the next five minutes."

Three minutes later the phone rang.

"I've never received a death threat before."

I recognized his voice. It had the same faint mockery,
that air of amused boredom. "I've never given one before.
Was that your wife?"

"Ah, a nosy death threat."

"Are you married?"

"A considerate death threat."

"Cut the crap, King Philip, this is the real thing."

"So who are you?"

"I'm someone with personal knowledge about some of
the land you're trying to steal. And it's no-go, Indian giver."

"Which land is that?"

"Mavericke's Island."

"We'll let the courts decide that."

"*You* will. *I* won't."

There was a moment of silence, "Is that you, Wheelwright?"

"Who?" I had the presence to say.

"Never mind," he said. "So what's your personal knowledge?"

"That legally the island doesn't belong to you *or* the state. It belongs to the heirs of Samuel Mavericke."

"Ah, a well-researched death threat. But there are no heirs."

"Then it would be sold at public auction, wouldn't it?"

"That *is* you, Wheelwright, isn't it? I've been watching you all winter playing around in the snow out there."

"I don't know what you're talking about."

"You should have that house of yours done just in time for me to move into it."

"What house?"

"Make sure the doorways are high enough. I'm six-six and the seventeenth century produced miniature men."

"I don't seem to have your attention, King Philip. This is a death threat."

"Death threats are old-fashioned, boy. It's car bombs today."

"I'm an old-fashioned terrorist."

"Well, you wouldn't be the first in your family to kill an Indian."

"You're not an Indian. You wear business suits."

"We've come a long way," he said and hung up.

• 3 •

"Did you go see her?" Mavericke asked that night back on the island.

"Yes."

"What did she say?"

"I didn't talk to her. I just looked at her through the window."

I could hear him sigh in the dark.

"I was getting *depressed*," I said. "I hadn't finished the interrogatories. It was getting dark and I was worried about losing the island. I started walking and wound up in the North End. That's where she lives now. She told me before about the Italians, how they yell and scream from apartment to apartment, across the street, from building to building. All day and all night long. She likes it. She says she feels safe walking home at night. There are always friendly people in the street. The last time I saw her, she said she was going to put a dark rinse in her hair so she'd look Italian. I was depressed, Mavericke, I tell you. I stood up on a door stoop across the street and looked in through her windows. It was just getting dark and she hadn't pulled the shades yet. Maybe she never pulls the shades, I don't know. I watched her for half an hour and then left."

"What was she doing?"

"Reading."

"Reading what?"

"How should I know? A book that says she doesn't need me."

"Was she alone?"

"Yes."

"She was alone and she was just reading and you stood on the door stoop across the street?"

"That's right."

"Some wooer you are."

"I'm not wooing anybody. I told you that. Now leave me alone. I feel sick."

I woke the next morning feverish and certain I had heard a knock on my door. It was storming, and when I opened the door I was met with such a fierce spin of snow and wind that at first I couldn't tell that no one was there. I was weak in my knees. I fell back in bed. The storm clawed and ripped at the Quonset hut and made such a windy racket along the rooftop that it sounded like packs of stampeding devils above me. In a dizzy half-sleep, I had a vision of the island wrapped in snow—the rest of the harbor quiet and winter-serene, but my island in the throes of white oblivion—lifting out of the water and floating in whizzing white chaos above the winter sunshine. When I woke again it was to a second knock, and this time I saw a shadow—shoulders and head—dart across the ice-coated window along the side of the hut. I sat up, wide-awake, and knew it was Philip come after me.

But by the time I was dressed and wrapped up in my winter gear his tracks were gone. I felt woozy with fever but I headed out through the driving snow all the same. I went up to the house site first and then down to the dig. I found footprints from time to time but they seemed like they were old ones—mine—uncovered by the wind. I kicked my way down to the dock, saw the *Pilgrim's Progress* rocking uneasily at her moorings, but no other boat. I called "Philip!" but the wind shoved the word back down my throat. I felt ill. My ankles were sweating inside my boots. I looked toward the city but it had vanished; turned toward Thompson's Island, but it too was gone. There was nothing but squalling snow, water, and the indistinct snow-image of the island.

I was alone.

Climbing back up the hill, I somehow got off the path. I knew it, but I didn't care. I kept on, breaking my way through the snow and the low bushes, passing the Quonset hut somewhere on my right and heading toward the interior lowlands. I was looking for footprints—stupidly, unthinkingly—but keeping a watch on the virgin snow for anything alien, wrong, un-Wheelwright. I got lost once or twice—the snow so thick that everything seemed changed around me— found my way, then got lost again. I was tired. I was hot. I stopped once and ate a couple of handfuls of snow, pressed it to my eyelids. I took my mittens off and snugged them over the ends of some fir boughs, and then a few steps farther, threw my hat away. When I tried to sit on what looked like a rock it turned out to be a bush covered with snow and it gave under me.

"Mavericke," I said aloud. "Mavericke, you got me into this."

But even as I said it I thought I heard someone in the trees off to my left. I sat stock-still and listened. The wind died and I heard it again—the hush of footgear through the powdery snow—but in the next instant all was bluster and gust again. I got up and crashed into the thicket.

"Mavericke!" I cried. "Philip?"

But there was no answer. I searched from tree to tree, bush to bush, caught a pine branch in the face so my eyes began to tear. I started running, breaking off branches that got in my way, running through the thicket trying to get back out to the clearing. I stumbled once, got snow all over the front of me, but got right up again. I kept coming across my own footprints, looking bizarre and confused in the snow. I tried following them, but they kept backtracking on themselves, crossing one another and stepping on themselves. Crazily, I started walking backward, trying to fit my feet into the footprints I'd just left behind me, counting as I went, counting each step backward: ". . . four, five, six . . ."

But I backed into someone.

It gave me such a start that I slipped and fell.

It was a woman. She had on a great gray cloak and cap with beaver fur tucked under the ears.

It was Hetty.

"Hetty?" I said.

"Honestly, Mr. Wheelwright."

It wasn't Hetty.

"Amias?"

"Get up off your knees, Mr. Wheelwright."

But I stayed where I was. "Amias?"

"Get up off your knees," she said again and started walking between the bushes and trees. I just watched her go. After half a dozen steps, she turned back to me. "Well?"

I was speechless.

"Coming."

"You're short," I managed to say.

She looked at me.

"You're short," I said again.

"Tall enough to handle you, Mr. Wheelwright," she said, and pulling her cloak neatly around her, started walking again. This time I got up and followed her.

"It's no use," I said once I'd caught up to her. "If Mavericke's been filling you in on things, it's no use."

She didn't answer, just kept walking, taking small steps, her tiny boots sending the powdery snow sizzling in front of her.

"I don't feel well."

"I should think not," she said.

"I'm sick and I don't feel well and I got lost."

"You were lost, Mr. Wheelwright, before you got lost."

I trudged along behind her.

"I must be right about *some* things," I said after a minute.

"You have your moments."

"What? What am I right about?"

But she didn't answer. I followed quietly behind her, trying to fit my big footprints into the delicate ellipses she left in the snow. After we'd walked another hundred feet, she pulled back the branch of a spruce tree and pointed the way in.

"What's in there?" I asked, peering in.

"Nothing," she said and gave me a push. I crouched and fit my way between the stiff branches until I was inside the little atrium that spread around the foot of the tree. Nearest the trunk, I could almost stand up.

"It's not snowing in here," I said with a look of wonder at the bare pine needles and the few crescents of snow arcing in from the outside. Amias sat down and started adjusting the fur inside her cap. I felt the top of my head, and then started brushing the snow off my hair.

"I lost my hat," I said.

"You threw it away."

"I lost my mittens too."

"You stuck them on the branches of a tree," she said, and she made a face.

"So you *were* out there. There *was* someone. You've been following me. You knocked on my door. *Twice*."

She shook her head. "I didn't knock on anybody's door."

"You did. I heard it. It woke me up. And then you knocked again and ran past the window."

Again she shook her head. "If you heard knocks, Mr. Wheelwright, they were inside your head. Now, please sit down."

I peered at her an instant and then sat on the stiff pine needles.

"It's no use," I said. "Whatever he's been telling you, it's no use."

She just smoothed the folds of her cloak and didn't answer.

"And besides, I told all that to Mavericke in confidence. In *confidence*."

"A married man and woman have no secrets from each other."

"Oh, God," I said, and we were quiet.

The snow made a hissing sound all around.

"Marriage," she began finally, "is the beginnings of society. It is the little commonwealth, the foundation of civilized behavior. To live alone is to live unnaturally, to do violence to the natural order of things. To live alone *in the midst of loving someone* is to do violence to your own self."

"I've heard all this before."

"*Marriage*, I repeat," she said with a stern look, "is a picture in miniature of society. It is a microcosm of society. Do you know your Greek?"

"No."

"Yes, you do. what does *microcosm* mean?"

"Small cosmos."

"And what does *cosmos* mean in Greek?"

"Order."

"That's right."

And we were quiet again.

"You don't have to convince the tenon," I said finally, feeling sick all over again, "of its need for a mortise. You'd do better to convince the mortise to stop trying the fit of every tenon that comes along."

"I'm trying to convince *you* to convince her."

"Impossible."

"Why? Why impossible?"

But I was helpless to answer. I looked across at her in the dim light. She had the same small bones as Hetty, the same quiet features. But there was none of the haunt of dissatisfaction and searching need about her face.

"It *is* possible," she said after a moment, "for a man to take pleasure in physical life, in a wife, and not necessarily succumb to the riot of the world."

I shook my head.

"Maybe you are just a coward, Mr. Wheelwright, too afraid to go after her."

"No."

"It looks that way."

"I just called up an Indian with a death threat. I'm no coward."

"There are all sorts of cowards."

I didn't answer.

"Maybe you're brave in the violent things of life—death threats and living on an island—but what about love? Love, Mr. Wheelwright."

"Listen here," I said. "I've loved her my whole life. I've loved her as long as I can remember. And I can remember her throwing peas at me from her high chair. You're no one to tell *me* about love. You switched beds awfully fast here in the New World."

"What?" she cried.

"You heard me."

"My husband died. He *died*."

"And I used to think you came here as Mavericke's young bride."

"I *was* young. I *was* his bride. We lived for three years alone and in perfect love before Winthrop came. You have an odd idea of purity, Mr. Wheelwright."

"And you have an odd idea of helping someone. I'm sick in the body and now you're telling me I'm sick in the soul."

"What I'm trying to tell you is that your cousin is just as sick in the soul, and you're the only one who can help her.

But you are a blind and selfish man." And she got up before I could stop her and made her way out from under the tree. I crawled after her.

"What did you say? *I'm* the only one who can help her?"

But she continued walking through the snow, keeping her back to me, turning this way and that each time I tried to come around to face her.

"*How* is she sick in the soul? What do you mean?"

"You have no right," she said.

"What?"

"You have *no right!* You have no right to accuse me—" She left off. There were snowflakes on her eyelashes and melting snow running down her cheeks; or maybe she was crying.

"David Thompson married me when I was fourteen and hadn't even finished my Latin primer."

"What did you mean—" I started to say, but out of nowhere she swung and hit me, and then broke into a run. I ran after her. The wind blasted all around us.

"He was a bully!" she said when I'd caught up to her. "Oh, he was just the sort of man for America. He brought me here when I was fifteen. When I was *fifteen!* I was a disappointment to him. I mean in the intimate way. I couldn't do things right until years later after I'd had Samuel's baby." And she flung me a look to see if I understood. "After I was big enough," she added harshly. "He started telling about it in front of me, when the other men were around after trapping or hunting. He'd say he preferred his Indian women. I was set to sail back to England more than once. But I didn't. I thought of putting myself before one of the other men just to have back at him. But I didn't. Once, when we were still at Wessagusset, I let myself get lost—stayed away for three nights—and when I came back only told him an Indian had taken care of me. *Let* his imagination rage. The morning he died he called me over to his bed and when I leaned over him, he hit me."

"But Hetty—" I started to say.

"Hetty has a city full of David Thompsons! She's drowning in them. She's being hurt and hit by every one of them. And she can't stop it."

"But there's a difference!" I cried.

"What? What's the difference?"

"She likes them! She likes her David Thompsons!"

"How do you know she does?" she cried back. We stopped and faced each other. "She's as hurt and as lost as you are. She's got an idea of herself as so broken and so unfit that she takes to her David Thompsons like she was slapping herself with each one of them. When I stayed on the island after David died it wasn't to catch Samuel even if he thinks it was. It was because I thought I was too soiled to go home. I was *seventeen*! I stayed to let myself be taken over by the woods and the Indians. When he asked me to marry him I told him I couldn't. When he asked me again I told him I couldn't be right with him at night. But he married me anyway. Love," she said—and now I was pretty sure it wasn't just the snowflakes in her lashes—"love is inspired by grace, Mr. Wheelwright. And grace is not merely portioned out to the individual soul. It needs the fertile soil of a second soul."

"But you don't know," I said. "You don't know."

"What? What don't I know?"

"You don't know the looks she gives me—has *always* given me—whenever I make a move toward intimacy. I don't mean trying to touch her or kiss her. I mean even when I try to remind her of old times when we were kids. Or when I try to hint at affinities in our lives. Or when I say that we know each other in ways other people could never know us. I've stopped doing it. She knows how to make me feel like what I'm thinking about her is dirty or obscene or unnatural or something. We're cousins, you know, goddamn it! We used to take baths together!"

"There's nothing obscene about a bath."

"*I* know that. Tell *her*."

"*You* tell her. Tell her that you love her and you're not going away until she loves you back. Tell her that you need her and she needs you. Tell her that your house is pointless, useless, nothing but a museum, unless she lives in it with you."

I just stood stricken before her.

"Tell her that she has to take you if she wants to find her way out of the wilderness. Tell her that you need her to find your way *into* the wilderness. Tell her that this is love at last. Tell her that you are *her* salvation and that she is *yours*."

I couldn't speak.

"Tell her, Mr. Wheelwright, that she doesn't have any choice."

CHAPTER
8

Courtship in the Wilderness

· 1 ·

I started with roses. I pilfered some money from my National Science Foundation account, and taking a deep breath, placed an order for half a dozen white roses to be sent to Hetty's North End address every morning for two weeks. When it came to the fourteen notes, I chickened out and signed them in a disguised hand:

Love, Your Future Husband

I went back out to the island, shaved my winter beard and waited for the fruits of love. After the first week I ventured in, docked my boat near Long Wharf and walked over to Hetty's place. The shades were pulled and I thought: There's a start. But inside I could tell she didn't know. She was coy about the flowers—all seven bouquets sitting around the room in different stages of beauty and decay—said they were from a friend. "An admirer," she said with a laugh when I pressed her. She smiled and flushed and looked all

111

abright with hope and excitement. It made me queerly jealous: What mad, handsome stranger was she imagining as the sender of those roses?

But I battled up my spirits, and instead of sailing back to the island that night went to my parents to establish a closer base of operations. I let the next week of roses run its course and then started sending notes to her by courier. I sent them to her place in the North End in the evening and to the third floor of the Baxter School in the daytime. I copied over some of Mavericke's notes to me on marriage, added some of my own, got out my Anne Bradstreet ("If ever two were one, then surely we"), and spent my afternoons in the controlled atmosphere of the Rare Books Room at the library, digging up and cribbing more quotes and sending them off to her in a bombardment of ardor.

After a week I got a note in return by the regular U.S. Mail:

Please, Wright, it's embarrassing.

But I didn't stop. I didn't care if she was embarrassed or disappointed or disheartened. I started sending her more notes, twice a day, even annotated them for her.

Husbands and wives should be as two sweet friends (*are we not, Hetty?*), bred under one constellation (*ha!*), tempered by an influence from heaven, whereof neither can give any great reason (*this is the very mystery of love*), save that mercy and providence first made them so, and then made their match; Saying, see, God hath determined us out of this vast world, each for the other (. . . *out of this vast world, my sweetheart*).
—Daniel Rogers, *Matrimoniall Honour* (1642)

And I wrote her on the very nature of marriage, of the Puritan companionate marriage, where the husband is friend and helper to the wife, and the wife is friend and helper to the husband, told her *that* was the sort of marriage *we* would have. And then I warned her of the dangers of living alone, that to live alone is to prepare the way for the triumph of lust (telling her too, in a very Maverickian tone, that there are all types of lust).

> Lust, that boiling putrefaction of the bloud, that raging, ruling *headstrong sinne of this age,* that is too likely to break out, though it went cloathed in sacke-cloth.
> —Alexander Niccholes, *Discourse of Marriage and Wiving* (1615)

I sent her newspaper clippings of the evil of our times: a pool-table rape (complete with morning-after picture of the pool table); gravestones at the Granary stigmatized with spray paint; bricks dropped from overpasses through the windshields of Japanese cars; articles about the death of the family, of God, of business, of America, of heterosexuality; postcards of the Hancock building with windows all set to pop. And then, as if to gather her with tender mercies, I began sending her presents: a dress from Bonwit Teller (size 5, my tiny sweetheart), a gold locket, a book on breast-feeding, various pearls of various great prices. I had to call an antique dealer to take away a Hepplewhite sewing stand to help pay for it all. (The next morning my mother looked at the empty spot in our living room but didn't say anything; my father walked right through it.)

"Please," I heard that night on the other end of the phone. "People at work are wondering who's sending me all this stuff. It's disruptive. I can't work properly."

"Where are you now?"

"I'm out."

"Where?"

"Never mind where. Just stop sending all this stuff."

"Let's meet."

"When?"

"Right now."

"No, not now."

"Now," I said. "Where are you?"

"At Goebbels. On Charles Street. But I don't want you to come."

"I'll be right there," I said and hung up before she could say anything else.

But when I got to the bar she was gone. There were Nazi flags and swastikas on the walls. Wagner was hammering out of loudspeakers at either end of the room. A big guy in a black flight jacket came over to me and asked if I was Wheelwright.

"Cut the shit then," he said, and he pushed himself against me. He smelled of leather and cologne. "She don't want you."

"Who are you?"

"You'll find out. We'll invite you to the wedding."

And he made a fat kiss in the air. I eased myself past him and took a quick look around the room. There were pictures over the tables—Goering, Himmler, Eva Braun—and on one of the walls a showcase with a Luger and an SS hat in it. A waitress dressed in black fishnet stockings asked if she could help me but I shook her off.

"Where is she?" I asked the big guy back near the door.

He shrugged.

"Where is she?"

"Maybe off somewhere having a laugh."

I took a step closer and peered into his face. "So you're David Thompson," I said.

"Who?"

"Who?" I mimicked.

"What're you talking about?"

"I'm talking about love in the wilderness, Thompson."

"Who the fuck is Thompson?"

"You're Thompson, Thompson."

"You're nutso, Jack."

"I've got friends who care about what you did to Amias, and they're not about to let you do the same to Hetty."

"Fruitcake city!" he called to the bar, but no one turned around, no one was listening to us. "I'll do what I want," he said, turning back to me. "And right now what I do is your cousin."

"My fiancée, you mean."

"I'm doing your fiancée, then," he said with a fat grin.

"She'll be my wife soon enough."

"Then I'll be doing your wife."

And he made an obscene gesture with an index finger and his hand. I pushed past him, went over to the ladies' room and opened the door.

"Hetty," I whispered into the reverberating white light. "I love you. I've loved you my whole life. And I'm not quitting until you love me back."

And then I left.

Half an hour later, lying in bed in my pajamas, I heard someone call my name down in the street. I hurried to the window and threw the sash up. It was Hetty, standing on the cobblestones four floors below.

"That was a rotten trick," she said, and she hit herself in the head. "I'm sorry."

"Marry me," I called down to her.

"No." Her breath made a puff of silver in the cold.

"Yes."

"Impossible," she said, and she tucked her chin in and stared down at the ground. The gaslight settled in a curly nest on the top of her head. She said something I couldn't hear.

"What?"

She looked up. "I said you can keep sending me stuff if you want."

I made a sign for her to wait and then grabbed my bathrobe. But by the time I'd run down the four flights, she was gone.

· 2

Bone of my bone, flesh of my flesh. Oh, Hetty, I have spanking dreams these nights! Dreams of flying, the two of us, winged and powerful over the exploding treetops. It's spring everywhere: the leaves under us, young and bright green, the brooks swollen with snow water, and the sky arcing above us like the great dome of heaven. Oh, we could have a life together! A marriage of souls that could tell the twentieth century to wait in the waiting room. We could love and live into the twenty-first century, bringing up a brood of beaming Wheelwrights, repopulating sweet New England with the moral bone of your bone. Think of the sweetness of the morning, waking beside one another, the screen doors slamming in the summer, the hot hearths in the winter. We'll have trays of warm tarts when little trick-or-treaters come to our door in October. In the springtime we'll pick red strawberries, blue blueberries in summer. These were the pleasures of our childhood, Hetty—why shouldn't they be the pleasures of our marriage?

It's happiness I want for you (that American pursuit), happiness and a clean life, a life of right angles (Wright angles, my sweet, my dove, my likely-to-be-angry cousin). We are two pursuers, you and I, Hetty, and our pursuits have led us into whoring after strange gods. I cannot fight the world alone; you are being bruised inside and out. But together, what couldn't we do? When our ancestor John came here in 1636 he came with his wife—he knew what the wilderness was all about. He knew that the true buffer for the soul is love. Now his two descendants are born exiled into this concrete wilderness, alone, without each other, and both are battered and afraid. I am building a house on an island, Hetty—a mere house by myself, but with you, a home. It will have square lines, rigid rafters, a ridgepole that will sing the heights of heaven, sills blessed by the bloom of the earth. It will have a dovetailed summer beam, a mortared chimney, a planked and shaked roof, enough windows to let the world in and thick enough walls to keep it out. And it will have room for a double bed.

You are my hope.

You are my salvation.

You are my love.

Wright

The next day I found a note dropped through the mail slot.

Dear Wright,
   If you like—and if you'll accept Isabel and Irene Steele as chaperones—I will be free this Thursday night.
                                                                 Hetty

• 3 •

When I saw them coming down the steps of the Baxter School I realized what was what, remembered Hetty telling me about the twins, and I felt my heart sink. She met me with a forced look, smiling but in no way soft in her movement toward me, as if she had something in mind and was determined not to let my letters and roses get in her way. She introduced me to each of the twins, but they just stared straight ahead in autistic oblivion. I leaned over and lifted each one's hand and made a show of shaking it—as if to prove to Hetty the largeness of my heart—but their wrists were limp and their small arms fell back to their sides like deadweight. When they walked they walked in step, shoulder pressed to shoulder, hip to hip, like cartoon characters except for the soulless, blank, screaming nothing that smothered their faces. I felt all the courting words and wooing I'd been practicing scatter around me.

"There are some studies of autistic twins in the literature," Hetty was saying. "But there is no systematic analysis or attempt at understanding the private language that seems to exist between them. It's a rare opportunity for gaining insight, I think." And she placed a loving hand on each of the twins' red heads. "With Irene and Isabel everything seems focused on twoness. They must always be together. They must always complement each other. I have this idea sometimes they're like those binary stars that orbit around each

other, each held in by the other's gravity. But beyond
that—"

"Are you seeing me the way I want you to see me?" I
interrupted. She looked at me with an expression of vague
distrust.

"We're talking about the twins."

I said it again: "Are you seeing me tonight the way I
want you to see me?"

She didn't answer.

"Are you?"

"I don't know," she said, looking straight ahead.

"Don't know what?"

"I don't know how I'm seeing you."

I made a face at that.

"If you don't like it, you know how to execute a one-
eighty."

"One-eighty," one of the twins said suddenly, in front of
us. "One-eighty," the other one repeated in the same dead
tone. It kind of spooked me, but Hetty made a bright face,
and then stopped and took a notebook out of her backpack.
The twins kept walking.

"A clue," she said, writing quickly, and then she skipped
after them, tossing me a look of such sudden pleasure that
my heart fluttered. I trotted after them.

"I made reservations at Locke-Ober's," I said when we'd
all fallen in step again. The Locke-Ober café is a ritzy res-
taurant just off the Common. "I didn't know then the twins
were the twins."

"Who'd you think they were?"

"Bridesmaids," I answered.

"One-eighty," Isabel said.

"One-eighty," Irene echoed.

Hetty seemed to be sizing them up as members of a wedding.

"I guess I should cancel," I said.

"I guess so."

We walked on in silence.

"Where are we going then?" I asked.

She shrugged.

"This is not quite the courtship I had in mind."

"I imagine not."

"Look," I said and stopped abruptly so someone nearly rammed me from behind. Hetty stopped too, but the twins kept going. She seemed caught an instant between us and then started after the twins, gesturing for me to come. "Am I making a fool of myself?" I called after her, holding my ground.

"I'd say so," she said. She hurried and caught hold of the twins so they stopped and stood stiffly in their tracks. "But I don't mind. Now, come on. I'll show you my new place."

"I don't want to see your new place," I said, running up to her so no one could hear us. "I want to know if you're going to marry me."

She looked me squarely in the face but didn't answer.

"Are you?"

"I don't know."

"Does that mean yes?"

"It means I don't know."

"What's keeping you from knowing? You know *me*, I'd say." And I hit myself in the chest.

"Maybe it's not quite the courtship *I* imagined either."

"It's the only one you're going to get."

"I've had a few others. How many have you had?"

"I only need one."

"Listen," she said. "About a thousand times now you've said that you've loved me all your life. Well, I have *not* loved you all my life, not in *that* way. This takes a little getting used to."

"How much is a little?"

"A little's a lot. I'll let you know when."

"Let me know now."

"I've let you know in two minutes more than I intended letting you know all night. So let's go. If you're serious about this, let's go." And she started the twins walking again. I waited an instant and then fell in behind them.

"*What* new place?"

• 4 •

It was being built with two-by-fours and Sheetrock. I wandered over PVC and coils of 15/3 wire while Hetty went on about how she had talked Mrs. Steele into it, how she'd already put in for a leave of absence from the Baxter School, how this would be the great experiment of her life, how she was taking a ten-thousand-dollar pay cut, and how it'd be worth it if she could understand the twins, bring them into contact with the world, maybe write a book about them. She showed me where the living room would be, how a drop ceiling would cover the basement pipes, showed me the dividing line between the twins' bedroom and hers, the bathroom fixtures still in their cardboard containers, and the kitchen. I picked up a framing square and checked the living-room wall for squareness, checked the doorway, the kitchen counters, rigged a plumb line and dropped it from the cupboards.

"You should've contracted me to do this job," I said. "I'd have built you a fine, beautiful, moral place."

"This is moral enough for me."

"I'd have built you one with love in it."

"There's love here," she said and gazed at the twins. They were each straddling a sawhorse. "Do you mean you couldn't live here?" she asked, turning back to me.

"Sure," I lied. (All's fair.)

"Could you?"

"His and her towels."

She let a doubtful look linger on me.

I went out for a pizza, and while Hetty sat on the floor picking off anchovies, tried singing for her, first an Elizabethan ayre: "If My Complaints Could Passion Move"; and then, while she fussed over the twins (who seemed to be trying to tie their hair together): "When Phoebus First Did Daphne Love."

"You can't sing, Wright."

"Sure I can."

And I tried again, but she was busy with the twins. "Sweethearts, sweethearts . . ." she whispered, combing her fingers through their hair. "They do this," she said to me. "They do it at night especially. They're always knotted together in bed in the morning."

I watched her. Her hands floated through their hair and she seemed to circle them with her shoulders, her arms. They were sitting in a violent torpor, their arms dead around them, their legs flat and lifeless on the floor and their eyes seeming to look inward, blind to the world but watching, watching, watching all the same. I wondered what they saw. The whir and shudder of their own brains? The shallow well of their souls drying out? Hetty petted them as if she were quieting a spooked animal.

"Sweethearts, sweethearts . . ." she murmured.

"So what're we doing now," I asked suddenly, bluntly.

"We're getting to know one another," she answered.

"And the twins are the worse to know about you?"

"The worst?" she said with a genuine look of surprise. "They're the best."

I considered a moment. "I'll show you *my* best," I said, and I got up and started for the carpenter's workbench. "Come here."

"What?" she said.

"I'm showing you my best. Come on."

"I can see from here."

"*My* best," I said, "requires close attention."

But she stayed where she was.

"First," I said, sliding open the cabinet door under the workbench, "tools. Good tools kept sharp." And I made a face as I hauled out a department-store handsaw and a plastic pouch of chisels.

"I don't think my carpenter wants you messing with his stuff."

"I'm not messing with it, I'm blessing it." And I held my hands out like the pope. Hetty kissed the twins each and then got up and crossed to me. "I'm going to show you the sort of work *I'd* do if you'd contracted this job out to me."

And I put a piece of scrap two-by-four in the vise. She stood a little distance off, arms folded across her stomach, watching me as if I were about to con her.

"The tenon," I said, making a layout with pencil and carpenter's square. "This is the joint that built America." And I balanced the saw on the wood at a perfect right angle. The teeth bit in, slowly at first, the rasp of the saw gradually filling the room with the sound of antagonism, the *yes-no, yes-no* of steel on wood.

"This," I said in my best Cotton Mather voice, "is the bite of moral man on the wood of the wilderness."

She watched the sawdust fall away.

I sawed all four sides of the wood a quarter-inch deep and then put it upright in the vise and carefully sawed the four cheeks so that all new wood was exposed. It had a sweet, vanilla look, smelled fresh and piny. I pared with a chisel and then held it out to Hetty.

"The tenon," I said again, "the male member of the mortise-and-tenon."

She looked distrustfully at it and then took hold of it, running her fingertips over the new wood.

"Very nice," she said with a noncommittal nod.

"Now the mortise," I said, getting a new piece of wood. I put it flatwise in the vise, laid out the size of the tenon on it, and then chucked a half-inch bit in the electric drill. "This should be done with a brace or a T-auger, but we are *in partibus infidelium*—" I said and squeezed the trigger.

She watched the whole time as if she could feel the wood's distress, the tear of the bit boring into her. I watched her out of the corner of my eye, feeling all the time the vibration of the drill running through me, watched her face follow each of the wood chips as it fell from the workbench to the floor. I bored five adjacent holes to the rough size of the tenon.

"Now we need to square it up." And I took a half-inch chisel and a hammer and started squaring the hole to the pencil line that marked the tenon. "The mortise," I said while I worked, "must frequently be made to fit the tenon." And again, I looked at her. She had hardened a little and a skeptical, suspicious look came over her.

"Just what kind of mortise are we talking about?"

"All mortises," I answered, trying the tenon's fit. "The perfect mortise. The universal mortise."

The tenon was still too big. I pared the mortise all around.

"How about taking some wood off the tenon too?" she asked.

I blew into the mortise to clear the shavings. "All right," I said. "This is the twentieth century. All right." I put the chisel to the tenon, shaving the wood neatly so that it peeled away in ribbons. "Now, a trick," I said and got a can of 3-in-One oil out of the cabinet. "Here," I said, handing her the oil, "try some of that." And I held the tenon out to her. She gave me a wary look and then squeezed some oil onto the wood. "Spread it around."

"I know how to do it," she snapped, and she put her fingertips into the pool of oil and started spreading it so the wood darkened. I turned each of the four faces to her, watching her rub the oil into the wood and down into the joints where the shoulders met the sides.

"Good," I said quietly when she'd finished. The wood glistened, the grain showing like veins. "Good. Now here." I handed her the mortise. "You hold that and I'll hold this." And then slowly, gently I put the tenon to the mortise. "Hold it," I said. She'd let it fall away when I first pushed. "Now, push. Gently. Easy." It began to slide in. "Easy." She had a tense look; her lips were parted and the tip of her tongue showed between her teeth. I could hear the two of us breathing, the sucking sound of the oiled wood between us.

It began to tighten. "Push," I said. Our hands quivered with the effort. "Push." And then, as if the will of the wood had been broken, it gave all at once and came together.

"There," I said and leaned toward her. "You see. It's possible. It's possible."

She backed off, letting me take full hold of the wood. She had a look of fear and suspicion about her.

"*This* is a joint," I said, taking the right-angled wood and trying to twist it apart. "*This* is a joint."

She kept her eyes on the wood, and there was dread in the way she looked at it, in the way she watched me prove its tightness.

"This is the way *I* build things," I said and took a step toward her. She backed away. "Now, you tell Mrs. Steele and your carpenter that you're having your cousin come in to finish this job."

"No."

"You tell your carpenter that he can finish up the kitchen and the living room and the twins' bedroom, but that *your* bedroom is going to be built by your fiancé."

"No."

"I'll build it with mortise-and-tenon joints all around, tight and true."

"I think we'd better forget all this," she said, looking me squarely in the face.

"I'll build it with frame and panels, drawbored and pegged together to last."

"It's been contracted out already."

"I'll build you a room sweet and square where you can keep yourself your self, and do it with beauty and cleanness. Planed and trued-up wood all around you."

"No," she said.

"I'll build you a bedroom where we can live in harmony, Hetty, where we can lie down and love and be right with the world."

"It's been contracted out already," she said again, coldly this time, and she turned away.

Over in the corner, the twins lay with their hair all knotted together.

• 5 •

But the next morning I got together my cabinet-making tools from my parents' cellar and called in an order for one hundred board feet of clear white pine to be delivered to Mrs. Steele's cellar. Hetty's carpenter watched as the deliverymen hauled in shoulderful after shoulderful of wood. I dragged in my chest full of tools after them.

"Who the fuck are you?" he asked. He had a body like an oil drum, a neck like a tree stump and there was a faint fog about his eyes. I threw open my tool chest and let him have a look at my antique planes, at the brass-decorated try squares and the ivory-tipped fillister.

"The exorcist," I answered finally. "And if you smarten up you might learn something."

He watched me a full minute and then kicked his way through the scrap Sheetrock into the living room and came back with my mortise-and-tenon joint.

"Did you do this?" he said, waving the wood around. "Have you been messing with my shit?"

"That," I said, "is the best job your pathetic tools have ever done. Now go back to your Formica and leave me alone."

"Have you been messing with my shit?"

"Yes, I have."

"Piss!" he said. "Who're you supposed to be?"

"Your partner," I said. "And I don't like it either."

"This is *my* job. I work with exactly zero partners. You can shove off."

"I am *trying,*" I enunciated carefully, "to integrate myself into the world. You are not helping any."

"Exactly zero," he said again, making a *0* with his hand.

"All right. You don't talk to me and I won't talk to you."

He looked at me a moment longer and then threw the

mortise-and-tenon hard onto the cement and left. I heard him go up the cellar stairs, knock, and when there was no answer, come down again and go out the street door. I taped the rough plans I'd drawn up the night before onto the cement wall and started arranging my tools.

Half an hour later I looked up from my planing to see Hetty in the doorway.

"What're you doing?" she asked.

"You look nice in white," I said. She had her lab coat on.

"What're you doing?"

"Making good on my promises." And I gestured at the smooth white pine stacked on the floor. "Did Thompson call you?"

"Who?"

I gestured toward the carpenter.

"Yes."

"We have an understanding now."

She eyed me.

"We must take the world in stages. A Formica kitchen, a frame-and-paneled bedroom."

Still, she eyed me.

"Come here," I said and crossed to the plan taped on the wall. "I'll show you."

She hesitated and then picked her way carefully across the room, standing a couple of feet from me.

"This is just a rough drawing. I didn't have time to really draft something up, but look." And I showed her each of the four walls, the frame and panels, the swan-necked pediment over the doorway, the dentiled molding that ran along the ceiling. "It'll be a piece of another time—order, harmony, intelligence—right here under Mrs. Steele's house."

"Didn't I tell you last night not to do this?"

"Yes, you did."

"And you're going ahead anyway?"

"That's right."

She looked at me with real wonder, and then shrugging as if to say it was my funeral, turned and left. I heard her say something to the carpenter and then head out the street door. I waited a minute before going into the living room.

"What'd she say?"

He didn't answer.

"What'd she say?"

"She said I'd get paid my full quote."

"I mean about me. What'd she say about me?"

"She didn't say anything about you."

"She must've."

"She said to let you do the bedroom."

"Were those her exact words?"

"I'm busy."

"Were those her exact words?"

"She said: 'Let him do the the bedroom.'"

"Let him do the bedroom," I repeated.

"I thought you weren't going to talk to me."

· 6 ·

So every morning I woke in my boyhood bed, break-
fasted with my parents ("Who is this young man, dear?" "He's
our son, dear"), skipped down Beacon Hill past the iron-
grilled windows, past the tired, genteel brick, the gaslights
humming with the night's work, past George Washington
astride his green horse, over the spring-frosted lawn, past
the Hilton into the flat Back Bay, and tiptoed down three
blocks through the dog-doo to Mrs. Steele's cellar.

And every morning I brought Thompson the Carpenter
a Styrofoam cup of coffee, set it every morning on one of
his sawhorses, and every morning he just let it sit and get
cold there. But I didn't mind. It gave me such a sense of
righteousness that I felt my old Puritan spirit scrubbed up
good by it. I was working on being a generous soul, listening with *tolerance* to the brainless complaint of his electric
drill and the whine of his router. At noontime I sat demo-
cratically in the Common and ate a democratic lunch (Ger-
man ham on Jewish rye with an Irish beer), urchins and
dopers all around me, three-card monte on the sidewalk,

the Hancock building like a great benevolent glass Magog
peering over the distant trees, a cocaine deal on my right,
Mohammet on my left, the ghosts of the Quakers hanged
in 1660 floating over the tennis courts, all around the great,
tumbling rumble of life. I forgave the world all the injus-
tices done me, begged forgiveness for my own trespasses,
for the uncharity of my soul, handed every derelict who
approached me a quarter as installment against my back-
sliding. I walked to the Hancock building and rode up and
down in the elevators, telling myself the whole time that I
was *not* in the belly of the beast but zooming up and down
the white spine of civilization. On the sixty-second floor I
paid my $2.50 and went out onto the observation deck,
looked harborward, and with a shiver in my soul, said aloud
into the wind: "Mavericke, I am a member of the world.
Love works wondrous changes."

For the first few days Hetty stayed away. When she came
finally it was on her noon hour and she was still dressed in
her whites. She treated me as though I were just a work-
man, asked how I was doing, how long I'd be, were there
any unforeseen difficulties? I whistled and worked and let
her have her way, let her walk with a proprietor's air amidst
my shavings and saw-ends. When she left, I hurried to the
door, skipped up the steps to sidewalk level and watched
her walk away, her smallish hips slicing from side to side
under her lab jacket, the neatly turned cuffs on her white
pants flapping in the April wind and her hair a surly scrib-
ble around her head. I let her have her way because I knew
with each plane stroke, with each saw stroke, with each tenon
drawbored together and each panel put squarely in place, I
was building love around her. And I knew that she knew it.

She came like that—at noon, dressed safely in her work
clothes—for a couple of days. Then for another couple of
days she didn't come at all. I bided my time, the wood curling from under my plane in precise ribbons. I went out to
the island one night, pulled my cot outside onto the wet
ground, the snow still lying in rags in the lee of my timbers,

and slept under the bright spring sky, the Big and Little Dippers wheeling overhead and the sound of Logan International reassurance that society was hammering on in my absence. "I think she'll come around," I said to a Mavericke who may or may not have been there. And I said a lot of other things, lying awake a long time, singing hymns and naughty Elizabethan lyrics, feeling all the while the bright air on my face, my cheeks numbing with health and goodness, and the moon rising white and whiter in the east. A tanker passed through the channel on my right, lit with carnival lights, red and blue and white, but silent, utterly silent, so it seemed it moved by spirit alone.

I spent the next day tinkering with my timbers, taking last-minute measurements, checking for fit: When raising day came (after Hetty had said yes), there'd be no time to pare and putter. I made up a bill of things to be done. I'd have to grade a site to sit the sills, trim some saplings into barn pikes, get some rope for the tag lines, make a great beetle out of a stump and rive out two hundred treenails to peg the joints. And then I would take out ads, post handbills, call up my graduate students, give flyers to the tourboat skippers to hand out (A HOUSERAISING!), drum up a couple of hundred souls, a whole host of shining hands to lift my moral wood against the blue American sky, to lift plate to post while Hetty moved among them mistress, madonna and angel of light, and while Mavericke looked on, proud of me and my hands amidst the multitude. I got so excited about it, trimming a tenon with a hatchet, I nearly cut my toes off. At the first trespass of dusk, I hauled my tools back into the Quonset hut, and instead of spending another night under the stars as I'd planned, hurried down to the *Pilgrim's Progress* and crowded sail back to the mainland. I thought I might make it back to Mrs. Steele's in time to meet Hetty if she were coming by after work, but I got there too late. I used my copy of Thompson's key, got my kippered herrings and grape juice out of hiding and had a bachelor's supper, and then dragging Thompson's tarpaulin out of the twins' room, curled up next to my lumber and drifted off to sleep with the sound of Mrs. Steele's high heels on the hardwood overhead. (Mrs. Steele: whom I'd never seen, just heard, heard, heard . . . her high heels, the rustle of her nylons, doors shutting behind her, footsteps going by on the sidewalk outside. Who was she? What was she like? And how did the twins come out of her?)

I woke the next morning to Thompson spinning me out of his tarpaulin.

"What's mine's mine," he said. "What's yours is a lunatic's." And dragging the tarpaulin behind him, he disappeared into the twins' room.

I lay for a time in a pile of shavings and then slowly got up. The sun was spitting through the high cellar windows and there was a great bluster of wind in the shrubbery outside. I took my shirt off and rubbed myself down, then went into the newly finished bathroom and filled the sink with cold water. I splashed myself—my face, my neck, my shoulders, my back—and then let the water out. I was standing dripping, wondering what I'd use for a towel, when I heard the street door open and someone come in. I heard whoever it was cross straight to the bedroom, then come back out, pass within a foot of the bathroom door and go into the twins' room.

"Not here again?" I heard. It was Hetty. I opened the bathroom door in time to see her start and take a step back.

"Oh!"

I didn't say anything, just started drying myself with my shirt, smiling at her, grinning even. She stayed as she was a moment longer, and then, tucking her head down, bulled her way past me, through the living room and out the door.

Thompson gave me a look that showed he was finally curious about what was what.

"We're in love," I told him.

He nodded and looked around himself. "Where's my coffee?"

I spent the day running molding for the cornice, making the wood spin off in neat spirals. I reminded it that it was the fierce wood of the wilderness, the sons of the tall timbers that had greeted ancestor John when he had led his banished congregation to the Maine woods. But with each pass of my molding plane it seemed to say that it too was part of the world, willing to be shaped and fitted to the crown of civilization. I hoped against hope that Hetty would be by for lunch, and when she didn't come, stood for a time with my elbows on the high windowsill, watching the ankles hurry past outside. It was windy still, last year's leaves scattering in cartwheels and the brown branches of April seeming to claw the brick façade across the way. Back at work, I got sadder and sadder as the afternoon wore on, as the light shifted and made the bedroom go from bright gold to cozy amber to a cool and brittle brass. I went out around three for a sandwich and when I got back asked Thompson if she'd been by, but he said no.

"Are you married, Thompson."

"Divorced," he answered.

"What's that like?"

"It's like being divorced."

I tried to go back to work, but my spirits kept sinking. I sat in a corner to rest and found myself getting drowsy, stretching out farther and farther on my new pine floor until I was lying down, face to the wall. I fell in and out of sleep, crowded with a whole landscape of dreams, the sound of Thompson—nailing, sawing, drilling—like the sound of some busy underworld, and in the heavenly distance, the Park Street carillon playing hymns. I woke from time to time, reassured by the sight of my frame and panels six inches from my face, tried to get up, but each time I was taken over by a new dream, drafted into some brindled landscape or wall-less room. When finally I heard Hetty's voice saying: "I'm not paying you to sleep," I thought it was just a dream with a sense of humor and I tried to answer something about not being paid at all, except I tried to sing it to a Dowland song. I woke for real with a nudging kick in the small of my back.

"I'm not paying you to sleep."

I rolled over and saw her in the soft dusk standing over me. She was dressed in a way I'd never seen before, in a velvet dress and a fur jacket, nylons with seams up the back, black high heels. There were gold hoop earrings hanging from her ears, and around her neck, a gold locket (one of my gifts!). The jacket was unbuttoned and I could see she had on a bra that lifted her breasts so a faint swell was visible above the black velvet neckline. She tapped one of the earrings.

"I've remade your reservations at Locke-Ober's."

"Yes?" I said dumbly.

"You'll have to change."

I hauled myself up so I was sitting with my back to the wall.

"A jacket and tie," she said and started walking away, the high heels making her little rear lift and kick. I got on my feet and hurried after her.

· 7 ·

She kept her eyes straight ahead as we walked, as if she were aware I was looking at her, trying to figure her out, and she liked it, but she wasn't going to give in and say something. It was just getting dark—that long, slow dusk of early May, the air with the reds of summer in it and the blues of winter still—and the streets were jammed with traffic, the taillights firing everything with a red haze, making our shins glow when we crossed Arlington Street between banks of cars. Inside the Gardens we stepped around a game of hopscotch, quick-timed past a pair of leafletted zealots trying to hook our souls, crossed the fairytale bridge that straddled the duck pond, curved around toward the dolphin boy and headed for the Charles Street corner. I was all aswoon: the darkening expanse of lawn, the globes of light turning on overhead, the wintered flower beds, the new-leaved trees, all ground up with memories of playing under those same trees as a boy, playing by myself, with my mother on a nearby bench, with Hetty in a bright yellow pinafore, eyes a spanking blue still and her hair tangled in illegible braids. I looked at her now, at her now-gray eyes, at the patches of color on her cheeks, the hollow at the base of her throat, her white neck, the silvery buckles of her collarbones, her breasts quivering with each stab of her high heels and her curly hair seeming sprung about her head. I was struck simple-witted with the joy of walking with her.

"This is *life*, Hetty!" I said, a sweet tear come to my eye. She tossed me a look and kept walking.

Life! Life! Life! We walked down past the small shops on Charles Street. I smiled at every woman who came by, nodded to every man. We saw businessmen with their young lovers cutting into bars, a handsome woman in a suit coming out of a market with a bag full of cantaloupes. The Park Street carillon was tolling over the building tops; a cheese store was exhaling ripe odors onto the sidewalk. A horn sounded; someone called out; a trio of pretty schoolgirls came by singing "Frère Jacques" in rounds. When we crossed Mount Auburn Street I put my hand at Hetty's back and, a little giddy with touching her, guided her uphill. I could feel her muscles working beneath the fur.

"I'll be right down," I said, escorting her into the second-floor drawing room and then turning and bounding up the two flights to my bedroom, stripping my clothes off as I went. I ran water for a shower, got in even before the hot water had made it up the five stories from the basement, soaped my head, my neck, my shoulders, my arms, my waist, my groin, my legs. I was starting over again on my hair when I heard the bathroom door open.

"Can I come in?"

I pulled my head out from under the water. "It sounds like you're in already."

"I mean in the shower," she said, and she started to pull the shower curtains apart. I cried out and snatched them back.

"You can't come in!"

"Why not?"

"You're dressed for one thing."

"I'm not," she said. "I took my clothes off." And again she tried to slide the curtains aside. I held fast to them.

"You haven't," I said.

"I have."

I didn't answer, just stood there, my body tingling all over. Was she really naked, just inches away?

"I want to see what you look like," she said.

"Will you marry me?"

"I want to see what you look like. Don't you want to see what I look like?"

She waited for me to answer but I couldn't.

"My thighs are skinny and my ass is so small you'll have to put a pillow under it, but my breasts—" she said and stopped. "My breasts are nicer than you'd think."

I stood there shaking.

"Don't you want to see what you're getting?"

"I don't need to see."

"I do."

I was shaking like a virgin. "Marry me and you'll see."

"See first, marry later. That's how we do it nowadays."

"No," I said.

"Let me come in and I'll soap you down."

"I'm soaped down already."

"You can soap *me* down."

"Hetty, this isn't funny."

"I saw you this morning," she said. "I saw you this morning coming out of the bathroom with no shirt on."

"Yes . . ."

"Let me see the rest of you."

"I can't."

"I want to," she said. "I *want* to."

I started to slide the curtains apart and then stopped.

"Yes," she said, "yes."

I tried again but couldn't.

"What's the matter?"

"I'm scared."

"Don't be."

"*You* pull them back and come in."

"No, *you* pull them. You have to if you're scared."

I didn't answer.

"Wright," she said, and then like a caress: "Darling."

I pulled them back.

She was still in her clothes, fur jacket and all.

"Christ!" I said and yanked the curtains closed again.

"Still want to marry me?" she fired at me.

"Christ!"

"Still want to marry me?"

"For Christ's sake, Hetty!"

"Still want to marry me?"

"No," I said. I shut the shower off.

"No?"

"No."

"Listen," she said, "quiet, listen." I heard something drop
on the floor: the fur jacket. "Listen." I heard the zipper in
her dress and then the velvet falling about her feet, then
what must've been her bra, then her high heels kicked off,
then the elastic static of her nylons.

"There," she said, "there."

"You can go to dinner without me."

"I'm naked."

"I know."

"I'm naked," she said. "Wright. *Darling*," she said.

"That won't work twice."

"Here," she said and she slipped her arm between the
shower curtains. "Here," she said, "kiss me. Why haven't
you tried to kiss me yet? Two months, forty-five letters, seven
dozen roses and you haven't tried to kiss me yet. Kiss me,"
she said and let her arm hang in the air.

"No."

"Wright," she said and she moved her arm blindly, her
hand, searching for me. "Wright?" She touched me on the

shoulder, caressed me so I shivered, then slid her fingers up and down my arm, over my shoulder and onto my chest. "Wright," she whispered. "Do you love me? Do you *really* love me?" she said. She let her hand drift down my chest, running her fingers lightly over me. I stood stricken, trembling still, a little dizzy. "Wright," she was saying, "Wright." She had her hand on my stomach now, then my hips, then down one of my legs. "What you *feel* like," she said. "What you *feel* like." She was on the other leg, running her fingers over the muscles there, up my thigh, inside my thigh.

"Oh!" she said.

"Hetty."

"Shh! Give me your hand, give me your hand." And she searched blindly for my hand, and then when she got hold of it, pulled it slowly between the shower curtains.

"Here," she said. "Sweetheart, here." And she kissed my hand and then put it on one of her breasts.

"See?" she said. "See?"

I started to pull the shower curtain back with my other hand.

"No!" she said and she held on to the curtain. "No," she said and pressed my hand back to her breast. "See?"

"Hetty."

"Do you love me?" she asked.

"Yes."

"Say it. Say 'I love you.'"

"I love you."

"Say 'I love you, Hetty.'"

"I love you, Hetty."

I could hear her breathing, feel her breathing under my fingers.

"Darling," she said.

I let my hand slip over to her other breast.

"Darling," she said, her voice husky and strained. "Call me darling. Call me sweetheart."

"Sweetheart."

"Yes," she said.

"Sweetheart. Hetty."

"Yes, yes."

"I love you."

"Oh, yes!"

"I'm coming out."

"Don't."

"I'm coming out." I was hoarse and out of breath.

"No," she said and she held on to the curtains. "No."

"Hetty."

"No," she said, and there was an edge of fear come into her voice. We tussled over the curtain. "We have to go to dinner still. I've made reservations."

"Hetty!"

"Don't!" she said and then: "Wait."

I heard her scuffle about.

"What're you doing?"

"Wait!"

"I'm coming out."

"No!"

"I'm coming," I said and I slid the curtains apart in time to see her hurry out of the bathroom, clutching her clothes in a great mass before her. "Hetty!" I called, but she was around the corner and gone already. I heard her bare feet on the stairs. One flight. Two flights. I ran to the railing at the edge of the stairs, shivering in the cool air, and listened. She'd stopped. She was back in the drawing room.

Fifteen minutes later when I came down the stairs she was seated in the chair where I'd left her, clothed again, her legs crossed smartly.

"You look sharp," she said with a nod at my suit, and when I made a face: "Well, you *do*."

CHAPTER
9

The Marriage Covenant

• 1 •

When we got to Locke-Ober's it was just past seven and the lower dining room was nearly full. Hetty had made the reservation in her own name, walking ahead of me and saying "Jenney" to the maître d' in such a way as to let everyone (me) know who was in charge. We were shown a small out-of-the-way table, Hetty slipping with a flourish into the seat held for her by the maître d'. She was nervous and excited by turns, ordering cocktails and getting me to try a sip of her tequila and then taking my Scotch from me. I held myself back, a little stung still and wary of her, watched her flirt, playful and scared at the same time, almost breathless with her own idea of what was happening to her. She seemed to be playing out some set vision of the evening—reading the menu to me in her lispy French, advising and counseling me—as if for the last several days she'd been imagining this scene, dressed the way she was, ordering the food she was ordering, me across the way from her bewitched, baffled and dumbly hopeful. And now that it was here she was

139

awed and frightened, so that she could barely keep herself under control, giddy with the idea of what she was about to do, the "yes" she was on the verge of saying. I watched her, watched her toss back her hair, finger the gold chain that ringed her neck, fix her eyes on me and then look away, laughing at me, or herself, or at the wild improbability of what was happening.

"So am I going to marry you?" she asked when our shrimp had arrived. "Hey?" she said and kicked me under the table.

"It's beginning to look like it," I answered.

"You're so sure? And how long do you think it'll be before we're divorced?"

I didn't answer.

"How long?" she asked, cocking her chin at me.

"No divorce."

"It happens every day."

"No divorce," I said and before she could kick me again leaned forward and grabbed her ankle under the table. " '*What God hath brought together . . .*' " I said. She tried to shake her foot free but I held on. "No divorce," I said, squeezing her ankle until she let out a little cry. When I let go, she looked at me a moment with her face coloring and changing and then stuck her fork into her shrimp.

"All right," she said under her breath. "All right."

"All right what?" I said.

But she didn't answer, kept her face turned down, jabbing at her food. When our waiter came with the main dish, she wouldn't look at him, and when he asked her something, I had to answer for her. I watched her eat. I'd forgotten how she did it, going at all of one thing first, say, her vegetables, then her potatoes, then her meat, cleaning her plate in neat wedges. She'd always done it that way, but I hadn't eaten with her in such a long time that it came as a surprise, something small and endearing.

"Hetty," I said gently once she'd started in on her asparagus, "this is serious."

"That's right," she answered.

"Don't . . ."

She stopped eating. "Do you know how many men I've slept with?"

"I have an idea."

"Do you know why?"

"I have an idea about that too."

"The *right* idea?"

"I think so."

"Maybe it's simply promiscuity. Ever think that?"

"Yes."

"And?"

"I don't think that's it."

She eyed me, rolling her lower lip under her front teeth. "Are you a virgin?"

"No."

She looked at me like she didn't believe me.

"But it's been some years," I said.

"Some years. How long is some years?"

"Eight."

"Eight years," she said. "I couldn't do that."

"It cleans you out."

"I couldn't do it."

"You won't have to. Monogamy will clean *you* out."

She looked at me as if I'd slapped her.

"I didn't mean it that way," I said.

She went back to her asparagus.

"I'm sorry."

She shook her head.

"I'm *sorry*."

Again, the same sad shake.

"Sweetheart," I said and touched her under the table. She started at the word as much as at my touch. I could see her skin change color and seem to melt.

"Say it again," she said, low and urgent.

"Sweetheart."

"All right," she said softly, almost exhaling the word. "Even if you meant it that way, all right."

"But I *didn't* mean it that way."

"If you didn't," she said, "maybe you should have." She kept her face down, talking into her food. "It isn't just sex, you know." And she looked up at me with pleading and urgency. "Do you think that?"

"No."

"It isn't. The sex is almost—" And she paused, thinking, and then didn't finish.

"Yes," I said. I was still touching her, petting her the way I'd seen her do the twins.

"Working at the school," she said, "with all that unfeeling and uncontact around you, when you leave at night sometimes you're just screaming for someone to touch you. I mean *really* touch you."

"Me," I said, "me."

"And so you do the awfullest things. And part of you hates yourself for it, and part of you likes it. Just waiting for that next touch, that next hand that says you're you because it's feeling you."

"Me," I said. "I'm the one."

"You," she said and she looked at me as if from a distance. "You," she said again, this time as if tasting the word, and for an instant she seemed poised on a thought. Then she put her fork down and picked up her purse off the chair beside us. She undid the snap and pulled out two pieces of paper, typewriter paper, folded in thirds.

"We'll see just how serious you are," she said and handed me the papers. They were typed, one a Xerox of the other. I had to read the first sentence three times before I realized what it was.

It was a contract.

"What's this?" I asked.

"What's it look like?"

"It looks like a contract."

"It's our *espousals de verba per*—what?"

"*Espousals per verba de futuro.*"

"That's right."

"One of my notes," I said.

"That's right," she said again, smiling. "The marriage covenant."

There were six items, prefaced by a paragraph that named her as Mehitible and me as John. At the bottom were two lines, one with my name typed under it, the other with hers.

"Are you serious?"

"Are *you*?"

We eyed each other.

"When did you do this?"

"This afternoon, typed it up on my typewriter and Xeroxed it downstairs, in Records."

I turned the paper over; the other side was empty.

"Aren't you going to read it?" she asked.

"I'll just sign it," I said with a touch of the bluff and held out my hand for a pen.

"Better read it," she said.

"I trust you."

"Better read it all the same. Aloud. Read it aloud and ask questions. And then we can both clarify our positions so there will be no misunderstandings."

I skimmed the paper.

"Go ahead," she said.

"I feel funny. *You* read it."

"I wrote it. You read it."

I stalled, took a sip of wine. "Should I skip the first part? Just read the items?"

"All right. Sure."

I pushed my dinner plate to the side. " '*Item One: that—*' "

"A little louder. I can't hear."

" '*Item One: that recrimination will be absent from the marriage; that John will not reproach Mehitible for her past life, for any indiscretion of soul and body she may have committed; and that Mehitible will not ridicule John for the solitude and celibacy with which he has misguided his life.*'

"Why do you get '*may have* committed,' " I asked, "and I get '*has* misguided?' "

She held out a pen to me. "You may make alterations, as long as they're agreed upon."

I waved the pen off.

"Go on, then," she said.

" *'Item Two: that Mehitible will be allowed to keep her maiden name.'* Fair enough. *'Item Three: that physical affection will be shown to Mehitible by John, frequently, and not withheld as revenge or punishment.'*

"Punishment?" I asked. She reached across the table and underlined a word with her fingernail.

"Frequently."

I read it over again. "How frequently is frequently?"

She leaned toward me. "I need to be made love to, Wright," she said. "I'm warning you. I need to be touched and I need to be—" she caught herself—"made love to."

I fingered the paper. "Give me your pen," I said after a moment. She handed it to me. "Here," I said and made a double line under *frequently.* She watched me, grave and intent.

" *'Item Four: that the having of children will be by mutual consent, and that should an unwanted pregnancy occur Mehitible has the right without recrimination to terminate that pregnancy.'* "

I looked at her but didn't say anything.

" *'Item Five: that as long as Mehitible's professional and personal relationship with Isabel and Irene Steele continues, they be considered as Mehitible's wards and included in all family decisions; that Mehitible be allowed to continue to reside with Isabel and Irene Steele; that consideration of consequences upon Isabel and Irene Steele be of paramount importance in any decision-making.'*

"I'm marrying *you*, Hetty, not the twins."

"Those are the terms," she said.

"But how long? I thought you'd only taken a one-year leave of absence."

"I have. But I intend on sticking to the twins as long as I can or as long as I can do some good. If I have to give up my position at the school, okay. But I *will not* leave them."

I studied the paper.

"Those are the terms," she said again.

"Do you expect me to live there too?"

"You can if you like. Or you can live somewhere else and just stay the night sometimes. Or *don't* stay the night if you don't want."

"That would conflict with Item Three, wouldn't it?"

She didn't answer. She was sitting all tight to herself, arms and legs drawn in, hugging herself.

"Those are the terms," she pronounced finally in a quiet, resolute voice.

"I wonder what's the point of getting married."

"That's covered in the last item."

I looked at the paper again. " *'Item Six: that John will love and care for Mehitible and that Mehitible will love and care for John.'* "

She was still hugging herself.

"Do you mean this?" I asked, tapping the paper. She just stayed as she was, pulled back from me, looking chill and elegant in her fine clothes. "Is this it?" I said. "I mean, the real thing?"

Almost like a dare she picked up the pen and held it out to me. I took it and, feeling a stir of excitement and dread inside, signed the contract. As soon as I had, a queer nervous bubble of syllables escaped her, not quite a laugh, not quite a cry, but like a ripple of nerves finally breaking out. Her face was tight and frightened. She smiled, tried to laugh and then licked her lips.

"Well!" she said, and again tried to laugh. "Well!"

She took the contract from me. I held out the pen, but she didn't take it.

"John Jen-ney Wheel-wright," she said, tracing my signature.

"Here's the pen," I said.

"Jay-jay Wheelwright," she said, musing and musical.

I put the pen down next to her.

"Wright," she said, trying the word out, and then again: *"John Jen-ney Wheel-wright."*

"Your turn," I said in a voice that was low and intent and, even in my own ears, scared.

"My turn?" she repeated. Her eyes were bright with something between mockery and resentment. *"My* turn?"

"Mehitible Constance Jenney," I said, reaching over and tapping the bottom of the contract. She looked at it as if surprised that her own name was there.

"Oh, that's impossible," she said simply and started fussing with her purse.

"Hetty."

"I have to go to the ladies' room. Will you order dessert?"

"Hetty!"

She got up. "Something light," she said. "A pastry. Or a glace."

And she turned and made her way through the tables, past the other diners, her steps quick and precise and provocative, disappearing into the ladies' room without looking back at me. For an instant I sat all stiff to myself, my legs shooting with anger, and then I turned toward the wall and started calling myself every name I could think of. Then I started in on Mavericke. I read the items of the contract over again, wondering with each one what Amias would have to say about *that* (hey, Mavericke?). The waiter came and asked if we would like dessert. In a barely civil voice, I told him no.

She was gone a good ten minutes. When finally I saw her coming back through the tables, pert and pretty and smiling at me over the heads, I felt such a perverse prick of love, I nearly spat in my plate. She slipped into her seat with a breathless, conspiratorial air.

"You'll never guess what I found," she whispered and let her eyes slip around the room. Her face was freshly made up, a little rouge on her cheeks and her eyelashes darkened. "You'll never guess."

"What?"

"What?" she mimicked and reached across the table and

tugged at my sleeve. When I didn't respond she sat back in her seat. "Well, never mind," she sang in a musical la-di-da voice. But she couldn't keep it up. "You'll never guess." And again she slipped a sly look around at the other diners. Then slowly, with a secretive air, she unlatched her purse and pulled out a gold hoop, a bracelet. She slid it across to me, keeping it hidden behind our dinner plates. "It was on one of the vanities. Just sitting there. Keep it down!" she said when I'd picked it up.

"It's solid gold," I said.

She nodded.

"It's worth two or three hundred dollars."

"More," she said and tapped each of the gold hoops that hung from her ears so they spun around. "Four hundred, at least."

"You'll put it back."

She ignored me. "Whose do you suppose it is?" she said, looking around the room.

"You'll put it back."

She let her gaze rest on me. "No." The word was hard and definite, I took the contract, and picking up the pen, wrote at the bottom: *Item Seven: that both Mehitible and John will play square with the world.* I shoved it across to her. She read it with her face going chill and remote.

"I'll tell the waiter," I said, feeling a flush of pleasure saying it.

She kept her face turned from me. I watched it pale and tighten.

"Put it back or I'll go around asking people myself if they lost it."

She'd gone cold, a dead, smoldering cold.

"I'm not marrying anyone who's a cheat and a thief," I said, feeling dizzy with my own words. "If she's a cheat and a thief in the mere physical things, what's she likely to be in the feeling things?"

Without warning she picked up the pen. For a wild, singing instant I thought she was going to sign the contracts. But with killing deliberation she drew a huge *X* through each of them. She threw the pen down and stood up. Then picking up her purse, the bracelet, her jacket, she cut coldly through the tables again, back to the ladies' room. I watched with my fists like clubs on the table in front of me. She was inside only half a minute. When she came out she made her way along the wall to the street door and, with a curt nod to the maître d', left.

I sat for a minute solid with anger. Then I stood up, took all the money out of my wallet—I knew it wouldn't make the bill—threw it down on the table, and with any number of eyes watching me, made my own way through the tables to the ladies' room. When I came out the maître d' was beside me. "Sir, the *men's* room," he said, making a gesture. I pushed past him and headed for the street door.

Outside I could see her a half-block away walking fiercely uphill toward the Common. I started after her, stepping quickly and then breaking into a run. There were cars and people in the street. I ran past a bookstore, past closed boutiques, the scissor-barricaded windows of a jeweler's store, nearly knocked someone over. At Tremont Street, just when I was almost up to her, she turned at the sound of my running, cried out and darted into the traffic, high heels and all. There was a screech of brakes, a horn blowing. She stumbled up onto the curb opposite and ran off into the dark parkland. I waited for a break in the traffic, and then ran after her.

"You leave me alone," she said when I'd caught up to her. We were hurrying down one of the sidewalks, the lamplights dingy and the benches on either side of us empty. "Don't!" she cried when I tried to grab her by the arm. She ran on a couple of steps. "I'll call the police."

I followed behind her, dumb and angry.

"A cheat and a liar!" she said. She was stabbing at the ground with her high heels. "A cheat and a liar! At least I'm not trying to fuck my sister."

"You're not my sister."

"Eight years!" she screamed. And then to some dark figure we passed: "This guy hasn't laid anyone in eight years. Eight years," she said again, almost to herself, and then, realizing suddenly: "You've been wanting *me* for eight years." And she shuddered as if it were a sickening thought.

I felt for the bracelet in my pocket but didn't take it out.

"I've seen you looking at me," she was saying, spitting the words out in spite and contempt. "For twenty-eight years you've been looking at me, watching me, wanting to put your hands on me. I've known it since we were kids. It made me feel creepy then. It makes me feel creepy now."

I tried again to grab hold of her. She whipped her arm away and ran a few steps off, stumbled, and then took off her high heels and threw them at me. One of the spikes caught me on the side of the head. She broke into a full run.

"You and your roses," she said when I'd caught up to her; we were in the Public Gardens now. "You and your notes. I used to lie in bed and read them to whoever I was with. Do you know that?" she said. *"Do you know that?"*

"I'm bleeding," I said, still walking behind her.

"How could you possibly imagine I would marry you? Why would I *want* to marry you? What could you *possibly* give me? How could anyone not see I was playing around?"

"Hetty!"

"Marry!" she cried, laughing and choking. "Marry! Marriage! A wedding! A wife! Husband!" And she laughed a bitter string of syllables. "God!" she said and started running again. "Don't!" she said when I started after her. She veered off the path and onto the dark grass. I followed her, matched her step for step. She was choking with spasms of laughter, darting this way and that, trying to throw me off. "You meticulous, moral bastard!" she cried. "I hate you and your fucking eight years!" She ran under a tree, the low branches catching her in the face. She cried out and ran on. "Leave me alone!" She turned and threw her purse at me. It glanced off my shoulder. I left it where it fell and kept

after her. We were running along the duck pond, the dark
water littered with red and green and white lights from the
street. "Mortise-and-tenon joints," she spat out. "It's cock
and cunt today. *Cock and cunt!*" she cried out, knowing I'd
flinch. "No fucking tenons and no fucking mortises. Not today." She was out of breath, half running, half walking, but
keeping herself ahead of me. I walked behind her, said her
name. "Don't!" she said. "Don't use my name. It's *mine*! It's
dirty. I'm dirty. I like it. I like being dirty. Don't!" she
screamed when I said "Hetty" again. She was crying now,
choking and spitting and trying to keep on her feet. I put
my hand out and touched her on the shoulder. She shook
me off and tried to run on. I reached out again. "Don't
touch me!" she cried. And with one last burst of strength,
she spun around on me. "Don't—"

I had the bracelet out.

For a moment we just stood where we were, both of us
out of breath, the shadows stilled and the water darkening.
She looked at the bracelet, up to my face and back down to
the bracelet. Her eyes were swollen and her cheeks were
wet, glistening in the lamplight. I took a step toward her
but she backed away.

"What's that?" she said.

I held it out to her. She had a confused, stubborn look
about her. She tried to say something else, stopped and then
wiped her face with the back of her hand.

"Why'd you do that?" she asked finally.

"I just did."

We both gazed at the bracelet. The lamplight spun off it
in white lances.

"You put it on," I said and made a motion toward her.

"No," she said and stepped back.

"It's yours," I said. "I stole it for you. It's yours."

She looked me in the face and then fixed her eyes again
on the gold hoop. I tried again, softly this time, without
recrimination or anger:

"It's yours, Hetty. I stole it for you."

She shuddered at the words, and then tucked her chin

in, away from me, and started looking around herself in confusion. "My purse," she said. "I lost my purse."

"You threw it at me."

She stopped and peered at me. "Yes," she said, not at all certain.

"It's on the other side of the pond."

She turned and gazed across the water. "Oh," she said. "Yes." And she started walking, limping a little as though one of her legs were hurt.

"I'll get it," I said.

"You don't have to."

"I will. You wait here."

I broke into a trot, starting around the water. In the center of the pond the swan boats that paddled children about during the daytime were lashed together and drifting in a slow circle. The light lit on the fierce wings of the giant swans and seemed to freeze them in whiteness. They arced as I arced, followed me with their eyes as I worked along the edge of the pond. When I'd found Hetty's purse and started back, they kept on, cool, indifferent, making their slow circle without me.

"I cut myself," she said when I was back beside her. She was sitting on the granite lip that faced off the pond, one of her feet in the water, the other pulled up beside her. She was peering at the underside of a toe. Her nylons, ruined from her running, were floating in a crazy huddle ten feet out in the water.

"Me too," I said and touched the cut just below my hairline. She turned her face up to me, wondering and concerned. I still had the bracelet in my hand. She opened her purse and, searching around, took out a pair of cuticle scissors.

"Do you think it's possible?" she asked after a time. She kept her head down, still fussing with her toe.

"Yes," I said, though I wasn't sure what it was she meant.

"Do you?" she asked and looked up at me, her face all innocent and white in the lamplight.

"Yes."

"Boy, I don't know," she said, shaking her head as if she were ten again. She patted the ground beside her. "Come here." I knelt on the grass. She swung her legs out of the water and knelt too, facing me. "Here," she said and she dabbed a little water on my cut. She held the back of my head with her other hand, tipping it downward so my face was just inches from her. I could smell the perfume around her neck. When she was done I took her hand and tried to put the bracelet on it. "No," she said and pulled back. Her face had quickened. I tried again. "No," she said and for an instant she tucked her hands up under her arms like we used to do in the winter when we were kids. She was flushed and uncertain. "Wait," she said and picked up the cuticle scissors from off the stone behind her. And then before I knew what she was doing she'd snipped off a length of her hair. "Here," she said, and with her hands shaking, she tied the hair around my wrist. She knotted it, and then shivering, still kneeling, held her own wrist out.

CHAPTER
10

Hetty Tossing Out Her Underwear

• 1 •

A HOUSERAISING! A HOMEMAKING!

You are invited to come and Cleanse your Souls at an old-fashioned Houseraising. Lift plate to post amidst a community of Shining Hands and feel the Spirit of America in you. Take the Harbor Islands Tour Boat from Long Wharf (10 am, 1 pm, 4 pm; $3.00—save receipt/get reimbursed by God), and debark at Mavericke's Island. There will be Food and Spirits to Nourish the Body, Square Joints and Square Wood to Nourish the Soul.

After the frame is raised John Jenney Wheelwright and Mehitible Constance Jenney will be united in Holy Matrimony by the Reverend James Wheelock of the Park Street Church. Revelry will follow.

PARTICIPATE IN AMERICA!

May 2   Dawn to Dusk   Mavericke's Island

I had five thousand of them printed up, and like a messenger of God with the Word tucked under my arm, went out among the people. I left off batches at the Massachusetts Historical Society and the Genealogical Society; at the pewter shop under Faneuil Hall, at the Paul Revere House, at the Harrison Otis Gray House, at Goodspeed's, at every antique store I came across; left a hundred with the lobby guard at the Hancock tower; posted one at the Old North Church, at the Park Street Church, the Arlington Street Church, a Catholic church or two, a synagogue; at the Old State House, at the new State House, stapled one up at the Public Library; across the river I handed them out to everyone I knew at MIT, left a ream at the Coop, pasted one to John Harvard in Harvard Yard; back in Boston I taped one to the statue of William Lloyd Garrison in the mall on Commonwealth Avenue, another to the bas-relief of Winthrop coming ashore in 1630 (Richard Mather behind him, Bible to bosom); left one at the Athenaeum, at Goebbels, taped half a dozen to the back side of the left-field wall at Fenway Park; stapled one up at the Christian Science Center, the Mount Vernon Street Firehouse, the Harrison Day School; risked my life and taped one up at the Harriet Tubman House in Roxbury, risked my health around the corner at Ricky's Soul Food; dropped a batch off at Katy Gibb's Secretarial School, another batch at a meat market in the North End reputed to be a Mafia headquarters; rode on the swan boats and surreptitiously taped one to the seat in front of me; rode the subways, the Red Line, the Blue Line, taping them over the graffiti, the trolleys on the Green Line that ran out Huntington Avenue; taped one to the base of the statue of the Indian out in front of the Museum of Fine Arts, and on Boston Common handed them out to the Krishnas and Moonies before they could hand their stuff out to me.

Then I got together a mailing list—had Hetty draw up one too—and together we stamped and sealed and sent out a hundred more. We mailed one to each of my graduate

students, to all my old teachers at MIT, to Hetty's col-
leagues at the Baxter School; sent one to the President of
the Society for the Preservation of New England Antiqui-
ties, to the people at the Restoration Lab; I sent a copy to
The Boston Globe and the *Phoenix,* hoping they'd give me a
call for an interview (they didn't); sent one to my contact at
the National Science Foundation (which was paying for
everything, after all), to the MDC historian, to the State Parks
Commissioner; I sent one to Mrs. Steele, to Thompson the
Carpenter, then to King Philip, and then one to the judge
hearing his suit.

"We shall be as a little commonwealth," I pronounced to
Hetty as we walked together to the mailbox. "The eyes of
the world will be upon us, so that if we fail at our love our
failure will be as a byword through all America."

She pulled open the mailbox's mouth; and never mind
the look she gave me.

Oh, the world was spring-bright with love! We walked
through the city as never before, up and down the for-
sythia-studded streets of the Back Bay, under the purple
haze of crab apple trees in the Fens, along the Muddy River,
by the banks of the Charles where the mallards courted and
sparked on the wide green lawn. The dogwood was in bloom,
the knuckled branches frosted with white flowers, and the
magnolias were opening their faces to the sun and smiling
on us as we passed. Hetty held my arm, took two steps for
my one, pointing out this and that as we walked. We had
coffee and Napoleons at a sidewalk café, sitting with the
other lovers in the brisk, not-quite-warm-enough air, watching the people parade past and keeping our held hands just
out of sight under the table. We darlinged and doted, talked
like children at the window of the world, marked the odors
and noises all around, the smell of a pizzeria, the *shoosh!* of
an espresso machine, the bonneted taxis spinning past, a
call, a cry, a siren screaming. I was all awhirl with disbelief.
Hetty was a bible of bright looks, her face scribbled up with
excitement, her cheeks ruddy with the spring chill, her knees

pumping under her skirt, her hair a great lovely mess around her head, talking and talking, teasing me each day with a glimpse of her underwear ("Underwear is my *passion!*"), showing me the lacy border of her bra, the bright nickel-plate of a garter, the breast-lace of a camisole, slips the color of burgundy, of cream, of ripe peaches.

Out on Mavericke's Island, we picnicked on my stacks of square beams, looking over the blue harbor to Boston sparkling in the sunshine. Below us, my graduate students knelt along the terraces of the dig, wriggling and squatting amidst the greening grass and the bobbing dandelions, sprinkling the air with the *chit-chit* of their trowels, and from time to time throwing a curious look up at us. I showed Hetty my model of Mavericke's house, took the frame apart piece by piece, naming each beam and showing her the joints that would hold it to the rest of the frame, and then post by post, bent by bent, rafter by rafter, performed a raising in miniature. She ate olives and celery and marveled at the snug fit, at the proportion and balance and rightness of it all. She was even in love with me enough to ask questions about Mavericke. I told her some of the old stories: how Winthrop came upon him and Amias living a life of love and light and election at the edge of America, tried to gain him points for his Christian conduct among the Indians during the smallpox epidemic, got the teary violins in tune for his outcast years, for his death at the hands (slightly removed) of our Cousin Isaac. While I talked she looked around herself at the scrubby shrubs that marched like dwarfs up the slope of the hill, at the ancient ravines and the distant trees, looked as if seeing the island for the first time, her eyes coming alive with the idea that it all really *had* happened, that the island *had* lived its life under Mavericke's feet, had witnessed Amias and young Samuel weeding the corn, had leached into its cold crust the dying warmth of one hundred Indians—those Indians, the very ones whose skeletons were being uncovered at the dig below—and had seen Mavericke himself weaken and die.

"Is that where the word comes from?" she asked on the ferry back. *"Maverick,* I mean. Loner. Outcast."

I told her that that was a different Maverick, a nineteenth-century Texan who hadn't branded his cattle. A Samuel, too.

"A descendant, maybe," she suggested.

"Maybe."

I still spent my mornings at Mrs. Steele's. Thompson was done and gone, leaving behind three rooms that might have been found anywhere in the United States, in Florida, in Montana, in Sam Maverick's Texas: cash-and-carry studs, phony chestnut paneling, garbage disposal, trash compactor, generic toilet and tub, exhaust fan designed to burn out in three years, plastic towel racks, linoleum made to look like tiles, tiles made to look like wallpaper, wallpaper made to look like linoleum. I got hives and had difficulty breathing whenever I came out of the woody sanctuary of Hetty's bedroom.

"What're you going to do when we're married and you want to stay the night?" Hetty asked, dropping by on her noon hour.

"The bedroom," I said, pointing. "Sanctum sanctorum."

"And what if you're thirsty?"

"A glass of water, please."

"And if you have to pee?"

"A chamber pot," I said. "We'll have to get a chamber pot."

The weekend before the wedding we moved her furniture from her North End apartment to Mrs. Steele's. We rented a U-Haul and I paid two teenagers off the street to help. Sunday night Hetty went through her closet and, while I ate cannelloni on the floor, decided what clothes to keep, what clothes to pack in her honeymoon suitcase and what clothes to throw out. I watched and didn't interfere. She seemed to study each piece as if trying to recall something about it, her face clouding from time to time just before she threw it into the "Out" pile. Sometimes I heard her say something under her breath—maybe "that night at the Dragon" or "Labor Day weekend"—wrinkling her face with each memory and then tossing out a pair of culottes or a Norwegian sweater.

"It's a clean slate," she said, turning to me with a fragile smile. "A new life. For both of us."

And out went some of her pretty underwear.

When she was done we packed everything into boxes, called a taxi, and then, kissing each other good-bye, went our separate ways: Hetty with her boxed-up clothes to Mrs. Steele's, and me with her honeymoon suitcase out to the island.

CHAPTER
11

*How the Marriage of the Lord and
Lady of Misrule Was Supposed to
Be Annulled by a Half-Lap
Dovetail . . .*

• 1 •

I'd been up for four eager hours by the time the ten o'clock
tour boat arrived. I had bowls of punch and Gatorade set
up, tea brewing by the jug in the sun, the coals for the hot-
dog roast set afire. From the top of the hill I watched the
boat nudge the dock, shivering with gratitude, with disbelief
almost, for there were people hanging from the guy wires,
packed onto the quarterdeck, hugging the stanchions. I called
and beckoned them up the path, strangers, acquaintances,
more strangers, Hetty's mother dressed in a neat tweed suit,
my mother bending over a wild rosebush that scuttled parallel to the path, my father gazing seaward; Thompson the
Carpenter came, hammer in hammer holster, Thompson the
Nazi too; my graduate students were there, the head of my
department, the MDC historian, Reverend Wheelock. I
greeted each with the news that they, indeed, were the elect,
and that maybe America was still blessed after all. Hetty
wasn't among them (neither was King Philip), but there was
the one o'clock boat still.

The first order of business was a lecture (Oh, I have the true Puritan soul!). Model in hand and congregation surrounding me, I pointed out the beams and how the bents would be raised, assigned certain men to handle the tag lines, others to be pikemen, others to swing the great beetles. We shunned block-and-tackle, come-alongs, a transit. This was to be an effort of body and soul united: The community come to receive the man, the man to baptize himself in the community.

When we'd got the first-floor frame down—the sills laid on the foundation, mortised and tenoned at their corners, and the girts tenoned into the insides of the sills—I felt such a strength driving the treenails home that I nearly drove them full through the beam. I barked and badgered like a drill sergeant as the end bent was raised, ten men at each of the corner posts, tag lines looped around the top ends to keep the bent from falling full over once it reached its height and pikemen pushing with their poles the last few feet. When it was done and braced upright I shimmied up the post, and standing on the end girt above everyone, cried out in my best Roger Williams voice: " '*Abstract yourself with a holy violence from the dung heap of this earth!*' " And I threw my arm out to indicate Boston, America, the world. They laughed and applauded and went for the chimney bent. I stayed up there while it was knocked together and raised. I was singing with strength, with vision, with soul. I could see my mother gathering a housewarming bouquet, my father drawing equations in the dirt, Hetty's mother ladling out punch and Gatorade. I looked harborward for the next tour boat—all the while shouting commands, cautions, encouragement—but it wasn't one o'clock yet. The chimney bent went up without a hitch, joined to the end bent by the front and rear plates, my winter joinery proving itself by the snug rub of wood on wood. Next I called for the summer beam, called for six hardy men to stand with me on the second-floor girts (threw in a hardy woman), and while the giant beam was lifted and pushed and cursed up to us, preached the virtues of the haunched half-lap dovetails that would hold it to the girts, winding up by telling them all that after today they would have such a picture of purity in their souls, they could never again go with quite the same heart to their Sheetrocked cubicles.

By the time the one o'clock boat was sighted, we had the final two bents up. I left one of my hardy men in charge of laying the second-floor joists and swung myself down, got my department head to start the hot dogs, kissed my mother and then headed down the path to the dock. I stood there alone, throwing looks back up the hill at the frame (so often imagined, and now there, there!), and then looking over the water to the ferry. There was another crowd aboard—more Americans sick to their souls—and I waved and tried to call to them over the snarl of the engines. When the boat had docked I halloed her captain and then greeted everyone as they came ashore, slapping the men on the back, kissing the women, telling them all that their mere presence numbered them among the elect, and then sending them on their way up the hill. But I kept an eye on the decks, along the rails, at the phony portholes. When the crowd began to thin and she still wasn't there, I felt an old fear lodge inside me, felt almost as though I'd known all along, or should've known. I let the last half dozen trot down the gang on their own— no slaps, no kisses—and then went aboard and had a look around. There were Milky Way wrappers on the floor, someone's thermos, the *Globe*, a Coke can—but no Hetty.

My mother met me climbing back up the hill, her gray eyes swimming with mist. "There's the four o'clock boat still," she said and reached out to touch me. I tried to smile at her, and then looked at Hetty's mother standing a few feet distant. But she just turned away: She knew her daughter. I kept on up the hill, and then stuffing my knuckles in my mouth so I wouldn't scream, spun off toward the Quonset hut.

Once I was inside I kicked my cot, the space heater and then ripped Mavericke's hammock down. I grabbed an Indian bone and threw it against the wall so it shattered and sent splinters everywhere, and then sat down and tried to cry. But I ended up just getting up and kicking things all over again. I broke the light bulbs in the ceiling, hurled my teacup at my toolbox and then hauled Hetty's honeymoon suitcase out from under the cot. I picked it up over my head and threw it down so it sprang open and then kicked it across the floor. I snatched up her clothes and started throwing them around: her blouses, her bras, her underwear. "That night at Denny's!" I spat out, rolling up some culottes into a baseball and throwing them across the room. "Labor Day weekend," I said and ripped a pair of shorts apart at the crotch. I pulled out a purple garter belt and yanked off the elastic garters: "That weekend at Cape Cod." And then tearing her panties with my teeth: *"That weekend at Hitler's!"* I kicked the suitcase so it broke along the spine and then stomped on the corners until it was just a mash of cardboard and Leatherette and phony chrome. I hurt my foot doing it, swore, swore again and then fell facedown on the floor.

" 'Abstract yourself with a holy violence from the dung heap of this earth,' " I said into the floorboards.

Outside I could hear voices and laughter.

"The bitch."

Someone was singing "The Yellow Rose of Texas."

"The dumb shits."

I stuck my thumbs in my ears and closed my eyes and then plugged my nostrils with the tips of my little fingers. It was a trick I'd seen one of the autistics at the Baxter School pull—either to keep the world from rushing in or to keep herself from spilling out, I didn't care. I lay that way for a long time: no sight, no smell, no sound except the roar of my own blood. This is it, I thought. If she doesn't come, this is it. I'm not going after her. Not tonight, or tomorrow, or next week. To hell with Mavericke, to hell with Amias, to hell with the little commonwealth. I'll stay here on my island. Finish my house now that I've tricked the world into helping me. I'll stay here and live my life, stretch out the dig for another five years, another ten years, get a grant to excavate the fort, anything, just so I don't have to go back.

I unplugged my ears to listen for a second, then re-plugged them.

" *'Abstract yourself with a holy violence,'* " I said out loud.

I listened to the sumping of my blood.

" *'Abstract yourself with a holy violence . . .'* "

I rolled over onto my side, curled up and just lay there, eyes closed, orifices stuffed shut, sneaking a breath from time to time through my mouth. I kept seeing things in my mind: the Milky Way wrapper on the boat, Hetty's mother turning away, the twins winking at me in some sort of collusion. Behind me I thought I heard something, someone at the window or the door opening, but I didn't unstop my ears: Even if something was there, nothing was there. I kicked the Milky Way wrapper overboard, made Hetty's mother say: "She's not worth it," got the twins to recite the Gettysburg Address. I was starting in on Hetty herself—getting her to fall down on her knees—when out of nowhere someone kicked me in the back. I unplugged myself and rolled over.

It was Thompson the Carpenter.

"You been left standing at the altar, partner."

I hauled myself up onto my elbows. The light hurt my eyes and through the open door I could hear the raising still going on. "Who let you in?"

"I let myself in."

"Then you can let yourself out."

"Listen," he said. He took his hammer out of his hammer holster and aimed it at me like a tomahawk. "Maybe you should try plywood. Maybe you should try Formica, Sheetrock. Cut out this timber frame crap and join the twentieth century before it gets to be the twenty-first century." He made to throw the hammer at me and then let it slip back into its holster. "You might have better luck with the ladies that way."

"I don't need luck."

He cocked his head. "You need something, partner."

"Nothing," I said. "I don't need anything." And I got up and pushed past him.

Back atop the frame I called for the rafters with a show of my old gusto, but inside I was thinking: "Raise it! Raise it! Do the work and then get off my island!" I spat on someone's shoe when he wasn't looking, ate hot dogs and cursed the wood upright. We got one bent up, then another, pegged the purlins between them and moved on to the other two. I was sweating, hurrying everyone. I wanted it over and done with. I wanted them off my island. I wanted to feel myself alone. I wanted their eyes off me and my eyes off them. I was holding myself in, keeping a regimen of blasphemy inside me, forcing it down while I forced the wood up, saying to myself as I worked: *"Who can find a virtuous woman? For her price is far above rubies."* And then a little louder so that one of my raisers looked at me: *"The heart of her husband doth safely trust in her."* And then practically spitting: *"She will do him good and not evil, all the days of her life."*

The rafters went up.

The collar ties were set in.

The ridgepole was laid in place.

And then without saying anything—just as the four o'clock boat blew its horn—without saying sorry to the Reverend Wheelock or good-bye to my parents or Hetty's mother, I climbed down off the frame, turned down the path and locked myself in the Quonset hut.

CHAPTER

12

. . . But Instead Was Annulled by a Cabin Cruiser at Midnight

• 1 •

"Any way you look at it," Mavericke said that night, "love's a wilderness."

We were on the top floor of the frame. It was near midnight and the spring moon was already setting in the southwest sky. Across the dark harbor the city looked like a landscape of electric Gargantuas—Gog and Magog—the strobes atop the tallest buildings probing the sky like Cyclopean eyes. The skyscrapers seemed to be tending to their own needs—lighting themselves, warming themselves, pumping air through their arteries, water through their veins—all without the faintest fingerprint of humanity anywhere about them: a great deserted city inhabited by the utter hush of electronic life.

"Your father and his unified number theory," Mavericke mused. "He'd be hard pressed to put a number to your pretty cousin."

"Zero," I said. "Absent."

Out over the ocean, away from the city, the sky was

frosted with stars, the Milky Way winding like a snowy street through Cygnus and Aquila and Scorpius. I could see where sky became sea, the airy blue-black meeting the watery black-blue in a neat pen line, Venus rising from the water and shimmering through the heavy atmosphere. Out past Nix's Mate, a freighter lay all lit up, awaiting the harbor pilot; and farther out, Boston Light winked on and off, the warm yellow a testament to older times—but it too, like all light-houses now, unmanned.

"So what's next?" Mavericke asked.

"Next?"

"Yes, next. Even a man left standing at the altar has to have a next."

I considered a moment. "Plank the roof, I guess." Then split shingles with my froe, stud the walls, plank them and get clapboards up, also split with my froe.

"I meant what next on the love front."

"I *have* no love front. I've given over imagining vain things."

He shrugged. Out in the harbor I saw a small boat headed toward us, or rather, I saw its running lights and the silvery bill of its wake. Mavericke saw it too, but didn't say anything.

"I tried my best," I said finally.

He nodded and kept silent.

"I gave the world a chance to give me a fair shake."

"You did," he agreed.

"So now the world and I part company."

He sighed.

The boat had veered off, going southward around the island. By the sound of it, it was a cabin cruiser, inboard, maybe twenty-eight feet. In the dark, I could see nothing or no one on board.

"Cabin cruisers," I said after a time, "are immoral machines."

"How's that?"

"You need only look at my sweet, silent, white *Pilgrim's Progress* to understand me."

He considered a moment. "Sometimes, Wheelwright, you carry your vocabulary of saints and sinners to an unnecessary extreme."

It was my turn to shrug. "I am currently crushed of spirit," I said, and for a time we were both silent. The cabin cruiser had reached the southern end of the island, but instead of continuing south, it kept to the shore, as if it meant to circle us.

"My heart is broken," I said out of nowhere. Mavericke looked back at me. "It is. It really is. I know what they mean by that. It's broken right inside me."

And I thumped myself on the chest. He just sat there with nothing to say. I turned and watched the boat round the northern part of the island. It *was* circling us, coming back toward the dock.

"I wonder where she is," I said after a time. "Right now. What's she doing? What can she be thinking?"

"I don't know."

"Is she even going to explain herself?" I said and kicked one of the rafters.

"Wheelwright . . ."

"Send me a telegram, goddamn it!"

"Okay, okay . . ."

"What's that fucking boat doing out there?"

And I jumped up and crossed to the end gable. The boat had passed the dock again, following its own wake back around the island.

"Get the fuck off my water!" I screamed at the top of my lungs. But there was nothing in answer, no horn blown, nothing. "I wish I had my bird gun," I said to Mavericke.

It hugged the island, the running lights disappearing from time to time behind a rocky buttress or a bushy sprit, only the gargle of its engines betraying its presence. I followed it as it slipped southward along the harbor side of the island.

"Maybe it's one of your house-raising Americans," Mavericke said behind me, "just a little tardy."

"I'm in no mood for visitors."

"Or one of those Indians trying to get their island back."

I turned around to him. "Their?" I said. I could barely see his face in the dark. "Their? What do you mean their?"

"Don't get worked up."

"I thought you said you bought this island fair and square."

"I didn't actually *buy* it."

"What do you mean you didn't actually buy it? What *did* you do? *Actually?*"

"*Vacuum domicilium* was the legal concept of the time."

"You mean it was vacant so you just took it?"

"I didn't *take* it. I *settled* it."

"Oh, God."

"With the permission of the Massachusetts Indians from the mainland."

"Oh, God!" I said again and turned back to the harbor, to the city. "Do you mean to tell me after all this time it really *is* their island?"

"It's their *continent* as far as that goes."

"I don't *care* about the continent. They can *have* the continent. I care about the *island.* If I lose my island as *well* as my wife . . . !"

"It was the smallpox, you see. The population of the whole bay area was decimated."

"Fuck the smallpox!" I said and started running around kicking the rafters. "You don't seem to understand, you Anglican moron! I'm being killed piece by piece. They're *killing* me! First they broke my heart and now they're stealing my soul!"

"Just which *they* is that?"

"*They!*" I screamed at him. "*They! They! Them!*" And I made a gesture at the cabin cruiser, at the city, at the whole world. "I'm dying and you're talking about smallpox!"

"You're getting hysterical."

I ran to one of the gables and cupped my hands to my mouth. "*Who are you?*" I shouted at the boat. It was rounding the northern point again, swinging around toward the dock. "*Who are you and what do you want?*"

"They can't hear you."

"I've got a gun!" I shouted. *"I've got a gun and I'll use it!"*
"Take a seat, Wheelwright."

"You Anglican toad!" I said, spinning around. "You Indian-lover! You goody goody do-good!" And I ran from one corner of the frame to another, looking for a fast way down, and then just pushed myself between a set of rafters and jumped.

For a second I felt the heady freedom of flight, and then the black ground was rushing up at me and I was hit and sent sprawling. When I'd gotten my bearings I rushed down the path. In between the bushes I could see the cabin cruiser coming around the near point, aiming for the dock. I felt all hot inside. I'd skinned my hands in the fall but I didn't care. I could see by the dim cabin lights a figure at the wheel, and by the red running light, another figure perched on the side of the hull. I screamed something, let out a war whoop, but they kept on, easing past the *Pilgrim's Progress* and coming around the end of the dock. I scrambled down the last rocky tumble of the hill and then knelt down and searched for a stone.

"Out! Out!" I shouted and threw the stone at the windshield. I heard a sharp crack and then someone—the helmsman—shouted and blew his horn. It made a bright quack. I dove for another rock, searched frantically while the other figure hopped out onto the dock. I found one, and letting out a second war whoop, hurled it at him. I missed, but whoever he was—instead of coming for me—turned instead and kicked the boat.

"Creep!" he said to the helmsman.

I had another rock, but checked myself. *He?*

"Bastard!"

I peered into the dark.

"Creep! Bastard!"

"Hetty?" I said.

"Throw it, for Christ's sake!" she cried, turning to me. The cabin cruiser was backing water, trying to get clear of the landing.

"Hetty?"

"Throw it!"

I threw it. Again, there was the sharp crack of the fiber glass. Hetty let out a cry of triumph. The horn quacked again. And then the boat was gunned, its front end rearing back and its rear end spinning out. It veered off across the water, blowing its horn the whole time.

I turned to Hetty.

"Item One," she said in a raw voice.

In the dark I could only see a suggestion of her face; her hair cast crazy shadows that seemed to grip and disfigure her. I didn't say anything, just stood there waiting. She tucked her head down, gazing at her feet, and then seemed to think better of it and looked fiercely up at me.

"Item One," she repeated, "that recrimination will be absent from the marriage." And she dragged her fingers through her hair, turning away so she had her back to me.

"Which marriage is that?" I asked.

"The one you're so crazy about," she answered. She took a comb out of her purse and tried to coax it through her hair, then gave up and threw it overhand into the water. "Have you got something to drink?" she said, turning back.

"No."

"No? Nothing?"

"Gatorade," I said. "Just Gatorade."

"Don't you have something . . . you know, something to *drink*?"

"This is a state park. No pets, no alcoholic beverages, no weddings."

She stood with her hands on her hips, purse slung over her shoulder, watching me. "Look, I know you're mad at me," she said finally, "but are you going to be *really* mad?"

I didn't answer.

"I'm just about dead," she said. "Are you? Are you going to be *really* mad? Because I can throw myself in the ocean just as easily as talk to you."

Still, I didn't answer.

"I hung around the marina for two hours trying to get

someone to bring me out here. Finally I get that creep. And once we get away from land he wants to get *paid,* for Christ's sake. Goes twice around the island trying to get his creepy hands on me."

"You should have tried the tour boat," I said finally. "It runs regular hours. In the *daytime*. No creepy hands allowed."

"You *are* mad at me."

"Not me," I said, shaking my head.

"It doesn't matter," she said. "I don't care. This is the stupidest thing I've ever done. I don't care. I've been thinking about it all day. I woke up this morning and said right out loud: '*What* are you talking about?' And then I spent the whole day saying: 'Never mind, never mind.' I stayed at Mrs. Steele's and put away all my silverware. I stacked my plates, hung my coffee cups, plugged in my Toast-R-Oven, got my bed knocked together, my microwave squared away, the television antenna hooked up, arranged my chairs, measured for curtains, went out and bought material, got my sewing machine set up, called out for Chinese food, and then right in the middle of sewing on binding tape I started crying. *I started crying, you bastard!"*

And all of a sudden she ran at me and started kicking me, kicking me and hitting me with her fists.

"I can't stand it!" she cried. *"I don't want to marry you!* Do you understand? *I don't want to marry you!"*

I covered up, like a boxer. She pulled at my hair, pinched me, tried to get at my face. I tried to break away from her, turned this way and that, but she turned with me, kicking and slapping me, screaming the whole time.

Then just as quickly, she stopped.

I uncovered and looked at her.

"I'm going to throw myself in the ocean now," she said. And she turned and very businesslike, started walking toward the end of the dock. I straightened up and watched her go. Her heels made a sharp attack on the wood and her rear end had that old slice and kick to it. "Hetty . . ." I said, but

I didn't say it loud enough. "Here goes," she said when she'd reached the end of the dock, but she just stood there, at the very edge, as if it were a diving board, and then sat down.

"Item One," she said when I'd walked out to her. "I plead Item One."

I sat down next to her.

"I can't help it," she said.

"All right."

"It won't last a month, you know."

"All right."

"But if you still want to get married, I'll marry you."

I could see her better now. We were facing Boston and the light from the city made a pale glow around us. She looked tired, battle weary.

"Do you want to marry me, Hetty?" I asked after a time. "I mean really?"

"Yes," she answered.

"Do you? Do you really?"

"Yes, I really do. I can't believe it, but I really do."

I put my arm around her.

"We could drive up to Exeter," I said. "Never mind our parents. We could drive up there and get married at the Congregational Church."

She nodded, staring into her lap, at her purse.

"And then we could honeymoon at the house."

"This is an ugly purse."

"Get the croquet set out and play on the lawn. Like we used to do. Would you like that?"

She held the purse out at arm's length as if to judge it better, and then unzipped it and started taking things out. She took out her compact and her lipstick, her keys, a library card, a tampon, her change purse, her ID from the Baxter School, a condom, a pen, a credit card, another credit card, a panty shield and finally her driver's license. She held the last up so the light from the city hit it.

"*Jenney, Mehitible C.,*" she read. "*Birth date: three, seven-*

teen, fifty-six. Height: five-one. Weight: ninety-five. Eyes: green. Marital Status: S."

And for a minute she studied the picture of herself in the upper left-hand corner, and then put everything—license, compact, condom, lipstick—everything back into the purse, zipped it shut and threw it into the ocean.

CHAPTER
13

The Devil in the Dooryard

• 1 •

All that summer and into the fall I kept a tally on how many times Hetty stayed the night on the island and how many times I stayed the night at Mrs. Steele's. I was the clear loser: twenty-eight to six.

And I kept a tally too (after I'd finally come around to recognizing I was not just careless) of every item that disappeared from the site—mortise chisel, vitamin pills, shoehorn—gradually realizing it was not some prankster, one of my graduate students or some Indian misfit, but my own sweet bride who was stealing from me. I wanted to ask her about it outright, but I was afraid I'd somehow manhandle her feelings: She seemed so secretive and pleased with herself. It was well into September before I thought to steal something of hers in return. When I did I took something I knew she'd miss, a Xerox copy of one of her articles on autism. But the next day when I came to stay the night (bouquet of fall flowers in one hand, Old Mr. Boston brandy in the other), she was seated at her desk—a new Xerox spread

175

before her—with such a warm, fulfilled look on her face
that I wondered what new well of affection I'd divined.

I spent the summer closing the house in, readying it for
the winter when I'd do the interior work. It took me nearly
the whole month of June to gather stones for the chimney,
to grind mortar out of clamshells and then lay stone on stone,
building scaffolding as I went. (But what a feeling when I
lit a smudge fire in each of the fireplaces, checked the flues
for draw and then stepped back and watched the pearly
screw of smoke twist heavenward!) I planked and shingled
the roof next, teaching Hetty on a June-buggy weekend how
to split shingles with my hand-forged froe (missing come
Monday). I put in studs and planked the outside walls, split
clapboards and nailed them to the planking, and then put
in oilpaper windows that swung open and closed on wooden
hinges. I made the front door out of three-inch oak, board-
and-batten, with three hundred hand-forged nails making a
heavy diamond pattern on its front face, a sign ("To whom?"
my party-pooper wife wanted to know) that this was not the
house of an ordinary man When the twins saw it—saw the
precise pattern, the exact points and angles of the dia-
monds, the faceted nailheads repeated in the faceted pattern—their eyes seemed to light with intelligence and they
stopped in their tracks in front of the door. They stood and
stared at it for upward of half an hour. (This was normal
behavior for them as far as my eyes could tell, but it sent
Hetty digging for her notebook.)

She kept a lexicon on the twins, writing down everything
they did and said, keeping whole columns of nonsense in
the hope that some pattern would discover itself. She tried
to educate me, to show me correspondences between their
queer litanies and quacky psalms—"one-eighty," "no de-
posit/no return," "Vermont/New Hampshire"—repeated over
and over again. She gave me articles and books to read and
out of love I plowed through them, through the case histo-
ries and the hypotheses, feeling all the time that there in
the raging animality of Christine W. and the buzz saw of

Jeremy T. and the clocklike mechanics of Helmut W. was the raw world picked, pickled and canned. "A self-chosen state of dehumanization," one Herr Doktor wrote; "the world as anti-self, bent on annihilation." I read about the autistic's fascination for wheels and fans and propellers, anything that revolves around itself; about their compulsive ordering of bits of reality, blocks, puzzles, words or songs sung by rote ("Order created to counteract a world that is perceived as run by hostile, uncaring, irrational forces"); about their total insensitivity to pain, a burn or pinch yielding no cry, no recognition even, as if the pain merely blended in with a roar of psychic hurt; about Kelly H. who drew nothing but pictures of eggs with herself inside them; about Richard S. who painted the walls, chairs, rug, everything about him with his own feces; and finally about little Holly K. who succumbed to the ultimate autism ("marasmus," Hetty had written in the margin), a state of total and absolute passivity, her mind so completely extinguished that her body dehydrated, her tendons and muscles shrunk so her limbs curled fetally in on themselves: suicide by total self-negation. I got so depressed I had to get up and run around the apartment, and then in quick succession: practice my pitching motion, do jumping jacks, look at my beautiful paneling in the bedroom, sing "Jabberwocky" to the twins and finally go kiss Hetty on the neck as she sat at her desk.

"There *is* hope, you know," she said, making some note or other. I bit the blond baby hair at the back of her neck. "Some autistics *do* get cured. If a professional is smart enough, imaginative enough and persistent enough, it can happen. Gradually, slowly, you can make connection, and when you make connection you can communicate with them in *their* terms, in *their* language, and get them to see the world as something other than destructive."

I pulled a little too hard on her hair so she said "ouch," and then stood up and looked over at the twins. They were lying on the couch as usual, side to side, knee to knee, toe to toe, their heads pressed to each other and their pretty red hair braided together (braided—by Hetty—not knotted).

"They look happy to me."

She gave me a doubtful look and turned to look at them herself.

"They *do*," I said. "They really do. They've got each other and that's all they need."

She seemed to poise herself on the thought.

"It's not impossible, you know."

"It's not likely either," she answered and went back to her notebooks.

I rummaged through them from time to time. She had them organized in columns:

Word	/Is./Ir./	Stimulus	Correlation	Cross-index

and under each column were bits and pieces of evidence (in pen) and (in pencil) attempts at making sense of them, at seeing in them some metaphor for human feeling or want or need. At times there'd be an excited flurry of ideas under *Correlation*, as if for an instant she'd thought she'd come upon the Rosetta stone of autism, before the pencil writing petered out into questions, inconclusions and erasures. At the back of the notebooks there were little scenes sketched in, vignettes that were like capsules of lunacy, cockeyed parables that made you feel if you only had the right angle, the right symbolic bent, the right dose of mooncalvism ("Mooncalvinism?" queried Hetty), you could understand them. Here was Isabel saying "Thirsty," and Irene getting up and getting a Coke, coming back to the couch, sitting down next to Isabel and drinking the Coke herself while Isabel smacked her lips. And here was Irene saying "It hurts, it hurts," and Isabel saying "It hurts, it hurts," and Hetty asking "Where?" so that each of them said "Here," and pointed to the other's chest. ("Are they getting breasts already?" Hetty wonders in pencil in the margin, and I add under it in pen: "Maybe it's their hearts they mean.") Scene A: Mooncalf No. 1 lies side by side with Mooncalf No. 2, inner ear pressed to inner ear, fingers stuffed in each other's outer ear. "As if," hypothesizes the pretty psychologist, "each means to keep the ocean of her soul open to the other and only to the other." (Scene B: Visiting Mooncalvinist, fresh from reading notebook, lies side by side with napping wife, ear pressed to ear, as if . . .)

Persistent psychologist to entwined twins: "She is she and you are you and I am me."

Entwined twins in unison: "She is she is you is you is me is me!"

• 2 •

Mrs. Steele bugged me right from the start. I finally met her after we got back from Exeter. I didn't like her Bonwit Teller clothes and her sneaky perfume; I didn't like the static crackle of her nylons, or the cold air that seemed to stream in behind her; I didn't like her smart bow ties and button-down collars, the starch she put in her blouses or her neatly ironed hems; I didn't like her hair-sprayed hair or the perfect wedges of rouge on her cheeks; I didn't like the way she was always wearing spike heels as if she were stabbing the world on the sly, or the way she seemed obliged to put a hand on each of the twins when she came downstairs. But most of all I didn't like the feeling I got that I'd seen her somewhere before, like a character from some ancient dream of mine.

"Maybe you've seen her around town," Hetty suggested. "After all, you've both lived here all your lives."

I told her I didn't mean in the flesh.

"What *do* you mean?"

I couldn't say.

I tried to remember some of our childhood books. What well-dressed witches were there? Mrs. Steele as Delilah in the *Illustrated Children's Bible*? as Mrs. Gog? Or my *American Heritage Book of Colonial America:* a head-bedeviled Anne

Hutchinson? Mary Dyer with a noose around her neck and
a shadowy Satan at her side? I grilled Hetty about her. When
did she meet her? (two years ago when the twins were
brought to the Baxter School); where was *Mr.* Steele? (divorced and living in California with the rest of America);
did she work? (she went out at night a lot); had she ever
seen her naked? (sweetheart?); naked, you know, with no
clothes on? (I've got work to do); if she *had* seen her naked,
were there any witch's tits?

"She's just a divorced, middle-aged, twentieth-century
woman who dresses a little too neatly and has had the rotten luck—"

"The divine retribution."

"—the rotten luck of having her two children born autistic."

"Autistics are not born, one of your books says,
they're made."

"Have it your way."

"I don't like her."

"I don't like her either, but I'm not here because of her."

I let it go for a while, busied myself the month of September out on the island, preparing the dig for the winter
and moving my stuff out of the Quonset hut—where my
graduate students would spend their winter days photo-
graphing and cataloging—up into the house. In October, I
was quizzed and prepped by one of the lawyers for the government. It took three days, him writing everything down,
underlining certain parts of my deposition, and me suppos-
edly memorizing my answers. I asked him how he thought
things would go. If the Indians won would they actually get
the land back or a cash settlement? Cash settlements were
the recent pattern, weren't they? But he was a perfect lawyer, equivocating and qualifying until I felt stupid for asking.

Back at Mrs. Steele's I took to prowling. When she went
out at night, I waited a decent interval and then climbed up
Thompson's stairway and opened the door into her house.
In the creepy streetlight I saw the same compulsive order-

ing as her button-down collars in the neat arrangement of settee to settee, of mantelpieces the very picture of a Georgian mind-set, of three- and five-armed candelabra, of an antique clock with its hands set exactly at twelve (midnight or noon?), of pewterware on a sideboard and thumbtacks holding up notes and appointment cards on the kitchen bulletin board. I went from room to room, floor to floor, careful not to disturb anything, not opening any drawers or closets, but all the same stalked by the feeling that nobody human really lived there, that the chairs in the living room had no depressions in their seat cushions because no one ever sat in them, that the soap bars in the bathroom still had cameo impressions on their faces because no one ever used them. I made it up to her bedroom on the third floor, but the light coming in the window looked so eerie, and there was such a witchery of shadows on the walls, that I spun around without going in and hurried back downstairs.

But I went up again the next night.

And the next.

"If she catches you—" Hetty said, making a fist at me.

"If she catches me I'll hold a crucifix up to her."

"Just leave her alone. I know what you're talking about. I've been up there. She's neat. If you want my professional opinion, she's *compulsively* neat. But so what?"

"So she's making up for something. *Compensating.* And I want to know for what."

"Why? What's it to you?"

"My wife lives in the same house with her, that's what's it to me."

"Neurosis is not contagious."

"But depravity is."

When I saw Mrs. Steele in the daytime I tried to catch her eye, to look her in the face and say with *my* face that I knew what was what. But she just glided past me, her blue eyes the color of ice and every inch of her body covered with clothes and makeup. Whenever she was around I noticed the twins seemed to lie even more still and lifeless than they usually did, as if they knew they were in the presence of something that especially wanted to blast them to nothingness. When she was gone I asked Hetty if she'd ever noticed the same thing, but she just grimaced and said, "No kidding."

• 3 •

I took a break, and for an antidote, started work on the interior walls of Mavericke's house, working with wattle and daub, sleeping on my cot still, rigging Mavericke's hammock for him and from time to time filling him in on the vicissitudes of married life.

• 4 •

But I couldn't help myself. Back in town, whenever I heard the street door shut and saw Mrs. Steele's high-heeled ankles stride past the windows above me, I was up the stairway and in among the dark angles and unlived air of her house. "What's the difference between her neatness and those right-angled joints you're so proud of?" Hetty had asked. I didn't know. But I felt in the clean order of everything in the house the mockery of blasphemy. I began to look for things—what, I couldn't say—but I voided my promise to Hetty not to disturb anything and started opening drawers and cupboards. I pawed through her blouses (ironed, every one of them), through her sweaters, through her underwear; I looked her silverware over, her jewelry, the shoes hanging in her shoe bag. I even looked in the back of her phone book for suspicious listings (Jeremy Baal? Hugh Leviathan?), but only found the usual scrabble of names, including Hetty's. I read the notes on her bulletin board, the appointments on her calendar, the ledger in her checkbook, letters, bills, Visa receipts—but everything was ordinary, just as it ought to be. And yet I couldn't shake the feeling that it was all an elaborate ploy—Mrs. Steele disguising her real self in the commonplace of a balanced checkbook.

"It's like she knows someone's checking on her," I said to Hetty, "and so she's gotten everything so perfect and ordinary no one can tell what—"

"You said you wouldn't mess anything."

"—what a witch she really is."

I took to sitting up there—in the dusk, in the daytime, in the deep night—just sitting and trying to *feel* a clue. In the shadowy light the furniture had the look of grotesque sentinels, legged, armed, blunt-shouldered brutes with brass escutcheons that looked like eyes that had healed over. I could feel a keen sentience in everything around me, in the dark mirrors, in the ticking clocks, in the hourglass drapes that were carved into a woman's body by the streetlight. It made me feel creepy, but I stuck it out, sometimes reading aloud like an exorcism *The Gentleman and Cabinet-Maker's Director* or *The Analysis of Beauty*. When after an hour or two I heard Mrs. Steele's steps on the sidewalk out front, I'd get up and slip downstairs, pulling the door closed behind me just as I heard her key in the front door.

"There's a secretary up there," I told Hetty. "A big, beautiful Boston bombé with an arched pediment and a gilded figure of Liberty at the top."

She peered up at me from her reading.

"It's a beauty, well proportioned, well carved, four drawers on the bottom, a drop-front lid, two doors above, drawer blades joined to the carcass with stepped dovetails, through mortise-and-tenons for the doorframes, flame finials on either side of Liberty, and Liberty herself proud and righteous."

"So?" she said finally.

"So it's locked."

I tried the keys from my parents' secretary and from the drop-lid desk in my bedroom, but they wouldn't work. I went to the period-furniture hardware store down on Charles Street and bought all the different size keys they had, but none of them fit either. I got in touch with the Restoration Lab, but they wouldn't let the keys they had for the museum pieces out of the museum. I called a locksmith, another locksmith, finally a third who said he kept rings of skeleton keys. I asked if I could borrow them, for a fee, but he said it'd taken him thirty-two years to collect them, he'd have to come by. I told him I'd call him back.

"Dinner," Mrs. Steele's calendar said under November 18, *"J. C. Hilary's, 7:00."*

"Can you come in the evening?" I asked the locksmith. He said he could. "The eighteenth then? At seven-thirty?"

· 5 ·

"The devil in the dooryard!" I cried the night of the eighteenth, running down the stairs and looking for Hetty. She was in the twins' bedroom, braiding their hair together for the night. "I've got it!"

"What?"

I took her by the elbow and pushed her toward the door and then started unbraiding the twins' hair, finally cutting a swathe between them with my hand.

"Get them to walk," I said.

She just fixed a stubborn look on me.

"You want to know why the twins are the twins?" And I picked each one up under the arms and set her on her feet. Hetty crossed back to the bed, and pushing me out of the way, whispered something in their ears.

"Vermont," Isabel said.

"New Hampshire," Irene answered.

I waited around long enough to make sure they were coming, and then ran back upstairs.

"Forget your psychologists' theories about voracious environments and crossed wires," I said once they'd made it up into the dead hush of Mrs. Steele's living room. I led them over to the secretary. "This is the real thing."

"Whatever you're going to show me," Hetty asked, "can you show it without gloating? And show it fast?"

"We've got plenty of time. Mrs. Steele is currently enjoying filet of sole." And with a dramatic display, I took the key I'd just bought from the locksmith and laid it conspicuously in the cove of the waist molding. Then, when I saw Hetty eye it, I picked it up and put it above the cornice molding where she couldn't reach it.

"Now, concentrate," I said. "This is mathematics with a touch of mysticism." And I crossed to Mrs. Steele's sewing cabinet and got out her tape measure. "Do you know what the golden section is?"

"No."

"It's the division of a line so that the smaller part is to the larger as the larger is to the whole. Medieval theologians called it the Divine Proportion. For a cabinetmaker, roughly five to eight." And I held the tape measure out, dividing it in illustration. "It's been found in the design of the pyramids, in Druidic monuments, in the proportions of the five orders of Greek columns, in Mayan temples. It's even been used to establish the true date of Easter."

"We're going back downstairs," she said, taking each twin by the hand.

"Vermont," Isabel said and stayed where she was. "New Hampshire," Irene answered. I gave Hetty a significant look, and went on.

"It's been likened to the Trinity, since it is one proportion in three terms, and for the same reason, to the Constitution of the United States. Aristotle drew ethical analogies from it and Leonardo da Vinci constructed his ideal man from it, using the navel as the center of a circle enclosing man with outstretched arms. It is, in short, a fundamental ratio of beauty and order in the Western world."

"You sound like your father."

"Now Mrs. Steele's secretary was built right around 1790, just three years after the Constitution, a time when even a middle-class tradesman could breathe ideas of Greek democracy and order right out of the air. So watch." And I held up the tape measure to the side of the desk section and then to the front. "Would you like to work out that ratio?"

"What's this all to me?"

I measured again. "Twenty-five inches deep. Forty inches wide."

She figured a moment. "Five to eight."

"The golden section," I said and put the tape measure to the width and then—standing on a chair—to the height of the bookcase section. "Thirty-six to fifty-four."

She didn't answer.

"Thirty-six to fifty-four."

"Five to eight, I'll bet."

I measured the quarter columns—the capital to the entablature—and while I was still on the chair, the height of the bonnet to the width of the bookcase; then I hopped down and measured the combined height of the four bottom drawers to their width; then, down on my knees, the width of the ball-and-claw feet to their height; then the desk lid; then each of the bookcase doors.

"The golden section," I said. "Each and every one of them. And there's more."

Hetty looked doubtfully at me and then scanned the secretary. "I'll bet you could take any ratio—any reasonable ratio—say, two to three, or three to four, and find just as many places where it fit."

"Want to try?" I said, holding out the tape measure to her. She didn't take it.

"North Dakota," Irene said behind us.

"South Dakota," Isabel answered.

Hetty eyed them a moment and then climbed up onto the chair. "Okay. So what's inside." And she ran her fingers along the top of the molding until she found the key.

"One more thing," I said. "And then we'll open it."

"What?"

"Do you know what the Fibonacci sequence is?"

She started to unlock the bookcase but I reached out and stopped her.

"The Fibonacci sequence is a sequence of integers in which each successive term is the sum of the two preceding terms: zero, one, one again, then two, three, five, eight, thirteen, and so on into infinity."

"So what?"

"So the ratio of any two successive terms, three to five, five to eight, eight to thirteen and so on, approximates the ratio of the golden section, *and* as the sequence proceeds it approximates the ratio more and more closely. But it never equals it. It never equals it because the golden section, like pi, regresses infinitely. It has no final, precise numerical value."

"Vermont," Isabel said.

"New Hampshire," Irene answered.

"But that sequence—one, two, three, five, eight, thirteen, twenty-one, thirty-four—is found over and over again in the natural world. Just ask my father. It's found in the reflection of light, in the breeding of rabbits, in the genealogy of the drone bee, in the number of axils in the sneezewort, in the spiral of the sunflower, in the inside chambers of certain seashells. My father has got Greek temples, medieval mysticism, Federal architecture and the sneezewort all wound together. And he's right, lunatic genius that he is. Because what we're talking about here is a fundamental order in the natural world reflected in the mind of man."

She looked at me as if I'd bitten her.

"Now you'd better let me do the unlocking."

But she just stayed where she was, still on the chair.

"We're going to take a look at *Mus musculus*," I said and held my hand out for the key. She hesitated and then handed it to me and stepped down.

"*Mus*," Isabel said.

"*Mus*," Irene repeated.

"*Mus musculus*," they said in unison.

Hetty didn't turn, didn't even look at them.

I unlocked the bookcase. There they were, maybe twenty in all, bottles and jars filled with a murky liquid and set side by side where books—*Pilgrim's Progress, The Spirit of Laws,* the *Bay Psalm Book*—ought to have been. Hetty looked at them, and then at me, then back as if it were a joke. She started to reach for one and then stopped.

"What's in them?" she asked.

"*Mus musculus*," I answered.

"*Mus.*"

"*Mus.*"

"*Mus musculus.*"

"What's *Mus musculus?*"

"The common house mouse," I said and reached up and took down one of the smaller jars. "Remember high school biology?" And I handed her the jar. She took it and peered through the dirty formaldehyde.

"It's a baby mouse," she said.

"That's right."

"Its eyes aren't even open."

"That's right."

"Oh, God!" she said suddenly. "Here, take it. Take it!"

"Don't like it?" I asked, taking the jar and putting it back on its shelf. "Don't like your *Mus musculuses* with two heads?"

She looked angrily at me, wiping her hand on her pants. "You could've warned me."

"Sorry. Now you're warned." And I tried to hand her another jar.

"I don't want it."

"Go ahead, take a look. People pay money for these things. At county fairs and stuff."

"No."

I opened the desk lid and set the jar down, and then started taking others down. And while I pointed things out— the three front feet, the two tails, the Siamese twins—I told her about Cotton Mather's wife and the devil in the dooryard; how pregnant Abigail had seen the devil in a whirlwind of north Boston dust and then three weeks later had given birth to a monster baby; and how Mather had maintained it was his *own* evil that had allowed the devil inside of his wife, and that the baby—eyeless but with a beating heart and teeth—was the devil within made manifest. She watched me as if maybe *I* were the devil, watched me produce abortion after abortion, her eyes lit with alarm and her face crumpled in disgust. Behind her the twins stood stockstill, their faces averted but seeming to say that even though they weren't looking, they were looking. Hetty took a step back and put an arm around each of them, but I just kept taking jars down—a chicken fetus, an un-Fibonaccied rabbit, a raccoon—saying that this was the *real* Mrs. Steele, this was what she wanted the world to be.

"Just *stop* it."

"Do you want to see the bottom drawers? That's where the really big stuff is."

"Wright!"

"A collie pup with its head welded to its ribs and a lamb with no eyes."

She put her hand to her face and closed her eyes, and for an instant everything seemed to well up inside her—stillborn babies, the golden section, *Mus musculus*—and then she spun around, and grabbing each of the twins by the hand, hurried down the stairs.

• 6 •

Here's what I dreamed that night, locked out of the bedroom and sleeping on the twins' couch:

I am floating in a big jar. There are other jars around me, and they are screaming, only they are screaming without making a sound, so that there is a great silent roar all around me. I am screaming too, screaming somehow without opening my mouth, screaming through my eyes, my ears, my temples. I can see the others, see them floating facedown, deadlike, sightless in their jars. And I know I look just like them. And I want to look just like them, so the world will think I am not born yet, that I will never be born. And all the while, I

know that at any moment the big door in front of me is
going to be opened, and that a giant Mrs. Steele is going to
peer in at me—Mrs. Steele, face painted, collar buttoned
down—Mrs. Steele unscrewing the top of my jar and mea-
suring out one perfect teaspoon of the water around me—
the water that is keeping me alive, the water that is keeping
me from the world, the water that I do not realize is for-
maldehyde—and drinking it like soup.

· 7 ·

"I had their dreams," I said to Hetty the next morning.
"I slept on the twins' couch and had *their* dreams."
   We were sitting at the kitchen table, the twins across from
us feeding Kix into each other's mouth.
   "It was like black magic," I said. "It was like being inhabited by another person's mind. Or having another person's
memory. Or spirit."
   She was looking down at her cereal bowl as if she didn't
want to hear any more about it. But I couldn't help myself.
   "It was like Cousin Isaac and going savage," I said. She
blew into her cereal so the milk rippled. "It was like Cousin
Isaac when he was taken into captivity and marched naked
through the woods. Remember how he says he slept on an
Indian pallet one night and dreamed he cut the living heart
out of a man and drank the blood so as to take in the man's
life and courage? Do you see? He lay on that Indian's pallet
and *dreamed that Indian's dream.* For the space of a dream, *he*
went savage."
   "It runs in the family, I guess."
   "And *I* dreamed *their* dream, the twins' dream, and for
the space of that dream, *I was autistic.* I knew what it was
like to be autistic!"
   She looked at me as if part of her wanted to ask me
about it, to hear the dream over again, but as if another

part of her were tired, weary of me, of Mrs. Steele and her jars, weary of the twins even. When she spoke she told me she thought I should go and stay on the island for a couple of days. Just to give us a break. Did I understand?

• 8 •

I stayed longer than a couple of days. I was thinking she could stew in her own juice. I finished the wattle-and-daub infill of the interior walls and started work on the partition walls. I made the buttery and the pantry just off the kitchen and the parlor door. I started to draw up plans for a bed—oak with an arched headboard—but in the mood I was in, I couldn't decide whether to make it a single or a double and so stopped. On December first it snowed.

When I went into the city, instead of going to see Hetty, I walked up sixteen flights at the JFK building, and in Courtroom E sat in the last row—in a stackable, molded plastic chair—and listened to the testimony in the Indian suit. Philip was there, dressed in a trim three-piecer, sitting at the plaintiff's table with attorneys from the Native American Rights Fund and the New England Native Task Force. There was no jury, just a judge, no big Indian contingent in the spectators, not even as many reporters as I'd thought there'd be—no cameramen standing outside—just a couple of bored print men with note pads on their knees and Nikons around their necks. They dealt with the southern lands first, with Betty's Neck and Assawompset (Mavericke's Island would not come up until February), introducing deposition after deposition, Philip's lawyers maintaining that certain transfers of Wampanoag land after 1790 never received congressional approval, were, in fact, merely private deals, and were thus void by the Indian Nonintercourse Act. They questioned and quizzed and qualified. I had a hard time concentrating. From time to time, Philip would turn around in his chair, surveying the courtroom, and, catching my eye, acknowledge me with a discreet nod: the lawyer all the way.

I would have kept it up—working on the house in the morning and sailing in to the trial in the afternoon—but one evening coming back to my boat at the marina, I found a note stabbed onto one of her cleats.

> Are we still married?
> If so, I request Item Three.

• 9 •

So back on Commonwealth Avenue I was buttered up and soft-soaped by my wife for some reason I couldn't figure. By wiles and smiles she got me to help with the twins: making their bed in the morning, brushing their teeth, spreading peanut butter on saltines for them. I caught her looking at me from time to time, as if she wanted to catch a glimpse of me in mock fatherhood and felt alternately pleased and unsettled by what she saw. When she asked for the key to Mrs. Steele's secretary, I gave it to her and stood harmlessly by when she dropped it into the trash compactor. At night, lying in the bedroom I'd built for us, she told me she loved me, ran her fingers along my spine and asked was I glad I'd married her? Did I love her still? Did she please me? I didn't ask how or why or what, but in the morning while she showered, kissed my mortise-and-tenon joints for their good work.

I kept my mouth shut about Mrs. Steele, contenting myself with sneaking upstairs now and then behind Hetty's back and unplumbing a candelabrum or setting the hands of the antique clock at thirteen past three. I laid off the twins too, pretending I enjoyed helping give them a bath, washing their flat chests and girlish legs and then shampooing their hair while Hetty held her hands over their eyes. And I did enjoy it, I guess—at least a little—but what got me was the way

Hetty watched everything I did, as if she were looking for evidence of something, or preparing to tell me something, only she needed just the right moment.

Then it happened again. Napping on the twins' couch I dreamed of some horrible devouring mouth full of circular fluorescent lights and car horns. It was chasing me, following me through dark, wet alleys—Fallopian tubes and uterine canals—until I was flat up against a wall of wiggling cilia. I woke in a sweat and rolled off the couch as though it were about to swallow me. Over at the kitchen table Hetty was looking at me over the top of some article she was reading. I sat up and almost launched into it—into the teeth and the neon tonsils—but caught myself in time.

"Dreaming," I said instead, making a silly smile. She went back to her reading.

But after that—even while I kept up my bathing and peanut-buttering duties—I took to napping on the couch at every opportunity, even evicting the twins themselves sometimes, compiling a whole catalog of bogeys—Vermont and New Hampshire opening like jaws along the Connecticut River, seesaws whirling off like helicopter blades—writing everything down when I woke so that at some point—at just the right moment—I could sit Hetty down and present her with irrefutable evidence. ("Evidence for what?" I could hear her ask. "Evidence for evil in the world," I'd answer. "Evidence for Mrs. Steele's contaminating everything around her. Evidence for the twins as infected goods. Evidence for your moving out to Samuel Mavericke's island.")

I'm the Hancock tower popping panes out on myself walking thirty floors below.

I'm a mortise-and-tenon joint being eaten away by bugs with Mrs. Steele's face.

I'm thirteen again, sitting at my usual place in the reading room, the green lampshade like a visor over my head and the Hancock building rising like a vertical aquarium outside the window, filled with human beings swimming in their business suits. I'm reading about Samuel Mavericke, imagining the snow-white skin of baby Samuel, and dreaming about the beauty of their island life in the midst of the bickering and bawling of infant America. But at the same time I'm keeping an eye out for Mrs. Steele. It's ten to four and she always comes at four, dressed in her neat orlons and rayons, slipping in between the reference stacks, taking down first this book and then that, and then finally—thinking herself unobserved, not worrying about the teenager in the school blazer and tie, maybe not even aware of his eyes riding over the top of his book—taking a razor out of her purse, and with a practiced hand, slicing a page out.

"And then she used to put it back."
"What?"
"She used to put it back."
"What back?"
"The page."
"What page?"

I woke up. I was on the couch. Hetty was sitting over at the kitchen table, looking across the room at me and frowning. It was night, eight o'clock maybe. The twins were gone, in bed.

"She used to put the pages back," I said, a little dazed still, and then more certain: "Only she'd put them back in the wrong spot."

"What pages? Who?"

"Mrs. Steele," I said and sat up. For an instant I thought to take it back or say "never mind" or something. But it was too late. "I *have* seen her before. In the library. When I was young."

She waved her hand like she didn't want to hear about it.

"She used to come in in the afternoon and cut out pages from the reference books with a razor blade and then slip the pages back, only in the wrong spot."

"You've been dreaming."

"She *did*!" I said and then stopped short. Did she?

"You've been dreaming," Hetty said again.

I tried to think. I could picture her gliding between the stacks, could picture the thin strips of her clothing above and below the rows of books, could even picture a face twenty years younger, but I couldn't tell if I was picturing the dream I'd just had or a real memory. I sat up and tried to shake off the sleep cobwebs. Was Mrs. Steele prowling in my brain as invited guest or intruder?

"Come on," I said and hopped off the couch.

"What?"

"Francis Marion."

"What?"

"Francis Marion. The Swamp-fox. I remember she cut out his page in the *Encyclopedia of American Biography*."

"Oh, Wright."

"I remember because it was the same volume as Samuel Mavericke."

"Even if it is, so what?"

"So it'd still be missing, wouldn't it? Now, come on."

"Where?"

"To the library."

She shook her head and squared herself in her chair. "I can't. The twins are sleeping."

"We'll only be gone half an hour. You've left them for half an hour before."

"No," she said. "I'm not going."

"Don't you want to know? Aren't you curious?"

"I'm not leaving them," she said and put her face back into her papers.

I hung fire an instant and then hurried into the twins' bedroom. "Come on, sweethearts," I said and started unbraiding their hair.

"Wright!"

"Well, *you* do it then. Get their clothes out."

She was standing in the doorway now. I picked up one twin under the arms and set her on the floor, and then went for the other. I pulled their nightgowns up over their heads and tossed them on the floor. They stood like statues, naked, eyes open and staring straight ahead of themselves.

"No deposit . . ." I said.

"Wright!"

". . . no return," I answered.

She pushed me out of the way and knelt beside them, combing her fingers through their hair. "If I go," she said, looking angrily at me, "if I go and the Swamp-fox is right where he ought to be, will you forget about it? Forget about Mrs. Steele and everything? Will you let me live here with the twins and just come visit like you were supposed to do?"

I didn't answer.

"Will you?"

I still didn't answer.

"Will you?"

I tossed the twins' clothes to her. "Come on."

Outside, we walked with Isabel and Irene between us. We were holding hands—the four of us—and I could feel Hetty's anger surging like electricity through the twins to me. The Christmas lights were still up, lighting the telephone poles and giving the snow a reddish sheen. It was cold, and our four breaths bubbled in four clouds before us: Isabel and Irene trying to eat theirs, Hetty walking with her eyes on her feet and me trying to remember how it all had happened.

"It didn't matter what book," I said. "As far as I could ever tell, she picked books without rhyme or reason. *The Book Review Digest, The Land-Use Planning Abstracts,* the *Bibliographic Linquistique.* Our Mrs. Steele has eclectic tastes."

She threw me a dirty look and didn't say anything.

"I remember I went and told the reference librarian about her but he just said it was a public library. And when I tried to get across to him that she wasn't just some case off the street he said it again. Like he was tired. It was a *public* library."

"It *is* a public library," she snapped.

We turned onto Boylston Street, the Hancock tower appearing suddenly before us, its glass side like plates of blue ice in the moonlight. We crossed against the light, jumping a snowbank in front of the library (the twins just plowed through it), and then ran up the cement steps past the iron griffins and the statue of Henry Vane.

"Closing, sir," the security guard called to us once we were inside. I flashed five fingers at him and started Hetty and the twins up the marble stairs.

In the huge vaulted reading room we went straight to where the *Encyclopedia of American Biography* used to be, but it wasn't there, so we had to start searching along the wall bookcase. It was Hetty who found it. She started thumbing through one of the volumes, but when I got to her, I took it out of her hands.

"Mavericke . . . Mavericke . . . Mavericke . . ." I said, jumping through the pages.

"It's *Marion* you want," Hetty said. "Francis Marion, remember?"

The twins were staring at a shadow on the floor.

"Marion . . ." I said, ". . . Marion."

My hands were trembling. I found Marbut and Marsh, Mays and Marshall, names on both sides of Mavericke, but I couldn't settle myself down enough to find Marion.

"For Christ's sake!" Hetty said and took the book away from me. "Marion," she said and started snapping through the pages. "Marion, goddamn you."

"Maybe it *was* just a dream," I said, almost to myself.

"March . . ." she spat out, ". . . Marchant . . . Marcy . . ."

"Maybe I've been dreaming about it for a long time—for years, I mean—so I just *think* it really happened." I was looking at the shadow along with the twins. It looked like an eagle with its beak open.

"Marden . . ." Hetty said, ". . . Marigny . . . Markham—" she stopped short, and then paged quickly back, and then forward again.

"What?" I said, looking up.

She just stared at me. I reached out and took the book from her.

There it was: the telltale strip of page at the binding and the clean slit in the following page. I stared at it an instant as if it too were a dream, and then gave out a little cry and held the book up like a trophy.

"What do you have to say about that?" I cried. "Page two-eighty-two, page two-eighty-five. What do you have to say about that?"

She didn't answer, but her face drained of color right before my eyes.

"You and Mrs. Steele. What do you have to say about that?"

She stepped back and took each of the twins by the hand. But I wasn't going to let her off that easily. I took a step toward her and held the book right in front of her face.

"No page two-eight-three. No Francis Marion. No Swamp-fox. No—"

She hit it. She hit the book so it flew out of my hands and sprawled on the floor.

"I'm pregnant!" she cried. *"That's* what I've got to say about it! Item Four! I'm pregnant! I'm pregnant and I'm living in Mrs. Steele's house! What do *you* have to say about that? You and your *Mus musculus!"*

And she spun around and headed for the door, yanking the twins after her.

CHAPTER 14

ITEM FOUR: That the Having of Children Will Be by Mutual Consent, and That Should an Unwanted Pregnancy Occur, Mehitible Has the Right Without Recrimination to Terminate that Pregnancy.

• 1 •

Item Four.

It was time for cool heads, I told her. It was time for a sense of proportion. It was time (I was thinking) for subtle persuasion.

I was extra nice to the twins. I bought them a Scrabble game, telling Hetty it could provide one more clue if they started spelling things. (*MKLSLKM*, Isabel spelled; *RPMXMPR*, spelled Irene.) I vacuumed, helped with the dishes, initiated family walks. I kept my mouth shut about Mrs. Steele, about the Swamp-fox, about *Mus musculus* of any description. (*"Mus,"* Isabel and Irene still said from time to time, *"Mus musculus."*) If I talked at all it was to coddle the twins, to tell Hetty I loved her, to tell her how good she looked, how I liked this dress or that skirt. I invited the twins onto our bed at night, held one on each side and told them about the mortise-and-tenon joints around them, how the wood was like a vault, that they were safe here. And I kissed them each on both cheeks. But when the trial came around to Mavericke's Island and I asked Hetty to come and sit in the courtroom for moral support—come so we'd present a unified front—she said no.

Item Four.

So I went by myself. I expected the same empty corridors and courtroom boredom, but when I got up to the sixteenth floor the lobby in front of the elevators was stuffed with reporters and spectators as if the world had finally wised up to the idea that my island was maybe going to be taken from me. I recognized some of Philip's comrades from Martha's Vineyard—dressed in suits and ties, most of them— some being interviewed by the reporters, others just milling about. When they caught sight of me, they started hooting and pointing. The cameramen spun around, and on went their lights. I started to edge my way toward the courtroom. Someone asked me something; a microphone was stuck in front of my mouth; then a little cassette recorder. Questions popped at me from all around.

"My wife's pregnant," I said, smiling and leaning into the microphones. I said it again: "She is. She's pregnant," and then ducked into the courtroom.

"I see you've got your playmates here," I whispered to Philip, seating myself behind the plaintiff's table. "Going to try to do with volume what you can't do with *veritas*?"

He didn't turn around, just flipped me the finger behind his back. From across the room the lawyer from the Bureau of Indian Affairs gave me a quizzing look and motioned for me to come to him, but I stayed where I was.

I didn't testify that day, had to sit instead and listen to depositions being read into the record, and then to the MDC historian recount how the island had come to be owned by the state and then included in the state park system. That night Hetty's phone rang and when I answered it, someone with a thuggy voice told me I was the last in a long line of fascists. He emphasized the *last*. On the local news a reporter who didn't look like she could even spell Wampanoag interviewed Philip, giving him such plums for questions

I could tell he'd coached her ahead of time. He talked about the concentration camp set up on the island during King Philip's War, about how more than one hundred Wampanoag Indians—*Christian* Indians, he'd emphasized—had died there of exposure and malnutrition, how Mavericke's Island was the great unknown atrocity of American history and had become a rallying point for Indians all over New England, how this country had to learn to recognize and compensate the moral wrongs of its past, and how the current archaeological dig on the island was insensitive to Indian spirituality, sacrilegious, in fact, revealing an ethnocentric arrogance and blindness to Indian customs and religious beliefs.

"Is that true?" Hetty asked.

"What?"

"About the concentration camp."

"Yes."

She made a face. "You never told me that before."

"I assumed you knew it."

"How? How would I know it?"

"I assumed you'd read Cousin Isaac's book."

She shook her head and looked back at the television. "All the *s*'s look like *f*'s."

We watched the Red Sox on the first day of spring training.

"They interviewed me, too," I hazarded after a moment.

"What'd you say?"

"I told them my wife was pregnant."

Her face clouded.

"And I smiled," I added.

But it was no soap.

· 2 ·

In the middle of the night the thuggy voice called and asked if I was getting a good night's sleep.

· 3 ·

The next day I was the first to take the stand. I was introduced by the Bureau lawyer as an expert in early New England history, in ethnohistorical inquiry, and in historical archaeology. He took me first over the familiar ground of the interrogatories, letting me fill the court in on Mavericke, on his legal and moral battles with the Visible Saints, on the "commandeering" of his island (that was the word I'd been coached to use) in 1675 by Captain Isaac Wheelwright, on the internment of four hundred Indians from the Wampanoag towns of Canaan and Goshen (I left out that they were peaceful, Christianized Indians and that Canaan and Goshen were praying towns), on Mavericke's death by starvation during the winter of 1675–76, on the vanishing (as far as historical record is concerned) of his son Samuel, and on the subsequent abandonment of the island by the Indians ("The *surviving* Indians!" someone called out from the back of the courtroom), by the *surviving* Indians, when the war ended in the summer of 1676. Then we danced around the question of Mavericke's right to the island in the first place, and I got a chance to bemoan the lack of historical record, and then went on to speak about the state of the Massachusetts tribe in 1624 when Mavericke took up residence on the island, how they were decimated by the smallpox epidemic of 1616 ("And who gave them the smallpox?" someone asked from the back of the courtroom; the judge banged his gavel). I drew analogies from Plymouth about how such decimated tribes often welcomed white settlers, giving them land and so forth, since in their weakened condition they were in need of allies against their tribal enemies—"Other Indians, I mean"—that although, of course, there was no historical record to prove such was the case with Mavericke's Island, Mavericke's subsequent relations with the Indians of the Massachusetts Bay area *was* a matter of historical record, and that record showed him to be on friendly footing with the Indians both before the landing of Winthrop and his one thousand saints in 1630 and afterward. I sneaked in Mavericke's humane care of afflicted Indians during the 1632 epidemic, his beaver-trading alliances in the early years and the fact that when the English traveler and letter-writer Michael Pettingill visited Mavericke on his island he was sat at table with Sunuhoo, a sachem of the Massachusetts. There was nothing, in short, to indicate that Mavericke was not on honest and equal terms with the Massachusetts Indians, which—given the lack of definitive evidence—indicated to me a general fairness and squareness in his dealings with the Indians.

"And they with him," I added diplomatically.

When it came time for cross-examination, Philip stood up. Throughout the trial he had left the questioning to the lawyers from the Native American Rights Fund and the New England Native Task Force. He was a witness himself, after all: He had spent the first two days of the trial on the stand detailing his claim of descent from Massasoit. I'd seen him question only one other witness.

"Tell me, Mr. Wheelwright," he said now, standing over me, "as an expert in colonial New England history, was Mavericke's Island the only place of Indian internment during King Philip's War?"

"No."

"What was the other? Or others?"

"Deer Island."

"In the harbor also?"

"Yes."

"Were they Wampanoags also who were interned there?"

"No," I said. "Mostly Nipmucks."

"Ah, the fierce Nipmucks. They were allied with Metacomet? King Philip, I mean?"

"Some were."

"Those who were interned, were they?"

"No."

"Who were they exactly?"

"Indians."

"What kind of Indians? All Indians aren't the same, are they? Otherwise we wouldn't need experts like you, would we?"

"They were peaceful Indians. They were converted to Christianity. Mostly by John Eliot."

"The Apostle to the Indians? The saint?"

"That's right."

He paused a moment. "Why were they interned if they were peaceful?"

"War hysteria."

"Similar to the Nisei panic during World War II?"

"I'm a colonial expert."

"Fair enough," he said and stared at his feet a moment. "Let me ask you about the fate of the Indians on Deer Island. The same as those on Mavericke's Island? I mean, roughly a quarter dead?"

"No," I answered. "Conditions were better."

"Why?"

"It isn't clear why. Probably through the intercession of Daniel Gookin, the Commissioner of Indian Affairs and a follower of Eliot's."

"God's providence, in other words?"

The Bureau lawyer got to his feet. "Are we in need of Mr. Safford's sarcasm, Your Honor? Or a history lesson? The morality of King Philip's War is not at issue here."

"Your Honor," Philip said, turning toward the judge, "it is crucial to the plaintiff's case that the facts of how four hundred Wampanoag Indians were interned on Mavericke's Island be established. We are trying to establish moral grounds for ownership of the island, as well as legal grounds, testimony for which will follow. I apologize if I've allowed a certain tone to enter my voice."

The judge nodded and Philip turned back to me.

"Let me understand you then, Mr. Wheelwright. The Indians interned on Deer Island were peaceful, Christian and not allied with King Philip's forces?"

"That's correct."

"And most of them survived?"

"Yes."

"Then the Indians on Mavericke's Island, they were hostile, heathen and part of Philip's forces?"

"No."

"No?"

"They, too, were converted Indians living in praying towns."

He seemed to consider a moment. "And what's a praying town?"

"A town set up specifically for converted Indians, where they had to dress like whites, go to church, adopt civilized names—"

"*Civilized* names? What's that mean? What's a civilized name?"

"Tom, Dick or Harry."

"I see. Go on."

"They had to work at some sort of job, basket- or broom-making or fishing, give up signs of their savagery—"

"What were some signs of savagery they had to give up?"

"Long hair."

"And?"

"Going around naked in the summer."

"And?"

"And cutting out the live organs of their enemies and eating them in front of their eyes. Also, flaying alive, frying, roasting—"

"Thank you."

"—toasting, basting—"

"*Thank you.*"

There was a rumble in the courtroom. The judge hit his gavel.

"So we have four hundred peaceful Christians in what amounts to a concentration camp on a confiscated island. How many did you say died?"

"I didn't. You did."

"How many would *you* say? As an expert."

"Roughly a quarter."

"A hundred or so?"

"Yes."

"And how did they die? Armed insurrection?"

"Mr. Safford," the judge warned.

"I'm sorry, Your Honor. How *did* they die, Mr. Wheelwright?"

"Exposure, malnutrition, starvation."

"And they were buried off the island?"

"No, on the island."

"*On* the island? How do you know that?"

"Archaeological evidence."

"Of what sort?"

"Skeletons."

"Can you be sure they're Indian skeletons? Is there a difference between an Indian skeleton and a Caucasian or Negroid?"

"Yes."

"What?"

"The bone structure is slightly different."

"Where? Can you illustrate for the courtroom?"

"I could if there was an Indian present."

"Let's just say *you're* an Indian, Mr. Wheelwright," Philip said over the clamor. "Demonstrate for us."

"There's no need to," I answered. "It isn't by bone structure that we know the skeletons on Mavericke's Island are Indian skeletons."

"How, then?"

"By the manner in which they were buried."

"And how is that?"

"They were buried in traditional Algonkian fashion. By chemical analysis of the surrounding earth we know the graves were lined with bark, the body itself is curled in the fetal position, the head toward the west, the fingers in the mouth, all symbolizing spiritual rebirth. There's often a placental red ocher surrounding them as well."

"I'm puzzled," he said, putting on a face. "Is that a Christian burial?"

"No, Algonkian, as I've said."

"Then they weren't Christian Indians, after all? I mean when push came to shove?"

"Evidently not."

"In the end they returned to their native ways?"

"Yes."

"Repudiated the teachings of the Apostle to the Indians?"

"None of this means Mavericke's Island is yours, Philip."

"Died as Indians on Indian land?"

"It just means you're a big showboater!"

"Your Honor," Philip said to the judge, "would you direct the witness to answer my questions?"

"Which questions are those, Mr. Safford?" the judge responded. "They sound like statements to me. And I'm surprised the state is not objecting."

The Bureau lawyer got to his feet. "The state is letting Mr. Safford have his day in court, Your Honor." And with a dismissive gesture, he sat back down.

"I'm finished anyway, Your Honor," Philip said and started to walk back to the plaintiff's table. "Except for one thing," he said, snapping his fingers at his memory and turning back. "May I, Your Honor?"

"Proceed."

"Mr. Wheelwright," he said, drawing up to me again. "Would you say that you are what is commonly called a Boston Brahmin?"

"Meaning?" I asked.

"Meaning a member of the Boston genealogical elite."

I looked for an objection from the state's table but none came. "I suppose so," I answered.

"As an expert on Boston social and cultural history, would you say that a stereotypical trait of the Boston Brahmin is the lionization of family ancestry?"

"That's the stereotype."

"Are you, Mr. Wheelwright, related to the Captain Isaac

Wheelwright who you've already testified was responsible in main for the internment camp on Mavericke's Island?"

"Not directly."

"No?"

"No."

"But he *is* related to you? He's perched in your family tree somewhere?"

There was laughter.

"Yes."

"Thank you, Mr. Wheelwright."

And that was it. The next witness was called.

· 4 ·

That night, a brick was thrown through one of the windows in Hetty's apartment. There was a note attached to it, but the handwriting was illegible.

· 5 ·

"Hetty," I said that same night in bed while she slept, "how can you even think it? He's the very testament of our love, growing inside you and asking only to be let into the world. I can't understand it. The very idea makes me shake. And yet it's you—sweet *you*, Hetty—who's thinking it. It's wrong. It's wrong, wrong, wrong! Baby John dropped in a wastebasket! Don't you understand that this is the real thing— the real thing, Hetty—and that it's time to stand up for life and love?"

And I put my hand on her belly, feeling the hum of the tiny soul inside.

"You have at least one rooter out here, Baby John," I said. "Though I am surrounded by Indians, I will see you through. The world is all right if you're choosy enough. And there are aspects of it—let's say, acorns plunking on the roof in summer—that are downright beautiful. You'll see. This is merely your first encounter with something that doesn't have your best interests at heart. But you concentrate on growing your arms and legs—two of each—and your fingers—five on each hand—and ditto your toes, and let me take care of your mother. I will keep her locked up for nine months if I have to. But I promise you, you'll get your turn."

The next morning I went out to get a pane of glass to reglaze the window and instead brought back a big color-photo book called *The Miracle of Life* that showed babies *in utero* at one month, six weeks, two months . . .

"Look," I said and hauled Hetty over to the couch. I pointed at the pictures and turned the pages. She watched with a look of suspicion, distant and a little angry. "First he was like this, and then he was like this. And now he's like this. And he's doing it all on his own. He *knows*. He *knows* how to do it. What to grow, and when and where and how much. Just like *that!*" And I snapped my fingers.

"How do you know it's a he?" she asked, her voice cool and bitten.

"I can *feel* it."

"What if it's a she?"

"No sweat," I answered. "I like shes too. I like you."

She looked back at the book. "Do you know how they take photos like that?"

"Microscopic photography?"

She shook her head. "Those are aborted fetuses. They take the photos afterward." And she got up and went into the twins' room.

· 6 ·

I went to the sperm bank down in the Fens and told them I wanted to donate. The pay was twenty-four dollars a shot they said, but I had to bring in a sample to be tested first, sperm count, etc. I told them they could keep their money, I was after populating the world with little Wheelwrights.

"Because we're the elect," I said with just enough of a

smile so they'd think I was joking. While they got the forms ready, I told the pretty LPN who came with a specimen jar about ancestor John and Oliver Cromwell and the soccer field.

I tested out in the ninety-ninth percentile.

• 7 •

Back at Mrs. Steele's, I left out things of mine for Hetty to steal, but it was no go.

• 8 •

On leap day I got her friendlied up enough to come out to the island for a picnic, invited the twins too to show I was in a democratic mood. I wanted to show her that we could still be happy, that we were still right for each other, that Baby John could only make us more right. I bought Lorraine Swiss cheese and Genoa salami at the corner market, some rolls and dill pickles, California raisins for the twins, also some Twinkies, a bottle of Spanish wine, some greenish-looking oranges, a little box of maple-sugar candies, paper napkins, paper plates, paper cups and a pineapple.

"Why a pineapple?" Hetty wanted to know as we walked through the Common.

"Because it's a New England symbol of welcome and good times." And at that I gave her a sly look. "Colonial sea captains used to stick a pineapple on their picket fences after returning from a voyage to the South Seas to let all the neighbors know that the venture was a success and to invite them over for the best pickings."

"Is that why I see pathetic-looking pineapples nowadays on phony colonial buildings, banks and such?"

I gave her a kiss for that.

On the sail over she worked the jib the way she used to

do when we were kids. The twins sat one at the fore of the boat, the other at the stern: "the seesaw principle," as Hetty remarked. We docked the boat and made our way up the muddy path. On either side of us patches of snow were still sleeping under the bushes and in the ravines. The pussy willows were out, early this year, popping fat and fuzzy on their stems, and the crocuses I'd planted around the dooryard were pushing their toy faces through the thawing earth. Inside the house I opened all the windows and showed Hetty around. She hadn't been out all winter, so the buttery and the pantry, the bed (double, after all) in the downstairs chamber and the rough oak table and chairs in the kitchen were new to her. I showed her the unfinished upstairs, almost said how another bedroom could be made up there, but thought better of it. Downstairs again I got a fire going in the fireplace to take the damp away, and outside, stuck the pineapple on a stake. Hetty got together a bouquet of pussy willows and last year's milkweed pods, showing them to the twins and getting them to feel the pussy willows' soft faces. ("Knives," Isabel said.) While we laid the table and made the sandwiches, I treated everyone to "April Is in My Love," all four verses.

"Which mistress is that?" Hetty wanted to know. I told her I only had one . . . and April was in her.

We sat at the open windows with the fresh air blowing in, kept the door open and the fire going, cold and warm at the same time. The twins fed each other raisins and chatted about the world of seesaws. They were sitting under a window so the tops of their heads were lit with halos of sunlight. Out the back window, I could see nothing but ocean and sky, the great pure blue of Heaven reflected in the reeling black-blue of Earth. There was such a smell of salt and muddy fecundity all around that my heart ached. I felt all filled up with the beauty of things, the smells, the sights, the sounds. I wanted to eat things—I don't mean my sandwich and orange and maybe one of the twins' Twinkies—but everything I saw and smelled: the mud and the salt sea, the stiff milkweed and the soft pussy willows. I thought: This is it. This is Paradise. Mavericke, the island, Boston, half-lap dovetails, vast America, Hetty, the earth, the air, the ocean, the fire: I am in a world of beauty and sense and love. I was so stuffed with happiness, I thought I would burst. Over in the corner the twins cooed and croodled like pigeons. Hetty was taking tiny bites of her sandwich, her overbite making her wrestle with the salami. Outside I thought I saw Mavericke and Amias walking arm in arm along the rise of the hill next over. Was this the world, then? Was this what the world could be if you were picky enough? Was this the world sweet John Jenney Wheelwright could grow up in? I could see him in the dooryard, mud-loved and luscious, dungarees cuffed to his shins, a Wheelwrightian tangle of hair, the sun beaming down on him like the face of God, the grass green for him, the sea salty for him, the sky blue for him. I almost said it to Hetty, almost said that this was the world I wanted my son to grow up in, this was the world he *would* grow up in, because the very purity of his soul could create no other. But I didn't. Instead I reached out and touched her hand.

"I love you," I said.

She smiled at me and kept chewing on her sandwich.

The music of the spheres rang all around me.

But afterwards—in the boat back—I was reduced to a normal-sized soul and I couldn't help myself:

"You wouldn't really do it, would you, Hetty?"

She turned her eyes over the gray waves. "I don't know."

"When will you know?"

"April ninth," she said. "If I'm going to do it, I'll have to do it by April ninth."

· 9 ·

March 9

I tried to talk to her, tried to get her to tell me really, really, really why she was so afraid. A father has rights too,

I said. She told me it was *her* body. I told her it was *my* son.
She told me her first allegiance was to the twins; she couldn't
take care of the twins and be a good mother too. She'd married against her will, she wasn't going to become a mother
against her will too. I told her all right then, what was she
waiting for? Why didn't she do it? Go ahead, do it! I said.
If it's against your will, do it! And I went and got my book
to show her what a three-month fetus looks like. She knocked
it out of my hands and ran out of the house.

I took to following her after that. If she went into a doctor's office or toward the hospital . . .

March 15

I told her *I'd* bring him up. I'd do everything. *Everything.*
We'd live out on the island, just the two of us. He wouldn't
even have to know she was his mother. She could visit, like
an aunt or something.

March 19

I followed her—left the twins by themselves and, keeping a block between us, followed her down Commonwealth
Avenue, across the Charles into Cambridge, down Massachusetts Avenue onto Inman Street to The Susan B. Anthony Clinic.

"Why?" I cried, bursting through the door into the re-
ception room. "Why does it follow that a woman who wanted
the vote would want her name on an abortion clinic?"

There were maybe five women in the room. Hetty was
standing at a Dutch door that marked off the receptionist's
desk. She'd spun around at my voice.

"Call the police, Gail," a nurse said, coming up behind
the receptionist. "We've got another one."

Hetty flushed violently, and then tucking her head in as
if she were making against the wind, walked past me and
out the door. I crossed to the receptionist.

"Did she have an appointment?" I asked.

The nurse stepped between us. She had a face like a
hatchet and breasts like splitting wedges. "Patients' records
are confidential."

"Did she have an appointment?" I cried, and I leaned over

the Dutch door and grabbed her by the lapels with both fists. She didn't bat an eye.

"Assault is serious business, mister."

"So is infanticide."

"She was just asking for information," the receptionist said. She looked between the two of us and then suddenly burst out crying. The nurse and I both looked at her.

"Gail!"

"What's up with you?" I asked.

"Information," she said again and held out a pamphlet to me. "Family planning," she sobbed.

I let go of the nurse and looked at the pamphlet. *FAMILY PLANNING* it said in big block letters, and it showed a happy family of three. I look it out of politeness and left.

March 29

I couldn't sleep. My heart felt as if it were about to burst through my ribs. My legs were shaking and my eyes were stinging with I didn't know what. Beside me Hetty slept as if there were no bombé secretary boiling two floors above her, no such thing as *Mus musculus* or the devil in the dooryard. I listened to her breathing, tried to breathe in time with her, but I kept seeing the tumbling, evil dreams of Mrs. Steele overhead. I saw them on the backs of my eyelids, like movies. In the next room, I could hear the quick, shallow breathing of the twins sleeping wide-eyed in their bed, could hear them listening to me listen to them. I felt as if the room were singing with darts, darts from Mrs. Steele's black soul, from *Mus musculus,* from the twins' lifeless eyes, darts piercing the paling of my mortise-and-tenon joints and stinging me, stinging sleeping Hetty, stinging unborn Baby John. I wanted to roll over on top of Hetty, to shield her with a second layer of muscle and bone, wanted to wake her and tell her for the hundredth time that this was *our baby* we were talking about, even thought for a wild moment of wrapping her up in the bedspread and carrying her down to the *Pilgrim's Progress.* Instead I did some sit-ups, hoping the bouncing mattress would wake her, but she's a heavy sleeper.

I got up and started walking along the walls of the apartment, walking along the far perimeter of everything—the
bedroom, the living room, the kitchen, the twins' room—as
if putting down a scent, a moral palisade, around everything and everyone in the apartment. I did it three times,
climbing over things that got in the way, walking like an
acrobat along the back of the twins' couch, stepping on Hetty's pillow, on mine, walking into the shower cabinet, into
the bathtub. I ended up in the twins' room, out of breath
and with my eyes still stinging.

They lay in the middle of their bed, arms and legs em-
broiled, hair embrambled, their eyes like flat disks reflecting
back the streetlight that streamed in through the window.
(Yes, they sleep with their eyes open.) They looked at once
unconscious and on guard. I could never escape the sense
of a stunned intelligence holding its breath behind their dead
eyes, engaged in some killer version of hide-and-seek, trying
to bilk the world into believing they didn't exist, and terri-
fied that at any moment the world would wise up to their
ruse, call "touch-a-bye!" and blast them into nonexistence.
In Hetty's notebooks there was the strange case of Julia J.—
a verbal autistic like the twins—who was obsessed with
weather. She had always to have a television or radio tuned
to the weather report and be near a window where she could
watch the blue or red or gray sky. Her psychologists and
workers were bewildered until some graduate student with
a knack for codes and crossword puzzles suggested that
weather separated spelled *we eat her*. Julia J. was watching
the world in order to intercept the first notice of her annihilation.

What "touch-a-bye" were the twins awaiting? What key
or clue of *we eat her* was hidden in their litany of "seesaw"
and "one-eighty" and "no deposit/no return"? Hetty studied
her notebooks like a codecracker, columns and columns of
words tagged with whatever variable was present when they
were spoken: the clothes they were wearing, whether Mrs.
Steele was home upstairs, the food they'd just eaten or were
about to eat, whether they'd gone to the bathroom that day

(and at my suggestion: whether the shadow of the Hancock building was over the house or not). Some words she'd seemed to solve; there were numerous examples of twoness, of twinness—bride and groom, bicycle, Ping-Pong, Vermont/New Hampshire—which seemed to be their way of naming themselves, of keeping their selves authentic, valid, real, without calling direct attention to themselves (and inviting the world's apocalyptic "touch-a-bye!"). She had taken a scaled-down list to my father back in the fall and asked him if he could help her find correlations, patterns, but he was so used to trying to codify the natural world that the introduction of the *un*natural left him dazed. So she took her list to a prominent crossword-puzzlist (a Harvard semiotician) who'd told her he couldn't make them into a pattern, but had whipped up a crossword puzzle with some of them. Would she have dinner with him? She told me she hadn't gone, but the crossword puzzle was taped on the wall above her writing table. Eight across: *Chinese diplomacy;* twelve down: *I ——, I ——, I sawed.*

"No deposit/no return" I said to the twins in the dark bedroom. "Ping-Pong. Bicycle." Then, feeling a dart of cruelty, I whispered: "Touch-a-bye!" But they just kept staring blankly up at me, asleep or not asleep, I couldn't tell. I sat at the foot of the bed and reached up and touched one of their ankles under the covers, then a shin, but neither of them stirred. In the streetlight their faces were like loaves of dough set on their pillow, their eyes the glassy death and blindness of a mannequin's. If their litany of words *was* a code, then it was a code that was beyond Hetty, beyond me, no mere *we eat her* (or Sammy T.'s terror of the queerly chiastic *Connect-i-cut*), but a jam and tangle of nerves and senses and feelings so extreme, so encrypted, that their unraveling was hopeless, more than hopeless: potentially a trap for the unraveler's own nerves and feelings. And if it *wasn't* a code (because a code meant the presence at least of some vestigial flame of logic, understanding, will, humanity), if it *wasn't*, then they were—well, they were what I claimed they were: children of Mrs. Steele, twentieth-century Pearls, poisonous flowers growing in the shadow of the Hancock building. And how—*how!*—could my squealing, panting, puffing, gurgling, sucking, blue-faced John Jenney Wheelwright be inoculated against that poison? How could he stave off the secret holocaust of *Mus musculus,* of seesaws and no deposit—no return? Wasn't he even now being infiltrated? *Right now!* Infected? Fouled? Weren't those same singing darts that I had felt lying beside Hetty singing after him? Seeking out his dear soul? His tiny, just-formed arms, his legs, his hands? I wanted to have hold of him, to hide him, to carry him out of Mrs. Steele's house, away from the Hancock building, down through the city to my white sailboat. I wanted to be gone, back on my island where I could feel the strong and honest joinery of my house around me. I wanted to talk to Mavericke, hear his clean and fine voice, hear him say that goodness was its own weapon. Hadn't he tied himself to Amias's loom?

Back in Hetty's room, I stripped my pajamas off and put my street clothes on. I was in such a swivet, I left my shoelaces untied. I crossed to the bed, and then carefully—depressing the mattress as much as I could—slipped my hands under Hetty. Her skin was hot with sleep. I rolled her up onto her side just enough to tuck the bedspread under her. Her eyelids fluttered and for an instant I thought she was going to wake up, but she didn't. Slowly, carefully, I started to lift her, cradling her head in the crook of one arm, her knees folding over the other. When I tried to wrap the bedspread all the way around her, her eyes opened.

"Sweetheart?" she said.

"Just rolling you over onto your side of the bed," I whispered. "Go back to sleep."

She smiled and closed her eyes. "You're picking me up," she said. "That's what you're doing."

I waited, but that was it: She fell back asleep.

Outside, the fresh air was like freedom. I carried her parkward along Commonwealth Avenue, the gas streetlamps decanting their nineteenth-century light on us, and the wide boulevard empty but for an occasional taxi gliding past. In the Public Gardens I retraced the steps we'd taken that night after Locke-Ober's—across the fairy-tale bridge that straddled the duck pond, across Charles Street and over the dark sward of the Common. Whenever we passed under a lamp, I looked down at her. She was like a sleeping child in my arms, her eyelashes curling over the tops of her cheeks and her forehead frowning with the effort of sleep. It made me all giddy inside. I couldn't get enough of her, watching the shadows and light pass in turn over her face, waiting for each lamp. I was looking at her so much, I tripped on a tree root.

"Sweetheart?" she said, starting awake. She tried to lift her head.

"It's all right," I whispered, bending over her. "I'm taking you out to the island. I'm stealing you. It's romantic." And I kissed her.

"The twins . . ." she said.

"I left a note," I lied.

Her face clouded.

"For Mrs. Steele," I said. "I left a note for Mrs. Steele."

She blinked several times, as if trying to force herself awake. "I don't have any clothes on," she said.

"You're all right."

"Aren't I heavy?"

"Light," I said. "As light as love."

"You're stealing me," she said and I could feel her relax. "You're stealing me. It's romantic."

And she closed her eyes again.

I carried her past the Park Street Church, white spire dueling the black sky, down into the financial district. She opened her eyes from time to time, looking dreamily around herself, smiling at me and asking every couple of streets where we were now. We made it into the gritty regions of the harborside, walking along the old brick warehouses, along the railroad sidings embedded in the tar. The moon showed itself around the corner of a building, yellowed like an antique and resting on the water. At the sight of it, Hetty sighed.

When we got to the marina, I laid her on the port gunwale seat, gave her a lifejacket for a pillow. I got the drop keel down and the mainsail up, left the jib in its locker. As the breeze pulled us away, Hetty lifted herself up onto her elbow.

"How beautiful it is," she said. She was looking at the skyline behind us.

"Lot's wife," I warned.

But she kept looking. The water burned red and yellow all around us. When I looked myself—looked at the land dropping away northward toward Salem, southward toward Cohasset—I thought it looked like a long electric serpent, the car lights moving on the interstate like the slither of its spine, its dark belly resting on the harbor water. I turned back around and bore toward Mavericke's Island where Leo was making his spring leap across the southern heavens.

We made a bridal night on Mavericke's straw tick, and when we fell asleep, we fell asleep entwined like the twins, legs and arms and hair.

And it was in that position that we woke the next morning . . . with King Philip pointing a gun at our heads.

CHAPTER
15

A TRIAL IN THE WILDERNESS: A Narrative of My Recent Captivity at the Hands of King Philip; Including: selected passages from A Narrative of the Aweful Methods and Mercies of God in the War with Satan's Red Armie, by Captain Isaac Wheelwright, reprinted from the First Edition, 1678

FIRST DAY, March 30

At first my head was so soggy, I couldn't tell if this was real life or just another dream. He had on a business suit, and he was standing in front of a window so the sunlight shining through the oilpaper made a rosy aureole around his head. For an instant I thought I was still back at Mrs. Steele's. I thought I was on the couch, and I wondered what the twins were doing dreaming *my* dream. Because this *was* my dream: wilderness, Indian, gun. Finally I looked at Hetty to see if she was seeing what I was seeing.

She was.

"You're not supposed to be here," I managed after a while.

"You're not either."

It was Philip's voice. And the gun was one of those light-

221

weight modern machine guns, Israeli or French or something. There were two others in the room, standing behind Philip—one of them a lean and mouthy bastard I recognized from the trial, the other a buffalo-headed guy I'd never seen before. They had the same kind of guns as Philip.

"So what're you supposed to be?" I said finally.

"Me?" Philip said, and he shifted his weight and seemed to consider. "I'm a marauding Indian."

"Couldn't wait for the judge to tell you it was no go, Indian giver?"

He held his gun up, turning it so he could view it from different angles. "I don't know how to use this very well, Wheelwright, but I think I could manage to part your twentieth-century body from its seventeenth-century soul." And he aimed it at me, up one leg to the crotch, then to my chest, my heart, my head, and then back down. He let a significant look linger on me and then turned to Hetty. "Don't you sleep in a nightgown, Mrs. Wheelwright?"

She was lying beside me still. The sheet had slipped down when I'd sat up so the knuckle of her shoulder was bared. She kept her eyes fixed on Philip, and slowly, without a trace of fear or anger—and without answering him—pulled the sheet back over her.

"I was under the impression," he said, "that you spent all of your time with those retarded kids of yours."

Still, she didn't answer.

"Let's cut the shit and move it," the skinny Indian said behind Philip. The buffalo-headed one just stood in the corner by the door, his gun pointed at us and his eyes hidden in shadow.

"I only mention this," Philip went on in his lawyer's voice (whether to goad us or the Indian behind him I couldn't tell), "because all winter long in my planning I had rigorously tried to keep the indictable offenses down. Kidnapping, hostage-taking, et cetera. In short"—and here he looked at Hetty again—"I was counting on your incestuous cunt keeping Young Goodman Wheelwright here in town. We expected a vacant island."

"They're not retarded," Hetty said.

Philip smiled, and with the barrel of his gun, dragged the sheet a little off her.

"And now we find it not vacant."

He pulled it until one of her breasts was bare.

"Knock it off, Philip," I said.

He bared the other. Hetty just lay there, cool and ungiving. I reached over and snatched the sheet back.

"Let's cut the clever shit!" the skinny Indian said. "We're on a timetable!"

Philip gazed a moment longer at Hetty and then turned around. "Did Vietnam teach you to talk to your officers like that?"

"You ain't my officer. Now cut the shit and let's go."

I heard the safety catch on Philip's gun click off. "What I am," he said, "is Metacomet. King Philip." And he let go a burst of fire. The wall two feet down from the skinny Indian splintered with bullet holes. My ears rang and the air smelled of burnt oil. I looked at the wounded wood and felt ill.

"When this is all over," Philip was saying to the skinny Indian, "and we're in court trying to save our asses, I'll work extra hard for you." He straightened his tie and turned to the silent Indian in the corner. "Get these two dressed and bring them down to the dock."

And he left without looking at us again.

*   *   *

My first guess was that there were thirty of them in all. I could see them up on Fort Bentley, at the north point of the island, down by the Parks and Recreation building. They had the Quonset hut jimmied open and my propane generator hauled out. I saw the lean black carcass of a machine gun taken out of a crate and set on its spidery legs. All around the island, at regular points, they were throwing up breastworks, setting up lookout points, gun emplacements. I had to keep looking across at Hetty to see if this was really happening, to see if she was really there besides me, dressed the way she was (in Amias's clothes: petticoat, gray gown, the cap pulled on with a grim smile), and for the reason she was (my stealing her naked the night before), picking her way carefully down the path in her bare feet, the ties of the cap flapping about her head and the gown catching from time to time on the bushes. Down below us, the tour boat sat at the dock, its diesels shut down and its top deck cluttered with cartons and crates. I could see one of the line's captains—a cranky old bastard—on the lower deck. The hatch to the engine compartment was thrown open and there were tools spread around on the decking. When he caught sight of Hetty and me coming down the path, he ran topside.

"Wheelwright!" he shouted. "Are you in with these bastard Indians?"

As if to answer for me, our guard gave me a shove from behind with his rifle butt. I heard Hetty say something to him behind me, and I turned in time to see a crisp look of hate pass between them. They stood a moment poised against one another—Hetty holding her gown up so the brilliant red of the petticoat showed, and the Indian's face pickling with anger.

"Indictable offenses," I said and hurried back to Hetty. I took her hand and led her down onto the dock. The Indian stayed where he was, at the narrow throat that led to the path.

"They screwed up my radio and took apart my blower assembly," the captain said. He was standing at the railing. I gave the *Pilgrim's Progress* the once-over: She looked all right, unharmed.

"They took apart my blower assembly so it'd take me a half hour to put it back together. A delaying tactic." He turned to the Indian and shouted. "*A delaying tactic.* That was real smart, Tonto. Just like in the movies. Only I can't see well enough to put it back together." And he pointed at his eyes. The Indian just gazed back at him.

"So now what?" I said. "Do we have your permission to get in our boat and go?"

He shook his head.

"What, then?"

He didn't answer.

"Tonto Goes to College," the captain shouted. He'd gone back down to the engine compartment. "Did you see him?" he called. "The one in the suit?" He picked up a wrench and then threw it down. "Do you know anything about diesel engines, Wheelwright?"

I shook my head.

"Well, you don't have to know. Just come down here and I'll tell you what goes where." He waved a rachet around. "I just can't see close up like I used to."

"If it's a boat, and it doesn't go under God's power," I answered, "I don't touch it."

"God's power?"

"Wind," I said.

"So who makes diesel fuel?"

"Not God," I said.

"Who else then?"

"Not *my* God," I corrected.

They started unloading the boat, coming down the hill in twos and threes and hauling up cartons of Campbell's soup, Froot Loops, toilet paper, hamburger rolls. There were crated five-gallon water jugs, big lemonade coolers, sleeping bags, tents, Coleman lanterns. Philip came and stood on the path above us, watching his men work and gazing harborward every now and then, keeping an eye out for anything that looked suspicious. When a television was unloaded I asked him if he was planning on watching reruns of *Cochise.*

"No," he answered. "I plan on watching myself. Every night at six."

And he turned around and headed back up the path.

"How!" the tour-boat captain was saying to any Indian whose eye he could catch. *"How!"*

We stood and waited. I asked Hetty if she was all right; she batted the ties on her cap as answer. When one of the Indians asked from the gangway if we'd had a good night's sleep and then laughed, I knew the thuggy voice was among us. I recognized others from the trial, one or two even from the old days at the Squibnocket site. But there were a dozen or more I didn't know.

"There are no women," I said to Hetty. "At least I don't see any."

She just nodded. "I'm hungry."

We stood and waited.

"Hey, Wheelwright," the captain said. He was smoking a cigarette now. "Help me with the goddamn engine, will you? Half an hour and we can get out of here."

I turned to our guard. He'd moved off a couple of yards, out of the way of the stevedores.

"Can I help?" I asked him.

He shook his head no.

"For Christ's sake, Tonto!" the captain said; and then he called up the hill. "Hey, you! Head honcho Tonto!" Philip had come partway back down the path. "Either get that asshole Indian who took apart my blower assembly to come back here or let Wheelwright help me."

Philip turned his gaze on me. "Are you an authority on diesel engines too, Wheelwright?"

"Not me," I answered.

He looked out over the water toward Boston—nothing coming—and then made a gesture with his thumb for me to go aboard.

Down by the engine compartment I knelt and looked at the monster. It was all warm metal and oily dirt, its forehead taken apart so the clean machined surfaces where metal occluded metal were bared to the air. There were parts spread around on the decking, heavy metal housings, rubber gaskets, bolts, washers, a mesh filter. The captain knelt beside me and started me on what he called the blower rotors.

"So what did they do?" I asked. "Hijack you?" I was thinking of indictable offenses.

"No, they hired me."

"Hired you?"

"They hired me! Someone called and said they had some equipment to bring out to Mavericke's Island. How much would it be? I thought maybe it was you and your archaeologists."

"It wasn't."

"No shit."

I busied myself with getting a gasket on squarely. "So what do you mean? You mean they just came in a U-Haul truck with all this stuff and loaded it on your boat?"

"That's right."

"In broad daylight?"

"Why not? Is there a law in this commonwealth against loading stuff on a boat in broad daylight?"

"Machine guns, yes."

"*I* didn't know they were machine guns."

"Did they pay you?"

"Yes, with a check," he said, and he took the check out of his shirt pocket and showed it to me. It had Philip's name and address and telephone number printed at the top, and it was made out for three hundred dollars.

"Do you suppose it's good?" he said, biting his lip.

I started on the intake adapter.

*   *   *

Here beginneth the Narration.

I was taken whilst bathing in the Lord's Streame. I was in my Innocence, as was Adam when the Serpent first whisper'd to his weaker Selfe. They came upon soften'd feet, so that I saw them only when they stood before me. I spoke to them as I would have of late, before the scent of Hostilitie had been breath'd through the Aire, but they made rough motions for me to come out of the water. When I made to pull on my cloathes, they push'd me along, making it known to me that there was no time. Since they could not speak English, I said to them in the savage tongue: "Sun aiyeuehteaenūog aūog Swansea?" (Or as we might say: "Do the soldiers go to Swansea?") But they push'd and sign'd me to go on in silence. I did so, feeling the first pinch and bite of my Captivitie in the sharp stones and nettles on my naked feet.

This was the twentieth of June of that aweful year, 1675. We had had some warning of the Mindes of the Indians, for it was reported on the eleventh that the Inhabitants of Mount Hope, under the proud Savage who was known to us as King Philip, had sent their Squaws and children to take refuge across the Narragansett Bay. Too, Rumor was among us that warriors from Cowesit and Pocasset had join'd Philip at his Seat on Mount Hope. We were in great Distresse, for our new town of Swansea was at the narrowest point of land leading to this peninsula, and we knew that should the Lord permit Satan the Rule of his Savages, we would be the first to feel the Smart.

And thus we did. March'd naked through the wildernesse, I had immediate worrie for my Wife and son who were not five hundred yards distant. But the Lord saved for later his Afflictions of them. I was taken down the peninsula and held there for three days. I was not at first mistreated, given cook'd bear's meat and Indian potatos (what we call groundnuts). But when they offer'd me garments to put on, a breechclout and moccasins, I denied them. And when they pursu'd me, still I denied them. For should I dye in my Triale, how could I come before my Lord in the cloathes of a Heathen?

On the night of the third day I witness'd such a Furie of Heathens, I had thought the gates of Hell open'd and Satan's dark Kingdome establish'd here on our green Earth. Nothing in Newengland's evil Mayday Revels might compare. They dress'd themselves in what I might call their Finerie and, with faces painted, danc'd and howl'd and hopp'd about a fire to singing and knocking upon a kettle. My master (as I must call the Savage who captur'd me) was among them. King Philip, too, dress'd in a Holland shirt, with great cuffe laces sew'd down from the back as if to make a tail; he had shillings hanging from his garters and girdles of wampum upon his head and shoulders. There were necklaces and bracelets of bone and some sort of metal, jewels in the women's ears. They danc'd and howl'd, the fire at their center licking them with devils' tongues, the embers cracking and popping and the smoke sending a dirty cloud heavenward—if Heaven be still there, for it was a starless night and I felt as Jonah must have in Leviathan, stolen from the sighte of the Lord.

That night I slept upon an Indian pallet, and whilst I slept I dream'd the most horrid Dreame. I dream'd I was cloath'd in the breechclout and paint of the Savages around me, that my soule was the evil red colour of the Savage's soules. And I dream'd I had cut out the Hearte of my Master, cut it out before his dying Eyes, and ate of it, that I might take in his Courage, his Fortitude in Battel, and that I might have the blacke Hearte of an Evil Man. And as I ate, his blood stain'd my skinne, stain'd my Tongue and my Lips, and ran down the sides of my Mouthe, until when I was done, when I was well-feast'd, my entire Bodie was red, inside and out. And in my Ears was a hellish Howl, a Howl that I did not know was my own voice, thick with Bloode and Lust and the Wildernesse.

*   *   *

Half an hour later, the engines were rumbling under us like the devil's foundry. Philip came on board and handed the captain a sealed envelope for the police. He motioned for Hetty to come up as well, but I told him we were going in the sailboat.

"You'll go the way I say you'll go," he said.

"You've got the gun," I conceded, "but if you're smart, you'll let me take away the one means your less-loyal followers have of getting off the island."

He seemed to consider a moment, and then with a smile that implied more of a brotherhood between us than I was comfortable with, motioned with his gun for me to go.

We got the sails rigged, the rudder in, and while the tour boat backed and farted water out its pump dales, swept cleanly away from the dock. When we got a hundred feet out Hetty called back: "See you in court!" and made a gesture unbecoming a lady. I tacked and came about as soon as we were out of rifle range, and then instead of heading cityward as the tour boat was doing, started sailing counter-clockwise around the island.

"Reconnoitering," I said when Hetty gave me a question-ing look.

"Reconnoitering for what?" she wanted to know.

"I don't know," I said and shrugged. "But when the po-lice come, I'm going to be here."

We slipped along the rim of the island. It was a breezy day, salty and with scuddy rags of clouds drifting across the water. As best I could, I made a quick audit of the island. The dock was cleared now, the equipment and supplies hauled uphill to the Quonset hut. I could see three or four Indians kneeling about the base of the Parks and Recrea-tion building—planting explosives?—and another crew up by Mavericke's house. I maneuvered a little closer for a bet-ter look, but someone—I couldn't see who or where—fired a warning shot, and I tacked away.

"Let's go," said Hetty.

"No."

"Why? Why stay here?"

"Because they shot holes in my house, that's why."

I went on with my inventory. There were only two or three out on the battlements at Fort Bentley (which faced the ocean, not the harbor), a gun emplacement on the northwest brow of the island (with nobody minding it), an-other gun in the low dell that swept down to the tide rocks, a third by the dig. When we came around past the docks again, someone shouted out to us, but I couldn't hear what they said.

"Let's go," Hetty said again. "I've got to get back to the house. This is dangerous."

"*I'm* dangerous."

"But you don't have a gun."

"This is *my* island," I said.

We started around again. Hetty strapped a life jacket on for warmth. I asked her to put one on me too, but she told me to get it myself, and then took her cap off and stowed it in the port locker. I started working in toward the island again, carefully, still coming about, but slipping in ten feet with each tack. No one shot at us this time. No one seemed even to be watching us now.

"This is my island," I said again.

We arced around the stone-and-earth battlements of Fort Bentley.

"I put all my money and all my heart into that house."

Again, the unmanned machine gun.

"I didn't do it for some one sixteenth of an Indian to come and take it all."

The low dell; the dig.

"Goddamn it! That's the last piece of pure earth in all of America!"

And with that I hard-ruddered around and started clockwise back around the island.

"Put a life jacket on me," I told Hetty.

"What?"

"A life jacket, goddamn it! Put a life jacket on me!" And I kicked the locker where the jackets were kept. "You're my goddamn wife! Do something wifely for once! Do what I say for once!"

She looked at me with astonishment, and then slid down her seat to the locker. She opened it, took out a jacket and threw it overboard. Then she slid back down her seat.

She folded her arms across her chest.

I belayed the mainsail, and then, keeping the rudder steady with my knee, leaned over and pulled out the last life jacket. I got it over one arm, then the other, and then one of the two buckles buckled.

"What're you doing?" Hetty asked.

I could hear a helicopter coming from the mainland.

"What're you doing?"

Whock-whock-whock.

"Get ready to take the helm," I said and steered toward the island.

"What're you doing?"

Whock-whock-whock.

I could see it, the machine gun on the northwest brow, still unmanned. It was about a hundred feet in from the shore—first a rocky upslope, then an easy grassy rise. The nearest Indian was a hundred yards away from it. He was looking at the helicopter.

"Wright!"

MDC-127 the helicopter said on its underside. When it passed overhead, the rotors screwed up my sails for an instant.

"Get ready to take the helm," I said.

"Wright."

Two hundred feet.

"Keep an eye out. If anyone starts toward that gun, tell me."

One hundred fifty feet.

"I'm going to clip along where that upslope is. When I jump, push the rudder hard to port and you'll clear."

"For Christ's sake!"

Whock-whock-whock.

"The surf!" she said. "What about the surf?"

I looked at where the waves broke against the rock. There was a headland that rose next to the upslope, brutal and unclimbable.

"I've got my life jacket on."

Fifty feet.

Whock-whock-whock.

"Get ready!" I kicked my shoes off.

"I hope you drown!"

Twenty-five feet.

Twenty feet.

Whock-whock-whock.

Fifteen. Ten.

"Go!" I cried, and I threw the rudder hard to port and jumped.

The life jacket smacked me in the chin when I hit. It kept me from going under, but before I could orient my-

self, a swell carried me toward the head. I got caught in a
tiny vortex and then spun out. I saw the top of a mast, a
sail luffing, and then I was being sucked down again. The
sky whirled overhead. I thought I heard a scream, then the
whock-whock of the helicopter, and down inside me somewhere I was saying: *"Indians, Indians!"* Or it was the surf
saying it: *"Indians, Indians!"* I fought against the undertow,
the deep liquid black under me, cold, like fingers pulling
me downward. My knee smashed into something. I tried to
grab for it, but it was gone. I swallowed some water, coughed
and swallowed some more. My life jacket was up about my
ears. I kicked and flailed and then out of nowhere, a swell
lifted me toward where the rocks swept down. I tried to
swim—*face down, stroke, face up, stroke*—but before I could
make any headway, a second swell came like the grace of
God and carried me clear to the shore. I banged my knee
again, and for an instant I didn't think I could make it up
the slippery rocks, but I managed to grab hold of some seaweed, get some purchase on a ledge that was still underwater, and pull myself up.

I lay in a tide pool a moment getting my breath. When
I looked around to see if everything was safe, I saw Hetty
trying to climb up the rocks behind me.

"What?" I said, and for an instant I couldn't move. "The
seaweed!" I cried and crawled down to her.

"You jerk!" she sputtered, taking my hand.

"What? What happened?"

I could see the *Pilgrim's Progress* fifty feet away, founder-
ing against the headland.

"Just throw the rudder hard to port!" she cried between
heaves.

"Your beautiful clothes!" I said with horror. "Amias's cap!"
And I looked to where my sailboat was listing.

"Fuck my beautiful clothes! I almost drowned!"

"My boat!"

"Fuck your boat!"

Her sails were luffing. She looked for all the world as if

she couldn't catch her breath, the boom swinging loose, and with each wave, her side grinding into the rock. I thought an instant of trying to make it back to her, but she was listing so much I knew she was taking on water. She'll go down, I thought. Amias's cap with her. And for a time I just lay panting and witless.

"Now what?" Hetty said.

Somewhere distant the helicopter was still reconnoitering.

"*Now what?*" she said again and jabbed me under the life jacket.

"I don't know," I said. I looked around. "Have we been seen?"

"I don't think so."

I tried to gauge sight lines from uphill. "I think the boat's hidden. They can't see it."

She nodded, still out of breath, staring at the ground.

"We've got to get that gun."

"Oh, Wright."

"We've *got* to."

"You don't even know how to use it," she said. "Even if you did, what're you going to do? Kill people?"

"I won't have to *use* it. I'll just *have* it."

"No," she said. "It's too dangerous."

"We don't have any choice now."

"Yes, we do. We could just hide someplace until the police come."

"This could go on for days, Hetty. We're wet. We're cold."

She started wringing out her gown.

"I'm going to make a run for it," I said.

"I'm staying here."

"It can't be two hundred feet. That way," I said, pointing to the grassy bluff of the headland. She grabbed another handful of her gown.

"I'm staying here."

I kept low, stooping as I made my way up the rocks, and then going on my hands and knees once I got into the shrubby thicket. I had to be ginger of my bare feet; one of my hands was scraped and the knee I'd banged on the rocks was stiffening. There was a fetid, stuffy smell so near the earth, the dead leaves still wet underneath from the winter, the milkweed and the Queen Anne's lace from last year brittle and colorless. I ran across some day-tourist's empty Budweiser can, then a weathered Twinkies wrapper and another can, and then, like a special providence, a little colony of wake-robins—early to be in bloom—their toylike faces peeping up at me out of the winter grass. I picked one for good luck.

When I reached the open land that led to the brow of the head, I stopped and, from behind a scrabble of laurel, surveyed the island as best I could. The machine gun was still there—a hundred feet now—still unmanned; I could see Mavericke's house and a band there in the dooryard, and on the hill distant someone pointing harborward; there were two or three still up on the battlements of Fort Bentley; but most important, the pair I'd seen from the boat on the knoll next over had their backs to me. They were maybe two hundred feet off, two hundred and fifty feet from the gun. Carefully—without making a sound, or letting the bushes move—I stepped out into the open.

But just as I did, one of the lookouts nearest me turned around. For an instant we both froze—and then he was shouting and shooting his gun in the air and I was running as fast as I could.

We converged in a *V* on the gun; but I was closer, and as soon as I got to it, he hit the dirt. I let out a whoop and grabbed it by its handles. I pressed the trigger but nothing happened. Was it on? I looked for a safety catch, slipped some sort of tiny lever and then pressed the trigger again. The gun exploded. I yelled and fell back, my hand stinging. When I looked up again, everybody who had been running toward me had dropped to his knees.

"This is *power*," I murmured, dazed and with my ears ringing. I put my hands on the gun again and swiveled it on its tripod. I aimed in the air and pulled the trigger again.

"Power!" I cried, and I felt so giddy I almost wet my pants.

"Philip, you bastard!" I shouted. "Get off my island!"

I could see him, him and his business suit. He'd been up at the house and had come running at the first shot. Now he was down in the interior basin, maybe two hundred yards away. Some of the others collected around him.

"No need to confer!" I shouted. "Just get off my island!"

They were in a huddle.

"Swim if you have to! Surf! Levitate! But go!"

And I let off a couple of rounds for punctuation.

"Wheelwright!" someone shouted. They were waving a white T-shirt.

"No quarter!"

"Wheelwright!"

There were four of them. They got up off their knees and started walking carefully, slowly, toward me, waving the flag. Philip was one of them.

"Do you surrender, King Philip?" I shouted.

"We want to talk!"

"No talkee!" I said, and then pointing: "Gun!"

"We can negotiate."

"Heap big bang!" I shouted. "Many braves dead!"

"Knock it off, Wheelwright," Philip said, and he took the flag himself and started striding ahead. I let him get to within one hundred feet and then told him that was far enough. He came on another ten and then stopped.

"So what do you want?" he said.

"What do you think?"

"No way," he said. "Besides, we don't have a boat. Remember?"

"Wright," I heard behind me. I turned and saw Hetty at the verge of the bushes. I motioned for her to keep down.

"I can wait," I said. "I can wait until the police and the National Guard come."

"So can we," he said. "We don't need this part of the

island. As far as anyone on the outside's concerned, you look like one of us, manning one of our guns. We'll just keep our distance from you and you won't be able to do a thing."

I thought about that.

"Now I suggest we negotiate."

I heard the helicopter again. Philip heard it too, but he didn't turn to look.

"What do you say?" he said.

I turned and looked at Hetty.

"Ask him to let us go again," she said.

I shook my head and turned back.

"All right," I called after a minute. "Philip?"

"I'm here, Wheelwright."

"You ever hear about Nantucket during the War of 1812?"

Someone behind Philip shouted an obscenity and pointed toward the city. There were some boats heading in our direction, an MDC patrol boat and what looked like a small Coast Guard cutter. Philip made a gesture of patience with his hand and turned back to me.

"I'm listening, Wheelwright."

"During the War of 1812, Nantucket's shipping and fishing industry got so screwed up because of Britain's naval superiority, the island negotiated a separate peace treaty with England. Nantucket was the only part of the United States that was at peace with England in 1812."

"I'm impressed with your learning, Wheelwright. So what?"

"So I'm suggesting we negotiate a separate peace treaty. You and me."

He seemed to consider a minute. "I might be favorable to that," he said. "What are your terms?"

"You give me back my house, its near environs, and a right-of-way down to the dock, and you can have the rest of the island. *Not* for good. Just until the National Guard comes and kicks your ass."

"Or until we kick theirs."

"*Until*"—I said with exaggerated diplomacy—"the outcome of this crisis is effected."

"The house," he repeated, "the yard, a right-of-way to the dock, and you'll keep out of our way?"

"Scout's honor," I said.

"You won't fuck with us behind the lines?"

"Honest Injun."

The helicopter made a pass overhead.

"Agreed." Philip said and motioned for the three men behind him to come up. I did the same for Hetty.

"How do you know he'll keep his word?" she asked when she was beside me.

"He'd better."

"He'd better or what?"

I turned back to where Philip and his three bullyboys were making their way up the grassy slope and a sense of misgiving lodged inside me. "What choice have we got?" I said, turning back to Hetty, but she was watching them herself, her face strained and suspicious.

"Keep your word," I said when Philip was before me.

"I've got more on my mind right now than you, Wheelwright," he answered. "Don't worry."

"All right," I said and stepped out from behind the gun. "Shake?"

"Sure," he said. We shook, both of us smiling. He motioned for one of his men to take charge of the gun and then looked harborward.

"That house of yours," he said, turning back to me, "it's got an attic?"

"Yes."

"With a trap door? Does it lock?"

"No . . ."

"Well, we can fix that." He turned to the other two Indians. "Throw them in the attic and make sure they can't get out. Then get to your positions."

"You bastard!" Hetty said as one of the Indians grabbed her.

"What about Nantucket?" I shouted. I tried to shake myself free, but I got a gun muzzle in my ribs. "What about Nantucket, you Indian bastard?"

"Nantucket," Philip said calmly, starting to stride back down the hill, "was stolen from the Wampanoag in the first place."

*   *   *

The next morning I was waken'd before Daylighte and sign'd to rise. But even as I came to Wakefullness, my dreame of the night before clutch'd at me as if with demons' claws and I look'd with Horror at the pallet I had slept upon. And from that day hence— until I was bequeath'd the death Garments of one of my poore Countrymen—I would let nothing of the Savages touch me, not pallet, not breechclout, not moccains, keeping about myselfe only an English blanket that did me service as both Waistcoate and Bedding.

But sore was my going! I had nothing on my feet, and they were greatly cut from the roots and rocks of the forest. I had thought I would have but raw flesh for soles, but the Lord caus'd one of the Savages to show a most unlike Mercie and instruct me how I might heal my sores by the laying on of oak leaves. And it was a sign of the special Grace of the time that they heal'd so hard upon, for who—in times less cursedly Bless'd, in the straight streets of the Towne—might not lay on bushels of oak leaves and yet have heal'd no more soles than a Papist Confessor: unless the Lord grace those same leaves with the balm of Christ?

But on that aweful day I had still the cuts and blisters, and travel through the woods was a great Trial. We came down Mount Hope peninsula and through the necke called Kickamuit. And I knew that this day must prove the mettle of Newengland, for the Savages were greatly Intent upon their Bearing. Their faces were painted and their weapons whetted. I pray'd as I walk'd that my wife and son had hied themselves to the Miles garrison house, where— with others of the towne—they might withstand an assaulte of the Savages. When we neared the first settlements, I began to walk some bit clumsilie, grabbing a sapling for support, or cracking a twig underfoote, making noise as subtile as I might to warn of our coming. But my Master grabb'd me by the hair and without saying a word—though he knew I understood some good part of their speech—put his Knife to my throat. Whereupon I went on in silence.

They first looted and burn'd the house of William Wilson, which was nearest the necke. There was no one of the Plantation there, which gave me great Hope for my family. The Indians broke what they could not carry, murthering the livestocke and strewing the cornmeal.

Then they looted and burn'd the house of John Winslow, some half-mile away. Alike the Wilsons' house, there was no one at home.

When they came to my House, I made no notice of it. But I could tell by the looks that pass'd among them and by their Manner towards me, that they knew who I was, and whose house it was they were Violating. I could do nothing but watch as the Fruites of my Labor were brought low, my cow slaughtered, and my swine disembowel'd, thankful only that my family had fled.

And so we went, from field to forest, from forest to field.

Shortly after mid-morning, we met up with another band of Savages, and then another, among whose number I recogniz'd a townsman of mine, Richard Sutliff, who was later ransom'd for £20; and yet another, a goodwife, whose face I knew, but name remember not. I would have made toward them, for they were in the first Grippe of their Woe and I might offer them Cheer by my being still alive, but my Master made it clear to me that I was to stay where I was and attend him. We rested some short time, and then went on.

The Savages number'd now over two hundred, and I could tell by the Tracke taken that we were headed for the garrison house. About a half-mile short thereof, I was told to halt, as were the other English captives, while the main Force of the Indians went on. An hour later, we heard the fighting begin.

I had help'd build the garrison house, and I accounted its timbers and joinerie as strong as might be. But what wood is so well-grown that it may withstand the Furie of the Lord? What joinerie so well-made that it may halt the Assault of Satan's imps? And though I listen'd to each gunshot as if it might be the one that drove a ball through the heart of my wife, through the head of my son, yet I revel'd with each, betokening as it did the fort's holding. Our guards treated us with great Crueltie, for they accounted it an Insulte to be left with us and not allow'd to join the fight. They made at us great motions of Injurie, telling us by turns what they would do to us—cut our fingers off and eat them in front of our eyes, strip the skinne off our arms, drink our blood—and what it was that was being done by their Kin to our Townsmen. I did not account it naught, for I knew that the Dark Souls did often perform upon their captives the very Acts of Horror they most fear'd themselves, yet I thought we might be spared. When dusk near'd and our numbers began to swell with returning Indians, and there were no captives among them, and no signs of English defeat, I exulted—but only inwardly. Outwardly, I kept a face of Tragedie.

That night they feasted upon the cattle and swine and fowl that they had slaughter'd that day. It was a great Orgie. The ground was dyed with animal Blood, the very Aire seemed roasted with Fleshe. My Master asked me whether he should mix English blood with that of the swine, but I did not answer him. I lay upon my Back so they would not see me kneel, and pray'd whilst gazing upward at the Stars. I saw the Great Beare, and then the little beare, and I thought of my son. And whilst Hell rang and burn'd and rag'd around me, and my five senses were assaulted with all the Carnalitie and Lust of Savagery, I blessed him and told him in my Heart that I lov'd him. I pray'd God to keep him.

The next morning they renewed their Assault; and this time, by mid-day, we could see a great Pillar of Smoke rising over the trees. How I felt my heart smitten! I could Picture in my Head how it was: the English families huddling on the floor until the Inferno became too much to bear, and then running into the open Aire, where the Savages awaited them, to shoot or stab or knock them or the Head. When Philip's men started coming back through the Wood I knew it was true, for they were Wild with Exultation. I saw on warrior with the gorie hand of one of the Townsmen tied about hi waist, another had a handful of fingers from which he crow'd h would make a Necklace. There were captives too, Goodman Bar rows and his wife, Mr. Johnson, Mary Pratt, Richard Sparr, some others, and children. I looked for my wife, for my son, but they were not among them, and I was both lifted up and thrown down, first, with the thought that they had escap'd, and then, that they had been murthered.

We were marched back through the Wood. But oh! How differently we went this time! For I might grab all the Saplings, break all the Twigs I wanted. We were as a Processionall of the Devil, winding our way through the tender green Forest as a serpent through grass. The birds flew at our approach, the quail started, the game broke. When one of the women could not walk fast enough because of her Infant, her Captor took the childe and hung him by the armpits in a fork'd branch, making his Mother move on, the little Lamb left to cry and starve in the Wildernesse. I saw Blood everywhere I looked, blood on the earth, on the heathen garments of our captors, blood on their hands, in their eyes, in their souls. And I felt Blood in myself, a raging red Furie that would have struck down the nearest Savage had it the chance. I made covenant with the lengthening shadows that I would take my Vengeance should the Time ever come, that I would make the wildernesse ring with the death Throes of the red Devils, the ground run with their Blood. And I bit myself—strange covenant!—that I might taste my own blood as Witness.

That night I saw my wife's head put upon a pike at Kickamuit.

"Have pity upon me, O ye my friends, for the hand of the Lord has touched me."

*   *   *

SECOND DAY, March 31

"You said you left her a note?"

The attic was windowless, hot and dark during the day, cold and darker at night. There was a scuttle in the roof, a small hatch I'd built as a spy spot, but it was seven feet off the floor and Hetty was refusing to be used as a footstool. Yesterday, when I'd hoisted her up, she'd described a merry-go-round of bright cabin cruisers and Coast Guard cutters circling the island. I'd been sick with the thought of it.

"What did you say in it?"

We couldn't really see each other. We'd folded up my belt and wedged it between the scuttle and the roof frame so a plank of light dropped to the floor, but it left the eaves and recesses of the attic dark. Hetty was sitting by the floor hatch, her legs grazed by the light that etched itself in a rectangle around the hatch, but her face in darkness. She'd been in and out of anger the whole day, pounding on the floor at one point, shouting and swearing, and then when nobody answered, peeing on the hatch in hopes that it would trickle down through the cracks on top of someone. I tried to get her to answer some riddles like we'd done the first day, maybe play word dominoes, but she couldn't sit still for it. More than once I tried to get her to lie down with me, tried to kiss her and calm her down, but she wouldn't be kissed and she wouldn't be calmed.

"What did you say in it?" she asked again.

"In what?"

"In the note. What did you say in the note?"

I shrugged. I'd been lying on my back under one of the gables, but now I got up and crossed to the scuttle. "Nothing. I just said you were spending the night away." And I jumped up and for the hundredth time did a chin-up on the framing so I could catch a glimpse of the world outside. I held on for half a minute and then let go. "Help me look out," I said. "I mean for real. I want to see what's going on."

"You didn't say where I'd be? You didn't tell her I'd be out here?"

"I don't know. Maybe. Now, really, help me look out."

"What do you mean 'I don't know, maybe'?" She leaned over the hatch so the light lit her face from below. "Did you or didn't you?"

"I don't know," I said. "I can't remember. I guess I did. Yes, I did."

"You said I'd be out here?"

"Yes," I lied. "Yes, I said you were spending the night with me. You'd be back in the morning."

"So she knows I'm out here? She knows what's happened?"

"I guess so. How do *I* know? Now *help* me for Christ's sake."

*   *   *

At the word that Soldiers were coming from New Plymouth, we mov'd from Mount Hope, cross'd in canoes to Aquidneck Island which is consider'd the countrie of the Pocasset. At Aquidneck the Savages met up with their Wifes and there was great Celebration amongst them so that my Eyes were witnesse to many perverse and evil Carriages. The Pocasset too were well pleas'd with Philip's Successes, which fact caus'd me to realize that there was Bondage between them, and that we fac'd a general Uprising of Satan's Fellows. I watched them in their Jubilation and felt all the more the Bitternesse of my Loss. With each Wife's Embrace of her husband, I felt the utter Povertie of my new Life, or as I might say, my new Life in Death. I was so black within I have not the words to Describe it. Grief is a great Darknesse of Soule. My feelings were as if made corporeal and then bludgeon'd until black blood ran. I spent a night in which I could not cast the grislie Image of my wife's head from my Mind. And I have hereafter, to this day, never been able to picture her without seeing her as she was upon that dreadfull Pike. I can never, never see her again. Her sweet face is forever lost to me. For in my Mind now I was not wed to young Mary Winslow of New Plymouth, standing at my side in front of our Congregation all atremble with Love and Happiness, but a gorie Head set upon a body running with Blood. And too, when we met that Night upon the Marriage bed, I did not kiss the snowy skin of her virgin necke, but the ragged Hackings of the devil. And this is the horrific Resulte of our Aquaintance with Sin, that it so poisons us that we are evil even in our Remembrance, that it makes not just the Future the planting-grounde of the Devil, but our Past too, stains even the white bridal cloathes of our virgin wifes and daughters, who can be Virginal no more.

But it was in just this Desert of Soul that the Lord touched me. For as new Bands of Indians crossed the Bay, the number of Captives was added to, and in one such Band I had sight of my Son. What a Sweetnesse watered in me! He was as a Flower come upon in the Wildernesse! I cried out and ran to him. My Master tried to stop me but I was not to be stopped. We embrac'd and weep'd and when they came to tear us apart I would not let go. I carried him with me as they beat upon me. Their blows were the mere Swats of children so strengthen'd was I. I turn'd him this way and that to keep them from him. I kiss'd his head, his sweet hair, his cheeks, and I kiss'd the tears in his eyes. I told him that we would save each other, that we must look to Christ in one another. When finally they wrested him from me, carrying him some Distance off to his Master and me back to mine, still my eyes would not let go of him, and follow'd him wherever he might be. So it was for the next several Weeks as we left Aquidneck and moved northward further into the Forest. I looked for him each morning, follow'd him through the day as he carried Water for his Master or gather'd wood, and at night I blessed him from afar as the Sunne dyed the Wood red. His young body was as a Salvation to me, the sight of his Fair haire, his young lips, his slender necke, shoulders, his white legs, and his eyes so full of the Innocence of Christ. He was my tender Lamb. I felt renew'd, christen'd, whiten'd in his sight. I felt as if a great Kingdome had been restor'd to me. And I was certain my Fortune would go no lower, that the Militia would come, or that my Wife's Father in New Plymouth would Ransom us and we would be restor'd to Civilization. I looked for a Messenger daily.

*   *   *

"There's something out there I didn't tell you about."

She had just dropped to her knees under the scuttle. I had had to bribe her by hoisting her aloft again so she could have another look herself.

"What?"

"You won't like it."

"I don't like the whole thing. What in particular am I not going to like?"

"Your skeletons. They've wired your skeletons together or something. And they've got them hanging from your clothesline."

"Hanging?" I said. "How? By their necks?"

"No. Just hanging. Like on display."

"So everyone can see? I mean they can see them from the water?"

"Yes."

"Shit!" I said, and I jumped and grabbed hold of the frame, doing a chin-up until I could lower my feet onto Hetty's back.

There it was. The world all over again, the harbor littered with boats, ketches, sloops, yawls, cabin cruisers by the dozen. I could see the skeletons: eight of them hanging from my clothesline, swaying in the breeze, turning this way and that as if nodding to one another. They looked silver in the sun, the light glinting in lances along their legs, daggers down their arms, and the grisly death grin iterated eight times over. When the wind blew in earnest they seemed almost to dance in the air. Out on the water I heard the crack and snarl of a bullhorn. We'd been hearing it on and off all day, thinking it was calling to the island, asking for negotiations, information, assurances; but now I realized it was just a police boat warning off a cabin cruiser that had strayed too near the island. I saw one of the tour boats go by, stuffed to the gills with paying passengers, a fishing boat with TV cameramen on board, others with binoculars, zoom lenses, a little hand telescope—anything that would magnify, that would bring the island within reach. I felt eaten by a thousand eyes.

Down by the dock there was a red banner spread from the Parks and Recreation building to a tree trunk ten feet away. I could see the black letters on the other side, only in reverse. WELCOME, it said. WELCOME TO something something. America. WELCOME TO something, AMERICA. I tried to make out the middle word, but it resisted me. It was long-ish, with an *A* at the front, a *Z* on the end. I started spelling it out letter by letter with my finger on the scuttle frame. And then it came to me that it might be an Indian word, an Indian name Philip had given the island. But even as I thought that, even as I started to feel satisfied with it, I re-alized what it was: *Auschwitz.* The word was *Auschwitz.* WEL-COME TO AUSCHWITZ, AMERICA.

Was this what the rest of the country was seeing, the rest of the world? Was this what America was being told about Mavericke's island, *my* island? Not my city upon a hill, moral beacon and trim model for a new America, but Philip's cir-cus of trickery and trumped-up outrage? I felt as if my is-land had become a forgery, had changed overnight from the sea-breezed sanctuary to which I had carried off my ex-pecting cousin to a theater of treachery and imposture: Philip a great moral quack, parading his tricked-out sympathy, his sham passion over the injustice done his ancestors, and so making a mockery of the suffering—the *true* suffering—not only of his ancestors but of Mavericke as well. I felt wounded inside, and a sudden picture of the island as it was in winter came to me. I seemed to see myself, ice-caked and woolly, trudging through utter whiteness: no skeletons, no Ausch-witz, no cabin cruisers. Just whiteness, cold, purity. What had happened? How had things changed so? I had been alone. I had listened to Mavericke. And then I wasn't alone. And now I was being raped, despoiled, stripped down and bereaved of everything that made me myself: my house, my island, my Mavericke. I had invited the world in, and the world had come. And now I didn't know how to get shut of it again, or even if I *could* get shut of it.

"Okay?" Hetty said under me.

"Another minute," I answered.

"You're breaking my back."

"Another minute."

There they were, in the dooryard below, maybe a dozen

in all, watching a game show on television. Who were they? Were they Indians really? And if they were, if they were not just the genetic shadows of their ancestors but the true possessors of Indian souls, of a rightness and reverence for the earth and the individual human spirit, if the one-eighth part Indian in each of them had conquered on some battle-ground of the blood the seventh-eighths part American, if they were truly the whole-souled inheritors of the Wampanoag who had spent their last days starving side by side with a seventy-three-year-old Samuel Mavericke, then maybe it *was* their island, or if not theirs alone, then maybe they shared it with me, shared with me the same moral right to possession. Was that possible? Was it possible that all this while I had had fellows in my fight and not known it? I didn't mean all of them, but some? A half dozen who felt damage in their hearts? I looked at them, looked at them seated in a semicircle around Philip's television. Did they feel the same outrage against an America fallen to evil that I felt? An America that had extinguished its own light of election? Did they feel wild with rage at the sight of their land taken over by a flat and soulless people? And if they did, why were they following Philip? Why were they watching game shows on television? Why were the two women I could see made up in Maybelline and Max Factor? And why—*why?*—had they strung up those skeletons? For I knew in my heart that no matter what wound I felt, no matter what outrage I had suffered, I would never have hung Mavericke's skeleton from a clothesline for the world to see. Never.

"The new savages," I said aloud.

"What?" Hetty said under me.

"The new savages," I repeated. "They're the new savages."

"You get off me now."

*   *   *

But that Messenger did not come. And I may say that he shall not come as long as we are mir'd in the Atrocitys of our Time. For it was God's great Planne (I do verily believe) to allow Satan to hide the Lost Tribes of Israel—those descendants of Cain—here in Newengland away from all hope of Conversion, until his Visible Saints arriv'd and met them in great Conflicte. And it was as a Trial of us, an Armageddon in Rehearsal (as I may say), in which the Antichrist wore the red face of the Savages and Christ the white face of his Saints. BUT WERE OUR FACES WHITE? Was not the Captivitie of Newengland in the recent Holocauste the Captivitie of a people whose Evils had provok'd a just God to the Administration of corrective Afflictions? Had not our new found land become a land of Spiritual Death, a land of Apostasie and Avarice, where horn'd Beasts walk'd our streets in the guise of Merchants, Serpents slither'd in the garb of Lawyers, where our Magistrates were become secret Userers and every daytime Goodwife a nighttime Whore? We were become a Countrie of unfaire Dealing, a Countrie built of shoddy Workmanshippe, a Countrie where doorways are larger than the just size of a man, A countrie of Land-lust, of Money-lust, of Body-lust. And I will say this—my Captivitie allows me to say it—WE ARE STILL THUS. The Lord has Afflicted us for our Provoking Evils, but the Cessation of that Affliction does not mark the Cessation of those Evils. We were—oh, Newengland!—a land of such Hope! A land where the Sins of the old might be cast off, where the Soule of Adam might again be water'd by the gentle Rain of Heaven, a land that might be as a Beacon to the rest of the world. Yea, are we right to stamp out the red Beast that haunts our Forests, but we must as well root out the white beast that lurks in our Hearts! The devil is not made merely in his own Image, but he may wear breeches as well as a breechclout, wield a Flintlock as well as a Tomahawk. For as long as we are Americans—as long as we are Possessors of this Miraculous land—then do our devils reside at our Hearths, in our molasses Pots and in our Mirrors, lie with their heads upon our pillows and kiss our Wifes goodnight.

*   *   *

That night we lay with the scuttle thrown open so that a twenty-one-inch-by-thirty-four-inch patch of night sky—a golden section of bright stars and milky moonlight—floated amidst the rafters above us. We could see scraps and crumbs of constellations—the handle of the Little Dipper, the head of Draco—but nothing in its wholeness. Lying alongside with her head on my shoulder, Hetty sketched with her finger in the darkness just over our heads, giving Draco his coiling tail and the Little Bear his body. And then she pegged the Big Dipper on the same imaginary sphere, and then Cassiopeia, Lyra, Hercules, Boötes, the Milky Way with a wash of her hand, until we had the entire northern sky shimmering above us, a counterfeit heaven sparkling on the underside of Mavericke's roof. We lay a long while, silent under it, and then each of us fell slowly asleep.

THIRD DAY, April 1

We woke the next morning to the anguished cry of the nails being pulled out of the hatch. We sat up and waited, and then for the first time in three days, the hatch was thrown open and Philip appeared. He let his head peep cautiously above the floor, and then when he spotted us some twenty feet away, climbed another couple of steps until he was visible from the waist up. He had on a different suit from the first day.

"How are my favorite hostages *this* morning?" he asked.

"Fuck you," Hetty answered.

He shook his head. "Unacceptable, Mrs. Wheelwright. They'd have to edit that out. The FCC and all. Now, make yourselves photogenic." And he tossed us a hairbrush—a women's hairbrush—and then disappeared back down the ladder. Hetty turned to me with a look of wonder.

"What's he talking about?"

After a couple of minutes had passed one of the other Indians—I didn't recognize him—came up the ladder. He crossed to the corner we'd been using as a bathroom and cleaned up with one of the little shovels from the dig. Hetty asked him what was going on, but he wouldn't answer, just pinched his nose, and with a laugh, headed back down the hatch. After another minute, Philip reappeared.

"Now," he said with the air of addressing a briefing room, "say something that will put us in a position of strength when it comes time to negotiate the film rights. Try to act like a good TV script would want you to act. Mrs. Wheelwright, a touch of hysteria would be in order. Maybe a teary lament for your crazy kids. And you, Wheelwright, give us some manly, protective action. Like Kirk Douglas. You know the sort of stuff I mean. Whatever will make video America fall in love with you. Do it right and you'll be invited on talk shows all across the country. You'll be the electronic equivalent of your bastard ancestor and his racist book. Understand? It's your big chance."

And he dropped down out of sight. I crossed to the hatch and shut it. Then I sat on it.

"What's he talking about?" Hetty said again. "Are we going to be interviewed?"

"Not in this house we aren't."

"What?" she said. "What are you going to do?"

"Just what I'm doing. A hundred and ninety pounds. If you'll get over here we'll be *two* hundred and ninety."

But she stayed where she was. "If we're going to be interviewed, we could say something."

"I've got nothing to say."

"I could get a message out."

"Just get off my island."

"I could get a message out to Mrs. Steele, to the twins."

" 'Get your stinking, polluted, immoral feet off my island.' That's all I've got to say. Now get over here."

But she didn't come.

"Hetty," I said. "We don't want them. We're being raped. The whole island is being raped. We have to keep something that's ours. We have to keep this attic ours, or we'll be raped up here too." I felt someone push on the hatch below, push harder and then stop. There were voices. "We can't let them up. They want to pollute everything. They want to take us and pollute us all over the country. Ugly, unsaved, unsouled eyes looking at us, at my house, at everything that's good and clean about us." They started pushing in earnest now. I could hear Philip's voice. I was rocked and lofted where I sat. "Come on!" I shouted. "Get over here!"

"I want to get a message out," she said.

"No messages!"

They heaved and pushed but I could feel already that they couldn't do it. I was too heavy and the hatch was too small for more than a couple of men to get under at a time. After another couple of tries, they stopped. There was silence under me.

"Wheelwright?" I heard Philip say.

I didn't answer.

"Wheelwright, this is your big chance. An electronic pulpit. And it's free. Free, Wheelwright. I'm going to have to spend a couple of years in prison to pay for mine, but yours is free. It's a special one-time offer."

"*Two* hundred and ninety," I whispered across to Hetty.

"If you'll take advantage of this special one-time offer we'll even throw in a couple of sleeping bags and a Coleman lantern for the duration, and a potty jar as a special bonus. Just let these nice men come up and talk to you. Let them ask you a couple of questions about how grand it was of me to let you leave in your cute sailboat and how it was your own idea to come back and start shooting at people. At me, for instance. Then you can say whatever else you want. You can lecture them on post-and-beam joints, seventeenth-century ethics, historical grave-robbing, and all the other subjects you're an expert on."

"Buzz off!" I shouted down at the hatch; and then again, whispering to Hetty: "*Two* hundred and ninety." But even as I said it, I felt them begin pushing again. "Come on!" I cried as I was jolted aloft. I came down hard and heavy on the edge of the hatch. Hetty started toward me. "One, two, *three*!" I heard below me, and on *three* they all pushed. I made myself into as dense a ball as I could. Hetty was coming slowly, uncertainly. I waved her on. "One, two, *three*!"

"Come on!" I shouted to her. She hurried the last few feet, and then—"one, two, *three!*"—pushed me, pushed me just as they said *three*, so that I toppled backward off the hatch. It banged open, and before I could scramble back to it, a head was thrust up.

"I want to get a message out!" Hetty shouted at the first man that came up; and then down the ladder: "I want to get a message out!"

They tramped up, one after the other, cameras locked on their shoulders and lights like vicious eyes, asking questions even before they were all up. I swung around to the far side of the attic, blinded by the light. I had one hand over my eyes, and the other giving them the finger so that whatever footage they got of me could not go out over the air. They made a ruckus getting in position. There were seven of them, three with minicams, the others with sound equipment. They seemed like one mass, a monster with fourteen arms and three blinding eyes.

"Are you all right?" they were asking. "Have you been mistreated? Were you forcibly—"

"I want to get a message out," Hetty said. "I'm not answering any questions until you agree to deliver a message for me."

I could see well enough to make out Philip's head just above the hatch. But the lights were so bright the men behind the cameras were nothing but shouldery outlines. The others knelt in front of them. One of them was a woman. They all talked at once, stepping on each other's questions. They had the cameras on Hetty now—I still had my finger up—and she was backing away from them, covering her eyes.

"My message!" she cried.

They shushed each other so that for an instant the attic seemed filled with a hissing sibilance. There followed an instant of silence, and then one of them spoke. "Ms. Jenney," he said. The others started in again, but he waved them quiet. "Ms. Jenney, are you all right? What's your message? Can we take a message for her?" he asked, turning to Philip.

"I don't see why not," Philip said with a magnanimous gesture. "Mrs. Wheelwright?"

She seemed to take a deep breath. "Rhodora Steele," she said. "Rhodora Steele, one-ninety-five Commonwealth Avenue. Tell her where I am. And tell her I'm coming back to Isabel and Irene as soon as I can. I'm coming back. Tell her that."

"Were you forcibly—"

"Tell her that! Repeat it back to me. Repeat it back."

There was silence and then one of them said: "Rhodora Steele. One-ninety-five Commonwealth Avenue. As soon as you can, you're coming back."

"To Isabel and Irene."

"To Isabel and Irene."

"Okay," she said. "Now you promise? You'll deliver it?"

"Yes."

"Okay. You can ask your questions. One at a time."

"Were you forcibly—"

"No questions!" I shouted, and I scrambled across to Hetty, still giving them the finger. One of the cameras shut off. "I've got my own question. What I want to know is whether you think his coming here"—and I pointed at Philip—"is a barbarous act. Taking people and locking them in an attic against their will. Is that an act of savagery?"

The camera turned back on again. They all looked uncertainly down at Philip.

"Well, *is* it?" he asked.

One of them began answering diplomatically: "They feel they have certain grievances—"

"*Is* it?" I shouted. "Is it an act of savagery?"

"*I'd* say so," Philip said in a reasonable tone.

"We're journalists," one of the reporters said. But another answered quickly: "Yes. It's an uncivilized act."

"Would you say anyone who violated a man's home is guilty of an equal savagery?"

They balked at that.

"He's getting around to telling you *you're* savages," Philip put in.

"I consider you all guilty of moral rape," I said. "*All* of you. And all the people out there in their boats. And all of you watching this." And here I looked successively into each of the cameras. "You. And you. And you. Get up and turn your televisions off. I am being raped and you're watching it. That makes all of you rapists. All of you! All of America! I'm being raped by America!"

Philip started applauding. "You're an Indian after all, Wheelwright."

"And don't listen to him. He's all show, no substance. He wouldn't shoot at anyone. He's too busy figuring the odds on how to serve the shortest possible sentence."

"But there was *some* shooting done," one of the reporters jumped in with. "Was that you?"

"Yes," I answered, and I stabbed at my chest as if to prove my own substance. "I did it."

"Did you consider it self-defense?"

"Yes."

"But you had already been allowed off the island, hadn't you?" the woman reporter asked.

"There are all kinds of self-defense."

"But was it legally self-defense?" Philip put in. "That's the question."

I turned to him. "This man," I said, pointing at him, "this American, this King Philip, claims to be an Indian. Where he gets the idea that the one-sixteenth part of his blood outweighs the fifteen-sixteenths part, I don't know. If there was something to be gained by letting the fifteen-sixteenths part outweigh the one-sixteenth, you bet you'd hear him change his tune. But what kind of Indian hangs up the skeletons of his ancestors for the world to see? For you and your cameras to paste on television sets all over the country? It was forbidden for the Wampanoag to even mention the name of a dead ancestor. It was an insult. A sign of a lack of reverence. So what does this imposter, this phony-ass, off-the-rack King Philip do? He hangs up his ancestors like it's a store window he's decorating. He's selling them. He's merchandizing them. He's merchandizing the tragedy of their deaths, using them to get invited on talk shows, to sell some book he's going to write, to sell film rights. There isn't anything—"

"You shame me, Wheelwright."

"—anything he wouldn't sell or swindle, all in the disguise of trumped-up morals."

"You *are* your ancestors' descendant."

"I want him out of here. I want you all out of here. This is *my* house. I live here. And you were not invited in. I want you out! Out!" And without warning, I stepped forward and kicked one of the cameras so that something cracked. "You are polluting the only piece of moral ground left in America!" And I started kicking at anything I could find, at the microphones, at the sound equipment, yanking at the wires. They started scrambling about. One of them pushed me so that I fell back. "Out!" I cried, crawling on my hands and knees toward them. "Out! Get out!" And I hit at as many as I could reach as they tumbled down the ladder.

"My message!" Hetty called after them. "Don't forget my message!"

They were still filming.

*   *   *

There came then amidst our Number some Savages with the look of Civilization about them. They had their haire cut short (long haire being a sign amongst the Heathen of Manhood and Prowess), and they were fitt'd out in the cloathes of Goodmen. I had first Hope that they might be Embassies sent from the nearby Praying Towns by the General Court to obtain our Release, but it was to come cleare that, though they were from the Praying Towns, they were not here to aide us. They were kept apart from the rest of the Tribe the first few days, and I could tell that there were many Councils and Meetings taking place about them. I could not divine their Meaning, but I knew all about me was an Increase in Excitement. When these Deliberations were over, there was set up a Gauntlet of every one of the old Savages, and each of the new Savages (or, as

I may say, the old Savages become new) were made to run through it. And as he ran, the old Savages hit at him with sticks or switches or the hafts of axes, the purpose (as I took it) being to knock the whiteness out of the civiliz'd Savages, to dislodge in them their new-learnt ways, and to extinguish whatever Pinpricke of Light the Holy Ghost had lit in their dark souls. Then they were undress'd and led full naked down to a nearby stream where they were wash'd in the water, every savage man making of himself a Baptist, washing the new Savages, their hair, their backs, their fronts, baptizing away the light of Civilization, as if here in the Newengland wilderness was to be found the devil's counterpart to the Jordan River. Then they were led up to the council fire and dress'd in new Indian cloathes, feathers, jewelrie and paint. And with every warrior from every Band gather'd in a circle around them, the Indian called King Philip made a great speech of which I could only understand part, but enough to realize that the civiliz'd Savages were being adopted into the Tribe, that they were cleans'd not only of Christ, but of their earlier Tribe (for we were in the land of the Nipmucks now). There follow'd a great Revelrie with Feasting and Dancing and much Lewdness as I had witness'd so often before.

It was shortly after this that a great Raid was made upon the towne of Lancaster, and many Captives were carried away, several of them at the Hands of the civiliz'd Savages. The night was spent in Orgie as was usual after Victorie, but the next morning when I woke there was already great Stirre to be going, for Word had come that the Militia was afoot. I was busied by my Master, making ready for a new Trek through the Wood, though I had Chance once to Sign to my son that everything was all Right. But as the day wore on, as we made our way along the heathen Pathways further into the Wilderness, we seem'd to lose Sight and Sound of the other Bands. I began to worry that a Strategem had been taken and that (as was often the Indian way) the different Bands were going Separate paths. I began to lag Behind. For what would I do, having found my Son in the wilderness, if I were to lose him to it? I fell behind unnotic'd—unnotic'd enough so that I thought that some day I might make an Escape—but there was no other Band behind us. I felt for an instant Frantick—and my first Desire was to run

*back after him—but I bethought myselfe. Where would I run to?
Belike they had taken a different way some miles back. And I had
not the Indians' eye to differ—in that great Desert of Wood—the
Track from the Trackless. I would lose myselfe, or I could come
upon a Savage in need of no Slave. All I could do was Wait and
Hope that the divers Bands would reassemble again. And I had
some Reason to hope such, for in the past it had happen'd so. Still,
my Heart was sore with a new Hurting.*

*That night I waited for him to come back. The next night I
waited also. And the third again when one of the other Bands join'd
us in a new Camp. But he did not come, and I began to Despaire.
I could not ask my Master, for having become, as it were, part of
his Familie, he did not like my Attachment to any other Familie,
even the pitiful Remnant of my own. I could do Nought but Ago-
nize inside. I prayed on my back as I had done since the very first
Night of my Captivitie. I prayed even as Sleep defeated me, so that
when in the morning I awoke, the Prayer was still upon my lips.
And that Prayer was always of my Son, that he would be kept Pure
of Heart and unsavaged in his Soule.*

*   *   *

I could get out if I had to. I could chin myself up to the
scuttle and somehow hoist myself out. I could. I could
get out.

April ninth was coming.

FOURTH DAY, April 2

"I want you to fuck me."

We had spent an awful night. Every half hour or so,
Philip or one of his men had pounded on the floor under
us with a gunstock so that we kept starting awake. It was a
kind of sleep torture. Toward dawn we had quit trying, and
now we were sitting as far apart from one another as the
attic would allow.

"I want you to fuck me and when I come I'm going to
scream so that they can hear me downstairs."

I couldn't see her in the dark, but I could imagine what she looked like. I could imagine her at the opposite gable, sitting on the floor with her knees drawn up under her chin, and I could imagine her looking at me, tired and angry and reckless.

"I'm going to scream so the television crews can get it on tape and all of America will know I'm being fucked and I like it."

"I've got one," I said.

"No more riddles."

"An archaeologist sets up housekeeping on an island where two Indian tribes live . . ."

"I'm tired of riddles. I'm tired of riddles and word dominoes and Botticelli. And I'm tired of this shitty food. And I'm thirsty. I'm thirsty!" she cried and stamped with her feet on the floor. There was no answer. Somewhere out on the water a bullhorn crackled.

"An archaeologist sets up housekeeping on an island where two Indian tribes live."

"I'm not listening."

"One tribe always tells the truth. The other always lies. The truth tellers live on the western side of the island and the liars on the eastern side. Got that? Truth tellers on the west. Liars on the east."

"They didn't deliver my message," she said for the tenth time that morning.

"The archaeologist is a man of few words. He wants to find out if his guide tells the truth by asking him only one question."

"I'll bet they didn't."

"So the archaeologist, seeing an Indian walking in the distance, asks his guide (who happens to be wearing a business suit): 'Go ask that Indian in the distance which side of the island he lives on.' When the Indian in the business suit returns, he answers: 'He sayum he livum on the eastern side of the islandum.' Is the Indian in the business suit a truth teller or a liar?"

I could hear her just sitting there, silent.

"Is the Indian in the business suit a truth teller or—"

"If I answer it, will you fuck me?"

It was my turn to be silent. She got on her feet and started toward me.

"I mean it," she said, and she groped for me in the dark and then sat beside me and put her hand on my leg. "If I answer it, I want you to fuck me. Okay?"

I didn't answer.

"Okay?" she said. She was breathing hard, frightened-sounding. "Tell it to me again. An archaeologist lives on—"

"Sets up housekeeping—" And I repeated the riddle.

"All right . . ." she said when I was done, and drew a breath. I could feel her beside me in the dark, somehow both fragile and violent. I wanted to put my arm around her, but I couldn't. She thought for a solid minute and then spoke.

"All right, if he asks a truth teller, he'd say the western side, right? Because he'd tell the truth. Right?"

"Right."

"And if he asked a liar, the liar would say the western side too, because he'd lie. Right?"

"You're getting this too easily."

"So no matter whether the Indian in the distance is a truth teller or a liar, he *has* to say he lives on the western side."

She was running her hand up and down my thigh.

"But the Indian in the business suit says the Indian in the distance said the eastern side. Which means he's a liar. The Indian in the business suit has to be a liar. Right?"

I didn't answer.

"Right? He's a liar."

"Right," I said, and I felt oddly defeated. She leaned over me and whispered in my ear.

"Now, I want you to fuck me. I want you to fuck me dirty. I feel dirty and I want you to fuck me dirty."

"Hetty . . ."

"I want you to. You married me. You *have* to. I guessed the riddle."

"I'll make love to you," I said and tried to kiss her.

"You'll *fuck* me," she answered. She was stroking both my thighs now. "I want you to make me come. I want you to make me come so the whole world knows it. I want you to make me come over and over. I want you to make me come in a Fibonacci sequence. First once, then again, then twice in a row, then three times, then five times, then eight, thirteen, twenty-one! Fuck me, goddamn you!" And she pulled me toward her. "Get hard," she whispered in my ear. "Get hard and talk dirty to me."

"Hetty . . ." I said.

"Talk dirty to me. Tell me how you want your cock inside of me. Tell me how you want to fuck me in these clothes. How you want to pretend you're fucking Amias. Seventeen-year-old Amias standing and playing her virginal while you fuck her from behind."

"Hetty!"

"You're hard. I can feel you. Say it! Say you're hard. Say you've got a hard-on and it's for me."

"It's for you."

"For me," she repeated, and she pulled me down on top of her. "I want them to hear us downstairs."

"No."

"I want them to hear us. I want them to know I've got something they don't have. I want them to know I've got a cunt and there's no vacancy."

She unzipped my pants.

"There's *no vacancy!*" she shouted. She took me in her hand and whispered in my ear.

"Hetty. Sweetheart," I said. "This is no good."

"It's good," she said. She was using me to stroke herself. "We're letting them know."

"What? What're we letting them know?"

"You're so hard," she said. Her voice shivered.

"What're we letting them know?"

"I'm going to come. I'm going to keep doing this and I'm going to come."

"No."

"Yes," she said. "I'm going to come! Say something to me."

"No."

"Say something!"

"I love you."

"Something dirty!"

"I love you! I love you!"

"Oh!" she cried and I felt her tremble under me. "You bastard! You bastard! You married me!"

"Hetty!" I said and cradled her head in my hands.

"Don't touch me!" she cried.

"Hetty!"

"Don't!"

I kept myself up on my elbows and let her use me.

"My sweethearts, my sweethearts," she was saying. Her voice was hoarse, swollen. "My sweethearts." She kept saying it, tossing her head from side to side, writhing and kicking and swearing at me until finally she lifted her head up off the floor, straining, crying, swearing one last time, and then fell back. She shuddered—once, twice—and then lay still. A helicopter flew overhead.

"They'll be all right," I whispered after a minute.

"You bastard," she said.

"They'll be all right."

"They *won't* be all right."

"They will. They will. You'll go back to them."

"I don't want you anymore," she said and let go of me.

"Yes, you do."

"No."

"Yes," I said, and I pushed myself toward her.

"No!" she cried and tried to squirm out from under me. I let my full weight fall on her.

"I'm going to make love to you," I said.

"I don't want you."

"I'm going to make love to you," I said and pushed so I felt the kiss of her insides. "I'm going to make love to you."

"I don't want you. You're raping me."

"I'm making love to you."

"Rape."

"Love," I said. "Love."

"I don't want it. I don't want it. I don't want to be locked up here. I don't want to be married. I don't want to be pregnant."

"I'm fucking you," I said.

"Don't say that."

"I'm fucking you, Hetty. I'm fucking you. My wife. I'm fucking my wife."

"I'm not going to come," she said.

The helicopter flew overhead.

"You are," I said. "I'm going to make you come in a Fibonacci sequence. Two. Three. Five. Eight. I'm going to make you come in a Fibonacci sequence with all my beautiful joinery around us. All my mortise-and-tenon joints, my rafters, my ridgepole singing the heights of heaven. And you in your Puritan clothes under me. I've got your red petticoat thrown up. I've got my hands on your lovely rear end and I'm fucking you."

A bullhorn crackled out on the water.

"They're announcing it. They're announcing that I'm fucking my wife and that she's about to come. They're announcing to all the television crews and all the people circling the island on their cabin cruisers that she's coming for the second numeral in a Fibonacci sequence."

"You love me," she said.

"They've got their cameras trained on us. They've got their microphones trained on us. Binoculars. Instamatics. Polaroids. The whole United States of America is watching and listening to us make love."

"You love me."

"I'm bumping John junior on the head."

"You love me."

"I'm telling him this is his father out here."

"You love me."

"I'm telling him everything's going to be all right."

*　　*　　*

There follow'd some weeks of Want, and I and the other Captives were made to feel it most. There were no more caches of Wheat and Corne to be had (proof, if proof is needed, that the War was meditated in Advance), and we were Reduc'd to eating stews of Frogmeat and chestnuts, lily-roots and groundnuts. Nor were we any longer near any Settlements whose swine and Fowle might furnish our Table. The Want lodg'd in my stomach like a demon, and I had great Feare of the Winter coming, for the Trees were alreadie turning, and if we were hard-press'd for Food now, what was it to be like when the Snows flew?

There happened now an Incident of whose telling I almost Quake. But I have been Witnesse to the Lord's Worke—to his Afflictions and his tender Mercies—and as I am escap'd to tell thee, so will I.

There was a Lancaster Captive amongst the Civilized Savages. I never learn'd his name. Nor do I know what set the Indians so against him, though I know the sight of his ever praying upon his Knees—to those who had so lately fallen from the Lord's Grace— was a great Sore to them. I tried once—when we had happen'd upon one another gathering brush—to tell him to pray as I did, on his back, but he answer'd that the Lord meant him to Supplicate Him, and that should he try to Avoide the Lord's Afflictions, then would not those Afflictions turn from Corrective to Destructive? For he consider'd his troubles a Badge of Grace, the Father's Rod upon an errant Childe, and so, proof of his Election. I answer'd him that the Savages might not be as Privy as he to the Lord's finer Distinctions, but he was all of a minde, and I saw him soon after again on his knees and some couple of the Christian Savages kicking at him.

But one night, with the Tear of Hunger in their own Bellies, they did not stop at kicking. I do not know how it began, for I was off tending my Master's fire, but the cries soon drew me. There were three of them, and they had him tied to a tree, kneeling. They first tore off his Fingernails, and then one by one, cut off his fingers, eating of them before his eyes, not, I believe, because of their Hunger (for surely there are better ways of preparing a Man for a meal), but to show their own Strengthe, and to show to the rest of the Band, and to themselves, that they had regain'd their Indian souls. Then they strip'd him and burn'd him with coals, all the while Taunting him with great Sacrilege concerning our Lord. And then as if this put them in Minde of something, they dug holes in his palms and in his ankles with their Knives, and with vines pulled off a nearby Tree, strung him to some bent-over Saplings, making a savage Crucifixion of him. He cried out then: "I know, O Lord, that thy Judgements are right, and that thou in Faithfulness hast afflicted me!" so that I wondered if I were beholding a Martyr, or a man so secretly Sinfull that he knew the Savages worked the Lord's Vengeance. All through the night he howled in his Agonie, until some time near Dawn he gave up the Ghost—whether to Heaven or to Hell, I do not know.

But I do know this. There is a savagery in the Hearts of Men which cannot be cured by Civilization. And though a man might be held in Captivitie by Civilization (as I may say), though he may live in the Towne and pray in the Church, still his Bloode ranges to the Wildernesse. For the Indian is the basic Element of Man, and though we put Palings around our Townes to keep the Indian out, yet even if we had Palings around our Souls still would he not be kept out, for he is alreadie within. The most Civiliz'd of men may be a Secret Savage. Or he may be a Savage in civiliz'd Cloathes, or a userer, a gossip, a fornicator. And he may be number'd amongst our most illustrious men, those who dress their Savagery in the guise of Business or Statecraft or Learning or Religion, and whose Acumen we Praise, never naming it for what it is: the Indian within, working his Savagery in the courts and shops, in the ways and byways of Civilization. For are not our Court buildings, our Shippes of Commerce, our Meeting Houses, yea, even our homes, built of the very Wood of the Wildernesse? And cannot we say that our townes are merely the dark Forest Reform'd, and that the tree carries its Darknesse to the sawpit and even after—squar'd up and tru'd—to our Homes? So do we make a wooden Palisade out of the very Wildernesse we mean the Palisade to keep out.

*   *   *

"I married you because you needed me. I married you because you wanted me. I married you because you asked me to."

She was sitting somewhere under the eaves and talking into her knees. I was standing on a gallon can of V-8 juice and looking out the scuttle at the civilized savages. I was wondering what it meant to be held captive by Indians in the twentieth century.

"I married you because you said you loved me and I believed you."

Was it a kind of trial? Like Jesus in the wilderness? Or Job? Or Jonah taken from the sight of God? Was it a loving rebuke? And by whom? God? America?

"I married you because I wanted to believe in you. I wanted to believe what you said about me. I wanted to believe that I was . . . you know, what you said."

Or was it what Cousin Isaac would have said it was? A corrective affliction. A punishment for provoking evils, for moral deformity.

"Chaste. You said I was chaste, *morally* chaste."

And if that was true, what evil had I committed?

"You said I was one of the elect. And I wanted to believe you. I wanted to believe I had an inner goodness that could cancel out all the things . . . you know, all the unchaste things."

And Hetty, what was *her* provoking evil?

"And I vowed, I mean I really vowed. You don't know this, but I vowed I would be faithful to you. I wouldn't go out with anyone else or anything. No matter how much they said they needed me. Because that's how they always get me, you know. If they say they need me."

Baby John? Was Baby John and the Susan B. Anthony Clinic Hetty's provoking evil?

"And at first it was all right. I was happy. I stole things from you because I was happy. I wanted to have parts of you around me all the time. I wanted to have the things you held and wore and worked with around me. I hid some of them in the couch, under the cushions. And when you made love to me there, it wasn't you on top of me I was thinking about, but you in your work gloves or one of your tools under me."

But what was mine, then?

"And when you started stealing things of mine in return, I felt like you understood me. I felt like maybe you really *did* know me, like you could see what was really inside me. And if you *could* see what was really inside me, then maybe you were right—maybe I *was* one of the elect, in spite of everything."

Or was it what Mavericke said? That the world will come and get you no matter what? That no matter what island of space or time you put yourself on, it will come after you in the flesh of your nightmares: Indians and cabin cruisers and TV cameras.

"But it scared me too. I was frightened that you would win me so much that I would lose the twins. Because it's seductive. Do you see that? It's seductive to be told that you're good and that you've got the power to heal. And that's what you were telling me. Whether you know it or not, that's what you were telling me. Never mind that *I* had to be saved. You were telling me that *you* needed to be saved. You were telling me that you needed to be saved and I was the one to do it. And I don't know even now if you realize it, if you realize just what it was that made me marry you."

It will come and pollute everything you hold chaste, everything you have fought for and tried to keep free of stain and taint and trauma.

"Do you? Do you realize it? Do you realize that it's you who needs to be saved?"

It will come and shoot bullets in your house, hang up skeletons in your dooryard and lock you in the attic.

"Wright? Do you?"

It will come and kill everything you love.

"Wright?"

*   *   *

When I saw my Son again I did not recognize him. There was snow on the Grounde and we were camp'd beside what I later learn'd was the Merimack River. For some days the other Bands had been Straggling in, looking like two-legged Animals in their great Furrs, and I was Keen to the Thought that he might be amongst them. But I was shrewde and kept my own Council until one day just at Duske, I saw my son's Master and his familie. I felt my Hearte leap within me. But when I went to them and ask'd for him, they answer'd that he was no more. And when I press'd them—a great Feare and Rage beginning to Boyle within me—they said that he was no more but that they had Naananto back. I did not Understand them at first. I began to shout at them, and to take Holde of them, each in turn, shaking him and asking where my Boy was. My Master came and tried to lead me back but I dealte Roughlie with him. They started Severalle of them to lay Hands upon me, but I broke off from them and started Running toward one of the Tents. But some Others lay holde of me and this time I could not Shake myself Free.

And that's when I saw him. I don't know if it was my Voice that made him come or if he was coming anyway, but I saw him steppe out of one of the other Tents. He was Dress'd as one of them, in an Animal Skinne, and his Haire was grown longe. He had Animal moccasins upon his Feet and a skinne for a Cap. And I don't know if it was the duskie Sunlighte or some Indian Paint or the Effects of his new Life in the open Worlde, but his skin look'd Redder than it ever had. He seem'd not to see me at first, but when I call'd him by his name, he stopped in his Tracks. I call'd him again, using his Christian name, but His Master came between us, saying that he was Naananto now. I called him a second time and told him to come to me. His Master equall'd me, calling him Naananto and telling him to stay. A third time, I call'd him to come. A third time, his Master told him to stay.

He stayed.

I was wilde for three days. They tied me to a Tree, my hands behind my back and three ropes around me: one across my Breaste, one across my Waiste, one around my ankles. I cried out and struggled so the Ropes burn'd through my Cloathes. I cannot remember thinking the Thoughts of a Man, not even the Thoughts of a Man in great Torment, as I surely was. Neither can I remember Sleep-

ing, though I am Sure I must have Done so, my Head slumping to one side, but I cannot say I remember it. I remember little but the great Howl of Madnesse within, my Brain like a fire feeding on itselfe, and the aweful Retching that wrack'd my Bodie, wrack'd it until—with nothing left of the outside world to throw up—it began trying to tear out the very Insides of my Belly, as if it would Rid me of my Bodie from the inside out. I could not remember my Lord. I could not remember my Towne. I could not remember my Wife. My Heart was a Cinder of Blasphemie, my Brain a hot Rock of Hate. I was so foul'd with Giant Despaire that I do not know if I even saw the Band of Indians into which my son was adopted leave the Camp, or whether I only came to that Knowledge in the days that follow'd. But I fainted at last (I believe), fainted from Want, from hunger and from the Torment of my Minde, for I awoke one day upon a Pallet of my Master's, too weak to move and with a Soreness of Thought which sapp'd me of my Will, but which was no longer the great Fire it had been.

*   *   *

"I've thought of stealing them, kidnapping them I mean. I mean just going and taking them and disappearing with them. She'd *know* who did it. But here's what *I* think: I think she wouldn't care. Or she'd *care*, but not in the normal way. She wouldn't do anything about it. She'd *let* me take them."

It was night, and I was sitting in a corner of the attic with the tips of my fingers snugged into one of my joints. I was trying to feel some strength, faith, power—something!—coming to me through the wood. And I was watching the darkness where Hetty was.

"I even think sometimes she's *waiting* for me to take them. Daring me to."

That's my wife, I was thinking.

"Like she knows what I'm after."

I've known her all my life.

"And she's enjoying it. She's enjoying watching to see if I can do it."

She's pregnant.

"Letting me have them, letting me wash them and feed them, touch them with my hands."

She's pregnant with my son.

"Because she knows if I *do* begin to heal them, she can step in at any time and blast them back to zero."

She's pregnant with my son and she's being held captive by two dozen civilized savages. I'm also being held captive by two dozen civilized savages, but I've got my fingertips snugged into a mortise-and-tenon joint in Samuel Mavericke's house.

"And what I don't know is: Is she doing it right now? While I'm stuck here, is she twisting them up all over again? Freezing them back to where they were when I first met them? Is she—"

"Putting them in jars," I offered.

"—ruining everything I've done? All the work I've put in over the last two years? Can she ruin it just by her presence? Just by being in the same room with them? Can she do it just like *that*?" And she snapped her fingers. "Is that how the world is made?"

I heard her get up and head for the far gable. I followed the moving darkness with my eyes. Was this my chance? I wondered. Was now the time to tell her it was Baby John she was meant to save, not the twins?

"I'm kidding myself," she said. Through the scuttle came the murmur and burr of cabin cruisers. "I'll never do it. They're locked inside themselves like their heads are dungeons. All my notes, my notebooks, my theories—it's all useless. They're dead."

"Don't say that," I said, but even in my own ears it sounded false.

"Maybe someone else could do it. Maybe someone who was more—" but she left off.

"More what?" I asked. I thought I could see her shake her head, declining. More what? I wondered. More hardworking? Who could be more hardworking? Smart? Pure? Had she meant to say pure? Was it like when we were kids with the music of the spheres? Did she think if she were pure enough she could cure the twins?

"More something," she said.

I kept my hold of the wood. I could just barely make her out. She was standing as far away from me as she could get, as if she wanted to muffle herself in the dark. She had her arms wrapped around her waist and she was leaning against the wall with her head tucked in so her hair hid her face.

"I thought I could do it. I did. I thought I could take one hurt piece of the world and by utter goodness, by hard work, and faith, and love, and by denying myself, I could heal it. I did. I thought that. I had dreams of myself, a content, middle-aged woman, celibate, taking Isabel and Irene Steele—leggy eighteen-year-old redheads—for coffee on Newberry Street, maybe shopping at Bonwit Teller's, spending my money on them, or visiting them at college, going over the course catalog with them, talking to them on the phone late at night, advising them on boys and birth control, being there when they married, when they had children. That was my dream. To bring them into the world and then watch them as they lived their lives, lives that *I* had made possible. How many people can say they've done that?"

She had turned her head. She was looking at me.

"But I can't go back to them."

I pulled my fingers out of the wood. "Why?"

"Because I don't believe anymore."

"Believe what?"

She shrugged and turned away again. "I don't believe it can be done. They're lost. It can't be done. *I* can't do it. I can't."

And she sat suddenly in a slump on the floor. I got up on my hands and knees and started crawling toward her.

"This is what I want," I said. It was enough to make her look at me again. I crawled faster. "This is what I want, Hetty. Just listen for a minute. I want to live together. I

mean for real, for good. As man and wife." I drew up the
last few feet to her. "Out here," I said. "I mean out here."

"What?"

"Listen," I said, and I knelt before her and searched under her hair for her face. "Think what it would be like." I
started to feel at her with my fingertips, her cheeks, her
cheekbones, her eyes. "Try to picture it, just the two of us.
Just the two of us on an island in the Atlantic. It wouldn't
be like it is now, Indians, guns, TV cameras, cabin cruisers.
It'd be just you and me. Just you and me and the wild roses,
the crocuses I planted, the pussy willows. We'd excavate
Mavericke's well, have our own drinking water. We could
plant a vegetable garden, have chickens, sheep for wool. I'd
build Amias's loom for you and you could weave for us.
Blankets and things. And in the fall we'd stuff the buttery
full of our harvest, hang up herbs and dyeweeds by the fireplace to dry, and settle in for the winter. We could do it.
We could."

And I pressed my palms to her temples. She was still,
quiet. She was listening. She was thinking about it.

"We could do it. We could build our lives completely out
of ourselves, make everything around us—*everything*—just
the way we want it. Our house, our hearth, our bed." I could
almost feel her imagining it, feel the picture of the island in
winter, in spring, humming inside her head. "There'd be
no one watching us, no one who could get near us. Can the
Hancock building swim? We'd be alone. There'd be no Mrs.
Steeles chanting hexes over our heads. No King Philips
pulling the rug out from under us. It'd be just us. Just you,
me and . . . and Baby John."

I could feel her stiffen.

"I've planted crocuses out here," I hurried to say. Had I
said that already? "And there are wake-robins in the spring."
I started feeling at her again, her eyes, her lips. "Wild roses,
Hetty. Mussels at low tide. Wild strawberries in the spring.
Blueberry bushes in the low dell." Her chin, the down sweep
of her neck. "We could invent America all over again, the
two of us, right here where it was invented in the first place.

Only we could do it right this time. A little community of
right thinkers—you and me, Hetty. We could have each
other. We could love each other. We could be true to each
other, heart, body and soul. We could—"

"I've got to get back," she said suddenly, and for an instant she tensed where she sat as if she were stricken with
something—and then she was squirming to get away. I tried
to stop her, tried to pin her against the studs, even tried to
kiss her, but she twisted and turned until she'd gotten onto
her hands and knees. "I've got to get back," she said and
she started crawling away. "They need me. They'll die without me."

"But you just said—!"

"I've got to get back."

She was crawling like a madwoman, heading down along
the eave, and then making a right angle when she reached
the end of the attic, crossing over and then coming down
the opposite eave. I started after her.

"Hetty."

"I've got to get out of here."

"Hetty!"

"I've got to get back to them. It's been four days. If she
didn't read your note to them. If they don't know . . ."

I caught her by the ankle, but she kicked at me until I
had to let go. She started crawling again.

"I've got to get back."

I sat on my heels and watched her go. "Sweetheart . . ."

"Philip," she said, almost under her breath; and then
louder: "Philip!"

"Hetty, no."

She crawled over to the hatch. "Philip!' she shouted, and
she started rapping on the trap door with her knuckles.

"Sweetheart," I whispered. I crawled over to her. "You
want to make a life possible?" I tried to pull her away, but
she shook me loose. "It's Baby John. Baby John you can
make possible."

"Philip!"

"It's Baby John," I said, and again I tried to grab her, but she hit me.

"Leave me alone. I have to go. I have to *go!*"

"It's Baby John," I said, but this time I didn't even get a chance to touch her. She wheeled about and hit me.

"I'll show you *Nantucket,*" she cried—and for an instant she hung fire—and then she started pounding on the hatch with her fists.

"Shut the fuck up!" someone called from down in the house.

"Philip!"

"Shut the fuck up!"

"Philip! I've got my own peace treaty I want to make!"

There was no answer. I just sat on my haunches and watched the furious darkness over the hatch. I could see faint strips of her—her arms, her legs—where the light around the hatch lit her.

"Philip! Open up!"

Still no answer.

"Philip!"

Still nothing.

"They won't answer," I said. "They'll just wait until you wear yourself out."

"Philip!"

"You'll hurt yourself. You'll hurt your hands."

"Philip!"

"Really. They'll just wait until you wear yourself out," I said again. But even as I said it, I thought I heard the scrape of my ladder on the floor below.

"Philip! Open the door!"

I heard the ladder again.

"Philip!"

"I can't open it with you on it, Mrs. Wheelwright."

She stopped and for an instant didn't seem to understand. Then she was scrambling off to the side. I heard the two nails pulled out, and then the hatch was thrown back and light blew into the attic.

"Are you getting hysterical, Mrs. Wheelwright?"

"Open up," Hetty said one last time. She was screwing her knuckles into her eyes like a child waking up. "I want to come down," she said.

"I'm afraid that's impossible," Philip said. He was standing on the ladder with his head poked through the hatch.

"Why?" she said. "Why? Let me."

"Well, for one thing, Mrs. Wheelwright, I have my pajamas on."

"My name is Jenney. *Jenney.*"

"And for another, you're my captive." He said the word with a pleased sniff. Hetty crawled a couple of feet toward him.

"I want to make my own treaty with you," she said. "My *own* treaty."

"Also impossible."

"A separate peace treaty."

He shook his head. "I'm afraid the general idea with treaties is for each party to give something to the other. And in the present instance, I don't see how one of the parties has much to offer. Sorry." And he made her an apologetic smile and then looked across at me. "How're you getting on, Wheelwright?"

"Never felt better," I said.

"Not too tired?"

"No."

"Cramped?"

"Nope."

"Bored?"

I shrugged. "Been doing a couple of math problems in my head, proving Fermat's last theorem, working out a few riddles, that kind of thing."

"I've got my own Nantucket," Hetty said between us.

"Here, listen," I said. "An archaeologist sets up housekeeping—"

"I've got my *own* Nantucket!"

Philip turned back to her, and she had such a look of

intensity about her—her hair hanging in front of her eyes and her breath coming in short stabs—a new curiosity came over him.

"Just what kind of Nantucket *do* you have, Mrs. Wheelwright?" he asked after a time.

"I told you, my name is Jenney."

He made a quiescent gesture. "All right. Jenney."

"I'm prepared," she said and took a deep breath. "I'm prepared to make a statement."

"Oh, a statement," he said.

"I'll go before whatever cameras you want and I'll say anything you want."

"Anything?"

"I'll say I wasn't held forcibly. I'll say I've joined you. I'll say I approve of you. I'll say something against Isaac Wheelwright, if you want. He's *my* ancestor too. I'll say whatever you want. But I've got to get off the island. I've got to get back."

Philip seemed to be considering.

"We could work it like I was in on it from the beginning," she said. "Like I helped you plan it. Like I was—"

"—sort of a fifth columnist?"

"Yes. That's it!"

"Hetty," I said.

"But I want to be allowed to leave."

"It's a very interesting proposition, Mrs. Wheelwright, but how do I know you won't renege once you're off the island? You could say it now, under duress, and take it all back once you're safe again."

"I won't," she said. "I won't."

"She will," I put in.

"Even if you didn't plan to take it back," Philip went on, "it'd be hard to withstand examination. You'd contradict yourself. Don't you think?"

"I won't. I know how to handle myself."

"She would," I said. "She doesn't."

"And if you were arrested," Philip continued, "why

wouldn't you just tell the truth? Tell them you'd said what you did just to get free?"

She seemed to weaken. "I want to leave," she said.

Philip made an appreciative gesture. "But your little plan," he said, and again he looked apologetic, "I'm afraid it doesn't bear up under examination."

"It would help you with your suit," she said suddenly.

"The suit?" he repeated with a puzzled look.

"It would help emotionally. With public opinion. It would help with public opinion."

"But didn't you know?" he said. "The decision's already been handed down."

"What?" I said.

He turned to me and then let a look of understanding come over him. "That's right. Of course. You wouldn't know."

I took a couple of steps toward him and then stopped. "You lost," I said with sudden certainty.

"On the contrary. We won."

"You lost. You lost or you wouldn't still be out here."

"We won," he said, but this time it sounded like a bluff.

"You lost. If you'd won, the police wouldn't still be circling the island."

He shook his head. "Incorrect, Wheelwright. The occupation would still be an illegal act."

"*Would?*" I repeated as if I'd nailed him. "You lost."

He just stared at me.

"You lost!" I cried. "You lost!" And I could tell by the look that hovered on his face that it was true. He *had* lost. He eyed me an instant longer and then turned back to Hetty.

"Do you really want to get off this island, Mrs. Wheelwright?"

"Yes."

"You lost," I said again.

"At any cost?" he said. "You'd do anything?"

"Yes."

He seemed to consider. "Perhaps I spoke too hastily before when I said one of the parties had nothing to offer."

She eyed him.

"What do you think, Wheelwright? You think your wife has something to offer me?"

I didn't answer.

"Some nice Nantucket of her own?"

"You lost," I said.

"We're talking negotiation here," he said, "and I'm asking your advice. Should I be interested in your wife's Nantucket? Is it a cute little Nantucket?

"Leave her alone."

"What do you say, Mrs. Wheelwright? Do you want to get off this island that bad?"

She didn't answer, but she was looking at him, pulling her hair with one hand and looking at him.

"Do you want to get back that bad? Back to your crazy girls?"

She turned to me, but I didn't offer anything back, not a hint.

"You'd let me go?" she asked.

"Bright and early in the morning."

"And what would I have to do?"

"Honestly, Mrs. Wheelwright."

"Tell me," she said.

"You need it itemized?"

"I just want to know what exactly you're talking about."

"You know what I'm talking about."

She sat back on her heels. She had suddenly a look of pleading about her. "Why won't you just let me go?"

"Can't do it," he answered.

"Why?"

"It's against the rules."

"What rules?"

"The Game of America rules."

She hit herself, slapped her thighs with her hands. "I am *not* playing a game."

"*We* are, aren't we, Wheelwright?"

"No."

He shrugged. "At any rate, it would add to the salability of the film rights. Add a touch of sex to the show. Infidelity. Bare shoulders. Best of all, miscegenation. America is fascinated by the racially forbidden. What do you say, Mrs. Wheelwright?"

She just sat there, but I could tell she was crumbling inside.

"They'd get some white-skinned Hollywood tart to play you."

"Get out," I said.

"The latest example of *Homo erectus* to play me."

She closed her eyes. I was pretty sure she was crying.

"We'd have to give them character tips, insight, tell them how it was."

"No," she whispered.

"No? No, did she say? No tips? Or no, you won't do it?"

She shook her head again.

"It's the only way for you to get off the island."

Still, she didn't answer.

"And you'd look noble. Sacrificing your chastity for your girls."

I thought I saw her shake her head.

"It might even be fun."

"Get out," I said again and stood up. He turned to me.

"Take it easy, Wheelwright," he said. "Your machine-gun stunt is about all we need to give things an edge of danger. Let's leave it at that." And he took a step down the ladder and then turned to Hetty. "But I'm disappointed in you, Mrs. Wheelwright. I thought you had more of what it takes." He waited a moment for her to answer and then reached out for the hatch. "But if you should change your mind, I'll leave the trap door unnailed. Just come down if you decide you'd like . . . well . . . to leave in the morning. All right?"

He waited again for her to answer.

"All right?"

She just sat with her head on her knees.

"The court interprets Mrs. Wheelwright's silence as acknowledgment," he said, and he ducked quickly down and let the hatch slam shut after him. The light flew out of the room.

"Sweetheart?" I said. I hesitated an instant and then started crawling toward the darkness where she had been sitting. "Sweetheart?" I said again, and I felt for her with my hands. But the instant I touched her, she seemed to shrink from me. I held back, and then without touching her again, sat beside her. Slowly, the light came back into the room. I could see her drift out of the darkness: her head, her shoulders, her knees pulled up in front of her. She was looking down at her lap still, her hair hiding her face. After a minute, I reached out and gently tried to sweep it away, but again she recoiled.

"Hetty," I said—quickly, as if I were calming a spooked animal—"sweetheart." But I couldn't think what else to say. She just sat as she was, huddled to herself. A minute passed.

"Let's go lie down," I whispered finally. "Let's go lie under the scuttle and look up at the sky." But when I put my arm around her and tried to urge her over, she thrashed about where she sat.

"This is just fine with you," she spat out.

"What?" I said and fell back.

"You'd just as soon be here. Locked up here. It's fine with you."

"Hetty . . ."

"I know," she said, and she shot me a look through her hair. "I know what's going on. I know what you've been thinking. The longer it lasts, you've been thinking, the longer we're locked up out here, the longer I'll be away from the twins and the bigger the wedge driven between us. I know what's going on."

I just stared at her.

"If it lasts a week it's okay with you. A month. A year's okay. Anything to get me away from them. You *want* Mrs. Steele to have them. You do."

I could feel my face heat up. "Hetty . . ."

"I know what's going on," she said again. "I know you're waiting for April ninth. I even think it's the first thing you thought of once we were up here. You thought: If this lasts until April ninth, she won't be able to do it. She won't be able to do it and then she'll have to leave the twins and I'll have her. And you got the whole thing costumed up like you always do, telling me about Cousin Isaac and corrective afflictions like it could hide what you were thinking. The justly afflicted saint, you said. A provoking evil, you said. Telling me that *I've* lived wrong."

"I didn't."

"You did! You *implied* it. But what I want to know is: How are you so sure it isn't you? How do you know this hasn't happened because of you and what you've done? The way *you've* lived? The way *you've* acted? If I've lived wrong trying to save the twins, how have you lived not caring the least bit what happens to them? Only caring about you and yours. In the middle of the night picking up you and yours, but leaving them behind. Leaving them alone. Leaving them to Mrs. Steele."

"You liked it," I said, and I felt the first flush of anger with her. "You liked my carrying you off like that."

"I was sleepy."

"You *liked* it," I said as if I wanted to peg her to the truth.

"I was sleepy. I didn't think. You said you left a note. I didn't think."

"You liked it."

"I didn't even get a chance to tell them I was going, and where I was going, and when I'd be back. I *always* tell them that. I always let them know if I'm going out. Even if I'm just going out to the store. I *tell* them. I let them know so they won't think I've left them. If they think I've left them—" and she broke off.

"Okay," I said. "You tell them. But what difference does it make? What difference does it really make? Who says they understand you? Who says they hear you? And if they hear you, that it makes any difference? What difference would it have made if I'd left them a note or not? What difference—"

"Or not?" she broke in; she picked up her head. "Or not? What do you mean, *or not?* You said you left them one. You said you left them a note."

I should've answered right away, but my voice stuck in my throat.

"You said you left them a note!"

"Yes," I said.

"But you didn't."

She'd said it like a statement. I just looked at her.

"You didn't," she repeated, and this time it was almost a whisper.

"This is all wrong," I said.

"You didn't leave a note."

I thought to try to touch her.

"You said you did. But you didn't."

"Hetty . . ."

"Don't!" she cried, and she pulled back from me. "You lied to me. You lied about *that.*"

"I didn't *lie,*" I said. "I didn't mean to. I just said it. On the spur of the moment."

"Oh, you just *said* it."

"I was carrying you. And you were sleepy. You were beautiful. I just said it because I wanted to keep you that way."

"I wasn't beautiful."

"You were."

"You lied to me. And what's more, you did it so offhand."

"It *was* offhand. But that doesn't make it worse. If I'd planned if, if I'd planned to lie to you, then—"

"Then it would prove you took me seriously."

"What?"

"It'd prove you understood me and the twins. But as it is, with your offhand lies—"

"Not *lies.*"

"*As it is*," she repeated, "with your offhand lies, you only prove that you don't understand what the twins mean to me. That you don't understand what it means to me to lose them. That you don't understand me."

"I do. I do understand you."

She shook her head. She had a chill look about her now. And when she spoke again, her voice came as if from a great distance.

"How much more they are to me than you are."

"Don't . . ."

"How much more they mean to me. More than you and your island and your Baby John."

"He's not just *mine*."

"To think I waited this long trying to decide." She said it dispassionately, as if she were watching herself, marveling at herself. "I should've taken care of it right away. I shouldn't even have told you. I don't know why I did. But I'm lucky. I'm lucky I didn't. Because now I know."

"What?" I said. "What do you know?"

"What else have you lied about?" she asked, and she looked up at me. Even in the dark her eyes had a cold, killing look to them. "I want to know."

"Nothing," I answered. "I haven't lied to you."

"You've told me you loved me. Was that a lie? You've told me I was one of the elect. Was that a lie? You've told me I was pure-souled in spite of how I've lived. Was that a lie?"

"I meant them. I meant them all."

"And I've lived with you chaste."

"Yes."

"Chaste."

"Yes, yes."

"Chaste," she said and suddenly she laughed. "Chaste!" she cried. "What a word!"

"Hetty."

"Chaste!" she cried again.

"Hetty!"

"Chaste!"

I reached out and tried to hold her, but she scrambled out from under me.

"I'm leaving," she said. She almost spat the words out. "I'm leaving for real." And she started crawling toward the hatch. I reached for her, caught hold of her ankle, but before I could pull her back, she threw the hatch open. "Philip!" she cried. I pulled on her, dragged her back a foot, but she kicked at me, violently, twisting her ankle this way and that so I lost my grip. She scrambled for the hatch but I got hold of her again, managed to pull her away and then get to the hatch myself and close it. I squatted on it.

"You're not going anywhere."

"Get away," she said. She was kneeling about six feet off. I squatted as hard as I could squat.

"You're not going anywhere."

"Get away!"

I shook my head.

"Yes!" she cried and she came at me, kicking and scratching. I grabbed her by the arm and shoulder and threw her so she skidded across the rough decking.

"You're not going anywhere."

But she got up and came at me again; and again I shoved her back.

"Exactly nowhere," I said.

But she did it again, and this time I didn't push her back. I tried to cover myself up and talk to her from under my arms, then tried to turn myself away from her, this way and that, and still stay on the hatch, but she slapped and kicked and scratched at me until finally I had to push her away again. I hurt her this time. She cried out and stayed on the floor.

"Okay," I said. "Just stop it. Just stop it now."

But she got on her feet and launched herself at me, shouting at me now, calling me everything she could think of, slapping and kicking at me until finally I started slapping and kicking back. I hurt her. I know I hurt her. But she stayed on me, striking out at everything near her, at my face, my chest, my arms, missing me half the time, pulling my hair, throwing her weight at me and stumbling, falling, and then getting back on her feet. She kept at me until she was crying, until she was out of breath and weak on her feet. I ended up just dodging her, warding off the blows, ducking my head until finally she tripped—or I tripped her—and she went sprawling across the decking. I stayed on the hatch.

"Now, stop it," I said. "You stop it now."

I heard her pick herself up in the dark. But this time she stayed there.

"You might be able to do this now," she said, breathless and impotent. "You might be able to do this now—" she said and didn't finish.

"We don't want this," I said. "We don't want this."

"I've left," she said. I could just barely see her, just the rough outline of her head and shoulders. She was kneeling all of a piece on the floor.

"We don't want to do this."

"I've left," she said again. "I want you to know that. I've left."

"No."

"I've left. I've left your house. I've left your island. I've left you."

"You're still here," I said.

"I've left."

"You're still here," I said again.

She didn't answer.

"Aren't you?"

Still, she didn't speak.

"Aren't you? Aren't you still here?"

*   *   *

"Thou shalt beget sons and daughters but shall not enjoy them, for they shall go into Captivitie." Deut. 28:41

I lay in a Torpor for some days. My Minde, I remember, was a Desert of Thought, stung from time to time with the Realization of

*my Loss, but for Hours upon ende, dead, lifeless, without the Stirre
or Faint of Pain or Hate or Hope. I remember the thought rising
within me from time to time that I must get off the Savage's Pallet,
that I must move myselfe out of his Tent and back into God's worlde.
But I could not. Neither do I think I wanted to, for I was sunk to
a Pit of Destruction, and such is the Power of the Monster Despaire, that we turn that Destruction inward upon us and eat of
ourselves, daring the worlde to Ruin us. Even when the strength
return'd to my Limbs (for so the Bodie will sometimes betray the
Soule), I did not move. I did not want to be Saved. And yet with
each day my minde grew to match my Bodie, grew until I could not
but admit to myselfe my own Health, though I might Rage and
Hate it as a thing sent unwanted. When finally I was made to rise,
my Master made it clear to me that my Son was gone, that he was
gone North and gone for good, that he was gone where the snake
(those stars which we call the Dragon) disappears beneath the Earth.
He was gone and he was not coming back. He was Wampanoag
now. He was Naananto come back to life. I did not answer.*

*And so as before I did my Chores each day, and each night lay
outside in the snow in my blanket. I kept the fire, and so, kept
myselfe from a Death of freezing. But my thoughts ran ever now to
Escape. The long months of my Captivitie, during which I had
never tried for Freedom, had made my Master lax about me. And
he had not the Intelligence nor the Humanitie (may I say?) to understand that it was my Son that had kept me from Violence against
him, and that now that my Son was gone from me, that I might be
alive with Plots. I dissembl'd and shamm'd, fit myselfe to the Picture
of a servante, aided the women, bow'd myselfe to the childish will
of my Master's two boys, but all the time look'd left and right about
me, and look'd with new eyes, eyes that were hungry for the chance
to do Violence.*

*Vengeance became my Mate. I slept with her, woke with her,
ate of her, breath'd of her. I dream'd of the feel of Murther, of the
crush of bone and the tear of flesh, of the feel of the gullet under
my Thumbs. I hatch'd a Hundred possibilities, some the chicks of
pure Fancie, some the thought-out plans of good Reason. I thought
of laying in a Store of dry twigs, that some night I might creep to
each of the tents (we were but five familys now), lay a wreathe of*

kindling about each, and then with a coal from the night fire I tended, create such an Infernoe that I could escape in the fierie Confusion. Then I thought too that I might simply make an Escape in the night, build the fire up so my absence would not be noted and set out, giving myselfe up to my Lord and to good Luck that I might put a distance of some miles between myselfe and the camp before note of my Absence was taken. But in any such Plot the snow was my enemy: the tracks I would leave might be follow'd by a childe. If I did not put a goodlie distance behind me before my Absence was discover'd, surelie I would be caught, and once caught, my Bodie subjected to the most hideous Torments.

The river was my real Hope. It lay about a quarter-mile from the camp, and though I did not know then which river it was, I knew the Lord's worlde, and I knew it must flow oceanward to some towne or citie upon the sea. I could work a canoe, and given some severall hours start, knew I could make a Headway back to Civilization. It was not uncommon for me to be sent to the river for water, or to help portage a canoe, or fetch some hunter's kill—but in all these instances, if I was alone at the water, there was no canoe nearby, and if there was a canoe, then I was never alone. They kept that much Watch upon me. If I was to Escape, it would have to be when there was a canoe by the River, and if there was a canoe by the River, then there would be someone with it whom I would have to kill.

And this is how it came about. It was growing to Duske one day—that earlier duske of November—when my Master's wife sent me to the riverside to await her husband who had gone with his two sons to the Falls upriver to fishe. But when I got to the waterside, they were already there, ashore, the canoe pulled aground. I did not try to disguise my approach, but drew up as I might have any other Daye. They were working apart, my Master and his youngest boy off by the woods and the oldest boy—who was about fourteen and so accounted nearly a man—by the rocks dressing the fishe. I signaled my presence to my Master with great Dissemblance and then drew up to the older boy. He glanced at me once and then went back to his labor. He had a knife, an Englishman's knife, and I knew I must Deal with him first before I took on his father. I asked pleasantlie if the Catch was good. He made no answer but merely swept the knife at the four or five fishe laid out Headless on the rocks. I knelt beside him, my heart knocking against my Ribs and my Throat swelling within my necke. (For I do not mind admitting that I was Frightened. I had never taken a Life before and did not then—in spite of my later worke—account myselfe a soldier.) I asked him would he like me to help. But he shook me off. I asked him again, saying something about women's worke, but again he said no, he would do it. He had been blessed in his fishing, he said. I agreed that he had been, and then looked over his Shoulder at where his father and younger brother were working. They were almost hidden now by the duske—as were we, I was sure, from them. When the older boy chanced to put down the knife, I took it up. He glanced up at me, but I smiled as if to reassure him and reached for a new fishe. And then, I don't know why, but instead of doing the Deed, I began to clean fishe. I cut the head off, split the Belly, cut the tail, and reached for another. I did three in all, my mind spinning inside my head, and a great voice shouting at me: Do it! Do it! Do it! until finally, just as I was to reach for the last fishe, I went for the boy, grabbing him around the necke, and then all in a motion— as if I was as practic'd at it as a Hussar—I slit his throat. The skin made the same pop and hiss as a fishe belly. He was so surpris'd he had not even time to cry out or struggle. I felt the life go instantly out of him. And it was my fancie that it slid out of him down through his Legs and out his Feet and into the nearby river which was black and hushed and somehow accepting of his Soule. I lay his head down gently on the Soile. And I think I remember saying that I was sorry. But I do not know to whom it was I said it: to the boy, to my Lord, or to myselfe.

I stood up and in an instant calculated that the Deed had not been Noticed. I felt a powerful Energie, like a Shoot of Lightening in my legs, and it was a great Effort to keep myselfe from running straight to the Canoe. But to do so was to invite Failure. Instead I began walking toward the woodside where my Master was still. I tried to keep an ordinarie Aire about me, but there was something wrong. I felt Hot and Dizzy, and somehow I knew I did not look Right. The harder I tried to seem at Ease, the more stiff and wrong I felt. I seemed to be shouting: "Murther! Murther! Murther!" with each step. My Master looked up and for an instant watched me come. And I remember thinking: "He knows. He knows. But how?" And then as if answering myselfe: "Does Murther change you so?" And the Truth is I do not know how he knew—whether he saw the Knife in my hand or if he had an Animal scent that something was wrong, or if I myselfe gave off the Odor of Treacherie—but he sprang to his feet and, first shouting something at his boy, ran toward the River.

I caught him just as he was swinging a firearm from out of the bottom of the Canoe. He wheel'd about and tried to hit me with it—there was no time to fire it—but I duck'd and then caught him with the Knife. He cried out and sprang away. The gun dropp'd between us. I kick'd it Aside and then dove toward him. I got him again with the Knife, but he manag'd to Wrestle me down. And then for some Time we lay in each other's Grippe while the boy ran in circles around us, shouting and crying in Terror, coming forward and kicking me, and then backing off and crying to his Father again. I felt match'd in Strength. I could not free myselfe nor use the Knife to Advantage. But I had cut him twice I knew, and hop'd that the Wound must begin to Sap him before too long. He shouted at his son, told him to run back to the Camp, but the Boy could not tear himself away from us. The Savage shouted again, and then again, until with a cry the boy ran off. I began to feel my Strength ebb, and as it went I could see a Light come into the Savage's eyes. It was a light of Bloodlust, of Hunger for me. And yet he could not force the Knife away from me. We were each of us caught by the other. He looked at me, looked at me with his eyes just six inches from mine, as if his greatest Strength was the Hate in those eyes. As if he meant to defeat me with Hate. And I saw in them, in their black Depths, not just his Hatred of me, but the Hatred of his Race for mine, the Hatred of the God-forsaken for the God-belov'd. It was the Blood Hatred of the Animal, the Soule Hatred of the Heaven-exspell'd. And it was Pleasure. It was Anticipation. It was Love for the Thought of Killing. But here is what I wonder now: what did the Savage see in my eyes? Did he see in me the same Hate, the Hate of the White Race for all who are bodied with the Impuritys of Color? And did he see the same Anticipation, the same Pleasure in Killing, the same look of Love as his Strengthe oozed out of him along with his Blood; the same look of Love as I forc'd him over and plung'd the knife into him again and again; the same look of Love as his Life left him—and the Earth was burden'd with one less breathing Speck of Impuritie?

When it was done, I left the Knife on the grounde and got to my feet. I was dizzy, breathless, and my hands were wet with the Savage's blood. But I knew I had to go after the Boy. I ran through the dark woods, along the path to the Camp. I tried to think how much a Head start he had, but I could not Calculate how long I had lain with the Savage, nor how long I had been in killing him. I ran as fast as I could, the branches whipping my Face, tripping once or twice in the dark, my Brain wilde with Fear and Violence and the Exultation of Blood. When I caught sight of him running ahead of me, I was wild with thoughts of stealing him, stealing him as my boy had been stolen, of taking him with me in the canoe downriver, and instead of putting him ashore after a safe time, taking him back with me, taking him so he would be mine as a Slave. I would hold his Soule as a Ransom, teach him the salvation of Christ, reduce him to Civilization. And I was still thinking it when I caught up to him and hit him, hit him so that he went sprawling across the grounde. I leapt upon him as I would have a man and took his Throat in my Hands, putting my Thumbs upon the Softness just under the Adam's-apple, and in a great Turmoil of Hate I began choking him. And I spoke to him as I did, my Mind all awry, scolding him one instant and loving him the next, all the while strangling him, speaking to him as if he were my boy, my lost boy, as if his frighten'd face were my boy's frighten'd face, as if his black hair were my boy's blonde hair, as if his black eyes were my boy's blue eyes, as if his dark skinne were my boy's faire skinne, spoke to him as if he were mine, and then again, as if I were the Savage who had taken him, the Savage who had stolen him, adopted him, and was now killing him, strangling the whiteness out of him. He was at once a Savage boy and my boy, and I was at once my Christian self and a Savage. I was a Savage strangling a white boy, a white man strangling a Savage, a white man strangling his white boy, a Savage strangling a Savage. And the whole time there was a Voice saying over and over: "Thou shalt beget sons . . . thou shalt beget sons . . . thou shalt beget sons . . ."

and it did not stop until the boy was dead, until I felt the muscles in his neck go soft, until there was no Life left to kill.

I pick'd him up and carried him through the woods back to the Riverside. I do not even now know why, but I did. I put him in the bottom of the canoe, looked for the knife in the dark, and then after hiding the other two bodys in the Bracken, set off downriver. I was too sapp'd of Strengthe to paddle, and so could only drift where the Currente would take me. I look'd at the boy's bodie by the Moonlight, watch'd him as if I expected him at any moment to move, or to say something to me. I do not remember thinking or feeling anything, not even Joye at my Freedom, nor Feare that I might be overtaken. All around me the Wildernesse seemed to breathe in and out, and in my Torpor, I had the Fancie that the Moon overhead was like a great savage Eye watching me, the Eye of a giant Magog standing upon the Newengland landscape, and the hoot of an owl like a Laugh frozen in the Aire. I spent the whole night drifting in and out of sleepe, waking from time to time when the canoe bumped the banks of the river, or when I heard the Roare of rapids ahead, making a portage over the rocks or through the woods—always with the boy's bodie still inside the canoe. When morning came, I felt no better, dazed still, and somehow unsure—in spite of the sun's rising in front of me—that the river was running seaward and not deeper inland.

Toward Noone, I came upon some cleared Land, and then a Homesteade, burnt-out and abandoned. Half-an-hour later there was another, and then severall more, one of them with a Cow standing inside the charred timbers. When I saw still another in the Offing, I pointed the canoe toward the Riverbank and put ashore. It was a small farm with fields along the river and a Croft behind the house. The land was charred under the snow: a queere sight, the Virgin spreade hiding the Ruin'd Black beneath. The house itselfe was nothing more than a black skeleton. I could tell by the Timbers that it had been a goode House, a well-built house. On one of the inside walls there was the remnante of white Plaster, blackened by the fire, and the Stairway that led to the upper floore ended in mid-aire. I kick'd through the Rubble, found a Trivett and some ironware, then a Bible burnt into a black Stone, and then a Bay Psalm Booke charred only at the edges. I opened the Psalm booke with my foot, let the dry, cold pages Leafe upon themselves. But I didn't picke it up. I stood and listened to the Chill winde whistle through the Timbers, looked out through the walls at the edge of the Wildernesse that stood Sentrie along the Rim of the fields as if readie at any Time to retake the clear'd land. I felt Queere. And I remember wondering to myselfe what Eyes there were in that Wildernesse that were even now looking at me; and what Ears there were that were listening to me. And what kinde of Heartes were there that beat in that Wildernesse? I even may have asked it aloud, spoken in the frigid Aire. But there was no Answer.

Back in the Canoe I look'd at the Boy. He seem'd asleep, his eyelashes just Grazing the tops of his Cheeks and his Mouthe dropp'd open. I felt neither Regret nor Griefe nor Triumph at the sight of him. Nor did I feel Sorrow. I have a Memorie of trying to move him a little, move him so his Head would be more comfortable, but he was frozen Stiffe. And yet I still did not put him overboard.

Night fell again, and again I let the canoe drift, wrapp'd in my Blankett and dozing on and off. I had a Dream of my Wife which I will not relate, and another of my son. And I dream'd I was back at Swansea, living in my burnt-out House. It was snowing and the snow fell through the black Rafters and drifted in through the Walls, covering me in whiteness. Somewhere out in one of my fields a wolf howled, and then howled nearer still, and then nearer until I heard its Paws and its heavie Breathe inside the house. But I was so shagged with Ice I could not rise to frighten him away. He lay down like a Dog at my Hearth.

When morning came I awoke to a Cry along the riverbank. I started up and for an Instant I was shot through with the Thought that the Savages had come after me. But I quicklie saw that I had travel'd into another Settlement and that an Alarm had been sent out—for in my Blankett, traveling in a canoe, I was being thought an Indian. I heard the Bell at the garrison House sounded, and across the way someone was running downhill toward me, shouldering a Firearm. I took up the paddle and paddl'd as hard as I might downriver toward a Stretch of trees. I heard the sound of the Flintlock fired behind me and heard the Ball pass hissing over my

Head. When I had made it to the Trees I paddl'd toward the shore where I might best be Hidden and bethought myselfe. Should I cry out? Should I wait until the towne had garrisoned itselfe and then go further downriver? Should I go ashore here, without the canoe, without the blankett, and make myselfe known as an Englishman? That latter would be best I thought. And yet I felt a Strangeness in me, a Reluctance, as if I wanted not to go ashore, but to paddle myselfe back upriver, back upriver past the burnt-out settlements, past the last char'd field, past the Savage's camp even, until there was only me and the empty Wildernesse. But I lay these feelings now to the Exertion of my extreme Condition. In the end I paddl'd downriver until I came to the clear'd field that fronted the garrison House and, throwing my Blankett off, stepp'd ashore. And then, so that the sentrys atop the garrison might Recognize me as a Friend, I push'd the Canoe back out toward the Middle of the River where it might catch the current and continue on its way. The Boy's bodie went with it.

So ended my Captivitie during the late war called King Philip's War. Of my Experiences as Captain in the Plimouth Militia, of the Encarceration of the Heathen in Boston Harbour, and of the Awefull Victorie at Great Swamp, of the Decapitation and quartering of Philip, and of the selling of his only son into West Indian Slaverie, I tell in the Second Part of this Narrative. The Reader is kindlie ask'd to turn thither.

* * *

When I woke it was to the sound of the nails being hammered back into the hatch. I sat up, and for an instant I thought Hetty was really gone, as if her saying "I've left" had been haunting me in my sleep and had somehow made itself true. I said her name in the dark, but there was no answer. It was night still, maybe only an hour or two after we'd fought. I wondered if she'd been asleep yet. Was she sleeping even now? Or was she sitting back awake and angry still? I called her name again, but again there was no answer.

"Sweetheart?" I said, and started crawling toward where she'd been last. I searched with my hands ahead of me, but there was nothing there. I sat back on my heels and looked across the attic, peered from one corner to the other, but it was too dark to see.

"Hetty?"

No answer.

"Hetty?"

Nothing.

"We'll do this systematically," I said, but my voice sounded odd, as if I were talking to myself, knowing she was awake and listening. I crawled to one of the corners of the attic, as far under the eaves as I could get, and then started a sweeping operation, crawling the length of the building, sweeping left and right with my hands, and then turning at each gable end, moving three feet farther toward the center of the attic and starting over again. I kept saying: "I'm coming to get you, I'm coming to get you," as if it were a game we were playing. I figured I'd catch her no matter what. But by the time I'd made five passes and was coming up along the opposite eave, I still hadn't found her. When I reached the end wall, I sat back and stared at the darkness. Had she been moving soundlessly out of my reach each time I came near her? Had she been listening for me and then slipping quietly to the side so that I missed her?

"Hetty?"

And for the first time, I felt a little panicky. I stood up, and thinking I saw a patchiness in the dark to my left, I leaped and swatted at it. But there was nothing there. I did it again, trying to catch her by surprise, and then again, and again, until I was leaping about the attic, swatting at the air, kicking it, feinting and dodging this way and that, trying to get her before she could maneuver away. I hit my head against the rafters, hurt my hand, tripped once, but no matter how fast I moved, or how wildly I swung or kicked, and no matter where I went, I couldn't find her. I stopped dead in the center of the attic.

Was she gone?

"Hetty?"

Was she really gone?

I tried to think, tried to remember how it had been. I'd
fallen asleep on the hatch. I was certain of that. But had I
moved off it in my sleep? And had she waited until I had
and then slipped downstairs? Could she have moved me off
it herself while I was sleeping? Was that possible? I tried to
remember back to when I'd woken up. Had I woken on the
hatch? The nails had sounded like they were right under
me, hadn't they? Or had they sounded just off to my left?

I couldn't remember.

"Hetty?" I whispered in the dark, and I felt a horrible
sickness in me. She was gone. Somehow she was gone, and
yet I couldn't shake the feeling that she was there in the
darkness somewhere, watching me. I started running around
again, kicking and hitting at the air, sending the can of V-8
juice flying against the wall, and then a couple of Coke cans.
But there was nothing of her there, nothing. I tried prying
the hatch open, putting my fingertips in the cracks, but I
knew it was senseless. When I ripped a fingernail, I started
in running again, shouting her name and shouting Philip's
name, and then screaming and yelling and hitting the roof
planking one minute and the attic decking the next until my
hands hurt and my knuckles were sore and bruised and, for
all I could tell, bleeding. I finally hit my head again against
a rafter, hit it hard this time so that I think I was knocked
out for the few seconds it took me to fall down—because I
seemed to come to just as I hit the floor.

I lay there for a long time in a kind of black spell, witless
and barely breathing. And then I was up again, up on my
hands and knees on the attic floor over the bedroom and
banging on the decking, banging with the flat of my hands,
with my knuckles, with the can of V-8 juice. I don't know
how long I kept it up, but it was a long time, half an hour,
maybe forty-five minutes, forty-five minutes of banging and
shouting over the bedroom, banging and shouting until my

hands were ringing with pain and my lungs were burning inside me, banging and shouting until I was exhausted in a way I'd never been before, every muscle and bone in my hands feeling on fire, and the muscles in my arms aching, aching in my shoulders and in my neck. I don't remember how it was or when it was that I stopped, but I did stop, because I remember coming to on the floor again, as if I'd fallen asleep or lost consciousness, although I don't think either happened. I think my mind just went empty, and for a time there was nothing but a roar of pain inside me. And then I did fall asleep.

When I woke, the attic air had that faint purplish haze of daybreak. My arms were sore and stiff, and my hands felt like clubs, the fingers grafted together. I sat up and looked around the attic. It was dark still, but I could see a little now. I found the can of V-8 juice and put it under the scuttle, but it was a minute before I could gather myself and step up. When I did, I couldn't see much, just the outline of the Quonset hut, the MDC building below, the running lights of the boats circling the island, but nothing of Philip or any of the other Indians. And nothing of Hetty. I stood there for a long time, waiting. I felt dead inside, dead in my thoughts, dead in my feelings, dead enough so that I wasn't quite aware of what it was I was doing when I stepped down and emptied out the chamberpot and then turned it over and put it under the can of V-8 juice.

It took me three tries—my hands hurt still and I skinned my elbow on the edge of a beam—but I made it, pulled myself up in a sort of iron cross, and then swinging a leg around, caught the lip of the scuttle and rolled onto the roof. I just lay there for a time, lay on my hand-split shingles, waiting for someone to cry out. But there was nothing, nothing from inside the house, nothing from the Quonset hut. I sat up, slowly. Straight across from me, on the mainland, the Hancock building stood right where it had always stood, spangled with lights, cool, electric. At the sight of it I felt something awaken in me. I was going to do something.

I didn't know what. But I felt it, felt something in me that was going to happen. There was a fire down the hill, a campfire, and I could see some people sitting around it. And there was a light inside the Quonset hut. But no one had seen me. I was safe so far. I began creeping down the roof, one course of shingles at a time, careful not to slip, careful not to make any noise. When I reached the edge, I stopped and began crawling along the eave. I made it along the front of the house, then up and down one gable, along the back of the house, up and down the other gable and back to where I'd started. There was no one outside the house, no guard, no sentry, no one. I looked for a good place to land—clear of any bushes and away from the windows—and then squatting at the very edge of the roof, jumped.

I hit the ground, somersaulted and got up as fast as I could and stood back against the house. But again, I hadn't been heard. I stood there trying to think what the best thing to do was. Where was Philip? Was he inside? Was Hetty? Were they in there right now not three feet from me? I crept along the wall to the bedroom window, but the inside shutters were closed. I kept going around the house, past the TV set and the generator, until I came to the keeping-room window. It was open, but there was no light inside so I couldn't see very well. I looked in at the next window, and when I came to the door, opened it, slowly.

There was a gun, right there on the table, one of the submachine guns. And there was no one near it. I crossed to it and picked it up, expecting the whole time to be caught, to be heard or seen, or to realize I'd been tricked. But there was nothing. I checked the gun over—was it loaded?—found the trigger, the safety catch, held it against my shoulder for fit. And then I looked around the room. There were all my things, my table and chairs, the settle, my iron cooking things, my workbench, my dough trough; and over everything was strewn the litter of the last four days, beer cans, Coke cans, someone's dirty clothes, a half-eaten hot dog. I picked my way quietly to the bedroom door and listened, but there was no sound from inside. I didn't know quite what to do. I had a picture of Philip standing on the other side with his own gun—Hetty behind him—waiting for me. In the end I put my hand to the latch, and holding the gun ready at my shoulder, slowly, quietly, opened the door.

There was someone there, two of them, in bed, and there was another on a cot. But they were sleeping. And they weren't Philip. They weren't Hetty. I crept a few feet into the room, looked around and then crossed to the foot of the bed. I felt a bloom of victory inside me.

"*By the shores of Gitchee-gumee,*" I whispered. No one stirred. "BY THE SHORES OF GITCHEE-GUMEE," I said again, louder; this time someone moved. "*BY THE SHORES OF GITCHEE-GUMEE!*" I shouted.

They jumped awake, all three of them. I held the gun up so they wouldn't get too eager.

"*By the shores of Gitchee-gumee,*" I recited. "*By the shining big sea waters, Sits the wigwam of . . .*"

They stared at me. I waved the gun about.

"Is this loaded?" I asked.

Still they just stared.

"Is it?"

"What?" one of them answered. It was the skinny, mouthy bastard from the first day.

"The gun. Is it loaded?"

"No," one of the others—the one on the cot —answered.

"No?" I said. I crossed to him and pointed the barrel at his head. "Then you won't mind if I—"

"No!"

I tried to keep the smile off my face, but I couldn't help it.

"Let's go find your King Philip."

CHAPTER
16

The Game of America

• 1 •

I marched them down the hill toward the campfire, keeping the gun at their backs and checking into the dark bushes on each side as we went. I told them to take it easy, to go slow, not to shout anything or try anything stupid. I told them I was a man at the end of my rope and who knew what a man at the end of his rope might do. The sun was just coming up, and out on the water the boats were beginning to attach themselves to their running lights. It was cold—I'd only just realized it—and the ground was wet. Ahead of us I could see someone sitting huddled at the campfire, and around him three or four sleeping bags stuffed with bodies. He had a gun. I could see it leaning against a sawhorse beside him. I told my three captives to close ranks around me, and then when we were about twenty feet distant, told them to stop. The man at the campfire had turned to us.

"Tell him what the story is," I said to one of my captives, and when he didn't answer, I jabbed him in the back with the gun.

299

"What *is* the story?"

"The story is I'm in charge."

"What's up?" the sentry called suddenly. One of the sleeping bags stirred.

"This bastard's got a gun on us!" my captive called back.

"What?"

"He's got a gun. You know, a gun!"

"Who?"

"The Wheelwright bastard! Who else?"

The sentry picked up his own gun. I let him.

"How'd he get a gun?"

"Who gives a sweet shit how he got it? He's got it!"

The sleeping bags were waking up. I told my captives to stay right where they were, hands in their pockets.

"Where's Philip?" I called from behind them. He didn't answer. "Where's Philip?" I said again.

"Dicking your wife, the last I heard."

I fired a couple of rounds in the air. A bullhorn crackled out on the water and I heard a faint holler from one of the hills where the machine-gun emplacements were. The sleeping bags had scrambled to their feet. But they weren't any of them Philip. Or Hetty.

"I'm a man at the end of his rope," I said. "Now, where's Philip?"

"I don't know," he answered. The bullhorn crackled again; I caught something about having come this far without anyone getting hurt.

"It's not that big an island," I said. "Take a guess."

"I don't know," he said again, but just as he did, the door to the Quonset hut opened. I saw Philip step out—in his pajamas—and then two others behind him. My name gargled through the bullhorn.

"Is that you, Wheelwright?" Philip called.

"That's right."

"How did you get out?"

"I levitated."

"You levitated," he repeated.

"That's right."

"And the gun? You've got a gun?" He couldn't see me very well; I was still behind my trio of captives.

"That's right."

"And how did you get that?"

"It was like the loaves and the fish."

"The loaves and the fish," he repeated. He took a couple of steps up the hill. "And what do you plan on doing with it?"

"I'm not sure yet. I might use it, and I might not. You'll have to wait and see."

He gestured toward the Quonset hut. "Do you mind if I change into my clothes while you're making up your mind."

"Yes."

"Yes, you do mind?"

"But you can tell your boys behind you to take a hike. That way," I said and motioned toward the hills where the machine guns were.

"Why?" he said. "They haven't got guns."

"And then you can tell these four around the fire to follow them."

He held off an instant, and then motioned for them to go. "Keep it smart," he said when they balked. "He just wants me."

"That's right," I said. "I just want him."

They started off, slowly, two of them taking their sleeping bags with them. I waited until they'd headed down the path that led to the little valley at the center of the island and then told Philip to come closer.

"And now you," I said to my three captives when he'd come up to the fire. "And don't any of you come back until I give the signal. Tell the others. And tell them to keep away from the house from now on. The house is off limits. Understand?"

One of them nodded and the skinny one started to say: "We know, you're a man at the end—" but I hit him. I hit him as hard as I could in the back of the head with the steel butt of the gun. He crumpled onto the ground and just lay there.

"Wheelwright!"

"I am not playing a game," I said.

The other two picked him up under the arms and dragged him toward the path. I waited until they were out of sight.

"It's just you and me," Philip said.

"Where is she?"

"Who?"

I did it again, this time right in the face. He fell backward and blood burst from his nose.

"For Christ's sake!"

"Where is she?"

"Shit!"

"Where is she?"

"She's gone! What do you think?"

"Get up."

"I'm bleeding. I need something to stop the blood."

"Get up!"

"My teeth!"

"I could kill you," I said, and I felt dizzy saying it. "I could kill you for free. Now, get up."

He had his pajama sleeve to his mouth. He got slowly to his feet. I motioned him downhill.

"She's gone," he said. "I told you. She's gone."

"I'd like to see for myself," I said and pushed him along in front of me with the gun.

"Fuck you."

When we reached the Quonset hut I told him to open the door and to go slowly in. I followed him, peering first around the jamb to see if there was anyone lying in wait for me. But there was no one. It was a mess, the cabinets of potsherds and bone fragments rifled, the floor littered with soup cans and half-empty bags of potato chips, a Coleman stove in the corner, sleeping bags, my cot commandeered. I picked my way through it, turning over a hamburger roll, a candy wrapper, with the point of my gun, as if I expected to find Hetty under them.

"Outside," I said when I was done.

We headed down the path toward the dock. There was a police boat out on the water, following us at a constant fifty yards. I motioned once for them to go off, but they kept idling after us. When we got down to the dock, I checked the Parks and Recreation building. But the city's lock was still on the door.

"I told you," Philip said. "She's gone. We let her go."

I looked up toward Fort Bentley. Could they have her up there?

"Why?" I asked. "Why'd you let her go?"

"Why do you think?"

"I'm asking you."

"Because she fulfilled her obligations. That's why."

I just stared at him. "If that's true," I said finally, "it'd be the first time you ever kept your word."

"Mr. Wheelwright!" the bullhorn sparked suddenly. There was someone standing out on the foredeck of the police boat. They were angling toward us, toward the dock. *"Mr. Wheelwright! Is that you?"*

I looked back at Philip, and then at the banner strung between the Parks building and a tree.

WELCOME TO AUSCHWITZ, AMERICA

"Take it down," I said.

"What?"

"The banner. Take it down."

"John Wheelwright!"

"Take it down," I said again to Philip. He climbed off the dock onto the rocks. I turned to the police boat.

"John Wheelwright!"

"Go away!" I shouted.

"Are you safe?"

"Go away!"

I heard the inboard kick in; they started coming faster toward the dock.

"We are the police!"
"No!" I shouted.
"Everything will be all right!"
"Go away!"
But they kept coming, arcing toward the dock, as if they wanted to rescue me on the fly. I lifted the gun to my shoulder and fired at them, a short burst over their heads. It took them an instant to react, and then they veered away.

"This is my island!" I shouted after them. They turned and idled a good distance off, their own guns up.

"Let's go," I said to Philip. He had stopped bleeding, but the arm of his pajama top was a bright red. "And bring that," I added, gesturing at the banner.

I marched him back uphill, and when we got to the campfire, told him to throw the banner in it. Then, back inside the Quonset hut, I found a cardboard box and got him to start filling it with food. He went about it wordlessly, getting out six-packs of Coke and beer, cans of sardines and soup, boxes of crackers, tuna fish, cupcakes, raisins. When he was done, he stood silently over the box. I motioned for him to pick it up.

"So what do you plan on doing?" he asked without moving.

"You'll find out."

"You're making a mistake."

I pointed the gun at him. "Do I need to inform you that temporary insanity is a legal defense in Massachusetts?"

"You're making a mistake," he said again. "We were negotiating. We were moving toward a settlement. Another couple of days and you'd have had your island back."

"I've got it back now."

"There was another session planned for this morning. In about two hours."

"I guess you'll miss it."

"I can't miss it. Not if you really want this island back."

"Let's go," I said.

"Look, Wheelwright. Those morons of mine will try to

hold out for the whole thing. We were moving toward a
monument or something. I was beginning to sell them on
the idea."

"A monument?"

"That's right."

"What kind of monument?"

"Who gives a sweet shit? A plaque or a stone or something. Something commemorating the Indian dead."

"And it'd be out here? A monument out here on my
island?"

"Where else?"

"A monument for more tourists to come see?"

"You could grow ivy around it. No one would even notice it."

"Let's go."

"Look," he said. "You won the suit. Of course you won
the suit. I never thought it'd be otherwise. And you can get
out of this whole goddamn thing with only a three-foot-by-
three-foot granite headstone saying something about the
Indian dead."

"Is that all?"

"For Christ's sake, Wheelwright, they died out here! One
hundred of them!"

"It'll be one hundred and one if you don't pick that
box up."

He stared at me and didn't move. "You're an asshole."

"I'm an asshole with a gun. Now pick it up."

Outside I marched him uphill past the campfire to Mavericke's house. I told him to clean it out, to put everything
back the way it was before he'd come. He started with the
trash, the beer cans and candy wrappers. When he was done
I stood over him like an interior decorator, pointing the
settle here, the candlestand there, the table and chairs, the
blanket chest, the spinning jenny, my Brewster chair. And
then I got a length of rope.

"Oh, for Christ's sake, Wheelwright!"

I pushed him into the pantry.

"If you let me go," he said, "we'll be off the island in two days."

I tied his wrists together.

"At least put me up in the attic. There's no need to tie me up."

I shoved him down onto his knees.

"What do you want? Do you want your island back or do you just want to humiliate me?"

I tied the rope behind him, up and around his neck in a way I'd heard about from Vietnam—if the prisoner tried to move, he choked himself—but I couldn't get it right. He kept gagging even when he wasn't moving.

"Wheelwright!"

So in the end I just tied his ankles together and pulled them up behind him so his knees were bent, and then tied his feet to his hands. That way he couldn't stand up and he couldn't sit down. He could only lie on one side, and then by a great effort, flop himself onto the other side. I pulled down one of the muslin curtains Hetty had made for the pantry window and rolled it into a gag.

"It's just the Game of America," I told him.

CHAPTER
17

Hetty Six Inches Tall

• 1 •

When it was over—after I had him tied and gagged and the
pantry door shut; and after the Indians had come back from
Fort Bentley and the hills; and after I'd seen with my own
eyes a brace of business suits land on the dock, folding chairs,
table and all—I put down my gun and was ill in a chamberpot. And then I slept.

And I dreamed. I dreamed I was back at Mrs. Steele's
sleeping on the twins' couch, but instead of ravenous fans
and whirling seesaws, I was dreaming of Hetty. And then I
dreamed I was still up in the attic and Hetty and Philip
were below me in the bedroom, a TV crew at each of the
windows, videotaping while he took her clothes off, first
Amias's lappet cap, then her satin overdress, then her lace
fichu, her petticoat. When he carried her over to the bed,
one of the TV men held up a sun-gun through the window
for better lighting.

"I remember on Martha's Vineyard when you hit me, "
she said. "I liked it. I liked it when you hit me."

And the TV crews chorused: *"She liked it when he hit her."*
"I wanted you to do this to me then."
"She wanted him to do this to her then."
"I wanted you to undress me right there in the street and do me up against that brick wall so my back got all scraped."
"She wanted her back all scraped."
"But I was too young . . ."
"But she was too young . . ."
". . . and scared of you . . ."
". . . *and scared of him* . . ."
When I woke, Mavericke was sitting at the foot of the bed. I called his name and reached for him, but he just shook his head and faded, faded right in front of my eyes.

• 2 •

"I want to know what happened."
He was lying on his side, looking up at me out of the corner of his eye. He was sweating.
"I'm going to take the gag off and I don't want to hear anything out of you except what happened. Got it?" And I waited for him to nod and then knelt down and untied the gag.
"Christ, Wheelwright!"
"What did you do to her?" I said and stood up.
"Christ!" he said again. "You've got to leave that off. I can't breathe."
"I want to know what happened."
"Leave it off. Okay? Leave it off."
I just stared down at him.
"Nothing happened."
I kicked him in the ribs.
"Really!" he cried. "Nothing happened. We let her go."
I kicked him again.
"You bastard!"

"I want to know what happened."

"Nothing."

I did it a third time.

"You bastard, Wheelwright, you bastard!"

"What happened?"

"You can go fuck yourself!"

I knelt down and tied the gag back on.

· 3 ·

"Mavericke," I said when I was back in the keeping room. "Mavericke." But the house was silent.

· 4 ·

I ate some cupcakes and sardines and then lay down again. This time it was Hetty and Mavericke—Hetty and Mavericke making love in midair, floating midway between floor and ceiling, their bodies as light as their souls, while I sat lumpish in the corner, earthbound, mud-caked, figuring out my own specific gravity and coming up with a figure well over a damned soul. When I woke, I couldn't help myself. I pulled the nails out of the attic hatch, opened it and popped my head through, but she wasn't there.

"Are you hungry?" I asked Philip back in the pantry. "Are you thirsty? Not too bored?"

I resisted the six o'clock news, resisted the seven o'clock, sitting out in the darkening dooryard with the generator stuffed in the bushes and the Indians' TV on a cardboard box. When the sun was down I went inside and built a fire in the keeping room. I took out some of my tools—my mortise chisels, my planes, my carving tools—but they felt alien and unbalanced in my hands. " 'Beauty is the visible fitness of a thing to its use,' " I said like an incantation in the dark room. But there was no answer, no Mavericke mimicking me, not even his house seeming to chorus an answer. I put the tools all back and went and sat by the fire. I waited until eleven o'clock.

There she was, six inches tall and imprisoned on the Indians' TV. I could barely hear the sound over the generator, caught something about a four-day trial as they showed her being led down to the dock and then helped into a police boat and sped away. I couldn't see her face. I couldn't see her face because it was too dark and the camera was too far away, and because I was watching with a deadness inside me, as if I didn't believe the tiny image on the screen was really Hetty anyway—my cousin, my wife—but some electronic impostor got up in Amias's clothes and wheeled into Mass General, a bogus Hetty that an eight-inch doctor had examined and now was telling me was all right. Because I couldn't shake the feeling that the real Hetty was hidden inside the house still, up in the attic, or down at the Quonset hut, or up at the fort; or she was home giving the twins a bath; or baking bisquits on Martha's Vineyard; or she was arguing the rules of croquet up at Exeter, kicking my ball into the bushes. I even said it out loud, said: "That's not her," as if it were a private understanding between me and the dead air there in the dooryard. "That's not her," I said; and then again: "That's not her." But when they started in on me—an impostor me hitting Philip in the face with an impostor gun—I picked up my gun and shot the TV. The screen shattered and one solitary spark flew like a released soul through the air. I got up and shut the generator down and then went back in to Philip.

"On the news they said she was sexually assaulted."

He was on his stomach this time; he had to strain his eyes at their corners in order to look up at me. I put the gun on single shot.

"Now I want to hear what happened."

He shook his head.

"I'm going to take the gag off and this time I want it straight."

He shook his head again, and then as soon as I had the gag untied, blurted: "She did it herself."

I stood up and pointed the gun at him. "What?"

"She did it herself. I was just screwing around. She should've known that. I told her I couldn't sleep with her unless she'd had a bath. So I brought her down to the Quonset hut and told her to wash up. I left her alone—I went to call in the police boat, for Christ's sake—and that's when she did it."

"Did what?"

"I didn't have anything to do with it. I can prove it."

"What? Did what?"

He rolled onto his back, his knees cocked in the air. "She bloodied herself."

I felt my insides turn over. "What do you mean, bloodied herself?"

"What do you think I mean? She bloodied herself. Do I have to spell it out?"

"Yes, goddamn it! Spell it out! What do you mean? Bloodied herself? Where?"

"Where do you think?"

I just stared at him.

"But she was all right," he said.

Baby John?

"She was bleeding, but she was all right. She was able to walk."

Baby John?

"Now let me go, Wheelwright. I'll settle on the monument and you can have your goddamn island back. We're both in over our heads."

It wasn't an accident. It didn't go off in my hands or something. I did it on purpose. I aimed it. I aimed it at his knee and when I squeezed the trigger, there was a scream and something—a piece of bone—hit me in the face. I remember thinking for an instant that it was the bullet that had hit me, the bullet somehow ricocheting off Philip, but it was the bone, I know. I remember bending over and picking up a splinter, and while Philip writhed and screamed on the floor, putting it in my pocket. And I remember looking at him as if I weren't really there, as if I were looking at him from another world, maybe from the world of the TV, the world where John Wheelwright was capable of violence and Mehitible Jenney was capable of betrayal, the world where four-hundred-year-old Mavericke's Island was reduced to a flat, flickering nothing. I was watching him from inside the TV; I was the John Wheelwright on the TV; I was the John Wheelwright who had knocked out an Indian with the butt of a machine gun, who had smashed King Philip in the mouth. I was the John Wheelwright who had fired on the police boat; I was the John Wheelwright who had wanted to stay in the attic, had wanted his pregnant wife to stay in the attic.

I watched him writhing on the floor, and I wanted to do it again. I wasn't repulsed or horrified. I wanted to do it again; I wanted to blow a hole in his other knee. I wanted to make him a cripple; I wanted to make him so he'd never be six feet six again. I wanted to kill him; more than that, I wanted to nullify him, to void him, not just the King Philip on the floor below me—the King Philip who had killed Baby John—but the King Philip of the past, the antlered King Philip who had strode through the sand and sea bracken down on Martha's Vineyard; the King Philip who had married Hetty under the Maypole; the King Philip who had danced with her on Alice's yacht, who had slapped her; the King Philip who had shot holes into Mavericke's house; the King Philip who had kept me in captivity, in torture; the King Philip who had kept Hetty. Because to kill that King Philip—the King Philip of seven years ago, of a year ago, of four days ago—was to let Baby John live.

But he fainted before I had the chance. I kicked him in the side, kicked him again to rouse him back into pain, but he was gone. Out on the water I heard the bullhorn spark and question. The sound of it made me straighten up. Was the world still there? Was the world still out there waiting

for me? I went to the window but all I could see were the
boat lights and a crew of Indians down at the campfire,
standing with their guns, looking up at the house. What were
they thinking? Were they thinking Philip had wrested the
gun away from me? That he'd shot me? "Do they think you
shot me?" I said to Philip back in the pantry. There was a
swelling of blood on the floor, on my hand-planed pine, a
blooming rose of blood. I bent down and untied him, first
his hands, then his ankles, and then took the gag off. He
was unconscious still. I shouldered my gun and got a good
grip under his arms and lifted him, and then, without care
for his exploded knee, dragged him out of the pantry into
the keeping room and then out of the house.

I think I meant to stop outside, to drop him in the dooryard, but once there I kept going. I dragged him past the
murdered TV set, past the generator and started down the
path. Someone called something to me as I neared the
campfire but I just kept going. "I've got him," I said when
they tried to grab Philip from me. "I've got him." The bullhorn quacked again. "Shit!" someone said. "His leg!" I kept
on down the path. I heard other voices, then the bullhorn
again. We passed the Quonset hut and started down toward
the dock. *"We are unarmed!"* the bullhorn crackled. *"We are
going to dock!"* "I've got him," I said. *"We are unarmed!"* We
made it down to the Parks and Recreation building and then
onto the wooden dock. I dragged him right to the end, as
if I meant to somehow drag him across the water, across the
harbor to Boston, to Hetty's, to Mrs. Steele's, to the Hancock building, but the police were there. They grabbed hold
of me, locked on to my gun and then grabbed Philip. "Are
you all right," someone asked. "Mr. Wheelwright, are you
all right?"

"I've got him," I said as they took Philip from me. "I've
got him."

CHAPTER
18

In Partibus Infidelium

• 1 •

It stared down at me from its perch on the wall like a blank
eye, or like a blank soul, or like some terminus of a great
optic nerve that cut and coiled through the city, under-
ground, overhead, up the spines of skyscrapers, through
conduits and cubbies into the meanest of homes, a great
electronic maze which conspired into every bar and motel
room, every house, hospital and hotel in the city. I watched
it that whole speechless first day, stared up at its blank screen
as if I expected to see on it or in it or through it into the
Mystery of America. But all I could see was my own face on
the gray-green screen, and the bed and nightstand next to
me. When the nursy-looking girl from Rentals showed up
and chirped that it cost a dollar and a quarter a day and
would I like service, it was Thompson my guard who answered.

"It's on the city," he said.

I tried to tell him I didn't want it, but my voice
wouldn't come.

"You've got to cheer up, Wheelwright," he said. "It's not everyone in this here new America who gets to shoot an Indian."

On the second day they came and asked me questions: doctors, detectives and assistant DAs. I lay the whole time with my face pushed into the pillow. They said in such cases their sympathies lay with the victim, but that I had to help them out. They said that they were working from the presumption that I had shot Philip in the knee to further immobilize him. Had that been the case? Had I been so frightened, so beyond logic, that tying him up had not been enough? Had I felt he could still harm me? Did I feel it even now? Such a reaction would fit the psychological profile on hostages. I managed to tell them I hadn't been a hostage. What had I been then? A captive, I said. They wanted to know how I differentiated being held hostage and being taken captive. Weren't they both victims of terrorism? It wasn't terrorism, I told them.

"It was the devil in the dooryard."

They ordered a psychiatric work-up.

No one mentioned Hetty.

I took walks in the halls, my hospital robe knotted around me and Thompson at my heels. I did it systematically, going from ward to ward, floor to floor, looking at the name cards on the doorjambs, sick humanity, sick America. On the sixth floor I happened through a pair of double doors into a squall of infant humanity, infant America crying *"Life! Life! Life!"* with such intent and destiny, I turned around and nearly ran Thompson over. On the fourth floor we came across Thompson-II, sitting in the corridor on a plastic chair. When he saw me coming he leaped up, but Thompson-I motioned to him that it was okay. I stopped a moment outside the open door. The privacy curtains were pulled around the bed but I could see a bare foot through the gap. I thought to say something, maybe just "Philip!" like the voice of a ghost or a vengeful dream, but I didn't have it in me.

When finally on the ninth floor I found it—JENNEY, ME-

HITIBLE C. (with a mocking WHEELWRIGHT after it in paren-
theses)—I couldn't go in. I don't know what I had intended
to do—beg her, scold her, hit her, kiss her, ask her: *Was it
true? Was it true?*—but whatever it was I couldn't do it. I
stood in the corridor a long time, walked around the nurses'
station once and came back, but I couldn't go in. She was
just ten feet from me, but I couldn't. I went back with
Thompson to my room.

When my parents came I had a bizarre, inexplicable urge
to show them the splinter of Philip's bone, to take it out of
my pants in the closet and show it to them, but I managed
instead to busy myself over the books they'd brought me,
and the potted orchid. *Cypripedium aucule,* my mother said.

They didn't mention Hetty either.

• 2 •

The California Psychological Inventory (CPI)

	TRUE	FALSE
There are forces in the world out to harm me.	o	o
Right and wrong are relative values.	o	o
The circle is more perfect than the square.	o	o
You cannot trust even those closest to you.	o	o

What had happened? How had I got here? I had carried
a sleeping Hetty down through the mazy streets of Boston,
sailed her out under a corn-colored moon and made love to
her on Mavericke's mattress. And now she was lying on the
ninth floor of Massachusetts General Hospital and I was here
on the second filling in a round dot that said, *Yes, there are
forces in the world out to harm me.*

	TRUE	FALSE
I am suspicious of others.	o	o
A machine can do a better job than a man.	o	o
Most people would like me if they knew me.	o	o

No, that isn't what happened. I had stolen her, stolen her from the twins, from Mrs. Steele, from the Hancock building. I had stolen her out to the island almost as if I had known that the next morning the haunts and perjuries of my historic nightmares would come in the guise of Indians and machine guns and helicoptors. Almost as if I had known that they would lock us in an attic into which no autistic twins would be allowed, no doctors with saline solutions, no Mrs. Steeles, no *Mus musculi*. Almost as if I had known . . .

People should listen to me.   O   O
I am often ill.   O   O

That isn't what happened. We were locked against our will in an attic together. I had hoped we would stay locked in the attic together. Hetty had wanted to get out.

Nothing is more important than anything
    else.   O   O
If I could live alone I would.   O   O

That isn't what happened. Hetty aborted herself. I tried to kill Philip. Samuel Mavericke ceased.

People need me.   O   O

That isn't what happened.

· 3 ·

Statement of John Jenney Wheelwright, *given this day* April 9, 1985, *in the city of Boston, Suffolk County, Massachusetts.*

I was held captive by Philip Safford and others whose names I do not know in the attic of Samuel Mavericke's house on Mavericke's Island. I was held there with my wife, Mehitible Jenney, for four days. We were allowed very little food and water and not allowed outside. We were allowed no sanitary facilities. On the night of the fourth day my wife was permitted to leave. I was kept locked up but managed to climb out the roof scuttle and reach ground. I gained possession of a gun and took Philip Safford hostage. I tied Philip Safford hand and foot and locked him in the pantry of the house. I slept on and off the rest of the day. I had bad dreams. At the end of one of these dreams I went into the pantry and shot Philip Safford. I felt I was dreaming still. When it was over I carried him down to the dock. I did not want anyone to take him from me. I do not know why.

There are forces in the world out to harm me.

Witnessed, *Signed,*

• 4 •

That isn't what happened.

• 5 •

They let me go. I saw it on the news even before Thompson handed me the papers. There was a statement from the DA's office about temporary insanity, about provocation, about the hostage syndrome. And there was an interview with the head of the New England Native Task Force calling me the latest in a long line of Indian-killers, then an editorial calling me a victim of our fathers' sins, then a man-on-the-street interview saying that if someone took you hostage I mean you had the right to blow them away, didn't you?

"Shoot 'em up, cowboy," Thompson said, winking at me and washing out his coffee cup. And then he was gone.

I just stayed in my bed.

• 6 •

He was calling to me, calling that it was all right. He was all right. He was still warm and safe inside and he was all right.

• 7 •

"I want to talk to my wife's doctor."
"And who is he?"
"I don't know."
"You don't know his name?"
"No."
"What is your wife's name?"
"Hetty."
"What's her last name?"
"Hetty."
"What?"
"Never mind."

• 8 •

I took the stairs, still in my hospital robe, climbed from the second floor to the third floor, from the third to the fourth, the fourth to the fifth, the fifth to the sixth, the sixth to the seventh, the seventh to the eighth, the eighth to the ninth.

JENNEY, MEHITIBLE C. (WHEELWRIGHT)

The room was vacant. The bed was being changed.

"Where is she? I asked.

"*¿Qué?*"

"Where is she? The woman who was in here?"

"Nobody."

"Where is she?"

"Nobody."

I looked in the bathroom, in the closet. On the night-stand I found her name band. JENNEY, MEHITIBLE C. I picked it up and went to the nurses' station.

"My wife," I said. "Where is she?"

"Who?"

I put the name band on the counter. "Nine-oh-six. Where is she?"

"She's been discharged."

"When?"

"Just now. This morning."

· 9 ·

Back in my room I got my things together—my pants and shirt, my shaving things—and packed them in the bag my parents had brought. I took my name band off my wrist, threw it in the wastebasket and put Hetty's on in its place.

On the first floor I searched out the records office and then looked for a mens' room nearby. I went inside and put my suitcase in one of the stalls. I left it there, the door pulled to and the suitcase visible down low, and then went back to Records.

"My doctor said I could get a Xerox of my records here."

"Your name?"

"Jenney," I said. "Mehitible Jenney."

"What?"

I spelled it for her. "It's a family name. They call me Max."

"I'll need some ID."

I started swatting at the pockets in my robe. "I don't have any on me," I said; then: "Wait!" And I held out my wrist for her to see. "Will that do?"

JENNEY, MEHITIBLE C.

"You're a patient now?"

"Yes."

"Then your records wouldn't be here. They'd be up on your floor."

"But I've just been discharged."

"They're probably still up there."

"Have a look-see," I said. She checked my name band again, and then disappeared down a row of file cabinets.

"They're here," she said after a minute, coming back with a folder in her hand. I leaned over the Dutch door that separated us.

"Good."

"There's a charge."

"That's okay."

She was opening the folder.

"That's okay," I said again. She stopped about five feet from me.

"Wait . . ."

"I just need them copied."

"These are for a woman."

"Oh," I said. "That's always happening."

She took a step toward me, still reading the folder. "Five feet one . . ."

"It must be a mistake. Can I see?"

"Five feet one," she said again and looked up at me. But just as she did, I lunged over the Dutch door and grabbed the folder from her. "Wait!" she cried, but I pulled back, and before she could get the door unlatched, ran out into the hallway. In the mens' room I sat trembling in the stall a minute, and then opened the folder.

JENNEY, MEHITIBLE, C.
3-17-56

5' 1"
BROWN
GREEN

*Admitted, one Caucasion female suffering possible psycho-
logical trauma. Upon examination patient proved to be
bleeding vaginally. After some questioning patient admitted
to having forced a miscarriage. Patient seemed depressed.*

CHAPTER
19

Strange Deliverance

• 1 •

" 'Abstract yourself with a holy violence from the dung heap of this earth.' "

I, John Jenney Wheelwright, descendant of the antinomian outcast John Wheelwright and of the Indian-killer Isaac Wheelwright, husband of Mehitible Jenney, former skipper of the *Pilgrim's Progress*, B.S., M.S., Ph.D., ask you, Samuel Mavericke, beloved of Amias Thompson, of the Massachusetts Indians, skipper of *The Royal We*, father of vanished Samuel: to where? What abstraction of self and soul could take me from this horror which in dreams and delusions is called America, could make me such a liquefaction that I might float just above the scurry and dirt of the world, could take me from the dung heap of my own hopes and keep me from hearing every night the voice of Baby John in my dreams?

And you, Isaac Wheelwright, tell me how a soul reconciles itself to its own darker shades? How does it live again in the town once it has wandered in the wilderness? Admit

325

its cousinage with the whole of humanity? How do you, Cousin Isaac, make fast your belt and buckles and buttons, haul in under the weft and warp of civilization the flesh and blood that has spilled its like on the forest floor?

And you, Mehitible Jenney, beloved of John Wheelwright, of Isabel and Irene Steele, five feet one, green eyes, brown hair, murderer of Baby John . . .

Where are you now? Are you back among the Thompsons, throwing yourself away in a dark booth? Or sitting on someone else's midnight dock tossing *Mehitible C. Jenney* into the ocean again? Or are you merely back with the twins and just not answering your phone? This is your husband calling, Hetty, your husband who, after everything, wonders if it is still possible to declare Item Six: that John will love and care for Mehitible.

• 2 •

I went up to Exeter. It was Easter weekend and I went to get away from everyone, but almost thinking Hetty would be there. I sought out all our old spots, the cow pasture, our observatory on the middle rocks, the stand of birches, the low dell where the spring mud used to suck our sneakers right off our feet. I stood in the graveyard in the woods out back where we'd played Saint and Sinner and tried to feel some breeze of health, of old friendship for the small stone markers—*Richard Packard, April 1784*; *Ruth, his wife*; *Edward, aged 2 wks*—feel some poetry of life and longing and destruction in the way the stones canted to one side. I could almost see the ghost of Hetty in the woodsy air, as if the atmosphere held in its mist and quiver the spring avatars of all our past Easters: Hetty at eight in a skirt and veil, at eleven in a sensible suit, and the high heels at fifteen that gave her such a jaunt and kick that I was filled with wonder and confusion. But no matter how I tried, no matter what cudgel of memory or imagination, I couldn't conjure the

Hetty I'd married, the Hetty who last spring had stood with me in that same graveyard, who had dressed the next morning in spring cotton only to find the world spitting wet snowflakes, the Hetty who that night on our honeymoon had worn the same seventeenth-century clothes which a year later she had put on under the black muzzle of Philip's gun.

Back in Boston I screwed myself up and went around to Commonwealth Avenue. I knocked on the apartment door and peered in at the windows, went up the steps and rang Mrs. Steele's buzzer. But there was no answer. I used my key and let myself into the apartment, calling Hetty's name quietly in case she was hiding somewhere. But there was no one inside. The bed was unmade, her dungarees hung still from the bedpost, her notes and notebooks lay untouched on her desk. It looked just as it had the night I'd carried her off, except the twins weren't there. Had she not come back? Had she not once been back? And if she hadn't been, and if she wasn't at her mother's, then where was she? And where were the twins? I started searching through her drawers, through her blouses and sweaters and underwear, and then the truth struck me.

She'd done it. She'd done it just like she'd said. She'd kidnapped the twins, and Mrs. Steele hadn't done anything about it, just like Hetty had said she wouldn't. I went into the twins' room and started opening their drawers. They were empty. I flung open the closet door. Empty. Could it be true? But what about her notes? And her clothes? What about her clothes? For a time I just stood there, my nerves stinging and my mind paging through thoughts of a broken Hetty clutching the twins and then hurrying them outside, and a Hetty so solid with intent that she could take the care to pack their things first. I went back into her bedroom to look again. No. Everything was the same. She hadn't taken anything of her own, not her clothes, not her shoes, not even her hairbrush. I checked the kitchen. Her silverware was still there. Then the bathroom, her toothbrush still next to mine. It was all as it had been, all there, all, except for

Hetty herself. I stood a moment in the center of the living room, and then almost by intuition—or by an old antagonism—I started upstairs to Mrs. Steele's.

I listened first, standing on the landing, the house breathing and seeming to whisper my presence. I could feel the same dead consciousness I'd felt all through the winter: the eyes in the curtains, in the mirrors, in the clock that still read thirteen past three. In the kitchen I found a litter of newspaper clippings on the table, and there was no shock or even surprise when I saw a picture of myself in one of them, then one of Hetty, then Philip, the island, a grainy telephotograph of one of the machine-gun emplacements, and finally, a reproduction of Mavericke's signature side by side with a portrait of Isaac Wheelwright. I went up the back staircase to the second floor, through the drawing room into the front living room. The secretary was still there, still singing with Pythagorean precision, with golden rectangles and American democracy, stuffed inside with gilled and headless horrors. Up on the third floor I looked through some of Mrs. Steele's drawers, her closet. I don't know what I was looking for—evidence, proof, page 283 of the *American Biography*—but I didn't find it. Just sweaters from Saks, skirts from Lord and Taylor, a winter coat from Bonwit Teller. I went back out through the sitting room, and in the hall, with a growing sense of being cut off should I hear the front door open, I started up to the fourth floor.

When I saw them, for some reason I thought it was Hetty, Hetty taken captive by Mrs. Steele and caged in an overturned crib. But it lasted only an instant, and then I saw the other crib, and then the red hair. The cribs were turned over so their legs and casters stuck up weirdly in the air, placed just out of arms' reach of each other and with the posts screwed to the floor with angle irons. Isabel was inside one; Irene inside the other. For a split second I couldn't quite believe that this wasn't just one more dream I was having down on the twins' couch, one more of their nightmares of chase and annihilation. I couldn't tell at first if they were

aware of me, whether in the last two weeks they had been
so blasted back to autism, so lost to the progress of Hetty's
baths and hair-braiding, that the world had ceased alto-
gether for them. But when I knelt in the space between the
two cribs, they each moved toward me. I held out my hands,
the left through the bars of Isabel's crib, the right through
the bars of Irene's. They each took hold of me, Isabel just
my fingertips, Irene my whole hand. "Sweethearts," I said,
and I could feel something travel through me, some substance of spirit or soul travel right through me from one to
the other. "Has she been up here?" I said. "Has she been
up here and found you and is that what's happened?" But
they just moved closer to me. "Hetty," I said, "Hetty," and
I could feel again a surge of spirit course through me from
one to the other. I held them for a long while, saying
"Sweetheart," and "Sweetheart," and then: "Hetty," until finally I had to let go and stand up.

"I'll be back," I told them. I reached in and touched each
of them on the head. "I'll find her and I'll bring her to you.
I'll be back."

Downstairs I had the presence of mind to take Hetty's
address book with me.

· 3 ·

And for the next two weeks I called every number she
had listed, went to the Baxter School, to Goebbels'. And I
went out into the city. Every day from early in the morning
until long after dark, going from street to street, store to
store, subway to subway, just to be out among people, out
where she might be, scanning each face coming toward me,
each going away. I went from the harbor to the Fenway,
from Charlestown to Harvard Square, into Roxbury, into
South Boston, over to Dorchester. I walked along the wharfs,
through the financial district, the North End, the Esplanade. I checked into Filene's Basement, struggled through

the mob of bargain hunters and came out topside by Jordan Marsh. I rode the T—the Green Line, the Orange Line, the Red, the Blue—burrowing under Boston, walking from car to car, traveling the whole length of each train, on each line, changing at Park Street, at Government Center. I stood outside movie theaters every night as they emptied, then moved on to the next theater, checking the playhouses at ten when they spilled their audiences into the street. But no matter what chunk of humanity I bit off, she was not in it.

And yet I couldn't get rid of a picture I had of her still dressed in Amias's clothes, wandering the city, going from street to street, bar to bar, bus to bus, Baby John three weeks dead but still inside her like a poison. Because what other pollution of self or soul could have kept her from the twins? What enormity of self-hate could do that if it wasn't Baby John? I couldn't begin to imagine it. And yet, I expected every minute to see her, to see her just as I pictured her, still with Amias's stomacher on, her red petticoat, looking for her health, for some old sense of herself in the noontime crowds, sitting in a booth in some luncheonette, in the next car, the next train, walking toward me around the next corner. I could even imagine her catching sight of me and following me, following me even while I was looking for her, keeping a half-block between us, waiting in a door stoop or behind a kiosk while I went into this store, that store; riding a car behind me in the subway; sitting a row behind me at the Planetarium. Sometimes the feeling was so strong I had to turn around and look. But she was never there.

And there were times when I could almost feel her in the people who passed me, as if they had just been somewhere she'd been. It was as if the whole crush of humanity had a fleck of Hetty to it, some grace or decoration that was hers, some whisper or breath, some faint breeze of her. I saw curly-headed women that were her, short women that were her, girls playing hopscotch on the Common that were her, Irish women in South Boston, Italian women in the North End, all of them Hetty. And yet the real Hetty—the five-feet-one, green-eyed Hetty; the patient who'd seemed depressed—where was she?

Every couple of days I went back to Mrs. Steele's, and up on the fourth floor talked to the twins through the door, told them that I was all right, that Hetty was all right, that we were coming to get them.

I started staying out at night, checking the bars until last call and then going out onto the streets, thinking that maybe that was what she was doing, sleeping all day in some rented room and wandering the city at night. I went down into the Combat Zone, past the flashing marquees and the photos of strippers, checked the all-night hot dog and pizza parlors, and in the bright fluorescent light, said "Hetty" under my breath. "Hetty, the twins are locked up and Baby John still talks to me at night. Where are you?" Or maybe I didn't say it under my breath. Maybe I was just one more muttering shard of humanity, saying, "Hetty," and again, "Hetty," and again: "Where are you?"

I slept sometimes, down by the waterfront, in the Fenway, along the Esplanade, waking cold and confused, and then walking again. I tried for a time to find her by concentrating on Baby John, going this way and that over the city like a douser witching for water, talking to him as I witched. And I talked to Cousin Isaac, to Mavericke, to the twins. " 'Beauty is the visible fitness . . .' " I said; " 'Abstract yourself with a holy violence . . .' " I said. And I spoke to King Philip—I mean the real King Philip—the King Philip who had returned to his home on Mount Hope when he knew the war was lost, and there, waited for Cousin Isaac's men to come and capture him, to kill him and sell his infant son into West Indian slavery. "Baby John," I said. "Baby John . . ."

And then it came to me. It came to me while I was half-asleep under an easement to Storrow Drive. She was on the island. That was why I couldn't find her. She was on the island living in Mavericke's house, sleeping in Mavericke's bed, breathing Mavericke's air. I woke with a hard vision of

her sitting by the keeping-room window, sitting in my
Brewster chair, the shutters open and the moonlight making nests of silver in the near bushes, the dark ocean in the
distance, and all around, the island quieted down to a
seventeenth-century midnight.

I got so excited I started running. It was drizzling, cold,
but I didn't care. I ran through the Back Bay, across the
Common, down into the harbor regions. I climbed over the
Cyclone fence at the marina and started searching the docked
boats, going from slip to slip, but they all had their rudders
pulled or their tillers locked and chained. I caught sight of
the tour boat, and in the next instant, thought of the little
showpiece gig that hung from the aft davits. I swung around
to the end of the dock to make sure she was still there.

It took me half an hour to get her in the water and get
her dwarf mast in place and the little gaffsail rigged. I turned
my eyes toward where Mavericke's Island was lost in the
weather, and pushed the tiller to port. "Sweetheart," I said,
and I felt the cold rain fall on me like a special grace. I
navigated by the lights of Boston, the sky starless, moonless,
taking my readings from habit, nearly feeling my way across
the harbor. After half an hour I made out an inky rise ahead
of me, a darkness darker than the surrounding sea, and
then a second darkness to the south: Amias's island. I began
to feel full of old inhabitations, Boston lost behind me, Mavericke ahead of me, and Thompson dying of gangrene;
Amias alone, the darkness, the solitude, the quiet, the hush
of history, America still a bud unbloomed, and all the turmoil and shame waiting its turn. And for a time out on that
dark water, I felt I *was* Mavericke, Mavericke sailing *The
Royal We* back to Amias, Mavericke standing on the door
stoop of America, poised on that one point in history when
the whole continent was unconscious still, that one point when
he could say: "*I* am America." And I still felt it even when
I neared the dock, and still when I got out and tied the gig
up. No longer that I was Mavericke, but that the island had
whistled back to some breach in time. "Mavericke," I was

saying, and then: "Hetty." And then, as I started up the path: "*Hetty!*" I could see the house ahead of me, potent with darkness. It was as if I expected not only Hetty to be there but Mavericke too, and with Mavericke, Amias, and with Amias, their son Samuel; and Cousin Isaac too; and King Philip's son; and the Indian boy Isaac had killed; and with them a host of shimmering souls from the dig down the hill. But when I got there, when I tripped into the dooryard crying: "Hetty!" what I saw was the silvery glimmer of an enormous hasp and padlock on the front door.

I lay for a time on the wet ground. I tried summoning an old incantation: "This is my house," but even saying it, I felt weak and beaten. I got up and hefted the padlock. It had the weight of hard reality to it. I walked around the side of the house, the rear, the other side. The windows were locked too.

"Mavericke," I whispered in the dark. "Amias."

But there was no answer.

I stepped back. Was this the house I'd seen in my fourteen-year-old mind? Was this the house I'd built over and over in dreams and in love?

"Just show yourself to me," I said. "Just a glimpse."

But again, nothing.

I sat down in the rain and the mud and looked around. The dooryard was lit with light from the city, a gold and silver wetness over everything, over my sledge, Philip's television, the chest and bundles of wood the Indians had hauled out of the house. I looked across the water. It was Boston still, but it was a Boston un-Hettyed, a Boston robbed of all my old envisionings, no Hetty livening the brassy rise of Beacon Hill, no Hetty lending her soul to one of the electric tombstones. I looked south to Thompson's Island. What would it have been like, Mavericke, with no pearly screw of smoke coming from Amias's chimney? What would it have been like, here at the edge of the wilderness, with no sisterly house a half-mile distant, just the barren land and you and nothing but wide water all around?

"She could be in the river, Mavericke," I said out loud. "She could be in the Charles and I wouldn't know it."

I picked up a piece of wood beside me, picked it up without thinking to, without thinking what it was, and I felt suddenly a sickness stick in me. It was part of the high chair I'd started to make, one of the legs, squared up and the mortises cut to take the rungs. It was wet and muddy. I put it down, and then after a moment picked it up again. I held it up to the light, let the rain run down it, washed it with my fingers. It was the front right leg; I could tell by the splay. I put it to my eye, but in the dark I couldn't tell how much the wet and the sun had warped it. Down beside me were the other legs and some of the rungs. I picked up a rung, washed it too in the rain, and then with half a heart, knowing it would be too swollen and unfit from the exposure, put the rung's tenon to the leg's mortise. But it slipped in, neat and true and square.

And that's when I heard him, Hetty.

I heard him just like I used to hear him, lying beside you at night while you slept, my hand on your belly, feeling the hum of his soul inside you. He said that you knew the twins were gone, that you had been up to see them, but that you were beaten, dead inside. He said that you had seen me come and go from Mrs. Steele's. He said that you knew I was looking for you, that you had followed me, had even been in Mrs. Steele's once when I came, and had hidden in a closet while I went and knelt at the twins' door. He said Mavericke was there with him. And the Indian boy was there. And Amias too. They were waiting, he said. Waiting for what? I asked. He said to keep working on the high chair. Waiting for what?

Keep working on the high chair, he said.

· 4 ·

They're out here. They're out here roaming my island with transits and tapes looking for a place to put Philip's plaque. The tour boats are back, the tourists tenfold, and my graduate students wonder at me behind my back. But I don't care, Hetty. I've got the locks off the door and windows. I've got Philip's TV thrown in the ocean. I've got Baby John's high chair pegged and trued up. And I'm starting on a two-seater settee for the twins.

Because this is what I'm going to do. I'm going to steal the twins. I'm going to do it just like you said you would do it. I'm going to steal them and bring them out to Mavericke's island, where they will live in Mavericke's house, breathe Mavericke's air, and watch me as I fit mortise to tenon, tenon to mortise, building them a double bed, a double chest, a table to sit their settee at.

And here's what I think: I think you're going to be there watching me when I do it. You're going to see me come with my hammer and punch, go in through your apartment and start climbing upward, up past the newspaper clippings of you and me and Mavericke and Philip on the kitchen table, up past the belly of the beast in the bombé, up past the bedrooms on the third floor to the fourth floor where I'll pop out the hinge pins and take a twin in each arm and start down again, down past the mirrors crying "Thievery!" down past the windows screaming "Rape!" down past the dead clockface crying "Thievery! Rape!" And I'll carry them out into the bright New England sun while you follow behind, carry them through the green Public Gardens, past the red and white swan boats, the Common, the Park Street Church, down through the glass Magogs to the harbor. And there we'll pay our fares and take the one o'clock boat out into the fair breeze and fresh sea. I'm going to do it. I mean it.

Because how else can I steal you back, Hetty? How else make Mavericke come to me again, Amias too? How else revirgin my island, my house, my hand-cut dovetails? Can you see it, Hetty? Can you see it the way I can see it? The twins sitting in the dooryard, their faces with a new bloom of life, and their hair all afire with the sun and wind? And

Mavericke and Amias strolling along the hill next over, the breeze blowing Amias's gown about her ankles and Mavericke leaning over to whisper in her ear? And can you see me by the front window, knocking out dovetails by the dozen, looking harborward for each tour boat, for each and every cabin cruiser, waiting for the one that will bring me a Hetty trembling with hope and wonder and maybe the first hint of a new Baby John?

Because beauty is the visible fitness of a thing to its use, goddamn it, and the human soul is fit to the human soul. My soul is fit to yours, Hetty. The twins' are fit to the twins'. Mavericke's is fit to Amias's. And Baby John's is fit to the whole world's. So I declare Items One through Six, Hetty. And I declare Vermont and New Hampshire make a golden rectangle. And to you, Mavericke, I declare life and love and the half-lap dovetail and even the devil in the dooryard.

I've got my hammer in hand.

The twins are waiting behind their door.

The tour boat's coming.